T0361687

Acclaim for

EMBERGOLD

"Rachelle Nelson has created a beautiful and memorable love story in *Embergold*. The danger is all too real, and so is the bravery of the young heroine, Gilde, who is determined to live up to the best in herself no matter what it costs her. My only complaint is that the book ends too soon. Dare I hope for a sequel?"

—CLARE B. DUNKLE, author of The Hollow Kingdom Trilogy

"*Embergold* is a classic tale with a unique edge. Nelson transports readers into a wonderful world of her creation, one where love and loss mold the characters within as well as the reader. Soar not only on the back of a dragon but through the pages of a book that feels as familiar and transportive as the stories that made us fall in love with fairy tales."

—MORIAH CHAVIS, author of *Heart of the Sea*

"*Embergold* is everything you want in a fantasy book! A heart-warming romance, beautiful prose, and spell-binding plot to keep you enthralled from start to finish."

—VICTORIA MCCOMBS, best-selling author of YA fantasy

Embergold

RACHELLE NELSON

Embergold
Copyright © 2025 by Rachelle Nelson

Published by Enclave Publishing, an imprint of Oasis Family Media, LLC

Carol Stream, Illinois, USA.
www.enclavepublishing.com

All rights reserved. No part of this publication may be reproduced, digitally stored, or transmitted in any form without written permission from Oasis Family Media, LLC.

This is a work of fiction. Names, characters, places, and incidents are products of the author's imagination or are used fictitiously. Any similarity to actual people, organizations, and/or events is purely coincidental.

ISBN: 979-8-88605-186-5 (printed hardcover)
ISBN: 979-8-88605-187-2 (printed softcover)
ISBN: 979-8-88605-189-6 (ebook)

Cover design by Kirk DouPonce, www.FictionArtist.com
Typesetting by Jamie Foley, www.JamieFoley.com

Printed in the United States of America.

For anyone who has been told to be afraid.

THE FIRST TIME I SAW THE DRAGON,

I was eight years old. It was also the first time I knew my father loved me.

Ice slushed over the edges of my shoes and clung to the hem of my skirt as I trudged from the trees to the house, arms full of splintered twigs. At that age, my main chore was collecting firewood, and I hated it in the cold.

Father said my heart had never been strong. Not even when I first learned to run on chubby toddler legs. My lips had turned blue. Now, my heart still fluttered at odd intervals when I worked, and the walk through the snow made spots dance in my vision.

I was used to that. It would ease with rest, like always. But the ice was new this season, brought by the first winter storm.

It might have been a little better if I had owned boots. Pretty ones, with fur on the inside. The kind that would go with lace underskirts and velvet bodices that I had never owned, either. I saw a pair of boots like that once, hanging from the satchel of a trader who came through the marshes. But Father wasn't interested in pretty things, so he drove the trader away. And now I had to collect wood with ice in my socks.

You'll never hear a dragon before you see it. Their wings cut through the air without a sound. But you might smell a dragon before it arrives. It's their only warning.

I hadn't reached the house yet when the scent hit my nostrils, acrid and deep, like a fire without the sweetness of wood. I looked for smoke but saw none. It was a smell I didn't recognize yet.

Isa stood at the door to our house, her stark blue eyes fixed upward, her slender frame rigid. She had left to visit the settlement the day before with her husband, Guntor. They must have come home early, arriving while I was out.

I called to Isa, my voice small in the wind. "What's burning?"

She looked at me but said nothing, motioning for me to come inside. I shook my head. Guntor might be in there, finishing a bottle of liquor he'd bought on their trip. I would rather stay in the cold than watch them fight, and Isa knew it. After a last unspoken refusal from me, she darted into the house, closing the door behind her.

The handle latch clicked into place.

Then I worried I'd gotten it wrong. Maybe Guntor was outside, and she intended to lock him out. I forgot about smoke and spun in a circle, searching. My stomach tightened.

Someone moved in the trees. I dropped my twigs and turned to the sound. But it wasn't Guntor. It was my father, marching toward me, ankle deep in frozen marsh, his jaw set in its usual way.

Why had I dropped the firewood? These twigs were from the dead trees, above the ground where the wind dried them. I'd had to climb. They were wet now, completely useless for burning until tomorrow.

And Father had seen.

"I'm sorry." My heart beat in its weak pattern, and my lungs protested. "I'll get more wood. I will."

Father put his finger to his lips, demanding silence, then wrapped a strong hand around my wrist, pulling me toward a crop of scrubby brush. My feet scrambled to keep up, my mind scrambling faster. What was happening?

He rarely touched me. If he wanted to hit me, he would do it and be done. This touch wasn't gentle, but it wasn't the hurting kind.

Once we reached the brush, father lowered himself beside me, crouching beneath the spindly cover. He went still, except for his hair shifting in the breeze. It was always combed back from his face, and it had a glossy, chestnut color I liked to look at.

"Don't move." He was barely audible.

I tried to obey, but my chest felt heavy, and I couldn't help shuffling my frozen feet in the slush, giving each sock a turn to be up out of the cold.

"Quiet." Father lifted me from the ground into his arms.

I went still. He was holding me, a thing that hadn't happened in a long time. I nestled my head against his warm cloak, and his heart beat steady beneath my ear. When I was smaller, he must have held me often, but it was hard to remember.

Then the dragon came.

I saw the shadow first, moving across the ground at an impossible speed. It seemed as wide as our house. Father's eyes flashed to the sky, and he put his hand over my mouth, muffling my rapid breath. The flutter in my chest turned to an ache.

I needed to calm myself, like Father had taught me. He got angry when I had an episode. Panicking, he called it. I laid my palm over my chest and took in long breaths, fighting the urge to gasp air through my nose. Father removed his hand from my mouth, but still held me tight, a warning not to move.

I tilted my head back and searched the air.

The dragon's wings moved in a swooshing rhythm, contracting the long muscles in its dark, glittering body. It wasn't as large as its shadow, but it flew closer to the ground than I had feared. Tree height. Thick smoke trailed from its nostrils, and its black tail curled into a glossy spike.

"Shh." My father made the softest sound, his arms squeezing me.

The silence stretched on, an endless moment, scarred by dragon stench. Finally, the beast disappeared into the horizon. Its smell lingered for a moment, then left, blown away by a chill wind.

Father let air escape from his lungs, then stood and hoisted me over his shoulder. He was so tall.

My pulse calmed, but fatigue flooded my body, the usual result of an episode.

"That was the dragon," I said.

Isa had told me about the beast. I twisted to see Father's face.

"Yes." He carried me in a straight line, up the hill to the house. "Next time, I expect you to hide on your own. I can't always be near you."

There might be a next time? I played the image of the black dragon over in my mind. My nose still itched from the smell.

"Will the dragon come down here?"

"Likely not. It hates touching water. But if it ever sees us, even with these marshes, it might be tempted."

"Isa leaves the marsh." I propped my elbows up against Father's back. "To go to the settlement. Won't the dragon see her there?"

"Isa isn't hunted."

This was a new idea to me. Isa had taught me to hunt rabbits with a sling. Compared to the dragon, I might as well be a little animal.

I hesitated. "Am I hunted?"

Father paused his steps. "Are you my daughter?"

"Yes."

"Then, yes. You're hunted."

His answer was so definite. A fact of life that hadn't been a fact to me until right now.

How many more questions would he tolerate?

"Why?" I asked.

He quickened his pace. "When a dragon hates, it hates forever."

What did he mean by forever? No one had ever told me I would get to travel with Isa when I was older. But the possibility always loomed in my mind.

I whispered my next question, so he wouldn't have to acknowledge it if he didn't want to. "Will we . . . always be in the marsh?"

"You have what you need, don't you? Food, clothing, servants to bring news and supplies."

They weren't my servants—the men who came and went from the marshes. They all belonged to Father. Guntor was the only man who stayed in the house, because he was Father's distant relative. We called him a cousin, but it was more complicated than that.

The others only came at night, wrapped in dirty cloaks, grip-worn knife hilts hanging at their sides. They always left before dawn, and they never slept.

Sometimes, when I was supposed to be asleep, I peeked out from my loft at the men. They all had the same deep-set eyes beneath their hoods. What would make someone look so tired? Most were missing teeth, and they whispered with Father in hissing tones.

Once, a man looked back at me, and the blank expression on his face made me hide in my blankets again. I didn't like thinking about that time.

But it was daylight now. And Father was holding me.

He set me down when we reached the door to the house, testing the latch. It was still locked. With one kick of his boot, he broke through. I flinched. Father didn't like anyone but himself to use locks.

The door swung open, crooked on its hinges. Splinters and dust fell like dry snow.

In the darkened interior, Isa hunkered beneath the table.

Guntor thundered down the stairs from the loft, then stopped when he saw us. "You found the girl."

He had a way of never fully opening his eyes, and he always let his yellow hair fall into his face. The effect made him appear to be mostly chin and nose, both of which were well defined. He might have been handsome, if he were someone else.

Father stepped through the doorway, into the dust. "Only a fool would hide in the house." He kicked a patch of ice off his boot. "No water in here. And it's flammable."

Isa crawled out from under the table. "It's not like I had someone to come looking for me. Where do you think Guntor was? Hiding." She brushed dust off her frayed skirt. "Without the wife he says he loves."

Love.

She said the word in a harsh way, meant to shame Guntor, but it stuck in my mind.

Was that why my father had come looking for me? He loved me? Unlike the way Guntor treated Isa. At the thought, an unfamiliar warmth filled me.

Guntor pulled his cap from his hair and threw it at Isa. "I'm married to you, aren't I? Despite everything."

Isa dodged the cap and said nothing.

It was their usual fight. When Guntor drank, he dreamed, and he took those dreams seriously. After he married Isa last year, Guntor's nightmares predicted she would leave him. He called her unfaithful, though she'd never strayed.

Isa called Guntor delusional.

Father said he was an oracle.

"Enough." Father didn't need to raise his voice. When he spoke, we all listened.

"Gilde," he turned to me. "The danger has passed. Can you gather more wood, and stoke the fire?"

I nodded.

"Good. I'll walk with you for a distance, then I'll go to the edge of the marsh. I have eyes in those trees, and they'll know which way the dragon went."

Father gave Guntor a long look, then took my hand and led me out the door. I barely felt the ice this time, my hand warm in his. My usual chore had become something more. Now, I was part of Father's plan. We were allies against the dragon.

Next time, I hoped Isa would remember to hide near the water. I would be sure to remind her when I got a chance. I wanted her safe.

When Isadora married Guntor and came to live with us, I had never seen anything more beautiful. She was the first woman I'd ever met, and I dreamed of growing out my dark hair like her golden braid. Mine never went past my shoulders.

We were a category all our own. Girls, separate from the men. But there was one thing about Isa I didn't want to emulate.

I squeezed Father's hand tighter. He had allowed so many questions today. Maybe I could get away with one more.

I tried it. "When I'm fourteen, will I get married too?"

I didn't want a husband like Guntor. He was a grown man, and Isa still seemed half child to me. She had grown an inch in the last year.

I didn't want a husband at all.

Father didn't get angry. "No. You have more important things to do."

"Like what?"

"You're my daughter. For now, that's your role, and it's important. Do you understand?"

"Yes." I smiled up at him.

"Someday, I'll take care of the dragon," he said. "Someday, we'll leave this place."

EIGHT YEARS LATER

"Isa!" I leaned over the railing of the loft, my face warm with anger.

She sat by the fire, neatly plaiting her golden hair. As I had suspected, she was wearing my dress. The one with the ribbons.

I was sixteen now, and we had both grown to our full height. We fit the same garments, though I was taller. I had two dresses. Isa only had one of her own, and she always dirtied my hems when she took my things.

"What?"

"You know what."

She didn't reply.

"Isa, it's my best dress."

"Your best, you say?" Her delicate mouth curved into a quick smile. "I'd better test the quality."

"No—"

Isa yanked a ribbon. Then her eyes went wide. A rip sounded with the tug, and an eyelet came loose from the bodice.

She hadn't meant to tear it out. I could tell she was only trying to stretch the ribbons, another of my complaints against her. But, whether she meant it or not, my dress was still damaged.

She looked down at the ripped eyelet, her face blank.

Then she laughed.

At twenty-three years old, Isa was still wild. Like a spring wind. Sometimes harsh and cold, sometimes soft and warm, and you never knew which it would be.

Today, I was tired of guessing.

Tears stung my eyes. "Wait until my father gets home."

It was an empty threat, and I knew it. But it was all I had.

Father and Guntor had been gone for three days at the borders of the marsh, where the water grew thin and the forest thickened. Men there traded news for gold, and I think Father liked to wander the marsh, testing the boundaries. He could be back today, or in five more days.

"What's he going to do?" Isa said. "Nothing. Not for a thing like you."

There were certain boundaries in our little cottage. Guntor left me alone, and Father ignored Isa. He ignored me too, most of the time.

Isa, on the other hand, had slapped me more than once over the years. But I wasn't a child anymore.

My anger flared, which made my chest tighten and my heart strain.

And then I said something terrible.

"He can't do anything worse than Guntor already does."

I regretted the words as soon as I said them. The bruise on her right cheek was only beginning to fade. Her slaps were nothing like Guntor's, and it wasn't something we spoke about.

We had both crossed a line.

Isa's face hardened and went cold.

"Out!" She stood and grabbed the iron rod from the fire. "Get out of here!"

I ran down the stairs, past Isa.

She swung the rod at me as I passed but didn't hit me. An empty threat.

I slammed the front door behind me as hard as I could, panting against my racing heart.

For a while, I stood there, one foot off the step.

Where was I going? I had no one to talk to besides Isa, and she was more than capable of holding a grudge.

There would be silence in the marsh.

My anger cooled as I imagined the day ahead, alone, locked out of the house.

"I'm sorry, Isa." I spoke loud enough for her to hear through the closed door, and I meant the words. "I shouldn't have said that."

The latch turned with a wooden clack, sealing the lock. Sealing me outside. It was too late.

A winged insect whizzed across damp grass, headed for the water's edge. Spring had arrived, and the waters rose up the side of the hill, almost to the house. Everything smelled wet and green. Alive and rotting at the same time.

I sat on the step, still in my nightgown, the morning sun warm on my bare toes. I went barefoot too much, and the tops of my feet had already darkened this spring, tanned with a scattering of freckles. My cheeks probably matched, but I didn't have a mirror to see my round face anymore. Guntor had broken it last autumn.

In truth, it didn't matter what I wore—my best dress, or nothing at all. There was no one to see me.

How long would Isa keep me out?

My anger with her was always quick. Hot and burning, then gone.

But I still had pride.

I wouldn't let her see me through the window, moping after our fight. I gathered my skirt and made my way through familiar trees, humidity frizzing the ends of my wiry hair.

Bright green algae floated on the surface of the water. Years of practice had taught me where to step. A fallen log could serve as a bridge through wet moss, and thick ferns kept my toes safe from the slimiest puddles. There were things in the marsh I didn't want to touch, sweet and decaying.

Only one stream flowed clear enough to bathe in, and it was a full morning's walk away from our cottage. Isadora and

I washed our clothes there, but she had never learned to swim and was scared of these greener parts of the marsh. I loved to swim, and wished everything could be clean enough to do so.

I climbed above the waterline onto a ridge and let myself fall into the grass, stretching out on the ground.

It was the same as any other little hill, but for some reason, I had always thought of this one as mine. When I was younger, it was my imaginary house. The grass had been my bed, made entirely of velvet, and the thorny bush was a golden armoire, full of satin dresses, all with ribbons.

I didn't play pretend anymore, but the hill was still a place to get away from the real house.

I relaxed onto my back and squinted up at a clear sky. I always searched the sky. Always using my nose.

At first, after that day with the dragon, it had been from fear. An expectation of seeing black wings.

Then, recently, the expectation had turned to something else. Almost hope. Almost like I wanted it to happen, after years of constant vigil. And I didn't fully understand that feeling.

Was the dragon a reminder of my identity? The daughter who had been protected.

If it came again, at least it would be a glimpse of something from outside the marsh.

I had learned more about our isolation over the years. Somehow, the dragon could track Father when he left the marsh. He had tested it twice when I was small, before I could remember. The dragon had come both times, and Father had escaped to the water again.

But I never forgot the promise. Someday, he would take care of the dragon and we would be free.

I rolled onto my side and peered through the budding trees, my eyes resting on the mountains in the distance. They were always there, blue slopes and white peaks. I loved Isa's nighttime stories about mountain caverns filled with treasure, haunted by ghosts.

How long would it take to walk to those peaks? If someone made it all the way to the top, would they really find gold? Would they be rich enough to buy their own house?

I laid on my hill for a long time.

No dragon came. Not even a whiff.

Eventually, my stomach growled.

Isa would be hungry too by now, and she couldn't say no to wild carrots. I had already spotted their lacy tops, growing among the grass.

I retraced my steps and dug my fingers into the soft earth, pulling out crisp roots. It was a meager harvest, but I found onions too, sweet from the spring waters. We could add them to the fermented cabbage in the kitchen and the potatoes from the garden. I washed the produce and carried it in my skirt, held up to form a makeshift basket.

But when I reached the house, I stopped at the step. I had swept it earlier. Now, it was covered in mud. Prints, from large boots.

Father was home.

The door latch turned easy. I opened it and went inside, my footsteps loud enough to be noticed, but still careful.

Guntor and Isa were already in the loft, evidenced by their harsh whispers, barely audible over the crackling fire. Isa had closed all the shutters, so my eyes had to adjust to the dim light.

I laid my harvest on the table and let my gaze drift to Father's chair, tucked in the corner beside the hearth.

He sat in the firelight, his spine straight, black eyes focused on nothing. Normally, he would have been relaxed already, resting after three days away.

Why was he sitting at that angle?

Then I saw the blood.

Dark and thick, it soaked Father's cloak from his shoulder

to his wrist. Little smears of tarnished red painted the scruff on his square jaw.

I took in a sharp breath and stepped forward, breaking the silence, cautious.

"You're hurt."

He looked at me for the first time since I had entered, his face tight. "I'm fine."

"You're bleeding . . ." I snatched a clean cloth from the kitchen board, knocking over a basket. "You're not fine." I held the cloth out to him.

He didn't take it. "I'm better than I've been in a long time."

I noticed another fleck of blood, daubed below his eye.

If I was going to get answers, I needed to keep my tone empty of emotion, the way Father liked. But underneath, my heart raced.

"What happened?"

Father looked back to the fire. "There are dangers outside the marsh."

Outside the marsh.

I wrapped my arms around myself. "You left?"

"Yes."

That was a heavy yes. More questions filled my mind, too many to ask. He was the one who had taught me to hide. He was breaking the rules. Breaking our way of life and acting like it was nothing.

"Your wound." I tried to give him the cloth again.

He pushed my hand away and pulled back his cloak to reveal skin beneath a torn shirt. On his shoulder, a bandage had been tied, clean and well secured.

"It's old blood," he said.

His cloak fell back into place.

But there were things I needed to know.

"The dragon came?" I breathed.

He laughed at me.

It wasn't funny. Not with russet stains that could change our lives forever.

"The dragon would do more damage than this," Father said.

I should have felt relieved.

He settled back in his chair, still stiff. "He's out there though. And I'm tired of hiding like a rat."

My voice shook, but I managed to sound docile. "And that's why you left the safety of the water?"

"It's why you're going to leave the marsh."

The whole cottage went silent. Even Isa and Guntor stopped whispering.

"What?" I could hear my heart in my ears.

"You're going to leave the marsh." He flashed a smile, his white teeth bright.

The smile told me he knew the weight of his words, and he didn't care. He said them like a usual order, as if he were telling me to cook a wild goose or bring water from the well.

And finally, all my questions tumbled out, one after the other, no room for answers. Maybe I knew I wouldn't get any.

"But why? What is going on? Did something change? And you've always said my heart is too weak to—"

Father held up a hand. "Stop."

My throat tightened, but I kept my tears inside. I tensed, expecting a punishment for my outburst.

But instead, he lowered his hand and reached to hold mine. I watched it happen as if it were someone else.

"Gilde, have I always taken care of you?"

"Yes." The tears wanted to spill even more now.

"Have I always told you what you need to know? Taught you what plants to eat and which water to drink? Taught you to calm yourself when you're weak?"

"Yes."

"Then listen now. It's time for us to deal with the dragon. Do you trust me?"

"Yes." It was the only answer I could give.

"Then that's enough. You'll know more in time. No more questions, until we leave."

I couldn't imagine leaving.

"When will we go?" I asked.

"That's a question." Father let go of my hand.

I flinched for what would come, but he didn't move.

"I won't disappoint you," I said.

"No, you won't."

2

I PACKED MY SPARE DRESS IN A
satchel. It was still my best, despite the place where the ribbon
had been torn. Isa had mended it, her silent apology, and she
had done a good job. If I was going to the cities, it would matter
what I wore. There would be eyes to see me.

While I packed, Isa sat on my sleeping mat, picking at a
loose thread in the blanket.

"I'm glad you're coming with us for once."

I folded my handkerchief and said nothing.

She lowered her voice. "Do you . . . know where we're
going?"

I packed the cloth and met her eyes. She nudged her head at
the railing of the loft. Quietly, I peeked over the edge.

"They're outside," I said. "We're alone."

Isa became very interested in the loose thread again. "So?
Do you know?"

"To the city?" I guessed. "To find the dragon fighters . . ."

She looked up and scoffed. "If your father could have taken
shelter there, he would have done it a long time ago."

Isa had told me about the fighters. Rumors she heard
as a girl.

An army had been contracted from the southern empire
to protect wealthy people in the north. The soldiers carried

weapons stronger than scales, but they had never been able to find the dragon. The beast avoided them.

Father didn't have that problem, except things were changing. The dragon hadn't come last time he left the marsh, and that thought weighed on me.

"Father's willing to risk the journey now," I said. "Maybe he'll offer the soldiers gold."

He always had gold, but he never liked to buy things. Only people. He gave coins to his men when they came. But some of those men wouldn't survive a harsh winter, let alone a battle with a monster.

Isa pulled the thread loose. "Some people can't be bought. There are hierarchies in the cities."

"Then you tell me where we're going." If I thought she knew, I would have already asked. But I didn't like her picking apart my speculations.

Isa shrugged and wouldn't meet my eyes. She was in the dark too, like I knew she would be.

"He has a plan," I said.

"If your father was smart, he'd stay in the marsh. He has plenty of food and a home. An easy way of life. That's more than most people can expect."

"But he's not most people. He's hunted."

The only thing keeping Isa in the marsh was Guntor, not a dragon. She had run away a few times over the years, but she always came back. And she was allowed to travel to the settlements. She didn't know what it was like to be trapped here.

Isa sighed. "He's been talking about the dragon for so long, but it's been eight years since it traveled this direction. Maybe the dragon doesn't even care anymo—"

I cut her off. "You don't know what you're talking about."

"I probably don't." She threw the blanket at me, a smile forming on her lips. "So that makes two of us."

I threw the blanket back. She laughed, and I couldn't help but smile in return.

"They say it can talk, you know," she said. "The dragon. They say it has the voice of a man."

"I know."

Except when I was young, she used to say it had the bleat of a goat. I had a hard time imagining any sound coming from the silent creature I had seen.

Isa was my best source of information, but her stories were as fluid as her moods. They changed sometimes between the tellings.

"You think that's really true?" I asked.

"I don't doubt it. There are men who act worse than dragons. Why shouldn't a dragon act like a man?"

I leaned back on the mat, beside Isa. "Tell me what the cities are like."

Right now, I didn't care if her stories weren't all true. They were my connection to the world, and I needed them more than ever.

"Well, we probably won't go to a city first. The closest settlement is an encampment. It smells bad, but there's good food and lots of people." Isa looked me up and down, a slight frown on her face. "Can you make me a promise?"

"What kind of promise?"

"Stay away from the men."

"I always stay away from them."

"Not those spooks who follow your father. Out there . . . it's different. There's young men. Tricky ones. I don't want to see you get tricked."

I held up my hand in the sign of an oath. "I promise not to get tricked."

"This is serious."

I met her eyes. "I know."

Three days had passed since Father's return. Three days to prepare for the journey. They went too fast. This was my last night in the marsh. In the morning, at first light, Father said we would leave.

I'd wanted a glimpse of the dragon, to see something from outside. But this was more than a glimpse or a story. I was going there.

Me.

Away from the safety of my cottage.

I hadn't learned anything more about Father's plan to deal with the dragon, but something about him had changed.

There was a drive in his eyes.

For three days, he had paced in front of the hearth, his mind working. Whenever fear welled up inside of me, I took comfort in that drive. He had a plan.

The night passed without sleep. Time slipped by me, and I felt every moment of it disappear.

Morning came, cool and gray. I tucked my last item in my satchel. Hearty bread, studded with seeds. Traveling food. The kind I used to pack for Father when he went to the borders.

There were a few chores to finish before we left. I poured water over the embers in the hearth. Isa locked the shutters from inside the house, and I swept the front step, even though no one would be there to see the dirt. It felt better to leave it clean.

How long would we be gone?

Father waited outside the house. He didn't acknowledge us when we approached, but he turned and took the first step of the journey. He went north. Toward the mountains.

There was nothing to do but follow.

We were a silent party, picking our way around the deepest

parts of the marsh, our shoes squishing in liquid. The sky was clear, promising a warm day as the sun rose. Father and Guntor walked in front, Isa and I behind. She still had crust in her eyes from sleep, and stray hairs had fallen loose from her braids.

Coins jingled in Father's bag. Gold to buy material necessities. Nothing more. Not a cow to keep at the cottage. Not brass pins for my hair. Just flour and oil.

I recalled one of his favorite sayings. "Attachment leads to suffering."

It was his reason for not buying things. We would get attached to them.

I took a deep breath. My lungs warmed and my heart labored to keep up. One foot moved in front of the other, repeating in a long pattern. I didn't mind the fatigue. It felt good to move. To do something after days of waiting.

We journeyed like that until after dark, stopping only twice to eat and drink water.

"The girl is slowing us up," Guntor remarked.

It was how he always referred to me. Like I wasn't there.

"Keeps her mouth shut though," Father replied. "Unlike some."

Guntor was quiet after that.

I made a fire that burned into the night. There were no roasted carrots or mugs of hot tea or stories from Isa. Just dry bread and rest.

By the end of the next day, the ground didn't slosh where we stepped and the trees grew less sparse. The marsh was ending.

"We'll reach the encampment by nightfall," Isa whispered. "Remember your promise."

My stomach did a little flip.

The first sign of civilization was smoke. It wasn't dragon smell. It was human. Wispy curls of wood-sweet gray twisted into the sky. We could see it at a distance, in the twilight. More fires and hearths than I had imagined.

I motioned for Isa to slow down, lagging behind so we could speak without bothering the others.

"Do Father's men live here?" I didn't like the thought of that many cloaked strangers gathered in one place. There was a constant rotation of new faces. The longest I ever saw one of them last was a year or two, and I never knew any of their names. Father wouldn't let me, and I didn't want to know. Their job was to do Father's bidding. To be his eyes in the world where he couldn't go.

Isa shook her head. "Those kind don't keep camp with regular people. But the folks here are also paid off by your father, so word doesn't get out about where he's hiding. These are still the type who can be bought, even if they don't have as intense of a hunger for gold."

"How exactly is a camp different than a city?" I stared out at all the fires in the landscape ahead of us.

"This place is on the edge of the wilds. It's where people come when they need to hide, or when they don't fit in the city."

Was I that type of person? Someone who wouldn't fit?

"They're not hiding from the dragon," I said.

"Some people hide from things they did. Or things done to them."

Sometimes Isa was young alongside me—following rules, squabbling over chores. Other times, she was a woman with a past I knew nothing about.

"I would never hide if I didn't have to," I said.

Her eyes snapped to me. "Listen, the camps aren't much, but they'll be something to you. There's decent people here, in their own way. And they might even play music for us tonight."

Music. The idea gave strength to my tired legs. Isa had taught me to sing songs, but I had never heard the instruments she described. Flutes and strings.

At the edge of camp, I encountered my first stranger of the journey—a child leaning against a tree. He spotted us from a short distance, eyes wide in the evening light. His messy hair was trimmed short, sticking up like straw, and his cheeks were round and smooth with a tinge of pink. I eyed his little feet, bare in the grass, and I felt myself smile.

I had only seen children once before, when I was twelve. A beggar woman had wandered into the marsh, seeking Father. He sent her away with a single coin.

Her two skinny children had watched from the trees, waiting in the shadows. That image stayed with me.

This child was thin, but not as much as the two I had seen. There was something about children that made even messy hair and dirty clothes look charming, while an adult with the same ensemble would have looked disheveled.

Like Guntor, with his newly graying hair.

The boy stood beneath the tree and said nothing, eyeing us. Father said nothing. Then the boy took off at a run, toward the smoke.

"He'll be spreading word that we're here," Isa told me.

Guntor spit into the grass. "Not every day the alchemist leaves the marsh." He looked sideways at Father.

"That's about to change." Father kept walking toward camp. We followed.

The alchemist. I had never heard that word before.

In the dusk light, I could see the shape of the encampment. One house was almost as large as our cottage, though there were gaps in the shutters. Spaces between lumber, as if it had been built in a hurry.

Most of the structures were shabby lean-tos, lining a bare earth clearing where cooking fires burned.

Beneath the smell of smoke, there was a mixture of aromas. Human sweat, latrines, and roasting meat.

People milled around the clearing, in and out of firelight. Tall and short and broad, they cast long shadows. Their voices ebbed into one sound, marked by a high laugh here and a low rumble there.

My eyes darted from one fire to the next.

Isa grabbed my arm and pulled me along. I had stopped walking without realizing, trying to see everything. Father led us through the camp, and I hurried my steps to stay close behind.

People watched as we passed.

I shrank beside Isa and reached to hold her hand. She gave it a comforting squeeze.

To our left, I heard a strange, breathy sound and looked to see an animal. It was like a deer, but larger and broader, with a tail as thick and beautiful as Isa's hair. Its whole body was golden, intensified by the fire glow.

Isa followed my gaze. "A horse."

Another first for me. Father didn't like animals, and they liked him even less. Wild creatures tended to stay away from the cottage. I only saw deer when I went into the trees.

I watched the way the horse flicked its soft ears and tossed its glossy mane.

"It's beautiful," I whispered.

We moved on, into the thick of the people. Sounds came from all directions now, and I wanted to look everywhere at once.

Each of my family had their own way of speaking and moving and being. Their own take on things. I knew when Isa was happy and when Father was thinking. I could tell exactly how much Guntor had drunk.

Here, in these huddles of people, were a hundred new ways and a hundred new faces. How could anyone learn them all?

Father stopped in front of a fire, and we stopped too.

A woman stood from her low seat beside the flames, her eyes on Father. She wore a stained apron, and her thin brown hair was twisted into a knot.

"Sir." She gave a little curtsy to my father. "We would be honored if you joined our fire tonight."

"That is why we're here," he said.

A pleased look crossed the woman's face, and she wiped her hands on her clothes. "I have seats for you and your girls, and a good stew brewing. Folks say mine's the best, and they're not wrong. Of course, supplies aren't always easy to come by . . ."

"You will be compensated." Father took a small coin from his purse and slipped it into her hand.

Her smile broadened, revealing a missing tooth. "Come, sit."

She ushered us to an assortment of places around the fire. A wooden stump, a log, a flat stone. Soon, steaming bowls were in our hands, filled to the brim with savory broth.

She was right. It was delicious.

"So." The woman sat. "You're traveling again after all these years . . ."

Father gave her a long, sharp look. One that I knew well, a punishment for her question.

The woman opened her mouth again but said nothing. After a moment, she looked away. "I do have business to attend to. Call if you need me."

She stood and drifted to the next fire over, sitting beside a man with white hair. They brought their heads close together, speaking low, careful not to look our way.

I sipped my stew, unsure where I should look. Isa kept her eyes to herself.

Father finished his bowl in three gulps. "Fill your stomachs and get your rest. I'm going to buy supplies."

He took his bag with him, leaving me beside the fire with the others. I wished he would take me so I could see more of everything. Guntor yawned and stretched out on the ground, using his pack as a pillow.

Isa motioned to indicate his open flasket, propped up against the bag.

"He'll pass out soon enough," she whispered.

"I heard that." Guntor kept his eyes closed. "It's not called passing out. It's called dreaming."

We both knew Guntor would drink whether he was an oracle or not, but it was his best excuse.

I examined his ruddy complexion. He rarely shared his dreams with me, except when he predicted the weather. He was never wrong.

A shrill voice spoke from behind. "You're still showing your face around here, Isadora?"

A girl approached our fire. She was around the same age as Isa, though shorter, with trailing black hair and a low-cut dress. Her shoulders sloped, and her eyes sat wide apart on her face.

Isa grinned and stood. "You've been showing off more than that."

She gave the girl a slap on the buttocks.

The girl took no offense, and they both laughed.

It was the kind of teasing Isa and I might have shared, but I had never seen her so comfortable with anyone else. I had never seen her around other girls.

Guntor opened one eye. "Quiet down. I'm trying to rest, as you should be."

The other girl linked arms with Isa. "Let her off her leash, Guntor."

He sat up, still hunched.

Isa gave him her most winning look, lashes fluttering. "A bit of gossip between women is a good thing. Saves you the chatter."

"We'll go to my fire," the girl said.

Guntor folded his arms. "I know the kinds of folks who gather at your fire."

"Ladies only tonight. Promise."

Guntor thought for a moment, his eyelids drooping.

He laid back again. "Keep an eye on Gilde."

"Both eyes." Isa winked and pulled me up by the elbow.

As we walked, we formed a chain of three, arms linked together with Isa in the middle. Our legs moved in time with each other.

The girl leaned forward so I could see her face in the night shadows. "Name's Emma."

I smiled. "Name's Gilde."

It was my first time introducing myself to a stranger, so I mimicked her phrasing to make sure I got it right.

"How do you know Isa?" I asked.

"We used to work together," Emma said.

"Enough about that." Isa waved a hand at Emma, as if swatting a fly.

I held Isa's arm tighter in mine. That meant this was the settlement where Guntor had found her. Isa didn't have parents, so Guntor had offered to marry her. To take care of her.

What kind of work did she and Emma do? But I didn't want to ask the question.

Soon enough, we came to Emma's fire.

She stoked the flames and added another log, then pulled a bottle out of a nearby tent. "Drinks."

I sat by the fire, following Isa's lead.

Isa shook her head. "Tea for us, if you don't mind."

Emma's face fell. "You used to drink better than the rest of them."

"Not anymore."

I didn't want a strong drink either. I had snuck a taste of Guntor's when I was young. It was bitter and burning.

"Such an honest woman these days." Emma sat beside us, her legs extended casually. She turned her gaze to me. "And this is the hatchling you've been keeping in the swamp."

I didn't like being called a hatching, but her tone was playful.

"She's the one," Isa said. "And if I could keep her there, I would."

Emma kept her eyes on me. "Tell me, Gilde, now that you're in the wide world, what do you hope to find?"

I paused. Did she expect an answer?

I wanted to find out why I was here. What did my father have planned for us, and what was my part in it?

But those were not things to discuss with Emma.

"I'm starting to think I'll find more than I imagined," I answered hesitantly. "Things I haven't thought of yet. But I would like to hear music. And stories."

Emma gave Isa a knowing smile. "For music and stories, you've come to the right place."

The girl cupped her hand around her mouth and yelled in the direction of the houses. Her voice was loud enough to carry. "Ewan! Get your sorry self over here!"

Isa flicked dust off her skirt. "I thought we said girls only."

Two figures emerged from the shadows and ran toward us, one tall, one short. They paused when they reached Emma's fire.

The boys might have been almost my age, but they looked young. The taller one had a long, thin face, his chin set too far back.

The shorter one spoke first, pulling his cap from his shaggy hair. "What a thoughtful invitation, Emma. I'm obliged to accept."

His sharp eyes went from Emma to Isa to me. Though small, he was square, with a strong jaw and a prominent nose. The more assertive of the two.

"Meet Ewan and Jonas," Emma said. "Best loggers in all the north."

They each gave a little bow at their names. Ewan was the shorter one.

Isa looked unhappy.

Emma nudged her with her elbow. "These boys are harmless." She shot them a teasing look. "Might as well be girls."

Ewan laughed at that. "I have wondered if skirts are more

comfortable than breeches. Might be time to make the switch."
He sat on the log beside me, closer than I would have chosen.

I pulled my arms in, making sure I wouldn't accidentally
brush him with my sleeve.

"Name's Gilde." I used my new introduction.

"Gilde." Ewan gave me a long smile.

Jonas settled on the other side, near Isa.

"Your services are needed," Emma said. "Hope you brought
your whistle."

"Don't I always?" Ewan took a wooden cylinder from a
sling on his back.

Emma gave him a nod, and he put the thing to his lips.

I watched, curious.

Sound came out, and I went still.

The whistle made a song that a voice could never sing, high
and pure. Ewan's arm touched mine as he played, but I didn't
care. I was caught in the music.

It was the kind of sound that made you think of laughing. Or
maybe crying. Even though there was no reason for emotion.

The music ended sooner than I would have liked, and Ewan
searched my face.

"What did you think?"

"Can you play another?" I asked.

He looked pleased.

"Don't let her flatter you," Emma said. "She's used to Isa's
singing. Pretty much anything is better than that."

Isa scowled.

"How about you try it?" Ewan scooted closer, our legs
touching, and held the flute to my mouth. It was too close, and
the flute was still damp from his saliva.

My skin went cold, and I leaned away. "I'd rather not. I
don't know how."

Jonas winked. "I'm sure Ewan could teach you a thing or
two."

Ewan laughed and placed his hand on my leg, as if I were conspiring with him in the joke. But it wasn't funny to me. I stood up and backed away.

Isa stood too. "Stop."

"He doesn't mean any harm." Jonas tossed a twig into the fire. "You're usually more fun than this, Isa. Except when you're with the old man you sold yourself to."

Everyone around the fire went tense for a moment. Silent.

Emma tugged on Isa's skirt. "Sit down."

Isa motioned for me to come to her log, away from Ewan. I did. Not because I needed her to shelter me. I didn't like the way Jonas spoke to her.

"Anyway," Emma turned to Jonas. "You're one to talk about Isa, when your mum's been clamoring for the alchemist's gold tonight."

Jonas's mother must have been the one who gave us stew for dinner. The lady with the missing tooth.

He clenched his too-small jaw. "Spends like any other gold."

Ewan spoke up. "I wouldn't touch that stuff, myself." His gaze shifted to Isa. "No offense."

"Look at her," Jonas said. "She hasn't had her hands on a single coin. You were better off working with Emma. At least you got paid back then."

Emma laughed.

Isa didn't. "You're too young to speak about the past, Jonas. You weren't there."

A knot formed in my stomach.

Emma caught eyes with Isa. "He's just jealous, eh."

Everything was a joke to Emma.

But Jonas had a mean look behind his long face, the kind Guntor got sometimes. Father was hard, and quick to bring punishment. But some people liked to hurt others for entertainment. Jonas was the type who did it with words.

And beneath the insults, there were things he had said that I didn't understand. Things I needed to know.

"What's wrong with the gold?" I asked, cutting the tension in the circle. "What is an alchemist?"

Isa's mouth formed a tight line. "People like to talk, Gilde. That's all."

"What do they say?" I was firm.

Emma answered. "The more gold you get, the more you want."

"We don't just say it," Ewan chimed in. "We know it. I've seen those men who go to the marsh. They gave their souls away for those coins. You won't catch me with alchemy in my pockets. No one knows where he got it from—"

"Enough," Jonas interrupted. "You want your talk getting back to the alchemist?" He glanced at me.

Emma took a bundle from near the fire, unwrapping the cloth to reveal a kettle. She poured hot liquid into a mug and handed it to me. "Well, there's plenty of other gossip to share," she said.

I held the mug in my hands, warming my palms. Nothing they had told me was a surprise, really. Alchemy was a new word, but on some level I already understood what the men gave to Father in exchange for the money. Loyalty. And, the longer they stayed, the sicker they got.

None of Father's men stayed in his employ for long. I had started to pay attention as I got older. At the one-year mark, they seemed to grow more desperate for the gold. They demanded payment the moment they reported to the cottage, and they didn't look well, with missing teeth and hollow eyes. Then, eventually, they stopped coming at all.

I didn't like thinking about what happened to them. I tried to imagine they moved on to work that wasn't so difficult, or they transitioned to only meeting Father at the borders. But their deteriorating health made me wonder.

What did Father have them do that could be so hard on a body?

None of them were kind. They scared me with their snarls and outbursts. That didn't mean I wanted them to suffer.

Guntor was different. He let Father buy him things, but he never touched the money.

Were there other kinds of gold in the world? Innocent kinds that bought innocent things?

Emma offered Ewan a mug, but he reached for a bottle instead.

"There is plenty else to talk about." He uncorked it and took a swig. "Strange things happening here of late. Wizard sightings."

"Not this again." Jonas took the bottle from Ewan, pouring liquor into his own mug.

Isa leaned forward. "What happened?"

"You heard about the new girl?" Ewan rested his elbows on his knees, settling into his story.

Isa shook her head. "There's too many girls out here as it is. Was she fleeing the prisons?"

"Don't know," Ewan said. "She was only seventeen and didn't last long. It happened in one night. They said it was sickness, but it's wizard work if you ask me."

Realization struck. He meant the girl had died.

"Go ahead and ask him." Jonas took another drink. "He has a whole list of evidence." He said the last word in a mocking tone.

Ewan sat up straight. "She was coming of age, and she may have had a spark. That'll draw a wizard like nothing else."

"Don't be stupid," Jonas scoffed. "What would a girl with a spark be doing out here with the rest of us? People like that don't end up in the wilds."

A spark. There were so many new words.

Ewan was undeterred. "I know what I saw. It was six days

ago. Early morning before the sun came up. I heard a sound outside my tent. Some kind of chanting, too close. So I get up to see, and there's a shadow in the bushes, peeping into camp like it's up to no good. I warned it. Told it to go, but it didn't listen. Just kept chanting in its way, and the sound made me feel sick. So I put an arrow in it. The worst part is, the thing didn't react. Not even a sound. Just turned and left. Unnatural." Ewan shuddered. "Next day, when I heard what happened to the girl, I knew I'd seen a wizard in its killing trance."

Jonas didn't look convinced. "You shot your own shadow."

"Then where's the arrow? There was blood on the ground."

"A deer, then."

I clutched my mug. Isa had never talked about wizards or killing trances. It was the kind of story that would have made me want to hear more. If it were only a story.

Something moved outside the firelight. A shadow beside a tree.

I startled and spilled tea on my skirt, staring into the dark.

"Gilde." It was my father's voice.

Low.

Hard.

The others went silent.

Father stepped into the light. In a swift move, he grabbed my hand, pinching the tender nerve between thumb and forefinger, forcing me to my feet. To anyone else, it would look like a light hold. To me, it was a jolt of pain. I kept my face placid, hiding the truth.

"Come." He led me away from the fire, back toward Guntor.

When he let go of my hand, I took deep breaths.

Isa followed behind us at a distance, and we reached the fire.

"Sleep," he said. "Tomorrow we head for the mountains."

3

ISA WOKE ME WITH A SHAKE
of my shoulders. The fire was dead, the morning pale.

A chill sank through my cloak, and I shivered.

The encampment still slept, tucked into tents and hovels, bundled in blankets beside coals. The smoke from so many dying fires made my eyes water.

We left without saying goodbye. Would Emma think of us? Or Jonas and Ewan? I would think of them. My first introductions.

Father walked ahead, his strides long and swift. Something was driving him forward. Something I wanted to know about.

He would tell me when the time was right.

I had never walked on such dry ground. The grass grew yellow, and the trees thinned. Near the middle of the day, we covered terrain without any trees at all. Only wide stretches of parched land, studded with sharp rocks. By evening, the boulders were as tall as trees.

Would the rocks hide us if the dragon came?

My throat felt scratchy in the dusty climate.

Mountains loomed on the horizon. Close.

They had always seemed a lifetime away. But after three days of walking, here they were. Right in front of us.

At sunset, Isa sat in the stiff grass. She chewed on a lump of cheese from her pack. "I've never traveled this way before. The cities are more to the northeast." She looked in that direction.

"What's this way?" I sat beside her.

"Nothing good."

We shared a look.

Father threw down his pack where he stood and called to me. "Gilde. I have something to show you."

Isa's eyes narrowed on him. I scrambled to my feet, kicking up dust. My heart quickened.

Without a word, Father made his way to the other side of a massive boulder, not waiting for me.

I left Isa behind with an apologetic shrug and cantered after him.

When I rounded the corner, he stood facing me. Father and I were almost alone now, hidden by stone.

I kept my arms behind my back so he wouldn't catch me fidgeting. I would wait to hear what he had to say. Anything to help things make sense.

My chest hurt.

"Look close." Father held out his hand, a glass object resting in his open palm.

Gold flecks tinted the translucent bottle. It was filled halfway with some kind of black liquid, and the glossy contents swirled, though Father's hand was still.

"Do you know what this is?" he asked.

I shook my head, not pulling my eyes from the black substance. The way it moved made me feel odd.

"Watch." Father's hand closed around the bottle. Too tight.

His arm tensed until it shook with the effort, and his eyes squeezed shut as if in pain.

I didn't breathe. It lasted so long, I almost reached out to stop him.

Then, the black liquid bubbled out of the opening. Instead

of falling to the ground, as it should have done, the black spread out and floated in the air. It became clear, a circle of water, spinning around my father like a wheel.

He opened his eyes, and I took a breath.

Wind blew his dark hair back from his face. There hadn't been any wind a moment earlier.

My eyes moved back to the water. It was beautiful in a way that told me it was dangerous. Like ice or fire or a sharp blade. Except those were natural things I had seen thousands of times before, and this was something else.

"So that's it, then?" Isa's voice came from behind. She had followed us.

Father looked past me, to her, and a dark smile spread over his face. He tightened his grip again, and the water snaked its way through the air toward Isa.

I turned and watched it move.

With a crash, it poured over her head, soaking her cloak.

She shrieked and brushed off as much water as she could. "I'll freeze!"

Father released his grip, and the wind disappeared. Isa remained wet, as if she had been dunked in a river.

Guntor hurried around the boulder. "What's this?"

Father brushed a droplet of water off his own sleeve. "Little mice shouldn't burrow where they don't belong. I was speaking with my daughter alone."

Guntor assessed the scene, then gave Father a curt nod. He grabbed Isa by the arm. "Come on."

She went with him.

"You could help make a fire," she mumbled as they disappeared around the corner.

"That's women's work . . ." Guntor's voice faded.

I examined the bottle in Father's hand. The black liquid swirled inside the glass again, though the volume did seem like it might have been diminished.

It was a portable body of water. A safety device, or a weapon.

"Where do you think we're going?" Father asked.

I could barely say the words. "To the dragon."

"The beast hasn't come for me, and that tells me something. It's weakened. And now I have this." He held up the bottle. "I waited a long time."

A far-off look passed over him, and I wondered where he found something like that bottle. What had he done at the border to get that wound?

"You mean to kill the dragon by drowning it?" The idea still seemed impossible. Even with what I had just seen.

Father shook his head. "I'll show it that the hunt is over. That we're not defenseless anymore." His voice softened. "Will you go with me?"

And suddenly, I was the little girl again holding my Father's hand in the marsh. I was part of a team, meant to do something important.

Even if I didn't know what that something was.

"Why do you want me to come?"

"When I ask something of you, you should say yes."

Dread welled inside me like the black liquid, swirling.

"I want to," I told him. "I'm worried it's not safe for either of us."

"It was never safe in the marsh. The dragon couldn't track me there, but it knew the general vicinity. Touching water burns the creature, and it can drown, but if the dragon had decided to risk the danger, it could have come to us. Things have changed, and it isn't as strong as it was. It's time to make a new arrangement." He looked down at me, his eyes hard again. "You will go with me."

If Father had to face this, it wasn't fair for me to hide. I wouldn't be a coward. I met that gaze and saw the unwavering intent behind it.

This was always the path I had been on, whether I knew it or not.

"Yes, Father," I said. "I'll go."

This time, Isa woke me with a hand over my mouth. Her face was inches from mine, her finger at her lips, demanding silence. I nodded, letting her know I would be quiet. She removed her hand, and I sat up, breathing through my nose.

I searched the sky. No dragon wings. No dragon scent.

The moon was high. Father and Guntor still slept, heads on their packs. Why would Isa wake me in the middle of the night without the others? Her boots were on her feet, her pack secured over her shoulders.

I gave her a questioning look.

She stood and motioned for me to follow, her steps light. I tucked my feet into my shoes, hoping my rustlings would blend in with the night sounds. Here, in the dry grass, wind made a different sound than it did in the marshes. It was raspy. Swishing.

We left the warm embers of the fire, finding our path through the boulders.

"Isa—" I started.

She spun and clamped her hand over my mouth again, pointing back toward the men. We were still too close. Her palms were damp with sweat, even in the night chill.

When we finally reached a distance suitable to her, Isa spoke. "Talk low. I don't want them waking up."

"I figured that out." I pulled my cloak tighter around my shoulders. "What's going on?"

She took a long time to answer.

Long enough that I started to get frustrated. Then I saw there were tears in her eyes.

"I'm leaving." Her voice was hoarse. "And I want you to come with me."

Part of me wanted to believe this was some kind of game, but I couldn't ignore her shaking fingers and her laced boots.

She was serious.

"Isa . . . I know it's hard sleeping on the ground—"

"It's not like that." She wiped her nose with the hem of her sleeve. "Your father plans to talk with the dragon. We're heading into its territory."

"I know."

"Then you know you have to come with me."

"He has protection." I struggled to keep my voice to a whisper. "You saw. Water burns dragons."

Isa let out a sharp laugh. "It's enough to protect himself for a quick getaway, maybe. But not the rest of us. Even Guntor's scared."

"You don't know that it's not enough. The dragon's weakened, and Father plans to intimidate it. He said."

"Why hasn't he brought his men with him?" Isa gave me a long look, her tears drying. "Why not have extra protection? Gilde, something's happening here that he doesn't want anyone else to see. And I don't want to find out what it is."

But I was glad the men weren't here. When I was a child, I once stayed out in the trees instead of making dinner at night. Father sent one of them after me, and the man dragged me back to the house by a fistful of my hair. When he came close, his mouth smelled of decay.

I shook my head. "Father doesn't need them."

Isa leaned closer. "He's never lived in the cities, even when he was free. Did you know that? There were always rumors about him. But now . . . Gilde, his mind isn't well. I think it hasn't been for a long time."

I was shivering. More than I should have been. "This has always been the plan. Then we'll get to be with people again."

Isa shook her head, and the tears came back. "Sometimes I hated you, and I think you could tell." She looked away from me, into the black of night. "It's not easy to be around a child when you never got to be one."

I had been able to tell, but we never spoke about anything like this. Why now?

Her eyes drifted back to mine, and a tear escaped down her cheek. "But mostly I loved you like I was your sister . . . or a mother. Not that I know how to be either of those." She paused, biting back the flow of emotion so she could quiet her voice. "It's why I stayed for so long. But Gilde, we can't stay anymore. Please." Her whisper cracked. "Please come with me."

Realization struck. She wasn't just going home. She was leaving for good. Guntor's prediction was coming true.

My lip trembled, and my throat ached.

"You can't . . ." I searched her face, pleading. "Isa, no."

"Come with me."

"We have no money." What could I say to stop her? "Guntor will find you."

She had run away for a night or two before. She always came back. But I had seen Guntor's anger. He wouldn't let her go for good without a fight.

"We need to leave now," she insisted. "We don't have money, but we have our lives."

Isa had never been protected. Worse than that, she had been hurt on purpose. That's why she was afraid now.

But I couldn't leave Father to do this alone. We were in it together.

"I made him a promise," I said.

"Gilde." She let out a curse word and spit on the ground. "You don't know what you're promising. What's his plan?"

"I won't live my life in hiding."

Isa's brow knit in anger, and she took me by the wrist, pulling me with her.

I reacted. "No!"

I spoke too loud.

We both froze, waiting to see if Guntor had heard. If I got Isa in trouble, the punishment would be my fault.

A moment passed, and all was silent. The men were still asleep on the other side of the boulders.

Isa's eyes went hard. "I never had the heart to leave you. I still don't, but I have to go, even if it breaks me. Remember I tried. At least I can say that."

"I'll find you," I said.

"I really hope that's true. I'm going to the city."

The city north of the marsh. The one she left as a child.

We looked at each other for a long time.

Then, she turned and left.

I stood in the moonlight, watching her retreat. She always walked so straight.

My face was damp with tears I hadn't noticed.

Eventually, I made my way back to the fire. Back to my satchel and my blanket. My mind was numb.

I couldn't lose Isa.

But I couldn't choose between her and the promise I had made to Father. The dragon would find us someday if we didn't stop the hunt now.

Isa could be caught in the attack, even.

This was what I had to do for all of us.

I told myself it was another of her shifting moods. She would come back, no matter what she said.

I settled under my blanket, eyes open, my body shaking.

She would come back.

4

I DIDN'T SLEEP THE REST OF THE
night. When Father and Guntor woke, I closed my eyes,
pretending. They searched the rocks for Isa, then went away
for a private conversation, their voices hushed.

I got up and packed my blanket. They returned, dark looks
between them.

"The girl knows something." Guntor spoke through
clenched teeth, like I still wouldn't be able to hear him.

Father tightened the strap on his pack. "She would have
alerted us."

He was so sure of my obedience. But I wouldn't feel guilty
for keeping Isa's secret from Father. I had my loyalties to
both of them.

I spoke up. "Should we wait here? In case she comes back?"

They ignored me. I was the child.

"It's not too late to catch her in the fields if we hurry back,"
Guntor said.

Both of us wanted Isa to return. Only I wanted her to
choose it.

We looked to Father.

"I told you." He set his jaw. "There will be opportunity
to find her after, if you can. But this might be the time she
disappears. Even you can't escape your predictions."

Guntor clenched a fist. We followed after Father.

Toward the mountain.

By midday, walking turned to climbing. Isa would have hated this, and my weak heart didn't like it either. We were gaining elevation, and my chest burned. I took labored breaths, and my pace slowed.

I removed the cloak from my shoulders and packed it away for the afternoon. Soon, we were high enough to look out over the whole valley. There was so much to see, it was hard to focus on calming my heart.

Was our house out there somewhere on the horizon? If we went high enough, would I be able to spot it? Isa had to be down there, even if I couldn't find her among the rocks and the fields.

Hills turned to cliffs. Father climbed up to one of the high ledges, wedging himself in a crack, then pulled his body onto the flat surface. I followed, and for a moment, I thought I might fall. But I dug my fingers into the cracks and made it to the top.

The ledge was backed by a sheer wall of rock. Guntor climbed up and moved as far from the edge as he could.

"Here," Father said. "This is where we'll meet the creature."

I tensed. "This is its home?"

The only plants were spindly pines and spiky weeds. It looked like the dragon here. Dry and sharp.

"The whole mountain is his." Father set down his pack and perched on the ledge. "But this place is as good as any." He tapped a knuckle against the rock face. "Keep the stone at your back. The dragon can't come from behind."

It also meant there was nowhere to run, except the narrow crag we had climbed up.

Father took his knife from its sheath. "The dragon will come at the smell of human blood on his mountain." He ran the blade over the back of his arm. The cut was deep, welling with red. Father's face showed no sign of pain.

I closed my eyes against the sight, turning my head.

"My blood won't be enough." His voice was firm.

I opened my eyes. Guntor backed away to the furthest corner. My stomach lurched, but I wouldn't show it.

"I need to cut you both," Father said flatly.

"I'll do it myself." I held out my hand for the knife. "I'll make sure it's deep enough."

After today, we would live out in the world among people. I would learn to play my own flute, not Ewan's. There would be dancing, and a thousand new stories to hear. I needed to think about that.

Father passed the blade to me, pumping his fist to make himself bleed. Droplets ran down his arm onto the rock at our feet. "Cut above your elbow. Not the veins lower down."

I gripped the handle so tight my fingers hurt. I had gutted plenty of fish and skinned rabbits. This would be like that. I moved fast, before I could think too much. The knife was sharp. I pressed it in a line against my skin, straight and hard. It took a moment to feel the pain.

A sting and then an ache.

Blood spilled from the cut, and I let the drops fall on the rocks.

For a moment, my legs felt weak. I steadied myself with a hand against the cliff.

Guntor didn't cut himself deep enough, so Father finished the job, gripping his wrist hard.

We waited in silence, our wounds exposed to the wind. I didn't move, as if the knife had gone all the way through me and pinned me to that ledge.

The scent came first. Smoke and metal and fear.

Guntor swore. Father held his golden bottle, knuckles white.

I couldn't control my breath. It was as ragged as the heart in my chest. Father's knife lay on the ground, damp with blood. I picked it up from the rocks and wrapped both hands around the handle. He had a better weapon, but I couldn't help wanting something of my own to hold.

A shadow passed over us. Black and silent.

My pulse thundered, then faltered.

It was finally happening. The beast was here, hidden by the cliff now. I leaned closer to Father, but he stepped forward, right to the edge.

The creature darted overhead again, and I glimpsed it this time. Its midnight wings were nothing like a bird's. The flesh was all sinew and armor. Its lithe tail glittered in the sun.

Then it was gone again, behind the rocks.

Father took in a breath and raised his voice. "I've come to talk, Dragon. You'll want to hear what I have to say."

Nothing happened. For a moment, I dared to hope it had gone. Given up already.

Fast as lightning, it careened into our line of vision. The dragon landed on a high cliff across from us, close enough for me to see its eyes for the first time.

I had imagined a reptilian face, like the snakes in the marsh. But the dragon's enormous yellow eyes were intelligent, bright, and contrasted against the black lids. There was a mind behind its gaze, not an animal.

When I was a child, I thought the dragon was as big as our house. Now I saw it was only as tall as two men. Sharp claws extended from its four paws, and it stood like a horse with fingers instead of hooves.

It opened its mouth, revealing pointed teeth. I braced myself, but no fire came out. Only words.

"Who is bleeding?" The voice was deep, but not so different from a man's.

So it *could* talk. I gripped the knife tighter.

Father raised his cut arm. "All of us. So you would come."

"You know something about dragons." The beast looked at each of us. First Father, then Guntor, then me. On me, he stayed longer than the others. "So you should have known better than to come here."

Those eyes were too human, like a trick. A monster shouldn't have anything familiar or beautiful in its face.

Father bowed his head. "Forgive the intrusion, please. But I didn't come with empty hands. I brought what you asked for."

I looked at Father's bottle, still clutched in his fist. The dragon had asked for it? Suddenly, all the hair on my neck prickled. This wasn't what Father had said would happen.

The dragon snapped his tail on the rocks with a terrible clack. "You seek a trade?"

"As—as we discussed." Father took a step back.

"I'm sorry to disappoint. I won't give you fire, no matter what you bring to me." It glanced at me again. "You'll have to cut it from my body. And I wouldn't try that if I were you." The creature let out a low growl, and smoke curled up around it.

Guntor cowered against the rock wall. I wanted to climb down the crag and run, but there would be nowhere to hide.

Father put a hand out toward the dragon, a placating gesture. "I didn't come for fire. I didn't know it could be given." He licked his lips, and a hungry look passed over his face. A look I hadn't seen before. He blinked, and it disappeared. "I came to trade for my life. I'm tired of being hunted."

The dragon folded its leathery wings flat to its body. "I could kill you and take what you brought. I would have my hunt and my present."

"You won't kill me. You may be a hunter, but you've always been true to your bargains." I heard the fear in his tone.

The dragon fixed him with a stare. "What have you brought for me?"

"You must already know. Don't you sense it?"

The dragon's gaze snapped to me. I stopped breathing. It should have been looking at the bottle.

"You think I can't acquire my own magics?" it asked. "From among the cities? I don't need your leftovers, wizard."

A wizard, like in Ewan's story. But the dragon was wrong. Father's water was unusual. But it was a treasure, not like the chants and death spells Ewan spoke of.

"You know you won't find power like this in the cities," Father said. "Not unguarded. We've both looked."

The dragon said nothing, and its smoke billowed. I kept my eyes on its movements, but my thoughts were on Father. Why hadn't he told me he would try to trade away the bottle?

Father broke the silence. "All I ask in return is that you keep your promise. Give your word that you will no longer hunt me."

The dragon bared its teeth, and I felt my body tremble.

"You're a fool." It crouched. Stone crumbled beneath its sharp claws.

It was going to attack.

Panic welled inside of me. This was it, just like my nightmares as a child. But this wasn't a dream, and I wasn't the one in the dragon's sights.

Father was.

Before I knew what I was doing, I raised my knife and stepped in front of Father.

The dragon paused, eyes narrowed on me. No one moved.

It bared its teeth. "You would try to protect this man?"

I spoke softer than I meant to. "He's my father."

Its eyes went wide. "Wizard. You still would make your bargain?"

"It's why I came here," Father replied.

The dragon sat on its haunches and something like a laugh came from its lungs. It wasn't a happy sound. "I'll take the present then. And I won't hunt you. I don't want anything to do with you."

"Give your word," Father demanded.

"I give you my word. If you leave your sacrifice and never come back to my lands, you'll never have to see me again."

I let out a breath. The danger wasn't completely gone. The dragon was still in front of us. But now, all Father had to do was give away the bottle. Then it would be over.

To steady myself, I laid a hand on Father's shoulder, his knife still in my other fist.

He took me by the wrist. "Don't run, Gilde."

Did he think I was such a coward, after everything I had stood through today? We were at the end now.

"Take what is yours," Father said to the dragon.

The creature unfurled its wings and lifted into the air. Then, it dove straight at us.

Father didn't move.

"Hold out the bottle." My words were a plea and a command.

Silence was the response.

He held my wrist at arm's distance, forcing me away from him.

"The bottle." I pulled at Father's grip, and my chest seized with pain.

The dragon slowed as it came within reach of us. It didn't snatch the bottle from Father. It didn't even touch Father.

Instead, it wrapped its bony claws around my shoulders, and Father let go of my wrist. For an instant, I couldn't react. All I could feel was the hard press of the dragon's talons against my body.

Then I thrust my knife at its leg. The blade glanced off polished scales and twisted from my hand.

A scream tore at my throat, and my feet left the ground, dangling in the air. Nausea washed over me, turning my sweat cold.

This wasn't how it was supposed to happen.

Gasping for air, I tried to dig my fingers under the dragon's claws to loosen its grip. But we were high now. If it let go, I would fall to my death. I stopped fighting, my eyes unfocused. Everything was a blur of blue sky and gray rock. I tried to clear my vision, and I caught sight of Father far below.

He didn't yell. He didn't run after us as we sped higher. He looked at the ground, his hand over the cut on his forearm.

"Help!" I sobbed.

He didn't look up.

Then we flew too far, and I couldn't see him at all.

I was alone with the dragon.

5

I VOMITED TWICE INTO THE AIR.

The third time, bile filled my mouth, but my stomach was empty. I wiped tears and sickness from my face.

My breath came in choked gasps. The attacks hadn't been this bad since I was a little girl, when Father had taught me to control myself. Slow, slow. Calm, calm. Imagine the breeze in the grass. I tapped my hand over my heart.

It wasn't working. Wind rushed over my face and fresh terror clamped down on me. The dragon's sharp claws held me firm, but I wasn't bleeding. It hadn't cut into me yet.

Spots filled my vision. With each gasp, the spots grew darker, until everything went black.

I awoke on the ground, grass beneath me, dragon stench in my nostrils. I didn't open my eyes. For a while, there was nothing but solid ground and breath.

Then I felt the swish of wings. Air gusted against my face, metallic and hot.

I pretended to stay asleep, but dug my fingers into the earth, claiming a fist-full of dirt. Anything to throw. My other hand wrapped around a fallen branch.

The dragon moved on the ground, its steps heavy in the grass.

It was time.

I counted to three, then stood and turned to face it.

The creature kept its head low, at my level, watching me. I didn't know where to look. The teeth? The tail? Or its huge, beautiful eyes.

Instead of lunging at me again, the dragon stilled and curled its tail against its body. There wasn't much space between us. In one move, it would have me.

"You're going to fight me with a stick?" The dragon's voice was quieter than it had been with Father.

It sent a shiver through me. I gripped the branch harder.

Night would fall soon. I wanted to search my surroundings, but I couldn't look away from the beast.

My voice was a hoarse whisper. "You promised to let us go."

The dragon's ears went forward. "I don't remember making that promise."

I thought back over the conversation on the cliff, and my head throbbed. The dragon had promised Father would never have to see it again. Father, not me.

I took a trembling breath. "You were meant to take the golden bottle."

For the first time, it looked down, as if calculating how to answer. I broke my eyes away and took in my surroundings. We stood in a clearing of trees. Everything was pine cones and high branches rather than the low, leafy foliage of the valley. We were on the mountain.

And there was nowhere to hide.

Except to the left, through the trees, I spotted a structure. It was something like a house, if the house had been built to hold hundreds of people. There were more windows than I could count, and towers rose high, peeking out over the forest.

The whole thing had been made of stone, carved into a cliff face. I wanted to look longer, but I didn't dare.

The dragon wouldn't have built the place. The front door was narrow, made for people. Even if it was abandoned now, there might be somewhere to hide in those walls. Somewhere too small for the dragon to follow.

I had to try.

I tossed my branch aside and ran as fast as I could, fallen tree needles poking through the sides of my shoes.

After five paces, hard scales wrapped around my waist. I was caught in the coil of the dragon's tail.

It lifted me from the ground and back to where I had started. I heaved breaths, and frustrated tears spilled down my cheeks.

For five paces, I had escaped. It might have been the closest I would come to freedom. They might have been my last steps before I would die.

"You'll make yourself pass out again," the dragon said.

"Then let me go." I spoke through gasps.

"So you can run back to the wizard?"

The dragon set me on the ground and uncurled its tail. I steadied myself and tapped my hand on my chest, breathing. But that old trick didn't work in the presence of a monster.

I looked up. "He has other things you might want, like gold coins. Anything you ask for if you take me back—"

"There's only one thing most dragons would want."

My heart quickened. "What is it?"

"It's standing in front of me." The dragon's keen eyes watched me again, unblinking.

A weight sank in my stomach.

"The wizard knew what he was offering," it said.

At those words, I wanted to press my hands over my ears.

Everything that happened on the cliff played through my

mind. The way Father held my wrist. How he looked away as the dragon carried me through the air.

A pain welled inside of me, growing sharper. My mind ached, but it was physical pain too. A thought that might break me. I stopped thinking.

I pushed the memories away. Swept them up and cast them aside like dust from the front step.

Things hadn't happened like that.

They couldn't have.

The dragon had broken the bargain when it took me.

"Why would a dragon want a person?"

"Certain people are useful for casting spells." It met my eyes again. "I couldn't leave you with him."

"You should have." My voice was softer than I intended.

"And that's why I couldn't. You wanted to stay with a wizard." It showed its teeth. "You defended the man who cut you open. If you'd give your blood so freely, you're as bad as him."

There was anger in its voice. I placed a hand over the place where I had spilled my own blood. The wound was clotted now.

The pain started to grow inside me again, threatening to make me remember things I wanted to ignore. I closed my eyes and thought back to Father in the marsh, cradling me in his arms.

That was my truth.

I was protected.

And yet here I was.

I opened my eyes again. "There are dragon fighters in the city. When they hear you've taken a girl, they'll—"

"They won't find me here. They never have. This part of the mountain is shrouded from outside eyes. Even if they could come after you, do you really think your disappearance will be reported?"

The dragon knew about the fighters. It knew more than I did.

The sun had almost set, turning my captor into a dark shape against the trees. A night breeze blew. The night would be moonless, impossible to see anything.

My whole body began to shake from the cold, and from something else.

I had left my satchel and my cloak behind. Had Father carried them on for me? Where was he now?

But those were dangerous thoughts again.

I wrapped my arms around myself.

The dragon shifted its weight. "I'll take you inside."

I stiffened. "Inside where?"

"The castle."

I looked back toward the house in the cliff, now hidden in shadow. So it was the dragon's house. I had been running toward more captivity.

"You fit in there?"

"In most of it."

All my life, I had known not to talk back. It never led to anything good. But now the dragon was in charge, and I would probably die. What I said didn't matter.

I lifted my chin. "What if I don't want to go?"

If the dragon locked me inside, my chance of escape would be gone completely.

"You can't stay out here in the wind," it said. "The nights are cold in the mountains. If you don't want to go, I'll have to carry you."

I did not like the thought of hot claws gripping my shoulders again. "I'll walk."

"Very well."

That was a strange walk through the trees, the scent of the dragon mixing with the sweet night air. It stalked behind me, watching every move. I walked as fast as I could without running, my heart straining.

When we reached the castle, the dragon didn't go to the

wooden front door. Now that I was close, I could see an opening had been broken through the side wall, rubble crumbling away.

A dragon-sized entrance.

The beast went ahead of me and stopped at the hole. "I don't know your name."

I stood in silence, shivering.

The dragon tried again. "Will you tell it to me?"

"Why do you want to know?" Names were too familiar. Too real for a nightmare like this.

"You're coming to my home." There was no warmth in that acknowledgement. "And I prefer to keep track of the people who associate with wizards."

Didn't the dragon know me? I had been hunted by it my whole life.

"Gilde," I said.

It blinked. "I'm called Wil."

Wil. Such a normal sounding name. Too simple for something so large.

I decided I hated the name, and I would never say it. He was a beast, not a person. Though, in my mind, I started to think of the creature as something other than *it*. He wouldn't have a name, but he was decidedly a male.

With a nod of his head, he turned and entered the castle. I considered running again, but I was already bruised from the last time he caught me with his tail. He would be watching from the shadows now. I could sense him there.

If only I had a torch. If only I were anywhere else. With Isa, curled on my blanket in the loft. My throat tightened, but I refused to cry.

When I reached the threshold, I peered into the dark, my feet frozen.

"Dragon." I squared my shoulders. "Can you breathe flames?"

There was a long pause before he answered. "I can."

"Will you light a fire so I can see?" It felt strange to make a request, and I didn't like the idea of his flame. But I was cold to the bone.

"I will never breathe fire for you, or any other."

There was a scraping sound from inside the castle, like scales on stone. Then, a small metal object landed near my feet, flung from the dark.

I picked up the flint and steel.

Such a human thing, like the flint I used at the hearth in the marshes.

"I'll find wood for you," the dragon said. "Inside."

Those weren't the words of a creature who was about to kill me. He seemed more intent on keeping me. At least for the night.

I shifted my weight between my feet. "If I go inside with you . . . do you promise not to kill me tonight?"

"I'm not sure the word of a dragon will mean much to you."

"It's better than nothing." He hadn't killed my father, at least.

A snort came from the dragon. "You have my word then. As long as you stay close to me, you won't be harmed."

Eyes wide, I took my first step into the castle.

6

I NAVIGATED AROUND THE DARK outlines of boulders and piles of stone.

At least, I hoped that's what they were.

My imagination tempted me to see worse things. Animal skulls. Human remains.

Perhaps the dark protected my eyes.

The dragon moved beside me, closer than I had thought. I let out a gasp, then stifled it. We were so close that I could have reached out and touched his scales.

We were both still for a moment. My chest went tight again, and I fought for control. The dragon breathed out.

"Come with me." He moved further into the castle.

His tail stayed beside me. I could hear it coiling on the ground. I walked with him, before he could decide to pull me along with that coil.

The air grew cool inside the house, and my teeth chattered.

It was a home carved into stone, which made it seem like a cave in my mind. Especially with the crumbling opening. Away from the entry hole, the castle was completely dark. I could no longer see the ground beneath my feet, and I stumbled. I hit the floor, and my left palm stung with grit.

The dragon stopped. "Why do you keep stopping?"

"It's dark." I stood and rubbed my palm on my skirt, wondering if there was blood. The dragon would smell it.

"Hold my tail and I'll show you where to walk. We're almost there."

Hold his tail? I looked back to the entry, tempted to retreat.

The dragon sighed. "Or you can choose to be blind. As usual."

I chose to ignore his implication and reached for his scales. They were smoother than I imagined, and almost too hot to touch with my bare skin. The edges should have been sharp, but they laid flat, linking together to form one surface.

We kept going, and my feet didn't encounter any more tripping hazards. His heat warmed my chilled hand, and I eventually put both of them on the tail.

"You can see in the dark?" I asked.

"I'm a dragon."

As if I could forget.

"We're here." He stopped and his voice grew closer. He must have turned. "I'll show you through a small door to your left. You will find a bed with warm blankets. In the morning, you'll have wood and kindling for your flint. I'll be here. Do not try to leave the room. There are dangers in this house."

What could be more dangerous than a dragon?

His tail guided me to my left, further than I expected. It was difficult to measure distance in the dark. My legs ran into something soft. The bed.

He paused. "You should let go of my tail now."

I pulled my hands away, instantly missing the heat. I looked back and found I could no longer see the faint light from the entrance.

Scales clicked against rock as the dragon settled outside the bedroom door.

Complete dark was an awful thing. My mind kept tricking

me. Telling me I could see light out of the corner of my eye. But there was none.

I ran my fingers over the bed. A blanket lay smooth across a thick pad, softer than Father's bed at home. I felt the entire surface in the dark, checking every corner. What was I searching for?

Spiders? What a thing to worry about with a dragon nearby.

Something like dust coated the blanket, grainy and pilling. It might have smelled musty if not for the dragon scent around me, overpowering everything else.

"Sleep." The dragon's command was deep.

I startled at his voice.

Was he watching me?

There was nothing to do but climb beneath the dirty cover and lay my head against the soft pillows.

When I closed my eyes, images came to my mind.

My father's hands, holding me at arm's length.

The dragon's talons, swooping toward me.

As I lay there in the bed, pain grew inside me again. Emotion that wanted to break free. But even if I cried—even if I screamed—it wouldn't be enough to satisfy the hurt.

So I didn't cry.

If I was going to survive, there was only now. Only this house and this dark and the coming morning. I would make it through the night and then I would find a way to escape. I didn't know what the dragon had planned for me, but it couldn't be good.

He was right about one thing. I needed sleep. But I couldn't relax my body.

Not because I was afraid and hungry. Not because a dragon lay near me.

It was the cold.

I tried curling in on myself to keep in my own heat. I doubled the blanket over, tucking it around my shoulders. It was softer than the scratchy wool blanket I had left behind with my satchel, but thinner also. Too fancy to help me. I shivered and clutched the flint.

I needed wood and kindling now, not in the morning. I thought about lighting a spark to see the room for a brief second. Maybe there was something I could burn nearby. But it might disturb the dragon.

Would he be angry if I left the bed?

Would he punish me? I felt the bruises where his tail had stopped me mid-run.

After a while, a soft noise rose from where the dragon lay. The rhythm of sleep-breathing.

An idea occurred to me.

A terrible idea.

My hands had been so warm against the tail scales as we walked through the dark. What if I lay nearer to the dragon? I could be quiet. He wouldn't know I was there.

No. That was insane.

Who would willingly sleep beside a dragon?

Time passed. The dragon breathed. I shivered. My fingers and toes grew painful, then numb.

And then my idea didn't seem so terrible anymore.

I sat up, the gauzy blanket wrapped around me. The dragon kept breathing. I rested one foot on the floor, then the next, moving in the direction of the breaching sounds. I found the doorframe and left the bedroom. With each step I took toward him, the air grew a little warmer.

The final distance, I edged forward bit by bit, afraid I would accidentally touch him. Finally, I could sense him in the dark, so close to my skin.

The warmth was bliss.

I stood like that until I could hardly stand anymore, then I lay on my blanket a short distance away. Would he roll on me by accident? I was too cold and tired to worry about it, so I tucked the flint into my pocket and fell asleep.

In my dreams, I lay next to the hearth in my father's cottage. The fire was too warm. I needed to move.

I woke to the sound of scales rustling. Daylight filtered into the castle from high windows, forming gray dust motes. It was morning, and the dragon was awake.

He stood on all fours, head low. "What are you doing out of your room?"

7

I STOOD. "I—"

His tail flicked back and forth behind him. "My skin is too thick for a blade to cut through. Did you discover that while I slept?"

"No." There was a tremble in my voice.

His tail stilled, and he watched me. "It's not safe to wander the castle. I don't want to have to lock your door, but—"

"I was cold." I raised my voice, pushing through the tremble. "You're . . . warm. And I needed to sleep."

The dragon's ears fell flat against his head. "You spent the whole night beside me?"

"Only some of it."

His tail twitched again. "There's a place for humans to sleep, and a place for dragons."

"My place was freezing. That's all." I held up my hands, the way I might have done to show Isa I didn't want a fight.

His eyes narrowed, and I wondered what the expression meant. It was hard to read the emotion on a dragon's face.

"You'll be thirsty," he finally said. He didn't sound happy about it.

"I am." My lips were dry enough to stick together. I couldn't remember the last time I had taken a drink from my flasket. The flasket I no longer carried.

"Come with me."

I thought he would lead me outside, toward a stream. Instead, he ushered me across the massive room, deeper into the castle. Now that sun shone through the windows, I could see this place was not the lair I had imagined in the dark. It was bigger than I had thought. Bigger than I knew a structure could be, with ceilings so high I had to crane my neck back to view them. They were carved in arching patterns.

There were no bones on the polished floor, though a thick layer of dust coated everything, including the windows. Even with a full moon, it would be dark in here at night.

A long time ago, the room must have been beautiful. It was still impressive. My eyes wandered as I walked beside the dragon.

Rows of wooden doors lined the walls, each embellished with floral designs. Pillars supported the high ceiling beams. Stones had fallen from above, leaving piles of rubble. Had it happened when the dragon broke open his entry?

I was most interested in the doors and the staircases. Routes of exit.

Two elegant sets of stairs led in opposite directions. What could be up there? Rooms too small for the dragon to enter? Long hallways that I could put between us.

It was a house built for humans, more finely crafted than I had thought possible. When had the dragon taken it, and why? A cave would be just as convenient for the beast as this grand entry room.

The stairs had once been painted white, though dirt and ash marked them now. Beneath the soot, gold inlay swirled over the rails.

Gold. In the mountains.

Like the stories.

The dragon stopped at a strange boulder, larger than the others. It hadn't fallen from the ceiling like the rest. Its rough shape would have come from the wilderness, not the polished home around me. The dragon must have brought it inside.

"Stand back." The dragon reared onto his hind legs and threw his weight into the boulder.

It made a painful grinding noise as it slid against the floor. I lurched away from the sound and pressed my hands over my ears.

The noise stopped, and I turned to see what the dragon had done. Dust motes swirled over a round hole in the floor where the boulder had been.

The dragon turned his head away from the hole and put a wingtip over his nose, as if he were trying to stanch a smell.

I smelled nothing but dragon.

"Look inside," he said.

I walked to the edge and peered in. Water bubbled below the rim, like a tiny pond with a stream flowing into it. This place was definitely built for people, not dragons.

My mouth felt like ash, and thirst gnawed at me.

"It's safe to drink?" I looked up at the dragon.

He closed his mouth and nodded his head. Such a human movement.

I knelt and cupped water to my lips. Sweet and cool, it eased my throat. I took gulps until I couldn't drink any more. Then I sat beside the well, gazing into the water.

The dragon's eyes were on me. I could feel them.

"Thank you," I said.

"I'll leave it open for you, so you can drink whenever you need." He snorted and wrinkled his nose.

I looked across the great room to where we had spent the night. It was the only interior door that was open. Outside the bedroom seemed to be the dirtiest area in the whole castle, strewn with black marks and scales. The dragon's usual sleeping place, a nest of filth.

The entry hole was beyond that, and I marveled at the

distance. You could have fit all the trees from our marsh cottage in this great room, plus the house and the streams. It was as big as our outside spaces.

There were other granite boulders in the room, probably brought in by the dragon to cover more fountains. This was the furthest one from the dragon's area, which was quite a ways.

"Water smells bad to you," I said.

"In a way."

"Is that all? Doesn't it hurt you if you touch it?"

"Are you so interested in hurting me?"

I said nothing.

"Come." With a flick of his tail, he turned away from the fountain. "I need to talk to you. Away from here."

We made the long walk back to his grimy space.

"Now." He sat. "You'll answer some questions, and I'll decide what to do with you."

He hadn't decided yet?

I stood at a distance from him. The day had brought warmth, and I no longer needed the dragon's heat.

"You believe the wizard is your father?" he asked.

I wished I could hide the truth, but I had already admitted it on the cliff. "He is."

"It would be a strange thing for a man like that to father a child like you."

What did he mean?

I should have been too scared to be angry, but I had endured two days of terror, and I was exhausted. I winced, anticipating the dragon's reaction to the anger on my face.

It never came.

"Where is your mother?" he asked. "Siblings?"

"I have no mother."

None that my father would speak of, though I must have had one somewhere.

At the thought of a mother, Isa's face flashed in my mind.

She really was the closest thing. And a sister, and a friend. Sadness hit me.

The dragon looked me up and down. "When do you turn seventeen?"

I wrapped my arms around myself. I would be seventeen when summer began. Soon.

"How do you know my age?"

"I'm a dragon."

Was that going to be his answer to every question I asked?

His tail moved at the end again, a motion I was beginning to recognize as unrest. "There's no one else? No family?"

"No," I lied.

I would never mention Isa to him. Not if it would put her in danger.

His tail stilled. "Then I'll have to keep you here."

His tone was controlled. Purposefully emotionless.

So this was it. The dragon didn't want me, but he wanted to keep me from my father. Was this his way of settling their old grudge?

"If you want to be rid of me, then take me to the city in the north," I said. "I know someone there."

The city of Isadora's childhood.

"What is the city's name? There are many in the north."

I paused. I knew there was more than one city in the world, but we had never referred to them by names. We didn't need to. There was only the closest one.

"If you fly me from the mountains to the East, I can find my home. From there, I can show you the direction of the city."

The dragon scoffed. "So you can find your way back to that man."

Heat rose in my cheeks. "If you have no use for me, then I'm not yours to worry about."

"He made you my problem when he cut you open and offered you up." Smoke rose from the dragon's snout.

"He didn't do it. I held the knife." It was true, though I hadn't known the dragon would take me when I did it.

The dragon looked down at the dried blood on my arm. He stared for a long while. Long enough for my courage to falter.

"If you let me go," I said, "you won't have to smell the water anymore."

He made a sound like a laugh, showing all his teeth. "It's breakfast time. I'll get wood."

I tensed. "Do you . . . Will you need to eat?"

"I'm not hungry."

I hoped that was true.

The dragon stretched out his wings. "I'm going to leave you here while I go get supplies."

My eyes darted upward, and my chest tightened. This was what I had waited for. It was too good to be true.

"Do not try to run off." He folded his wings again. "You're not a prisoner. I rescued you."

Then why would I want to run off?

He turned his head and fixed me with one eye. "It's a death sentence if you climb down the mountain. The nights are cold, as you found out. The rivers here run underground, so you have no water. The cliffs are steep, and there are beasts among the trees."

Again, a dragon was warning me of danger. Wild animals were natural, and often scared of humans, like the deer in the marsh. But the dragon was intelligent, which made him the worst creature I could imagine.

"If you leave, I'll have to bring you back," he said. "You'll be easy to track from the sky."

"What should I do while you're gone then?" I wanted to sound compliant.

"You could rest, and you should drink more water while I'm not here to smell it. But do not explore the other levels of this castle."

I looked to the gilded stairs. "What's up there?"

The dragon's brow creased. "Nothing you should know about. Promise you won't go up."

"I promise."

He watched me for a moment. Then, as if satisfied, he turned to go.

I stood still as the dragon picked his way over rubble, hoping that it would be the last time I would see him.

From the castle opening, he looked back at me, sunlight reflecting off his glossy scales. "Drink water."

And then he left.

8

I DIDN'T MOVE UNTIL DUST

rose outside the opening, the only sign of his silent flight.

The dragon was gone.

How long would it take him to collect wood? I needed time to gather my own supplies.

Food was important, but I could go a few days without. I had done it before, and I knew how to make a sling to kill rabbits with stones. Water would be the challenge.

I hurried to the edge of the fountain and drank as much as I could, then splashed some on my arm to wipe away the dried blood.

I wasn't foolish enough to leave the castle today.

Like he said, the dragon would find me from the air.

Instead, I would hide, somewhere deep inside where the dragon didn't fit. When he returned, he would assume I had run. His senses were good. Night vision and blood-smell. But I would be silent, hidden behind stone walls, covered in dragon soot to mask my scent.

As long as I didn't bleed.

He would search the mountain, but he wouldn't find me out there. Then, when he came home, I would hear him. He was a heavy sleeper.

Once he settled for the night, I would sneak out and run. At least it would give me a head start.

I took one last gulp of water from the fountain, then headed to the bedroom to look for blankets. Something thicker than the one I had slept under last night.

I crossed the threshold. The dragon scent still lingered in the grand entry where he lived, but it had dissipated in the bedroom. I took deep breaths, savoring the fresher air.

By the light from the doorway, I crossed the bedroom and flung open heavy curtains that had made everything dark last night. In daylight, the bedroom was lovely. A far cry from the spider-cave I had imagined in blindness.

There was a large hearth, built from smooth, square stones. On either side of the window sat beautiful wooden drawers, carved with a maple-leaf design. I pulled them all open.

They were mostly empty, except for the very last one, which held a pair of men's breeches. I tied the legs together and knotted the opening, forming a makeshift satchel. Then I pulled one of the velvet curtains from its rod and stuffed it in my pack.

A cloak and a blanket.

The flint was still in my pocket. Now I just needed something to carry water.

I searched the other rooms, running from one to the next, making sure to close the doors behind me. Some were for sleeping, each with the same kind of silky blanket on the bed. Some rooms contained cushioned armchairs and chaises. It was all finer than anything I had ever seen.

But there was no flasket. Not even a crock or a goblet.

Then, in a sitting room, I found an empty wine bottle with a cork. It was more than I had hoped for, though I would have to be careful not to break the glass.

My chest blazed with pain as I sprinted to the fountain. How much longer did I have before the dragon came back?

I filled the bottle and returned to the dragon's sleeping place, scooping up a handful of ash and dirt. For a moment, the caustic scent stole my breath. When I regained control, I poured the handful over my hair. I took another fist of soot and ground it into my dress. I dusted the rest over my neck and wrists, where my veins pulsed with blood. Soon, I was caked in toxic black.

It itched, but I wouldn't scratch. Not if there was a chance it might draw blood.

Dragon scales littered the floor. Despite the filth, they still glittered iridescent and black in the dim light. They were well formed, without chips or wear.

I reached down and felt one, chafing my finger over the edge. It was hard as stone and sharp. Perfect. I selected the largest scale, the length of my hand, and secured it in my bag. It would be my knife.

Now, where to hide?

None of the rooms I had explored were ideal. The dragon would see me crouched beneath a bed or quivering behind a curtain.

I needed something deeper in the castle, without an easy door to peek through.

On the other side of the entry room sat a large black doorway made of metal rather than wood. I hadn't looked there yet. I ran to it and grabbed the handle, then pulled away. It was hot, as if a hearth blazed in the room beyond. Curious, I wrapped my hand in my skirt and tried the handle again. It wouldn't unlatch. I pushed and pulled, but the door was locked. A dead end.

I scanned the empty room, my eyes landing on the golden stair rail.

Gold. If I reached the city, I would need money of my own. Treasure from a mountain.

I tried to pry the gold swirl from the rail with my nails, but it was stuck tight. It would require tools and time. I had neither.

I peered up the staircase. At the top, a stone archway led to a shadowy hall. A narrow place.

I set my foot on the first step, then paused.

The dragon had warned me. I had made a promise.

But why should I trust his warnings? I was his prisoner, and I still didn't understand his full reasoning for keeping me. If he wanted to take me away from Father, he could have flown me to the other side of the mountain and left me there. Instead, he brought me to his home.

He seemed to want me alive. But that might change, and I didn't want to be here when it did.

Once I made my decision, I climbed the stairs as fast as my weak heart would let me, only stopping once to rest.

The shadowed hall opened wide past the arch, creating plenty of space for a dragon. But first he would have to break through the narrow entrance to get there. I took comfort in that.

At the end of the corridor, a small window led to a balcony, overlooking the forest. Trees grew up around it, branches touching the rail. I would be able to climb down there in a pinch.

Around the corner where the hall split, the dragon wouldn't be able to see me from the stairs. I chose the left, then sank to the floor, my back to the wall. Doors lined the hall, made of the same carved wood as downstairs.

There might be smaller spaces to hide behind those doors. Better places. But something stopped me. The dragon's warnings had worked on my mind to an extent, and this hall looked safe enough.

I sat there and took stock of my supplies again. Could I sell my dragon scale in the city? It had to be a rare thing. Why hadn't I thought to take more than one? But it was too late now to go back.

All I had to do was wait and stay silent. I pressed my palm flat beneath my collar bone, over my heart, tapping.

No memories. Only the rhythm on my chest.

The tapping never affected my heart in a physical way, but it calmed my mind, and I needed that right now. The dragon didn't terrify me like he had at first. The escape scared me, though.

I was disobeying. I was on my own.

But I had to try.

Then came a voice in the hall, shaky and dry. "Hello?"

9

MY HEAD JERKED UP. I SAW NO ONE.
The voice was male, but not deep enough to be the dragon's.

Someone else was in the castle.

I stood. "Hello?"

"I'm in here," the other person said. "Will you let me out?"

Footsteps padded on the other side of the nearest door. The dragon had a man locked up in here. No wonder he had told me to stay away.

I wasn't alone. I almost laughed from relief.

"I don't have the key," I answered. "Do you know where it is? The dragon will be back soon."

The footsteps paced again, and this time I noticed a strange clicking noise. What kind of shoes made that sound?

"The door isn't locked. Just open it."

I took a step forward and lifted my hand to the knob, then paused. "How did you get trapped if it's not locked? Are you hurt?"

Why was I hesitating? He needed help.

"The dragon trapped me with magic. But you can open the door. Hurry, turn the handle." The man's tone shifted. "If you do, there will be a reward. I promise."

Magic. The hairs on my arms tingled. "You're sure it's safe?"

There was a hiss from inside the room, then a pause. "Very safe."

I needed to hurry. But something was odd about the man.

"Who are you?" I asked. "How did you end up here?"

"You're young, aren't you? I can tell from your voice." The man was pressed close against the door now. "It's a frightening thing, to be in a dragon's home. I know from experience. We can help each other."

I wouldn't have to escape by myself. "I was going to hide here while the dragon searched the mountain for me. I thought the hall entry was too small for him. But he must have come up here somehow if he locked you in."

"I have not seen the dragon in a very long time."

I considered that for a moment. "Can you think of a place to hide?"

"I can do anything," the man whispered. "To help, I mean . . ."

Except to open his own door.

My fingers closed on the knob. I turned it slowly, as if my hand didn't want to obey me.

The man's voice grew syrupy. "I can take you back to your father. Just open the door."

My breath caught. How did he know about my father? I wanted to ask more questions and to keep the door closed.

But it was too late. The latch had already been released.

The door swung inward.

I backed away.

A dirty, elongated hand wrapped around the doorframe, and a man's head pushed through the opening. His skin had a flushed pallor, and black circles shadowed his eyes.

The eyes.

They weren't right. They stared at me unfocused, as if he were looking through me.

The man was taller than the doorframe, ducking to fit as he peered into the hall.

I edged further away. "Who are you?"

He flashed a huge smile, showing yellowed teeth. "I told you if you opened the door there would be a reward."

The syrup was gone from his voice.

"I only want to leave the mountain." My back came into contact with the other side of the hall. Why was he keeping his body hidden behind the frame? I tried to keep my voice from shaking. "How do you know my father?"

His eyes focused for a moment, then unfocused again. "Oh. The reward is not for you. It is for me."

I tried to breathe, but my heart seemed to stop and then skip on. "What do you want?"

"It's not a matter of want." He leaned further out of the door, focused again. "It's a need. I have not had a meal in a very long time."

I noticed his nails. They were long and jagged, like rodent claws. He stepped from behind the frame and straightened his body to his full height. Collar bones protruded beneath his ragged tunic, and his feet were bare, gnarled with the same claws as his fingers. They clicked against the ground as he took a step forward.

"I don't have any food." I could barely speak. "But I have water."

I fumbled for the bottle.

He laughed, dry and throaty. "I was right. You are young."

I took a step to the side, down the hall. He matched my step, halting my progress. I slid my hand into my bag, gripping the dragon scale in a tight fist.

"I am thankful you let me out," he said. "But you must understand. I have to eat. And I like my meals young."

What had I done?

The man opened his mouth wide. Then wider still. Then his jaw unhinged and became something black and gaping, lined with teeth.

He was no longer a man, but something worse than I had known could exist. A grotesque thing.

I stared into that mouth, horrified, and something strange happened. I lost track of where I was.

Memories came to me unbidden. Flashes of images that didn't belong in this moment.

Isa cried and Guntor yelled. I saw her crumpled in the corner of the cottage, kicked there by her husband. I stayed hidden in the loft. Father watched from his chair, and neither of us moved to help her.

We never did.

Shame washed over me.

It should have been fear. I should have been terrified. What was this creature doing to my mind?

I blinked, and the trance broke. I saw the man again.

He lunged forward.

I screamed and swiped the scale at his face. It met his cheek, and he hissed. Before I could run, he caught me by the arm, his grip like steel. Black liquid oozed from the place where I had cut him.

"It will be over soon." The man's tongue flicked across his stretched lips.

I took another swipe at his hand. He shrieked, then knocked the scale from my fist with his claws. His nails dug into my wrist, and they burned like fire, cutting deep. I pulled away with all my strength, but his grip was too strong.

The black mouth opened wider, and he pulled me close.

Everything smelled like decay.

Then a sound pierced the air, rock colliding with rock. The floor shook beneath our feet, and the creature stumbled.

I broke free. And then I was drowning, my lungs frantic for air, my heart failing. But there wasn't time to calm my chest. I needed to run.

Blinding light filled the hall. Where a stone wall had been, now there was open air, the forest stretching out below. The castle had crumbled away.

I backed against the inner wall of the corridor, away from the destruction.

Wings flashed through the air. Black smoke blocked out the light.

The dragon had returned.

His tail whipped against stone, widening the opening in the wall. The castle wasn't crumbling. He was breaking it.

He landed on the balcony, his talons gripping the ledge.

In the corner of my vision, the man-creature moved toward me. I braced for another attack.

The dragon's golden eyes burned red, then a stream of fire erupted from his jaws. Flames blew past me, heating my skin but not burning. The fire collided with the creature.

He howled, clutching a blackened shoulder.

"You will not touch her." The dragon took a breath, ready to flame again.

He was armor and fire and fury. The hunter I had always feared.

But the man didn't seem afraid. It opened its dark mouth and laughed, a stringy, vile sound.

I stepped over rubble, putting distance between us.

As the man-thing laughed, it changed again. Its dirty feet left the floor, hovering in the air. It turned white, then transparent. I could see straight through its body, to the other side of the hall.

The dragon's fire erupted, but the flames couldn't touch the creature. They passed through.

Hot wind whipped my hair from my face.

It laughed again. "Your kind never could touch a ghost."

The dragon glared. "And you won't be able to touch anything for days, now that you've transformed. Maybe months. Your kind always were better as phantoms."

"Wil?" The thing cocked its head to the side. "It's been years since I've seen you."

The dragon let out a low growl. "It should have been never."

"But your girl let me out, fair and square."

It grinned at me, and my stomach sank.

The dragon's tail twitched, breaking part of the balcony rail. "And you would have thanked her by ending her life."

"She never asked the rules." The ghost focused its wide eyes on me. "It can't hurt to tell you, now that my other options are closed. I owe you a wish for my early release." Its tongue flicked out again.

I took shallow breaths.

"She doesn't need your wishes." The dragon kept his gaze on the ghost. "Gilde, don't listen to him. You should have figured that out by now."

The specter bobbed up and down in the air. "Ah, but you could make a wish to escape. I really could take you to your father. I wasn't lying about that part."

"He'll never lie," the dragon said. "But he'll never tell the truth. If you ask to see your father, he'll do it in the worst way he can. He'd let you see your father from the air, then drop you to your death. Or let you see him, and then take you away."

The creature laughed.

After everything, I more than believed the dragon. I edged further from the ghost.

The dragon spread his wings and stood to his full height. "You should leave."

"I've traveled the empires and dined with queens," the thing said. "You think I'd want to stay in this mountain? But I really should leave a gift . . ."

"Don't." The dragon's eyes lit, warning fire, though it wouldn't do any good.

"Not a wish then. A revelation. Don't you want to know what your future holds, Wil?"

"You can't see the future any more than I can."

"True." If possible, the creature grew more transparent. "But even trapped, my eyes saw far. Things in the world beyond the castle. Things you don't know."

He had known about my father.

"What things?" I asked.

The dragon's voice was low. "Don't answer that."

"She deserves her reward, Wil. She deserves to know that a wizard is coming. He's preparing now. When summer arrives, so will he."

That's what the dragon called my father, though I didn't like to think of him that way. "Which wizard?"

"I think you know," the ghost said.

A strange sound came from my chest. An almost sob.

The dragon leaned further into the castle, his face nearing the creature. "That's impossible. This place is shrouded so no one can find it."

"Ah, but he already has." The creature gestured toward me. "You think he wouldn't track her with his spells? You're too late—even if you kill her now, he already knows. When he's ready, he'll come."

"What does he want?" the dragon asked.

The ghost looked him up and down. "I've said enough. Unless the girl wants her wish?" Its eyes shot to me.

I backed away.

"Goodbye, then." It bent forward in mock deference, lowering itself. "Remember, I see things, and I hear things. If you're ever in need, call for me to pay my debt."

"Go." The dragon bared his white teeth.

"With pleasure."

The ghost cackled, then disappeared into nothing.

For the first time since he got back, the dragon looked at me.

10

I STOOD THERE, COVERED IN soot, the incriminating bag slung over my shoulder. I stared at my feet.

There would be no running now. Would the dragon lock me up? Or something worse than that?

Dust settled and smoke hung in the air, filling my throat with dragon smell. I coughed.

"You're hurt," he said.

That wasn't what I had expected.

I hid my bleeding wrist behind my back. "It's not bad."

"It's a lot of blood."

I pressed the wound into my skirt. Did he like the smell? That thought made me queasy.

"That's how you found me," I said. "The blood."

"Yes." The dragon's eyes were golden again, the flame-orange gone.

I pictured the wet jaws of the ghost, and my stomach felt sick. "Was he . . . was it a dead man?"

"Not that kind of ghost. Though he'd probably like you to think he was human once. He's never been anything as good as that."

"What then?"

"Something very old and very wrong, but he's gone now. The world is worse for it. We're probably better off."

The world was worse because of me. The dragon had been right. There were things to worry about in this house besides him.

He took a breath. "Did you . . . see anything? When you looked into his mouth?"

How did he know? I stanched my wound against my skirt. The shame came over me again. The same I had felt so many times when Isa was beaten.

"No," I lied. "Why do you ask?"

"It's one of his tricks. He shows you the parts of yourself that you hate the most. It's a venom that paralyzes his victims."

That was more than a trick. I blinked back emotion and wondered what a dragon would see in a ghost's mouth.

My voice wavered when I spoke. "Thank you. For saving me."

Even though I had broken my promise. I wouldn't mention that part, though the truth of it lay between us, unspoken.

"You thought the ghost would help you escape," he said. "That's why you opened the door."

There wasn't as much accusation in his tone as I would have expected. More a statement of fact.

"No." I shook my head. "The way he talked scared me. But I couldn't leave him in there."

"So you'll defend wizards and phantoms."

We were both quiet for a moment.

I looked around at the broken and charred rocks. "Your castle . . . I'm sorry."

The dragon should have been angry. Maybe he was good at hiding it.

"This castle's been ruined for a long time." He eyed the mess. "It's better for dragons like this."

There was another long pause, and I began to wonder if I should speak.

"I brought food," he finally said. "It's out front. I could carry you down." He shifted from one foot to the other, lifting his wings.

I pressed against the stone wall behind me. "I'll walk."

He blinked. "Clean your wound at the fountain, then meet me at the front door."

I walked down the stairs, my fingers tracing the golden swirls in the rail. When I had climbed up, I was running. But now, something had changed.

A wizard was coming.

A wizard I knew, and he would arrive at the start of summer. The dragon seemed to believe the revelation, and so that made me believe.

Had Father known all along that I would survive?

A stream of hope trickled inside of me, enough to soothe the pain that began on the morning the dragon took me.

I went to the fountain and peered down at the water. It flowed and gurgled, never still. An underground river.

My wound had already begun to harden at the edges, a dark gash, jagged and deep. I dipped my wrist under the surface of the well, scrubbing with my other hand.

Red blood floated into the clear water, then disappeared in the current.

I scrubbed longer than I needed to, digging in. I washed myself everywhere the ghost had touched me, splashing water on my face and wiping ash from my neck. The rest of me needed a bath and a clean dress. But that would have to happen later.

The dragon was waiting.

I walked the distance to the front opening, feeling hollow and unwell.

After everything that had happened in these past two days, it felt like a lifetime since we left the encampment.

At the entry hole, I squinted into warm sunlight. The dragon was there.

He lay upside-down on the ground, rolling back and forth, scratching his spine. I paused, surprised. It was such a vulnerable thing to watch.

I had seen a dog do the same thing in the marshes when I was little, before Guntor killed it for stealing food. Its name had been Twig for the three days it lasted. I had never forgotten it.

The dragon's eyes were closed. I gave a cough to announce my presence.

He rolled onto his feet and shook his wings, then eyed me. "You didn't wrap your cut."

"Everything I have is dirty." The blood would dry in the sun.

"Do you know how to start a fire yourself?" He tilted his head to the ground toward a stack of dry pine branches.

Limp rabbits lay beside the wood. Three of them, neat in a row, all dead.

"Yes." I pulled the flint from my pocket, holding it out for him to see.

"And you can cook?"

I gave a nod, my eyes on the rabbits. If I were still in the marsh, I would have stewed them with parsnips and herbs.

"I'll need a knife to skin them. I could use one of your scales . . ." I held my breath.

It felt like an intrusive thing to ask. I wouldn't like it if someone collected my fingernails to use as tools. But I had left the other scale where the ghost attacked me, and I didn't want to go back.

"I've noticed you like to have a blade," he said. "The sharpest come from my neck. I have a loose one now. You can pull it free." He bent his head low and closed his eyes. "It's the third down from my left ear."

I stared. Touching his face was different than touching his

tail. There were teeth and flames. He opened his eyes, and I made myself take a step forward.

I located the scale and pulled hard. It came free easier than I expected. He stood and scratched at his ear with his front talons.

As I skinned all three rabbits, my hands remembered what it felt like to cut the ghost. I bit the inside of my mouth, trying not to picture the black ooze.

The dragon watched me work. Neither of us said anything. After, I washed up with the water from the wine bottle. He turned his head away for that part.

If he couldn't drink water, did he drink blood? My heart raced.

The rabbits crackled over the flames.

"Do you prefer the meat on the bone?" I turned the roasting stick.

"I won't be eating."

I fidgeted with my skirt. "I can't eat three rabbits."

"I'm not hungry."

Those words should have been comforting to me. Somehow, they weren't.

The dragon lay in the shade, his tail curled beside him. "It's been a long time since I've seen human fire."

"Is it different?"

He was quiet for a while before answering. "It moves different. Like a dance instead of a battle."

I hadn't paid attention to how his flame moved. I didn't want another chance to see.

When the rabbits were done and cooled, I cut a piece for myself. The dragon watched me take the first bite. The meat was tough and needed salt.

"Thank you," I said. "For the food."

Isa had always made sure I thanked her when she brought wheat home to the cottage.

The dragon said nothing. My stomach ached for another bite, but it was hard to eat with his eyes on me.

"I don't want to eat alone." I lifted one of the roasting sticks toward him.

"What you want is reassurance that I don't eat humans."

The dragon took the roasting stick in his mouth and leapt away, turning his back to me. I heard bones crunch between his teeth.

He came back. "There. I eat animals."

I stood. "Good. Because I'm staying here until my father comes."

The idea had been growing in my mind while I cooked the rabbits. My only other option was a dangerous escape and a long journey to a city without a name. The dragon wanted me alive, enough to breathe his fire even.

He had said he would never do that for any human.

But when I was in danger, he broke his promise. For me.

He turned his face to me. "This isn't a place for humans."

What was that supposed to mean?

I lifted my chin. "First you won't let me go. Now you won't let me stay?"

In the past, I might have spoken to Isa like that. But no one else. I tensed my whole body.

A tendril of dark smoke curled from his breath. "You have no other option except to stay. But there's a reason no other people live here. I'm only warning you that life on the mountain won't be easy."

I had spent my whole life away from people. Most of them, anyway.

"I could be helpful." I lowered my eyes, the way I might have done with Father. "I can cook and work. You said some girls are useful for magic. I could—"

"No," the dragon growled. "Magic takes more than you're prepared to give. And I don't use it."

"How did you trap the ghost then?" I wanted to know what he was capable of. And I wanted to know why this castle was here.

"It's best not to speak of magic."

It was the same as always. Don't ask questions.

"Then there's something else I need to ask you about," I said.

"You didn't believe me about the dangers in the castle. Why should I tell you anything if you'll just disregard it?"

"I didn't disregard it." I lifted my gaze to the dragon's. "I verified it for myself."

"At the cost of almost losing your life."

There was silence.

Then he growled. "What do you want to know?"

I answered immediately, "When my father comes, will you try to kill him?"

I also wanted to know why he had taken me, but I didn't have the courage to ask that yet.

The dragon's brow furrowed. "If the wizard gives me any other choice, I won't hurt him."

Could that be true? This wasn't the dragon I had known of all my life. The one that would kill the moment it had the chance.

"Also," he said, "you shouldn't assume the wizard is coming to take you back. Even if he is, you're better off here, whether or not either of us likes it."

He hated me being here, but he wouldn't let me go. And now I felt the same. Stuck.

"Summer's almost here," I said. "Two more cycles of the moon. Then I'll leave you alone again."

The dragon looked away.

I sat down to eat my first meal in days.

11

I DIDN'T BOTHER BANKING THE coals to keep them hot for the next meal. If I had my way, I was moving into the castle. The next time I cooked, it would be over a proper hearth.

The dragon looked like he was asleep in the shade, but his breathing wasn't deep enough. Every once in a while, one eye would slit open.

When everything was cleaned up from breakfast, I gathered brush and weeds along the edge of the trees. I sat in the afternoon sun, a ways from the dragon, and wove the stems onto a stick handle.

A broom. It was time to make myself useful.

I stood and cleared my throat. The dragon kept his eyes closed.

I walked closer and coughed loudly. "I'd like your permission to clean."

He opened both eyes and sat up. "Clean what?"

"Everything." Would he be offended? "Not that it's too dirty . . . but I could freshen things up for you. It won't involve water, I promise. I'll start with my room so you can see how it goes."

Then maybe I could sweep out the great entry and remove

the rubble around the fountain. And I needed to wash my dress. Did soapwort grow in the mountains?

The dragon rose to his full height. "If you're going to stay, there are things you need to see."

Then he turned and walked toward the castle.

I watched him go, his scales glittering in the sun, each one a weapon. I would be living with a monster. I should have been more afraid, but it was difficult to be scared for so long, and now I was in the sunshine with a full stomach.

He paused to look back at me.

I followed, broom in hand.

We didn't stop until we reached the bottom of the staircase. The one I had climbed earlier that morning.

He sat. "There are twelve doors at the top of these steps. Six on the left, six on the right. You already opened the second on the left."

And now the ghost was free to wander the earth again.

"How did you go up there before you broke the wall?" I asked. "The entry is too small."

"If I tuck my wings, I can fit in small spaces."

I eyed the dragon and the archway, doubtful.

He folded his wings flat against himself. They almost disappeared, black on black. He stretched his torso and legs, straightening his spine until he was long and thin.

Then he shook his tail and returned to his normal shape.

My stomach sank. The escape plan would never have worked.

The dragon sniffed and turned his nose away from the nearby fountain. "But there are places you shouldn't go."

"I won't go—" I started.

"You've made promises before."

That was fair. He held all the physical power. But I had released his prisoner. I was in his home, and that made him vulnerable to me in a way I hadn't considered yet.

"I'm not going to ignore your warnings again," I said.

"Then listen. The left corridor is the most dangerous, as you found out. The ghost is gone, but we won't go inside his room in case he left any surprises behind. The third room on the left is full of poison. We'll start there. Open the door, but don't touch anything. I'll meet you at the top of the stairs. I prefer to fly rather than crawl."

He turned to go outside.

"Wait," I called. "I don't need to see it."

His eyes met mine. "I need you to see it. To verify some things for myself."

"To verify what?"

"That you will actually listen."

The dragon flew to the exit, his dark wings gliding through the grand entry. He disappeared faster than I thought possible, and there was nothing for me to do but climb the staircase. Again.

I gripped the broomstick, and when I reached the top, the dragon was already waiting near the hole in the wall.

"Which room has the poison?" He was testing me.

"The third door."

"Open it." His tone was firm.

I took a left and rested my hand on the knob. The dragon followed, his bulk more imposing in the small space.

The door opened easily, just like the ghost's had. I backed away, my chest tightening. This was too familiar.

The dragon pressed in closer, almost touching me with his snout.

"Look," he said.

I knew there wasn't another ghost, but my body remembered the attack. The gash on my wrist throbbed, and my heart fluttered. I made myself peer into the room. It was empty.

"There's nothing," I said.

The dragon came closer, until he was one pace behind me. I was trapped between him and the door.

His tail curled forward, flinging a leafy branch onto the stone floor in the room. As soon as it landed, steam poured into the air, accompanied by a sizzling noise. Within a breath, the branch wilted and turned ashen.

Then I noticed the black sludge that coated the floor of the room.

The dragon stepped back. "You would have opened that door and thought it was safe. You could have tried to hide in there. I wouldn't have made it back in time."

He was right. I could have run straight in there. Nausea hit me as I pictured what the poison would do to a human.

"Why would you have a room like this?" My voice was strained. "Unless you wanted someone to get hurt."

"I doubt it was created on purpose."

I turned to look at the dragon. "It's not your poison?"

"Surely you've noticed that this castle was built for humans." His enormous face was close to mine. "They abandoned it, and now I live here. But they left some terrible things behind."

"Were they terrible people?" I asked.

Not that a dragon would be the best judge.

"The things they left aren't all bad. I want to show you a room in the other corridor." He backed down the hall, unable to turn around until we reached the broken window.

He led me down the right-hand corridor, then stopped. "The first room is empty. The second is my favorite. It's more than safe. Open it." His command was softer this time.

I stood in front of the second door, then turned the handle.

This room was much larger than the others, with several bright windows that looked out over the forest. There were so many items in the room, I found it hard to focus.

My eyes landed on all the treasure first. Gilded candlesticks sat on tables. Silver curtain rods hung over the windows. There were silver quills shaped like bird feathers, sticking up from glass ink pots. The stair rail was nothing compared to this.

"A treasure room," I breathed.

"In a way. Go inside and look around."

I stepped in. The dragon pressed his head and neck through the door, but his shoulders didn't fit.

Rows of shelves lined all the walls. Paper was everywhere. More than I had seen in my whole life. Some shelves held baskets of scrolls. Some held books bound in heavy leather.

My father kept a book under his armchair. In it, he wrote the names of his men, and he tallied their wages. I had learned to count, but never to write numerals. Sometimes, when he was gone, I liked to look at the shapes of the numbers. His book held rough papers. It was a practical, useful thing.

Nothing like the smooth pages around me.

I spun in a circle, taking it in.

"Which book looks interesting to you?" the dragon asked.

I searched, then pointed to a large one with golden inlay on the leather.

"You can read it if you'd like."

"Oh." I tucked my matted hair behind my ears. "I can read my name, but I doubt it's written anywhere in here."

Isa had taught me. She could do hers too.

"And you can read nothing else?"

"No."

The dragon blinked. "I'm sorry."

Of all the things he could have apologized for, he chose this?

I glanced at the shelves. Infinite rows of names and numerals. "What could be written in so many books?"

"All kinds of things." He wriggled further through the door, his shoulders squeezing against the frame. "Poetry. Astronomy. Stories."

My gaze went to the dragon. "Stories?"

"Not in the book you chose."

"You mean someone wrote down a story, like they'd tell it out loud? And you can read the words?"

"Yes . . ."

Isa's stories were limited. I always wanted more. There was the same one about the ghosts that only came out at night.

They were nothing like a real ghost.

And then she used to tell snippets of her real life, but never as much as I wanted to hear.

My eyes traced the books. How many people would it take to write all those words? How many stories were there?

"Can you show me how it works?" I asked.

"I need to ask you something first." He took a deep breath. "You don't have the stink of magic on you. You can't even read. But I need to hear you say it. Have you ever practiced wizardry?"

"No." The question was absurd. "I hardly understand what magic is."

He let out the breath. "Let's keep it that way." He pointed with his head. "You see that red book? The one near the window? That might be a good story."

I crossed the room and slid the book from the shelf, handling it as if it were made of butterfly wings. Slowly, I opened the binding, and my eyes went wide.

More than letters and numerals lined the pages.

There was an image traced in black ink. It depicted an enormous fish, five times the size of the man drawn next to it.

I stared for a long time, inspecting the lines that somehow made a whole picture.

Back in the marsh, I had sewn the shapes of flowers on my dress with thread. I painted images of animals onto rocks with mud and let them dry in the sun. But I had never seen anything like this.

So real.

The dragon didn't interrupt. He let me look through the

pages, pausing at each new drawing. There were swirly clouds, black mountains, and creatures I didn't recognize.

I squinted at the letters, wishing they would make words for me in the same way the drawings made landscapes.

After a while, I closed the book and placed it in front of the dragon. "Will you read it?"

A strange expression crossed his face. I couldn't guess what it meant.

"You should hold it for me," he said. "My hands are sharp. I've destroyed a few books from reading them. I'd rather keep the rest intact."

I had never thought of him as having hands. They were talons. "How did you learn to read human letters, then?"

"My mother taught me."

Like Isa had taught me so many things. Where was she living now? I couldn't picture it. She probably couldn't picture me having a conversation with a dragon.

My thoughts stirred. What did Wil's mother look like? She must have been a grand, smoldering creature.

I opened the book to the page with the large fish and held it up, close to the dragon's eye.

"You don't have to put it in my face," he said. "I have dragon vision. I could read that book through the window from the sky if I wanted to."

"Is this better?" I sat on the floor, ankles tucked to one side, the book open on my lap toward him.

"Yes." He took a deep breath, then began to read.

> "I heard it told long ago of a warrior
> brave and fair
>   who battled in deep waters with a
> monster living there . . ."

The dragon's voice settled into an easy cadence as he continued the story.

I watched his mouth and the letters in the book. All those little strokes of ink were coming to life. I found myself breathing in time with the rhymes. It was like a song without a tune, but still musical.

In the story, the man fought a fish called a whale. Both of them almost died. After a night and a day, when the warrior had won the respect of the whale, the fish showed him how to swim to a special place where water cured sickness. The man carried some of the water home to heal the woman he loved.

He had fought the fish for her.

> "And when the water passed her lips,
> full of salt and life,
> she laughed and wept, and she agreed
> to be his loving wife."

There it was again. That idea of love, like Isa had spoken of.

I tried to imagine Guntor fighting a whale for Isa. I had once imagined Father fighting a dragon.

The dragon rested his chin on the floor. "Did you like it?"

"Yes." I had. "But what if the warrior was sick instead of the woman?" Would he send her to fight the whale?"

He closed his eyes for a while, then answered. "That would be the woman's decision. If it's forced, it's not love."

I fingered the leafy pages of the book, my wrist aching where the ghost had cut me. I moved my arm from beneath the binding and saw fresh blood. It had spilled on the leather.

I pressed the wound against my dress, wiping at the stain on the book cover. As if I could hide it.

Slowly, I raised my eyes. The dragon was watching. He had seen.

I rubbed my skirt on the stain. "I—"

He interrupted. "I have one more thing to show you, then you need to wrap that cut. With clean cloth." He pulled his head out of the doorway.

Nothing was clean in this place. Leaving the precious book behind, I followed him into the hall.

"You see the third door on the right?" he asked.

I walked toward it, but the dragon thrust his tail in my path.

"Never open that door. Not even to look. A wizard used magic in that room, and the evil lingers."

"I believe you," I whispered.

He backed down the hall. "You can visit the library whenever you want. The rest of the rooms are empty. But don't forget about the third door. Or the left hall."

"Will you . . . read the book to me again sometime?" I looked back at the second room on the right. The library.

"I'll do better than that. I'll teach you how to read it yourself."

My pulse quickened. "I'm not sure I'll be able to do it."

But if I could, a world of stories would be open to me. A thousand lives of a thousand people I had never met.

"Are you afraid of failing?" the dragon asked.

"No." I wanted to try.

He looked me in the eyes. "I think you've had bigger things to fear in your life."

12

I WASHED THE CUT AGAIN.
It burned, and blood flowed. As I splashed water, the dragon
wrinkled his nose and disappeared up the other staircase. The
one I hadn't climbed yet. He had to make himself sleek to go
through the halls.

While he was gone, I washed more thoroughly than I had
in the morning, scrubbing my hair and the hems of my skirt in
the cold water. When he returned, he carried a white bundle
in his talons.

"You'll need this." He lowered the bundle to me.

I stretched my arms up and took it in my damp hands.

A linen shirt formed the outer layer, and the weave was
softer than even my best dress had been.

Ash marked the fabric in two places, left by the dragon's
claws. The untouched fabric was pristine. But I would stain it
with blood.

"It will be ruined." Water dripped from my hair.

The dragon made space between us, turning his face to
the clean air at the entrance. "I have no need for fabrics and
clothes."

I tore a strip free and knotted the gorgeous cloth around my
wrist. Red seeped into white.

Inside the bundle, I spotted something smooth and pale. A bar of soap. There were also more clothes. Something dark and silken.

"Is there poison up there too?" I nodded at the other stair. The one we hadn't explored.

"No. But the second door on the left is a bad one. Don't open it. A nest of giant spiders were trapped in there once. I hope they've starved by now, but I can't be sure, and I don't want to risk any escaping."

A shudder ran through me. How big would a spider have to be for a dragon to call it giant?

"Which door did I say?" the dragon asked.

"The second on the left."

"Good."

He quizzed me on all the doors. I rattled them off, along with the reasons they were dangerous. At the end, he seemed satisfied.

"What about that big metal door?" I pointed to the one across the great room. "The handle is hot."

"That door will always be locked." He laid his ears flat. "You don't need to worry about it."

I didn't like that.

The dragon stood on all fours. "It will be dark soon, and I need to hunt. Be safe."

Without a goodbye, he flew out of the castle.

I shook out the rest of the cloth from the bundle and looked closer.

It was all one gown.

Maroon silk flowed from the bodice to the generous skirt, lined with ice-white fur. I ran my fingertips over the draped sleeves. Everything was softer than spring tree buds.

It was more lovely than anything I had imagined.

And completely impractical for cleaning. I hung the dress

on the stair rail, high enough that it wouldn't touch the dirty floor. Night was coming, and the air was cooling.

First, I needed firewood. Wrapped in my curtain-cloak, I carried in branches and twigs, stacking them near the hearth. Next, I beat the dust from four thin blankets, making a clean pile on my bed. I swept every surface of the pretty bedroom, then wiped it with the outer cloth from the bundle.

Once the area around the fountain was swept, I scanned the great room.

An evening breeze blew outside.

All the doors were closed. I should have changed in the bedroom, but I would soil the new dress if I wore it while I washed my old one. The dragon hadn't been gone for long, and I was alone.

I shivered in my underclothes, the air cold against my bare shins.

The bar of soap from the bundle smelled like mint and clover. I breathed it in as I lathered my travel dress in the fountain.

Then, I heard a noise. Dragon talons on stone.

He was back.

Before I could move, he appeared at the entrance, and his golden eyes found me there, undressed. My underskirt and bodice hung close to my form in a way that made me feel exposed.

I thrust the soaked dress I had been washing in front of me.

Did dragons even understand privacy? He wore scales.

His eyes went wide, then he shut them tight.

Smoke poured from his nostrils.

I stood frozen, clutching my dress.

He turned away, his eyes still shut. "I didn't know."

Then, he disappeared out the front of the castle.

I scrambled for the silken gown hanging on the rail. It

slipped on warm and dry, and I removed my wet underdress from beneath it. My cheeks burned and my heart skipped.

I would act like nothing had ever happened. I hoped the dragon would do the same.

He didn't come back for a long time.

When he did, I was tucked into bed, a fire crackling in the room. I heard his footsteps.

Without a word, he lay down outside my door. My cut throbbed beneath the bandage as I pretended to sleep.

And that was how we spent the second night.

I woke in the dark from dreams of ghosts and spiders. Dreams of glass bottles and Guntor's bloody cut on the mountain cliff.

But then there were dreams where I heard a steady voice speaking rhymes. That dream didn't wake me up, and I didn't want it to end.

In the morning, when I got up, the dragon was already gone. Two rabbits lay outside my door. I roasted them for breakfast on the hearth in my room, wishing for porridge instead.

I explored the second staircase. The halls were wider, the rooms more lived in. I opened all the doors except the second on the left. There was a room with a large hearth and dozens of cooking pots. I took one for my room. At least I could have stew now.

Behind another door, I found ladies' clothing. There must have been more than a hundred gowns, and I spent the whole morning looking through them. This was a treasure I hadn't imagined.

In the end, I selected three that looked the most practical

for working, though I admired the long trains and full skirts on the others.

The practical dresses were still immaculate. White lace covered one, rising into a high collar. There was a gown the color of summer sky, and a thick woolen dress for cold evenings.

And boots.

None of the shoes had fur, like the ones I longed for as a child. But the leather was embroidered with silk roses, and the boots laced well above my ankles.

In a drawer beside the bed, I discovered my first piece of gold for the day. A thin chain with a lovely flower pendant. I spun it between my fingers and noticed a little clasp on one side.

When I pressed it, the pendant sprang open, revealing a hidden interior.

I laid the delicate thing flat in my palm and inspected it. Inside the two halves, someone had made a painting.

The perfect image of a little boy with round cheeks.

His blond curls matched the center of his eyes, a sunny yellow shining in circles of blue that winked up at me.

A lump formed in my throat.

Someone had loved this boy enough to make the drawing. Who was he? And why had they left it behind?

If he had been real, I imagined he would have a dusting of freckles over his nose. Like Isadora.

After looking for a while, I fastened the chain around my neck. My own gold, as long as the dragon didn't find out.

I tucked the pendant under the neckline of my dress, where it would be hidden.

I would have never stolen gold from Father like this.

Thinking of Father wasn't unbearable pain anymore, like it had been three days earlier, when the shock hit me. But it still cut, and there were things I didn't want to face.

So I kept moving through the castle.

In the library, I explored drawings of mountain ranges, giant birds, and people with odd clothes.

None of them gazed back at me the way the boy in the pendant seemed to.

Dried herbs filled one book, pressed flat between the pages. The drawings showed how to boil and bottle the leaves. I couldn't read the recipes, but I thought they might describe medicines.

High on the walls of the library, other paintings hung. Richly colored images of men in fine clothes. Several of them were of the same man, with high cheekbones and black eyes.

I didn't like any of their faces. I opened the pendant again to look at the boy.

Day turned to evening.

The dragon never came.

Before sunset, I scavenged greens from the forest and boiled a stew with the leftover rabbit. I ate by myself.

When the fire burned low, the sound of dragon steps thudded outside my room. I flung off my blankets and went to the door.

"Where have you—" I started.

But he was already gone. A silent shadow in the night.

The next day went the same. The dragon left rabbits again, but I never saw him. What happened to his promise of more stories? Of teaching me to read the letters?

I thought of his shut eyes when he saw me changing. Of his almost-apology.

In the marshes, Father left me alone for days at a time. Sometimes even Isa went. But that was my home. This place was something else.

I had fought to get away from the dragon. I had wished he would leave me. Now, my eyes searched the castle entry, hopeful for a glimpse of black scales.

The next day, I stole all the silver buttons from the ladies' gowns and sewed them into the hems of my own. There were twenty-two buttons, plus one gold clasp with a green gem.

When summer came and I left the castle, whatever I wore would be lined with treasure.

And treasure meant options.

That night, my wrist ached too much to sleep. In the morning, I peeled off the bandage. Something black and thick crusted my skin, too dark for blood. The edges were yellow, the wound still open.

I washed it and bandaged it with a fresh shirt, trying not to remember the ghost's fingernails. What kind of filth had it left behind in my body?

Two more days passed. Five days in total since I last saw the dragon.

Red lines streaked my arm.

I lost my appetite for rabbits, though I still cooked them in case the dragon came back to stay. Would he be hungry?

By the seventh morning alone, I vomited at the hearth and clutched the bed post for support. My body shook. Heat and ice washed over me, and a foul smell came from my bandage.

I laid on the bed and tried to sip water from my bottle, but it didn't stay in my stomach for long.

Sleep came.

In my dreams, Guntor's jaw opened wide, lined with sharp teeth. His claws sliced Isa's pale skin.

I shivered under my blankets, even though the day was warm. I had been this sick once before with a fever, but it wasn't from a wound. And I hadn't been alone. Isa had placed wet cloths on my head and made me drink a thick paste mixed with water. Medicine from the encampment.

In the castle, I strained my ears, listening for dragon steps.

But no one was coming for me.

Not even a beast.

The red marks covered my arm now, streaking toward my elbow. Without medicine, what would happen?

I would have to be my own help.

I rolled out of bed, landing on my hands and knees. It took me a while to stand. The foul bandage fell from my arm onto the floor, and I left it behind.

Step by step, I made it to the well. The room spun.

Water burned my cut. I scrubbed anyway, then vomited nothing onto the stones. My breath came in heaves.

The staircase wasn't far now. I forced myself to move up it, then toward the hall. Toward the library with the book full of dried leaves.

I hadn't touched them before. I didn't know what they were. But I would study the drawings again and look for anything familiar.

Maybe one of those leaves would smell like Isa's paste.

My head pounded. I squeezed my eyes shut and took a right, leaning against the library door to catch my breath.

With a final push, I turned the latch.

But there were no shelves in the room.

No books.

Swaying, I looked down the hall.

I had gone one door too far. The third on the right. The door I had promised to never open.

13

I LET GO OF THE HANDLE

too fast and lost my balance, falling to the hall floor. I needed to close the door, but it had swung into the room, and I didn't want to reach inside.

Evil magic.

That's what the dragon said was in this room. I had no idea what that meant, only that it was dangerous.

I pulled myself to standing, using the wall for support.

Blood rushed from my head and my vision went fuzzy. When it cleared, I searched the doorway. Would closing it be enough to stop the magic from escaping? It had been too late with the ghost.

I leaned over the threshold to grasp the handle. My hand closed on the knob. I swung it toward me.

That's when I saw what was in the room.

Bones. Human bones. The white remains of skulls and bodies strewn across the floor. I had never seen a human skeleton before, but these couldn't be anything else. All charred with smoke and ash.

Dragon ash. The smell was overpowering.

My eyes wouldn't leave the bodies. Dozens of them, killed in this castle by dragon fire.

By my dragon.

The one I had hoped to see again. To read with and to speak with.

My stomach churned and acid filled my mouth. The fever washed over me, hot and cold all at once.

Then someone was screaming.

I faintly recognized who. It was me. I fell, unable to hold myself up anymore. For a long time, I lay there, shivering in sickness and sweat.

Scales coiled around me.

"No." My eyes shot open, and I struggled against the dragon. Pain throbbed at my temples.

"You're unwell," he said. "I'm trying to help you."

Like he helped the victims in the third room to the right? That hadn't been magic. It was fire.

But I couldn't stop him from scooping me up in his tail. The warmth felt good, and my body went limp. We started down the stairs.

Fever pulled me into a half dream.

How strange that the dragon's scales and claws had never cut me when he picked me up. They were knife sharp, yet somehow gentle.

I lay on a flat surface again and opened my eyes. We were near the fountain. With a flick of his tail, the dragon draped a wet blanket over me. The water soaked to my skin, deepening my chill.

"It's cold," I slurred, shaking.

"Cold is good. You're burning."

I lifted my head. Pain shot through my arm.

"Don't move." The tail rested on my shoulder, easing me down. "I'll be back."

But he hadn't come back before. He had left me. Which was good, because he was a killer. And it was bad because I was dying.

"Don't go." My voice sounded far off to my ears. "I need—"

"I know. I won't leave you for long."

"But you did."

I shuddered under my icy blanket in the great room.

The dragon bounded to the enormous iron door at the far end of the room. It creaked open, though it had been locked when I tried the fiery handle. Black smoke curled from the other side, leaving soot on the white walls around it.

What was burning?

I imagined a cellar full of dragons, all scorching human bones.

The dragon disappeared into the smoke.

I drifted in and out of awareness. The castle was dim, the sun setting outside the windows. How long had I slept beside the door with the skeletons? When the dragon returned, heat wafted across the room as he closed the door behind him.

His tail curled around something silver. It clanked onto the floor beside me. A bowl filled with white powder.

I wanted to ask what it was. I only managed one word. "Salt?"

Salt could prevent infection, but I was beyond that.

"Silver salt from the mine," the dragon said. "It fights disease from the inside and the outside. How long have you had a fever?"

"A day. Maybe longer."

The dragon closed his eyes, his mouth in a tight line. He let out a growl, then took a deep breath. With his tail, he picked up my empty water bottle and plunged it into the fountain. Hissing steam erupted into the air where his scales touched the surface. It smelled like burning hair and sulfur.

When he pulled away, his tail scales were white and charred. One had fallen away, revealing angry red skin beneath.

"Show me your wound," he said.

I pulled my trembling arm from beneath the blanket.

He poured a small amount of water over the cut. I winced. The dragon lifted the bowl and sprinkled half the silver salts into the bottle. It was a clumsy process without hands. He spilled a lot of salt on the ground.

"Can you drink this?" He set the bottle beside me.

I lifted my head and brought it to my lips, taking small sips. It tasted metallic and bitter. After a while, I vomited. But only a little. Not all of the liquid. Encouraged, I drank the rest and laid down, mouth clamped shut. I had to keep the medicine in.

"Good," the dragon said. "The next part won't be easy."

With his scalded tail, he lifted the salt bowl and poured the rest over my outstretched wrist. I gasped. It burned. First on the surface of the skin, then deeper, where the crystals settled into the wound.

My eyes went wide and my chest ached.

I saw white skulls and dragon ash. Then I slipped from consciousness again.

Time passed in snippets and moments. The sharp pain of fresh silver salts. My legs tangled in blankets. Golden eyes, rimmed in blue, watching me.

Periodically, the dragon brought my bottle. In a haze, I swallowed liquid. Sometimes it was water, sometimes bitter medicine. I didn't vomit again.

Then, one night, my mind cleared, and I woke up. A fire burned low in the dark room. Did the dragon use a flint, or his own breath? My bed had been pulled at an odd angle near the door, where he could reach me more conveniently.

He was there now, out of sight, sleeping. I could hear him. I lay back and rested without pain. The fever was gone.

That morning, yellow sunlight shone through my window where I had pulled the velvet curtain off. The dragon came to the door, his head filling the frame.

I pulled the covers close around me.

He crouched with his arms in front of him. One of the claws was charred, the scales flared near the knuckles. Had he dipped it in water also?

The dragon followed my gaze, then tucked the charred arm under his body where I couldn't see it.

"You should have told me you were sick."

How could I have told him? He was the one who left.

But that didn't matter anymore. Not after what I had seen.

"You found me in the hall," I said. "Did I . . . did anything escape from the room?"

The dragon took a long breath. "Nothing like that."

Then there was nothing in that room but the truth. A truth he wanted to hide. Why keep me alive when he had burned the others?

"Why did you open the door?" he asked.

"I thought it was the library. I wasn't myself." I looked away. "But I fainted before I could see what—"

"We both know you saw what is in that room. I can hear it in your voice. I see it in the way you look at me. Lying doesn't become you."

My chest felt tight. "I'm not the one who lied first."

I went still, waiting for the dragon's anger.

His ears went back. "I never lied. Not once. I told you evil magic had been done there, and it has."

Evil? Yes. And this dragon had done that.

The dragon who charred himself to give me water. Who brought me food and fought the ghost. The dragon who had never scratched me once with his scales.

"Why?" My voice was a whisper, and tears blurred my sight.

One tendril of smoke curled from the dragon's nostril. He pushed his head further into the room. "What do you think you saw?"

I avoided his eyes. "The marks from your fire."

"And how do you know it was mine?"

Because I had a nose. Nothing in that room was natural. "It smells like you."

The dragon closed his mouth, his jaw muscles working. I eyed the window, wishing it had hinges to open. I was trapped in the bedroom.

After a silence, he spoke. "I know you need time to recover from everything that's happened—"

I spoke under my breath. "It's still happening."

I was still alone on a mountain with a dragon.

"Which is why you need to slow down and think. Ask questions and evaluate your situation. Stop acting on fear."

Fear was good. It told me when to stay silent and when to fight. It kept me moving when I wanted to give up.

If I was honest, it always had.

But the dragon was right about questions. There were answers I didn't want to face, so I hadn't asked.

"Here's a question then," I said. "Why haven't you burned me yet?"

"Because I'm not going to."

I couldn't believe him. And the worst part was that I wanted to. I tried to keep emotion from showing on my face.

The dragon raised his head as high as the door would allow. "Did you ever consider that maybe I'm not the only dragon to ever exist? That another might have made those scorch marks?"

More than one dragon?

I searched his face, and the golden eyes were soft.

Father and Isa had always called him the dragon. The only one. Like the sky, the marsh, the house.

The dragon. Single and solid.

But, he had a mother. Which meant there were others.

Hardly breathing, I thought of the dragon from my childhood. The one who came every time Father left the marsh. Then, one day, he didn't.

What had changed?

Then, a truth came to my mind. A truth Father had never considered.

I looked up. "You're a different dragon. Father meant to call someone else with our blood."

"Ah." The dragon's eyes crinkled. "So you are capable of reason. I had never seen that wizard before. But he couldn't tell the difference between me and his enemy."

"Where is the other?" I asked. "The smoke behind that silver door . . . The smell—"

He cut me off. "That door leads beneath the castle. Fire burns in the mines. Nothing else."

"If those are not your fire marks . . . then he was here?"

"The other dragon is long gone, though he did live here once."

Humans had lived here, then a dragon, and then another dragon. What was this place? How long had dragons owned it?

"You knew him?" I asked.

"Yes. But we parted ways." His tone lowered. "I won't have anything to do with magic."

"Will he come back?"

"No."

I waited, but the dragon didn't offer anything else.

So I asked another question. "What was my father's debt to him?"

"I don't know. At first, I thought the wizard was after dragon fire. Wizards used to seek it, a long time ago, before the knowledge was lost. When I saw you, I feared your wizard had rediscovered certain things."

My father's face had changed when the dragon talked about fire. "You told him it was possible to have it for himself. He didn't know that before."

Muscles tensed in the dragon's neck. "And now he does. Because of me. I think that's why he's coming back. Wizards fear death more than anything. They can put it off for hundreds of years, though they pay for it in the end. It's fear that drives them to become wizards, to seek out power at all cost. Before, he wanted his freedom. But now . . . there's fire in his sight."

"He's always been too scared to fight a dragon."

"He wouldn't be the first wizard to become foolish when he smells new magic. It's intoxicating."

"Or he's coming for me," I said.

The dragon gave me a direct look. "Anything is possible. Not all things are likely."

"So," I ventured, "if it had been the other dragon, he would have burned me right away?"

"Yes."

That familiar pain built in my heart, but I pushed it down. I tried to imagine it was a made-up story. That some other girl had been on that cliff. Not me. Not with my father.

It worked. The wave of pain disappeared.

"If the other dragon liked magic, maybe he would have wanted my father's golden bottle instead," I said.

"Between you and the bottle, there would be no competition." His expression changed. "There's power in killing. More than you know."

Did the dragon know what the golden bottle could do? That my father could summon water? I didn't ask. It was a secret, and if I let it out now, I would never be able to put it back.

There was something I wanted to know. "You never burned anyone?"

"Never," the dragon said. "And I hope I never have to."

In that moment, something shifted inside me. All my life, I had learned to ignore what I thought. I had believed what Father told me. He said his men were good, even though I wanted to hide from them. Guntor was to be trusted, even though he hurt Isa. Questions were wrong, though I longed to ask them. The dragon was evil, though his eyes told a different story.

A story that argued with everything else.

"I believe you," I whispered.

I was done being afraid of this dragon who gave me medicine.

"Thank you." The dragon's words held some kind of emotion.

"Thank you for saving my life." Even though he had taken my freedom.

"Let's not do it again. No more opening doors. And tell me if you start to feel unwell. I wouldn't have left."

"Where did you go?" I asked. "It was so long."

His ears twitched and he shifted onto his front feet. "After we last spoke . . . I thought it might be best for you to have some time . . . to yourself."

Was it the water that bothered him, or the lack of propriety? I didn't want to talk about this with the dragon, but something had to be said.

"I promise to warn you when I bathe or wash my clothes from now on."

He gave a slight nod. "Dragons aren't used to living with humans. But I will try."

Did I make him uncomfortable? That was hard to imagine.

"You can start by keeping your promises," I told him.

"I have kept every promise."

"You said you would teach me letters."

A little steam escaped. "It isn't easy. You may regret reminding me."

I straightened the collar of my beautiful gown, making sure the necklace was still tucked away. It was.

"I'll take my chances."

I would wait for my father. No matter what he had done or what he intended, I needed to see him again. There were still too many questions. Until then, the dragon and I would have to pass the time somehow.

14

LESSONS BEGAN AS SOON AS THE
dragon deemed me well enough to leave my room. Which took
three days—longer than I would have liked. While I recovered,
he brought roasted meat each day. At my insistence, he also
brought greens, and they made him sneeze. I would cook them
and eat, then I would need to rest again.

He never used his flame to make my work lighter.

"Let me see your wound," he said on the third day.

"You've seen it enough. We both have." I rose and took a
deep breath, tracing a finger over the pink skin of my healing
cut. "I'm ready."

The room spun a little when I stood, but I wasn't going to
let the dragon know.

"Barely." His teeth showed.

It wasn't exactly a dragon smile. More of a grimace. I was
beginning to think I could discern either.

"Which books should I get?"

He backed out of my room, clearing the doorway. "We're
not going to the library. Not yet anyway."

"Where, then?" I wanted to hear more stories.

"Outside."

With a swish of his wings, he was through the castle entry.

I followed behind at my human speed, picking my way around the larger boulders. What would it be like to have wings?

Outside, the dragon waited in the shade of the trees, protected from the warm sun. He didn't like to be hotter than he already was. When I reached him, his curled tail extended, holding something out to me.

I took the stick from him.

He flicked his tail down and began tracing lines in the soft dirt beneath the trees. He drew the characters in a long row, each one larger than my outstretched hand. When he finished, I counted them.

"Twenty-three." I already knew a few of them. "Are these the easiest ones to start with?"

"That's all the letters. You won't find more in any of the books. Or less."

Only twenty-three letters to make all those words? I examined the shapes and tried to calculate how many combinations there could be.

With the tip of my stick, I drew the first letter in the dirt next to the dragon's lines.

"Do you want to know their names?" he asked.

I let out a short laugh. "Letters have names? And then you have to use the other letters to write their names down?"

"I never thought about it like that. You can't really write down the name. The letter is the name."

He pointed to each one, pronouncing it slowly. I repeated after him. Then, he went back through them and showed me how their names connected with the sound they made.

Sound.

Letters represented sounds, not just words. I hadn't realized that before.

He made me draw them more times than I could count, until I got them all right from memory. I messed up a lot, and I began to grow tired.

Finally, I interrupted the lesson and wrote my own name in messy strokes. Something easy.

"G-I-L-D-E." I said the name of each letter, then made the sounds, seeing how they fit together. The shapes could speak.

He traced three letters in the dirt. "Try this one."

I made their sounds. "W-I-L. W-i-l. While."

"What other sound could the middle letter make?"

I answered quickly. "Wil."

Heat rose to my cheeks. It was his name. The one I had vowed not to use.

The dragon's tail rested on the ground. "You've never said that aloud before."

"Oh."

How long had it been since someone had called him by his name? How long since he had seen another of his kind?

The lesson had taken most of the morning.

I put my stick into the dirt and drew meaningless swirls. "Stories don't have to be in books. They can be from your memories too."

"A life story."

I looked up. "I'm sure yours is very interesting."

The dragon lay down and folded his wings. "Not as interesting as you might assume. Why don't you tell me a story first? It will give me time to think of my own."

Now I needed to think. I decided on a story inside of a story.

"When I was little," I began. "Isa married my cousin and came to live in the marshes."

I actually didn't understand exactly how I was related to Guntor. He was called a distant cousin, which meant Father might have siblings and family somewhere. But those were things I had been punished for speaking of.

"The wizard lived in the wetlands?" The dragon's tail twitched. "A dragon's magic wouldn't find him there. It's diminished by water. That was smart."

"And lonely. When Isa came, she brought stories and songs and . . ." I stopped myself.

"And what?" the dragon's ears perked up.

I bit my lip. "No one ever gave me a kiss before she came. I remember her hair was so soft and long, and she used to pick me up and carry me, and she would kiss me on the cheek." I swallowed back emotion. "She hit me too sometimes. She was only fourteen."

The dragon's tail twitched again. "So young."

"She didn't want to come to the mountain with us, and I can't blame her. I don't know where she is now. Maybe somewhere in a city north of the marsh."

"You once denied having any family besides the wizard."

"I didn't think it was safe to tell you."

I tensed. It was admission.

The dragon breathed. "Thank you for sharing that story."

"That's not the story," I said. "I'm going to tell you one of the stories Isa brought to me. That's why I had to bring her up."

His tail settled, and he rested his chin on his front talons. "I'm listening."

The words came without thought. I had heard them hundreds of times during chores and before bed. It was my favorite story.

I told the dragon about the treasure in the mountain, deep in a cave, guarded by ghosts. About how anyone could enter the cave, but you needed a secret password to exit. During the day, the ghosts slept. Countless treasure hunters entered and saw the gold, but when night fell, they didn't know the password and they couldn't leave. The ghosts would wake at night, stealing the hunters' souls into the afterlife.

When I spoke of the afterlife, the dragon's ears came forward. "And no one ever got the treasure?"

"Wait and hear the rest of the story."

Next I told my favorite part, about the boy who asked too

many questions. No one in the city liked him. But one day he struck up a curious conversation with a far-off traveler, and the boy learned something about the password. It was written on the back of a turtle who lived at the bottom of a lake at the top of the tallest mountain.

After a long and dangerous journey to retrieve the password, the boy went to the cave and returned home with all the treasure he could carry.

"What was the password?" the dragon asked.

"It wouldn't be a secret if everyone who heard the story knew." That was the answer Isa had given me when I asked.

I sat on a fallen tree trunk, careful to gather up the hem of my fine gown from the dirt. The hidden buttons clinked in the skirt, and I thought of my own journey to treasure.

"Real ghosts are worse than the story," I said.

"Maybe not. I'd rather fight something with teeth than have my soul taken."

I picked up a handful of pine needles and scratched at the ground with the sharp points. "That's because you have teeth too."

His nostrils flared. "Do you think Isa made the story up?"

"No. I tried to get her to make up stories sometimes, but she couldn't do it. She only knew a few good ones from the cities. None of them seemed true."

"There's more truth in myth than people often guess."

I let the pine needles fall through my fingers. I looked up. "It's your turn to tell a story. A true one."

"What do you want to know?"

I thought for a moment.

"I'd like to know about the other dragon. You were . . . friends?"

"Not exactly."

"What then?"

It took him a while to answer. "He collected knowledge,

and he used it to help someone in my family. I was grateful, and I learned from him. That was before his knowledge turned dark. In the end, he crossed too many lines, and he fled."

Was the other dragon out there somewhere, living a happy dragon life? He didn't deserve it. Were any dragons happy? There was a sadness in this one.

"Where is your family now?" I asked.

"I'm the last dragon. The other is lost, if not dead."

The last. There really was only one now.

Silence fell between us.

Did I have a family anymore?

A song came to mind, and I let it hum from my chest for a while. The dragon didn't react to my hum, except to close his eyes. After a while, I grew comfortable, and I sang the words.

> Friend of old, years long,
> I am not dead but only gone.
> I traveled past the endless sky,
> to the land where no one cries.
> No more hunger. No more strife.
> My first breath here was my first alive.

It was a sweet melody, sung as a message from the afterlife. When I finished, the dragon opened his eyes again.

"You have a beautiful voice."

I clasped my hands together. "Maybe you can teach me a dragon song sometime?"

"Dragons don't sing."

Then how would he know if my voice was nice?

He sat up. "Gilde. There's something I need to say to you. I don't think you want to hear it, but I'm going to tell you anyway"

I blinked up at him.

"When summer comes," he said, "I don't want you to go with the wizard."

"I need to speak with him," I said. "There are things I need to ask."

He took a slow breath. "It's going to be your choice . . . but only if you can be honest with yourself. I need to know that you understand what happened the day I took you. That you understand the danger he is."

The dragon waited, expecting a reply.

But I didn't understand what had happened that day. I couldn't hold my question back anymore—I was ready to face the answer. "Why did you take me?"

"I couldn't leave you with a wizard. He could use you—"

"No," I corrected. "Why did you take me here, when you could have flown me anywhere? Why are you keeping me?"

He took too long to answer, but I was used to that now. He would reply if I gave him the time.

"You tried to defend him with your knife," he said.

"And it bothered you."

"In a way. But at the same time, it hinted at something. You would protect a man who was betraying you, even though you had no real defense." His voice was low, almost a rumble.

"And that made you keep me?"

"It made me suspect you might be innocent, though I had my doubts. And innocence is a rare thing in this world. I . . . wanted to know."

"You were curious enough to risk a wizard tracking me here?"

"Tracking spells are dark and rare things. I didn't think he would be that deep into magics. And now that I know, I won't leave you somewhere for him to find again."

Wind blew, warm enough to be considered summer. Puffy clouds passed overhead.

So it had been curiosity that made him keep me. And now obligation.

He spoke. "You didn't protest just now when I said the

wizard betrayed you. What do you really think happened that day?"

But that question was still too much.

I refused to show the pain that threatened to crack me open. I slowed my breath, then rehearsed the answer in my mind. After a few repetitions, it was just words. No emotion attached.

"I think my father didn't tell me everything." Then came a truth I hadn't rehearsed. "And . . . he didn't fight for me."

"That's something."

It was an evil something.

I stood and dusted needles off my skirt. "I want to talk with him. Beyond that, I'm not sure what summer holds for me." I felt the buttons in my skirt. My future security.

The dragon stood too. "Seeing him will be dangerous."

"He may have new names now," I said. "Wizard. Alchemist. But I called him Father. I'm not scared of his magic."

The worst had already happened.

A dark look came into the dragon's eyes. "Alchemist?"

I didn't answer.

Smoke poured from his nose. "I won't have you here when he arrives. I can't guard you and the mines at the same time, and he's tracked your location there. He will search the castle first before paying the cost to track you to your next location."

What was in those mines?

"You want me to hide while you fight." My heart stopped. "And I'll be left with whoever survives."

"No." His tail swished over the ground, erasing our letters. "I'll hide. Deep in my caverns where I can defend my position. I'll be able to call out to him so we can speak."

Father's water wouldn't be enough to kill the dragon. The charred scales had healed quickly from their dips in the fountain when he filled the bottle for me, nothing more than surface wounds. Still, it made me uneasy.

"He could hurt you."

"He can't. If he's after you, I'll tell him a place where you can meet, and I'll follow from the air. But if you get too close . . ." The dragon swallowed. "Try to keep your distance. You can change your mind about meeting him. Even up to the last. There's a place nearby where you won't be found."

That didn't assure me. "He could track me again, like you said."

"No." The dragon shook his head. "He won't have the resources on my mountain to cast the spell. I'm sure he has plenty of things from you. Bits of hair and personal belongings. But there are other pieces to the magic that he can't find here. He'll have to go to the cities to do that."

I tried to remember Father's face but found I couldn't see it in perfect detail. Had I never memorized him? What would he say when I met him? What could I say?

The dragon moved slightly, fixing me with one golden eye. "Is he holding something over you to make you go to him? The life of a loved one?"

He did have something over me. "I'm his daughter."

"He doesn't own you."

I found my arms were folded tight around me, as if I were in pain. Maybe I was.

I looked up at the dragon. "It's a good plan."

"It's your choice. You don't belong to me either."

Belonging.

Some part of me had started to think of the dragon as mine. My dragon. My teacher.

But he didn't see it that way. I had been a thing he couldn't leave behind. And then I caused trouble, opening doors I shouldn't have.

"Whatever happens," I said. "I'll be gone from your castle."

To that, the dragon said nothing.

15

WE DIDN'T SPEAK OF FATHER
again, and the days passed. Time was a strange thing, and it
seemed to move at different speeds. My first few days in the
castle were long in my memory, especially the uncertainty
when the dragon abandoned me.

But now that we had settled into a routine, time sped up. It
went faster than I could have imagined.

Every morning, we practiced our letters. Before the sun
went down, the dragon read stories to me in the library while
I held the books and turned the pages. After a while, I could
read enough to pick the story titles.

After that, I could read full sentences.

Spring was passing. Summer would come soon.

When it rained, the dragon hid inside his castle until the
skies cleared. Once, he was caught in a drizzle, and little white
scorch marks speckled his scales for two days.

"If you were stranded outside, would you be hurt?" I asked.

"I would be in pain, but it wouldn't injure me."

On a day with clear skies, he brought me a bag of milled
flour, an enormous crock of cream, and a bag of cellar potatoes,
still crunchy from last year's harvest.

I eyed them, my stomach rumbling. "You didn't hunt those in the wild."

His tail scooted the gift toward me. "There's silver ore in the mines. The farmer who lost this produce is better off after my visit."

The potatoes lasted, and I didn't take another bite of rabbit until they ran out. The cream was better than I remembered, and something I had rarely had, even in the marsh.

Every day, I discovered some new trinket to steal from the castle. In the kitchen upstairs, beneath the pots and skillets, there was a set of twelve silver spoons, each with a tiny gem set in the handle.

I sewed them all into my skirts, padding them with thread so they wouldn't clink. The dragon and I never spoke of this either. Did he notice his treasures disappearing?

Mostly we talked of stories. The dragon knew some of the names of the people depicted in the portraits on the walls, and I found out they weren't all people who had lived in the castle. Some of them were characters from the fables in the library books. Illustrations, in their own way. He liked to talk about them most of all.

The real ones who had lived in the castle were dead now, and the dragon didn't have much to say about that.

Then, little pieces of our own lives would find their way into the conversations. I learned that my dragon had never known his own father and that his mother was something of a scholar. It was difficult to imagine her reading, all claws and teeth and ripped pages. Had there once been a better relationship between dragons and humans? Had someone held the books for her too?

"What happened to her?" I asked the question as gently as I could.

"She got sick."

"I'm so sorry," I said. "That must be a terrible thing for a dragon. You could fight off any other danger, except that one."

He lapsed into one of his silences. The kind that could last a long time when I asked the wrong questions. But his silences weren't like Father's, which had been a punishment. I felt the dragon needed to be quiet sometimes so that he could come back to me refreshed, and I didn't mind.

After I learned of his mother, a thought intruded into my mind. Would it have been better if my father died? I would have remembered him well, rather than living through the confusion I felt every day since the cliff.

But that thought was selfish. I made myself forget it as soon as it came.

Some evenings, I took walks among the trees. The dragon liked to follow behind or fly above to watch for beasts.

One night, he came nearer and walked beside me, and I found I didn't mind the closer proximity. I trotted next to him, pine needles crunching under my boots. My lungs filled with ease as I raced along. My heart beat steadily, stronger than I could ever remember. The mountain air was healing me.

The first stars appeared in the sky.

I stopped in a meadow and arched my neck to look up. "In eight more days, it will be summer."

The dragon sat. "Do you keep a calendar?"

"What's that?"

"A way of tracking time on paper."

I shook my head. "No. I can tell by the moon. I always count."

"Who taught you?"

"Isa taught me to count. Then I figured out how to watch the sky on my own."

He looked down at me. "Will you ever stop surprising me?"

I didn't know how to answer, so I didn't. "It's been five moons since midwinter. When the moon is full again, I'll turn seventeen, and summer will come."

Summer was a weighted word, full of the unknown.

"Your birthday," the dragon remarked.

"I guess so."

I had never thought of it like that before. It was a day when something happened to me, not a day that belonged to me.

"I would have given you a present," the dragon said.

I stiffened, thinking of all the stolen treasures in my three skirts.

"There's no need."

"I know. When you were sick, I noticed the necklace you wore."

My hand flew to my collar where the pendant was always hidden. "It was with the gowns. I can put it back . . . if you want me to."

"No. I'm saying I would have given it to you for your birthday, if you hadn't already found it. You can have anything in the castle you want."

Now I really didn't know what to say. All the silver. All the beautiful things I had thought I was stealing.

"It's a lovely necklace." I pulled it from beneath my dress and held it up in the starlight.

"It belonged to another human I knew. You're different from her, but I think she would have liked you."

I wasn't his first human . . . companion? I didn't know the word for what I was. Friend seemed too familiar, and yet too small of a word. He had confined me, and abandoned me, and then saved my life. There was nothing casual about our intersection. Prisoner didn't feel right either, or student. Maybe I was all of those things.

Who had the other human been?

"She used to live in the castle?" I asked.

"Long ago."

I couldn't stop myself from picturing the scorched bones. "How old are you?"

"Older than you. Young for a dragon."

I wanted a more specific answer, but he interrupted my thoughts.

"There's another gift I want to give you right now." He unfolded his wings. "It's a good one, though you may not think so at first. I want to take you flying."

My whole body went tense. "I thought you said it was a gift."

On the flight from the cliff, his claws hadn't cut, but they had gripped hard, bruising my shoulders.

"In eight days I'll need to fly you over the top of a peak," he said. "It would be better if you sat on me, rather than hanging from my hands. I'll flatten my scales for you." His ears twitched. "Haven't you ever thought about flying like a bird? The stars are brighter up there."

I had thought about it when I was little. I had even imagined flying like a dragon. But in my imagination, I was the dragon. Not the passenger.

I stared up at his gentle eyes. I had trusted him with my life every day I lived here. Why not with this?

"Lie down," I said.

The dragon's face fell.

"I mean lie down so I can climb onto your back." My stomach fluttered, but my heart remained steady.

He lowered his belly to the ground.

I looked him up and down, then stretched my hands to where his wing met his body.

"Will this hurt you if I pull myself up?"

"You couldn't hurt me if you tried."

I swung myself over the wing, wrapping my legs on either side. From there, I climbed onto his back, settling between two sharp spine ridges. His scales lay smooth, the knife edges tucked flat, just like he had promised.

The dragon extended his wings to their full width. "You really will never stop surprising me."

Then, with a ripple of powerful muscle, we were flying.

The ground fell away, and I screamed. Not from fear this time. It was so different from when I flew with him before.

Something wild and free rushed through me as wind blew over my face. I was safe, and alive, and soaring. The dragon could have rolled, and I would have fallen. But I knew he never would.

"Are you frightened?" His voice was deep and close in the air, with nothing else around. There was a smile in it, as if he could tell my scream was a happy one, despite his question.

"No!" I let out another whoop.

He laughed and rose higher. I gripped his spine ridge and dared a look down.

Darkness spread out below, and stars spun around us. The dragon slowed. We were wrapped together in the night sky.

"You were right," I told him. "The stars are closer."

"It's the best part about being a dragon."

"What is the worst part?"

I expected a retort about water fountains in his castle, but instead the dragon's body stiffened. He turned in mid-air.

"Hey!" I gripped hard to maintain my perch. "What are we doing?"

My eyes landed on a tiny pinprick of light in the distance. Something orange and flickering.

Fire.

"I'm taking you to safety," he said.

"Is the forest burning?"

"No. There are men on the mountain. At the base."

Men. Fire.

Father.

I held onto the dragon's spines until my hands hurt. I didn't let go. Not even when blood trickled down my fingers.

16

WE DIDN'T GO TO THE CASTLE.
The dragon flew over a high ridge and landed in a valley on the other side, in a wide meadow beside a stream. Bathed in moonlight, the place felt a world away from the torches at the base of the mountain.

"Do you see that shadow in the tree line?" The dragon pointed with his snout.

There was something large and dark, like a boulder.

"Yes."

"That's the house where you'll hide. You'll have everything you need provided. If you see a fire on the ridge, it means the wizard wants you back. He's signaling for you, and you can go to him if you choose. I'll tell him to wait three days after he lights the fire. If you go, I'll watch from above." His tone deepened, and extra smoke curled from his nose. "If you bleed, I'll know. The wizard won't harm you on my mountain if he wants to live."

I pulled my hands from the dragon's spines, knowing he could smell the little drops of blood now. But my cuts were shallow. They had already begun to seal.

"And if I don't go?" I surprised myself with the question. But I needed to know my options.

"He won't come looking for you. I'll make sure."

The dragon was setting me free. He had said I didn't belong to him, and I had thought he wanted me gone. But I didn't want to believe that anymore. Not after all our days in the library. And the gift of the necklace.

It was everything I had wanted. Escape. So why didn't I want to get off the dragon's back now?

"Can't I stay with you at the castle?"

If they fought, I could tell Father to stop. I could argue on behalf of the dragon.

My heart fell. When had I ever argued against Father?

The dragon settled into the grass. "I'm guarding more than my own flame. There are things in that castle no man should have. Especially not a wizard-man. I'll protect it with noxious smoke, and you wouldn't be safe."

"What if the men bring water? Or dragon fighters from the city?"

"The fighters are ambassadors, and they spend their spring in the western isles. I used to watch their travels from afar. They will already be gone on their ships. As for water, I would die if I were submerged in a lake for a while, it's true. And before my body cooled, someone could cut the fire from my chest. But men can't carry that much water."

"What about a wizard?"

"I've read hundreds of books of spells, and I've never come across that kind of magic."

Father didn't have a lake in his gold bottle. Maybe a small well. But it wasn't enough to submerge the dragon.

I should have told the dragon. He said he wouldn't hurt my father if he didn't have to. But what if he had to? If my father was stupid enough to force a battle, I wanted him to survive. So I kept his awful secret.

I sat on the dragon's back, and he sat in the meadow. Neither of us moved for a while.

"I wish I could stay here with you," he said. "I wish the men would leave us alone."

And there was a softness in him that I had never heard before.

"I'm sorry." My words came out in a hush. "I brought them here."

The dragon's breath rose and fell beneath me. "They brought themselves. I'm not afraid to face them, but I am afraid of the choice you have to make. You'll either trust a dragon or a wizard. Neither is usually a good option."

"There should be more dragons like you." The pain in my hands was gone, but still they quivered.

"Then you don't despise me?"

I wished I could see his eyes.

"No. I don't."

His rumble deepened. "What will you choose?"

"I don't know."

"Then this may be the last time we speak."

"We should have had eight more days," I said. "More time before summer arrived. But the ghost probably doesn't count by the moon."

"You should know," the dragon said, "I will never regret taking you from the wizard. Even if I can't keep you forever."

I had almost died. I'd lost Isa and lost Father's love. But I found I couldn't regret the dragon, either.

"Wil." The name was foreign on my lips, but I finally allowed myself to say it again. "You are the kindest creature I have ever known."

And as I spoke the words, I knew they were true.

He went still. "You haven't known many creatures."

"Thank you for showing me stories." My throat ached.

"You reminded me why they matter."

The dragon leaned to one side until I slid down his scales onto the soft meadow. Somehow, I landed on my feet.

The blue-rimmed eyes looked at me. "Time is running out. The men will arrive in two days, and I need to prepare." He spread his wings. "Go to the tree line. They're expecting you."

With a gust of hot air, he shot into the sky.

I was alone again. Even the scent of dragon was gone, the strange smell that had become my companion.

I wrapped my arms around myself and shivered.

Then the words Wil had spoken registered in my mind.

They're expecting you.

I swiveled to face the dark trees.

17

AFTER A MOMENT, I NOTICED
movement in the shadows. Whoever it was, they were small.
Although anyone was smaller than my usual company.

Wil wouldn't have left me here if it was a beast in the woods.
I watched the shape move closer, and decided I wouldn't
be afraid.

I would trust my dragon.

It was a woman. She stepped out of the shadows into
starlight, and I let out a breath.

How strange to see a human after all this time. Even in the
night, I could see deep wrinkles lined her face, burying her
eyes in folds of skin. A plait of thick, silver hair hung past her
shoulders.

I had never seen anyone like her.

So thin and sharp and soft, all at the same time. Then I
realized why she looked that way. She was old. Older than
anyone I had met.

And she was on the dragon's mountain. Another human.

As the woman approached, she threw one arm in the air
and waved. A greeting. Instinctively, I raised my hand in reply.

The woman stopped and called to me. "Are you going to
make me walk all the way over there?" Her voice was raspy
and thin.

"Oh." I hurried to meet her.

"My name is Gilde."

It was the introduction I had learned in the encampment.

The little woman blinked up at me. "That's what the dragon said. Though he didn't mention you'd be coming in the middle of the night. It's a good thing I was awake or you might have gone up to the house and scared the stuffing out of us."

"I'm so sorry . . . I didn't know people lived on the mountain."

"Most people don't live here. Not anymore." She turned back toward the trees. "Come on, I'd rather not stand out here all night in my sleeping gown."

The dress she wore was loose and shapeless, but still looked like an outer garment. Much nicer than the underclothes Isa and I always used to sleep in.

I walked beside her, matching her pace. She was faster than I would have guessed.

She breathed heavily as she trudged through the meadow. "We saw you out the curtains. Hans wanted to fetch you before the dragon left, but I wouldn't have it."

There were at least two of them.

"The dragon wouldn't hurt you," I said.

Didn't she know that already?

"It never has, but we keep our distance if we can."

"But you still live on the mountain." I hoped my comment held a tone of appreciation rather than any kind of judgment.

"We keep more distance than you, girl." The lady took a turn and led me into the forest. Everything was black in the tree shade. I might have tripped, but the path lay smooth beneath my feet, cleared of branches and stones. "I hardly believed it when I heard there was a human in the castle again. But here you are. And you flew on the thing."

She had been here when people used to live in the castle?

"You never told me your name," I said. "How many people

do you live with? How many years have you been in this forest? How often do you talk to the dragon?"

She laughed. "The girl rides dragons, and she thinks we are the ones who need to be interrogated."

But she hadn't asked me anything.

"Maybe we can both answer each other's questions," I said.

"Maybe." The woman stopped.

Hinges squeaked, and a door swung open. My eyes squinted against sudden light. This was the house, hidden in the dark.

Through the door, I could see it was built of wood, and it had shutters inside like our home in the marsh. A fire burned low in the hearth.

I followed her, and warmth washed over my skin. I hadn't realized it was cold, but even summer air chilled in the mountains at night.

There were no stairs and no loft, but two doors hinted at other rooms. A dining table sat in the corner, lined with long benches. Enough space for a whole family to sit.

I stood on the woven rug in the middle of the floor, uncertain.

The elder woman poured something into a mug from a clay pitcher. "I can't count the days since we've had a guest up here." She handed the drink to me.

"Thank you." I took a sip, my throat dry after flying. The drink was creamy and smooth. Milk.

"Hans." The woman raised her voice. "She's here!"

I clutched the mug.

A door creaked like the hinges, and a man emerged from the back of the house. He was as wrinkled as the woman and almost as short.

Despite their aged skin and sharp angles, these two didn't look nearly as worn out as Father's men. There was something bright in Hans's eyes.

He shoved a cap over his sparse hair. "You don't have to yell, Petra. You'll scare the girl."

So her name was Petra.

She glanced at me, her mouth twitching up at the corners. "Hans worries that you're easily startled. That's why he sent me to get you."

"The girl's had it hard enough," Hans said. "I thought a female presence would be soothing."

"If the girl's not scared of a dragon, I don't think you'll give her much of a fright."

I expected Hans to get angry. Guntor would have if Isadora spoke to him like that. But he gave Petra a crooked smile, and she laid a hand on his back. They stood close together, like that was their usual state. Near. Next to.

"Suppose we ought to let her sleep," he said.

"Or suppose we could have a chat," came the response. "She's already got us out of bed."

I spoke up. "I'm not tired."

There was too much in my mind to allow sleep.

Hans lowered himself to sit on the bench beside the table. "What is your name, child?"

Petra answered for me. "It's Gilde."

His eyes twinkled. "Anything else you should catch me up on?"

Petra thought for a moment. "No. That's about it."

"Good enough, then." Hans pulled one of the wooden benches near the fire. "Gilde, will you sit?"

I sat and took another long drink of milk. Petra joined Hans on the bench across from me, and his hand rested on her knee. I couldn't look away from that hand—such a small, gentle touch. She didn't seem to notice.

Petra spoke first. "The dragon told us you're not a wizard." There was a question in her tone.

"I'm not." My eyes roamed around the room. Plank floors.

A basin of water. Everything was small and plain. So different from the castle. My eyes went back to them. "What else did he tell you about me?"

Hans leaned forward. "Not much. And I can't deny we've been curious."

"Why would you come to the area?" Petra asked.

The milk went sour in my stomach. How could I describe what had brought me to the castle? A rescue. An abduction. A lie.

"The dragon brought me," I said. "My companions were . . . unusual. The dragon meant to help by giving me space from them."

The two elders gave each other a long look.

"But you're free to leave the castle now?" Petra asked.

Freedom.

It's why Father had sought the dragon in the first place. Now, when I thought of my days walking in the forest and reading stories in the castle library, they felt more free than any I could remember. Even though I hadn't been allowed to leave.

"My family is coming for me," I said. "The dragon will let me go if I want to."

"Why wouldn't you want to leave?" Hans took his hand from Petra's knee. "Tell me, is there still a hole instead of a door in the front of the castle?"

"Yes . . ." Why would that matter?

Hans shook his head. "Dragons can't build anything. They only destroy it. It's not a place for someone like you."

Now it was my turn to lean in. "Petra says you've lived here a long time."

"I was born on this mountain," he said.

"In the castle?"

"Near to it."

Petra laid her hand on Hans's shoulder again.

"It must have been full of people once," I said, watching them. "Before the dragons came?"

"One dragon came at first." The lines deepened on Hans's brow. "The bigger one. The one that caused it all."

"All what?"

Petra patted Hans. "You'll have to start at the start."

"I'd like to hear from the start." I set my mug on the bench. "Please."

He studied me, then gave one curt nod. "Only seems fair for you to know what you're in the middle of."

It had to be late, past evening and well into night. But I didn't care.

I would listen as long as he would talk.

"Thank you," I said.

Hans sat up straighter. "Like I said, I was born here. Clear air, blue skies, and pine needles as far back as I can remember. My mother served in the castle, and so did I when I was old enough to carry a rubbish pail. They said it was made by magic, but no one worried about that much when there was silver to be had.

"The people used to come up for the summers to work in the mine. The castle would be full, the meadows pitched with tents. Each fall, the miners would leave with pockets full. Those were rich times. Plentiful. Before the curse came."

"Curse?" This felt like one of Isa's stories.

"It started with the bad fumes," Hans explained. "Toxic smoke poured from the depths of the caverns, and men died. Then, the first dragon came. We thought Edric, the lord of the castle, would call us to fight. Instead, he welcomed it into our walls. Told us to obey the dragon, as if it were Edric himself. A lot of people left. And then later, they say people started disappearing."

Petra stood, her mouth tight. "I'll boil water for porridge. No sense in being tired and hungry. And no sense in digging up grief. Those times are past."

"She has a right to know," Hans said.

Petra did not respond as she hung a kettle over the hearth.

Hans went on. "Pretty soon, most people were gone. They either fled back to the cities or were taken by the dragon . . ."

I had seen them. What was left of them.

"But you're still here," I said. "Why?"

"The first dragon was a wizard. It really didn't care about people like us. Not a spark in any of our family lineage. By the time the last humans were leaving, Petra and I were in love. Ready to get married. But what did we have in the cities? No land. No family. Here, we had a house. A forest rich with furs and metals to trade. Our parents were buried on this land." He rubbed his head. "We were the last ones like that."

Petra set a mug heavily on the table, hard enough to make a loud thud. Hans looked her way, then continued.

"So we made our wealth and raised our family in the shadow of the castle. We just had to stay out of the dragons' way. Both of them. It wasn't hard to do once they decided we weren't worth paying attention to."

Petra stoked the fire. "Fought among themselves is more like it. The first one got more and more sickly. Then, in recent years, the new one came and the old one disappeared. Probably killed off. Eaten."

"We don't know that," Hans cautioned. "But the current dragon is a different sort. I haven't heard of anyone disappearing from the base towns in a long time. And no one with a spark has been hunted that I know of. I doubt this dragon's even a wizard. He brought us a sheep or two over the years."

A spark. That's what Isa's friends had spoken of in the encampment. And a girl killed by a wizard.

Petra stirred bowls of porridge with a long wooden spoon. "Just because a dragon's neighborly doesn't mean it can be trusted. This one's taking girls now." She nudged her head in my direction.

"She looks alive to me," Hans remarked.

"For now." Petra's eyes shifted to the window, then the door.

The way they spoke, even I felt a chill. But if Wil came, I wouldn't be afraid. How could I be?

"Please," I asked them. "I need to know about sparks. What can you tell me?"

"That would be something your family should have told you." Petra handed a bowl to me. "They'd know if it's in your line. Though you look old enough, so it would have shown by now. Perhaps the dragon got it wrong when he took you. So now he's giving you back."

This was like trying to catch a waterfly in the marsh, the truth fluttering out of reach.

"I don't know what a spark is at all." I set the bowl beside me. "I don't understand what it means."

Petra looked me up and down. "There's no way a girl your age hasn't heard about the sparks."

"Well, I haven't." I didn't want to tell her that I had spent my life in a marsh. That I didn't know the names of any cities, or even many people.

Petra began eating her porridge.

Hans only held his, eyes thoughtful. "I've never had to explain it before. The best way might be to tell you about some folks. There was a man, when I was young, who lived in the basetowns at the bottom of the mountain. He never was good at chopping wood or heavy work. But when he came of age, around the time he was sixteen or seventeen, he got fast."

He raised his brows with meaning, as if he had shared something important.

"Fast how?"

"You really haven't heard." Hans shook his head. "At first, he could run faster than any of the other men. Then, he could run faster than horses. I saw it with my own eyes. He used to carry messages between cities. Got paid good silver too, from emissaries and magistrates."

"So a spark means you're fast?"

"Not just that. There's all kinds. Some can sing so pretty you'd give them your soul if you heard it. There's a woman in Dampftal who can weave fine clothes from straw and scratch."

Petra scraped the last bite from her bowl. "I heard of a man on the coast who can breathe underwater."

"Now," Hans admonished. "That's not been confirmed. But the point is, some families have a spark, and a sparked person can do certain things better than other people. Beyond what any regular person could hope for. It's in their blood."

Better than others. I thought of Father's gold and the power it held over men. "Like an alchemist? Does that come from a spark?"

Petra and Hans exchanged glances.

"No," Hans answered. "Some folks revere alchemy, but it's wizardry through and through. If you've been around long enough, you see things. Power like that—the greedy kind— doesn't come from anything good."

"How then?" I swallowed a bad taste in my mouth. "How would someone become an alchemist?"

"Like all wizardry. Power like that only comes from leeching blood. That big kind of magic requires killing."

18

THIS WAS THE TRUTH I HAD been ignoring.

I had seen how dragons made magic. All the brutality of it in the castle's skeleton room. But I had hidden my mind from Father's part in it all. I felt sick.

"You're sure?" The words were shaky.

"Yes." Hans frowned. "There are chants involved, and sometimes symbols, but decent men don't know the details. I do know the wizards only get a small fraction of the spark when they bleed their victims. They can get more if they kill. Still, it's a lot of sacrifice for only a sliver of power. To become an alchemist . . ." His voice slowed. "I think many people would have to die."

Father's gold. His circle of water. They weren't miracles. They were gravestones.

And somewhere in secret, I had known it.

Wil said girls like me could be useful for magic. Evil magic. "How do you know if you have a spark?" I asked.

It was Petra who answered. "Wizards can tell. And people know if they can do something special. But having a spark is nothing to be prideful over, and not having one is nothing to be ashamed of. You're either born with it or you're not. It doesn't say anything about your character. Like looks. You're a pretty young thing, but you didn't do anything to earn it. And plain folks are just as good as anyone else."

I startled. No one had ever called me pretty. Isa was beautiful, not me.

"All that said," Hans interrupted, "I'm glad I married a beauty."

He gave Petra the warmest smile, and her face lit. For a moment, anyone would have believed she really was a beauty. Wrinkles and frizz and all.

Petra looked back to me. "But of course, our sons grew up and married women from the valley. One of our granddaughters, Anna, may have a touch of the spark from her mother's side. She's fifteen now, and when she cooks, it's better than anything you've tasted."

"So it can really be anything," I mused.

"They sent her to be a chef in a grand house on the coast, away from here. It means she'll have plenty of options for a marriage too. Lots of wealthy families would like a spark in their line. To the rich, a spark is a shiny, useful thing. It comes with status in those walled-up cities. For country folk, it isn't so easy. We don't have armies and walls to scare off the wizards, and a spark can mean you have to move somewhere with protections. It ends our way of life."

Hans stirred his spoon around his bowl and tilted his head at me. "Do you think you have a spark, Gilde?"

"Someone thought I might," I answered. "But I don't think so."

"You're better off without." Petra stood with a groan. "We'd like to know more about you, Gilde-girl. But we all need a rest now that we've eaten."

That's when I saw there was a faint light around the edges of the shutters. Morning was on its way. It had already been late when Wil took me for a flight.

"You'll be in the boys' old room." Petra opened the furthest door at the back of the house. "The blankets are clean. Let's all have a good sleep and wake for supper." She eyed my untouched porridge. "You'll be hungry."

Yesterday, I would have loved to eat porridge. Now I couldn't manage it.

I let her usher me into the back room and close the door behind me. The room was dim, barely lit by the dawn outside. I settled onto a lumpy mat, thick blankets spread taught.

My body wanted to sleep, but my eyes didn't close.

Petra and Hans.

New people. New stories.

There was a strange warmth between them, something unfamiliar and soft. Was that what marriage could be?

Was that what it was supposed to be?

I forced my eyes shut and listened to the elder couple close the door to their own room.

Then, in the silence, I couldn't hide from my own mind anymore.

In the encampment, Ewan said he shot a wizard with an arrow. Father had returned home with a bloody wound. That wizard had killed a young girl.

That was how Father got his magic water.

Enough to ward off the dragon for a moment. Enough to defend one person if needed. Himself.

I was his daughter. Fathers don't give away their daughter's life to save their own. But that's what had happened.

I curled myself into the rough blankets and clutched the fabric in closed fists.

Sobs came, unhindered.

All the tears I had held back soaked into this stranger's bed. I cried for longer than I thought possible, and the pain built into a flood. Then it drained from me, finally relieved. All used up.

The truth was now in the open. Fully seen, and just as terrible as I had feared.

But you can't fight a ghost while it hides in the shadows.

Eventually, cheeks damp, I drifted into an uneasy sleep.

And I dreamed.

In the dream, a girl lay in a field, her skin gray, her body lifeless. Beside her rested another girl. And another. All dead.

I wanted to run away, but I was hiding in the bushes. Hiding from something, and I had to be silent. The thing flew overhead, casting a shadow on the field. I held my breath and dared to look up.

It was water.

An enormous gathering of magic, as wide as a lake, churning like a river. Large enough to drown a dragon. Enough water to kill.

I woke up in a sweat, the room flooded with afternoon heat. I sat up and pulled my knees to my chest.

Even in my dreams, the scope of my situation wouldn't leave me alone.

I had always thought of the magic water as a limited resource. Now I knew it was only limited by how many people Father could kill.

After the cliff, why had he taken so long to come after me?

With all that time, while I had learned to read stories, Father might have gathered more water in his golden bottle. Enough to stand a chance in battle.

And I hadn't warned Wil.

I hadn't thought I needed to.

The sweat on my brow turned cold. I pictured his charred scales and blistered skin.

I flew to the window and threw open the shutters. I had slept too long.

At sunset, it would be almost a day since we saw the men's

fire on the mountain. They had been near, with maybe two more days to climb before they reached the castle.

How long would it take me?

A gentle scraping noise came from the main room. Someone else was awake. I opened the door and hurried through, almost colliding into Petra.

"So you're up." She crossed her arms and held her ground, inches from me.

"I am." I looked past her and scanned the room. What would I need for the journey back? I had good boots on my feet, and the treasure sewn into my dress, but nothing else.

Petra stepped aside. "I've put the kettle on. Take a seat."

But I didn't sit. I couldn't.

The small woman looked up. "What is it, girl? You're spooked."

"I have to go."

She shook her head. "The dragon said the others won't arrive on the ridge for days. No sense in getting hasty."

"I'm not climbing the ridge." I shifted my weight from one foot to the other. "Well, I am. But then I'm going back to the castle."

The back door flung open, and Hans strode into the room. "You're going where?"

"The castle." I stopped my shifting. "Thank you very much for taking care of me. But I have to leave now."

Hans frowned. "Back to the dragon. When so many others never escaped." He edged toward the door, cutting off my path. "Are you mad, girl?"

I squared my shoulders. "Will you try to stop me?"

No one moved.

Hans finally let out a breath. "I should try."

Petra spoke to him. "The girl rides dragons."

"I haven't forgotten."

"There's more here than we understand."

"There usually is."

They both looked to me.

There wasn't time to tell them everything. "I need to warn him," I said. "And I'm running out of time."

"Dragons need no warning," Hans told me. "They face no dangers."

"The alchemist." That was something these two understood. "He's coming to the mountain. He has water. Magic water."

Even now, sharing my father's secrets felt like a betrayal.

Petra came over to me and studied my face. "We lived this long on the mountain by staying out of the dragon's business. But staying out of this doesn't feel right. You're such a small thing."

Next to Petra, I was anything but small.

I looked into her bright eyes. "I may already be out of time."

Something shifted, and Petra went to her cupboard in quick strides. "Well, you won't make it far on an empty stomach." She wrapped a loaf of bread in cloth, then took a small crock from the lower shelf. She placed everything in a brown sack.

Hans was still watching me. "If you could tell us more, it would be easier. We have no claim on you. But we should know the full story if we're going to send you to the dragon."

"I will tell you," I promised. "I'll come back when it's done, and I'll explain everything."

I liked the idea of returning to this little place. I liked the idea of seeing these two again.

He shook his head. "We may not be here. This was our last spring on the mountain. Our bones are getting too old for the high places. Soon, we'll start down to the valley. Then, we'll follow our children to the coast. If we don't leave in a few days, we won't finish our journey before the frost. We move slow. And with an alchemist coming . . . None of us should be here."

Petra thrust the bag of food into my arms. "We thought you

might come with us. There was supposed to be more time to discuss everything."

I stood there longer than I should have, taking them in. Hans and Petra. Willing to bring a stranger to their family. To a city. A community of people.

It was everything I had wanted. To move away from the marsh and be among music. I could go with them. I could go to Isa.

Without thinking, I ran my fingers over the golden pendant that hung around my neck beneath my dress collar.

The dragon hadn't left me when the ghost attacked. He hadn't left me when I was sick.

And he needed me now.

"I should pay you for the supplies." I held the food in one hand and fumbled for my skirt with the other. "I have silver."

Hans's expression hardened. "No. We won't take payment for sending you. It could be blood money."

But my blood wasn't at risk. At least, not from Wil. I didn't know what lay in the forest.

"I was thinking it will take me all night to reach the castle," I said instead.

"If you're lucky," Hans replied. "We're close enough to the shroud that you shouldn't have forgotten where the castle is quite yet. You slept inside the walls too. The longer you stay the less you forget it later. But it's been too long since Petra and I have seen the place. We can't remember the way anymore, and it's forgotten us too. I don't think it would let us find it."

I did know the way. And I couldn't imagine forgetting it.

"Are there animals on the ridge?"

"Do you have a flint?" Petra asked me.

I nodded and felt the tool in my pocket.

"You'll do well enough, then. The beasts won't come near a fire at night. And they don't hunt in the day."

There was nothing left to say. I gave Petra and Hans a last

smile, trying to look more calm than I felt. If they sensed my fear, they might argue further.

"Thank you," I said. "I truly mean it. I would have liked to see you both again."

I would have liked to know people like them all my life.

I imagined a false history. One where Petra was my neighbor, and I brought her potatoes, and she gave me warm milk next to a lovely fire. I might have slept in their back room when Guntor was angry. I might have played with their sons.

Petra's eyes welled, but no tears fell.

Her eyes welled for me, someone she barely knew. If I didn't leave now, I would cry too.

"I don't know how long my journey will take," I said. "But I am glad I met you."

Before either of them could reply, I slipped through the door and closed it behind me. Now, it was time to face the mountain. The rest would come after that.

19

IN SOME WAYS, THE JOURNEY
looked like any of my evening walks. Except I was alone. And
I ran.

When had my heart grown so strong? A few moons ago,
this pace would have left me breathless and weak.

The sun dampened my hair with sweat, and I drank Petra's
jar of cool milk.

Looking back into the valley, the cottage disappeared
among the trees. It was part of the mountain, like Hans and
Petra. Chimney smoke might have given it away, but none
curled into the clear sky.

Father wouldn't have found me if I had chosen to stay hidden.

That would have meant choosing safety and comfort. And
it would have meant not choosing Wil.

But now I was choosing him by leaving safety behind.

On the ridge, the trees grew thick and the ground sloped at
a steep angle. I used arms and legs and even elbows to climb.
Soon, the air cooled, and the birds sang their twilight songs.

I found a spot on the ridge where a boulder jutted out from
the earth. It wouldn't be comfortable, but at least it was flat.
Sort of.

In the remaining daylight, I gathered as many fallen

branches as I could, stacking them at the boulder. They would be my light.

My protection against the beasts.

By the time darkness fell, I had the beginnings of a fire. Smoke from the wood burned my eyes, but I stoked the flames higher.

A knobbed tree served as my back rest. I should have slept, but every time I dozed, I dreamed the fire went out. My eyelids flew open, and I added another branch to the flames.

The forest had never been so loud. Twigs snapped and leaves rustled, but I saw nothing in the dark ring of pines around me.

If only the noises in the forest were Wil. If only he were here.

But he wasn't. I had scratched myself on the climb, and he might have smelled the blood on his mountain, but he never came. Maybe there were too many people on this side for him to be alarmed at the scent. I doubted he came every time Petra accidentally cut herself with a kitchen knife.

And maybe his mind was on the wizard now.

I thought of spilling more blood. Enough to alarm him. But what if the men had climbed quicker than I predicted? What if the dragon was already facing my father, and I weakened myself too much to finish the climb?

To pass the remaining time, I sang under my breath, my voice husky from smoke. I mouthed the story about the whale and the warrior, setting it to an old melody.

Dawn arrived. Thanks to Wil's flint, I never saw a beast.

I stretched my stiff limbs and resumed the climb, stopping only to take a mouthful of Petra's bread. As I went, I practiced what I would say. It would have to be fast and clear. A warning. Then Wil would know what to do.

Sharp rocks scraped my hands as I crested the ridge. If he hadn't smelled me yet, he wouldn't. Now what if Father was making his own cuts to draw the dragon out of hiding? Would Wil be able to tell the difference?

The trees thinned up here, opening to a craggy perch. I would have stopped to take in the view, but there was no time. How long until the men arrived?

Going down the other side, my calves burned less. Pebbles slid under my feet, leaving steep trails of loosened earth. Dust billowed around me, filling my nose.

By midday, the spiraled towers of the castle came into view, spiking above the trees.

I let myself slide now, catching my fall on tree branches. My sleeves tore.

Soon, the ground leveled. These were trees I knew. Ones I had walked through with Wil. I sprinted, despite my aching feet. One more gully and hill, then the castle would be in full view.

But when I finally saw it, things had changed. It wasn't the same castle I remembered.

I came to a standstill, then crouched behind a tree, panting.

Rocks and rubble barricaded the castle entrance. Most of the front room had collapsed, along with the side of the tower where the ghost had lived.

They were gone. Destroyed.

I thought of the library and the beautiful books. But mostly I thought of Wil.

My eyes swept over the scene, and a deep cold ran through my veins. Dead campfires and travel packs littered the grass.

Signs of men.

They were here.

I thought of every moment I had rested on the journey. I should have run faster. I should have carried a torch through the night.

My chest ached, but not because of my weak heart. This was something different.

I hadn't come fast enough.

I sank lower, and tree bark skinned the backs of my arms.

More useless blood. What if Wil hadn't smelled me because his body lay underwater?

But he couldn't be dead. I wouldn't believe it unless I saw it.

I took a deep breath.

When Father used to give me bruises, I still smiled for him. I was good at pretending, and this was no different.

I would pretend I was brave.

Where were the men? Blinking back tears, I stood and scanned the castle. Then I listened.

Thumping sounds came from the far right, near the castle, above the mines. I took off in that direction.

Darting from tree to tree, I crept to the edge of the forest and peered out.

Men gathered around a mound of loose dirt at the base of the castle. There were at least thirty of them, and they hacked at the earth with picks and shovels, sweat soaking their filthy shirts.

Among them, I recognized one face. Guntor. Father was nowhere to be seen. Guntor looked smaller than I remembered. And older, though I doubted he had changed. My perspective had shifted.

If they were digging, it meant they hadn't killed Wil and cut out his fire yet.

Because he was down there, protecting secrets deep in the castle.

He would billow his own acrid smoke. Even if the men tunneled in, they wouldn't be able to breathe.

He thought he was safe.

He thought he wouldn't have to burn anyone.

But water could pour down tunnels. When the smoke cleared, before Wil's body went cold, they would cut his chest open.

And I was powerless to stop it.

20

THE MEN WORKED THROUGH
the evening, crawling deep inside the hole to dig further. They
cut tree branches and used the wood to fortify their tunnel.

I watched from behind pine needles, careful to keep my
distance. A few of the men had climbed up on the castle walls
and looked out over the forest. They would see me if I left the
cover of trees.

By sunset, more than half the men returned to the camp
in front of the castle. Smoke drifted into the air from their
campfires.

Human smoke.

But my father was nowhere to be seen. I was looking for
him, and I was afraid to find him.

As it grew dark, I moved closer, hidden in brush. I crawled
beneath a low branch. Even if a man walked right by, he
wouldn't know I was there.

But they never came.

They talked around the fires and ate chunks of cheese,
smacking their lips. They urinated in their own camp, like
animals. I looked away.

This close, I could overhear conversation.

"Not that you did much of the work."

"Hey!" a man with a high voice retorted. "Shut up."

"Listen." Another speaker joined the bickering. "You think we could strip a bit of gold out of the castle tonight?"

"Naw. It's all caved in and blocked off. Even up top. Found it like that. Besides, you want an alchemist to catch you treasure hunting? His gold's the only gold in his eyes. Best not to stray."

So they hadn't been the ones to collapse the castle. Wil must have done it. A defense.

There wasn't as much treasure left as they might think, after I had squirreled away my silver pieces. Unless they considered books to be treasure. Which I did.

The man with the high voice piped in. "Well. I wouldn't mind getting in there after he gets what he wants."

He meant after Wil was dead. I swallowed back disgust.

One by one, all the men laid on the dirt and went to sleep.

On the dirt where Wil and I used to draw letters.

Before first light, I moved to a new hiding place, high in the branches of a sturdy pine that overlooked the tunnel. I drank the last of my milk from Petra's crock. There was no more bread, and my stomach felt hollow.

The sun rose, and the men gathered to work again.

I watched and listened. What else could I do? Sometimes, panic threatened to well up, but I pushed it down.

Wil was still alive. I was here. That was something.

Late in the afternoon, voices shouted from inside the tunnel, and men scurried out. Black smoke trailed behind them.

One man yelled at the others. "Where's Guntor? And Fritz?"

"Didn't make it out. The smoke choked 'em."

It took a while for me to process the words. The man had said it so casually. So devoid of emotion.

And when I understood, I felt numb. Nothing. I should have felt something.

But I noticed my hands were shaking.

All the men backed away from the hole, and it belched dark clouds. They had reached the mine.

I inhaled the scent of dragon.

Another two men ran away, to the backside of the castle. Had they decided to escape after seeing the smoke?

They all should have gone. This wasn't worth any amount of gold. This wasn't worth the cost of a life.

But the men returned, and someone familiar came with them. The most familiar person in the whole world to me.

Father.

It was like seeing him for the first time. His dark hair had never grayed. He stood there, appraising the scene with youthful, unlined eyes. The strong lines of his jaw should have softened over the years, like a younger version of Hans and Petra. But his skin was smooth.

Why hadn't I understood before? He didn't age, and it wasn't natural.

Like a wizard.

Like my father.

Part of me wanted to climb down and run to him. To show him I was alive. Another part of me wanted to run away.

I trembled, but I held tight to the branches of the tree I sat in. My father didn't know I was here. He couldn't see me.

Tree sap stuck to my fingers, sticky and fragrant. Pine needles brushed my skin. I was safe.

For now.

My mouth went dry, and I searched the gathering for golden hair. For Isa. If Guntor was here, she might have come. He might have found her.

But all I had seen were men. I took comfort in that, for her sake.

Father stood near the hole, feet planted wide, hands clasped behind his back. His voice rang out with a cold undercurrent.

"I know you're in there, Dragon. Will you come out and face me, or are you a coward?"

Father always liked to do things the easy way. If he sent his water down the tunnel to drown Wil, he would have to search a fiery mine for the body. Coaxing Wil out would be less work.

Wil's voice echoed from the hole. "You're free to come down here, if you'd like. My home is open to you."

I thought I heard a smile in his words, and I ached at his confidence. He didn't know.

Smoke poured from the hole.

Father faltered back, then held his ground. "After all your years alone, I'm surprised you remember how to speak to someone else, let alone host a guest."

The smoke dwindled a bit, but still filled the tunnel.

"Why have you come?" Wil asked.

"You said if I ever came on your mountain again, you'd kill me. So why are you hiding in a hole? You have a promise to keep."

"You hid in your swamp. And now you'll fight a dragon after all these years?" Wil paused. "Is it to avenge Gilde?"

Father's unclasped hands dropped to his sides. I couldn't move.

"It wasn't a fair trade," Father snapped.

Once, when I was young, I fell on a piece of firewood. It pressed deep into my abdomen without piercing the skin, leaving a dark bruise.

I felt like that now.

Injury without blood.

"She was valuable," Wil said.

"She's gone." Father's voice hardened. "I waited a long time for my freedom. But now I find I want more than that for what I sacrificed. You can give your fire to me, or I'll kill you for it. It's that simple."

The smoke billowed. "You don't know what you're asking. It burns the one who holds it."

"They say that about all magics, but the reward is worth the loss. I'll test the fire for myself."

"No. You won't."

Father went rigid. With his back turned to me, I could still picture his face. I had seen it too many times. The dark eyes threatening punishment.

"You have until dusk to come out and breathe fire for me. If you don't, I'll take it from your carcass."

He turned on his heel and strode off in the direction he had come. I watched him disappear around the castle.

My body went from pain back to numbness. I hardly felt the spiny branches against my skin anymore.

The reward is worth the loss.

Those words carried the answer to all my questions. Yes, Father would trade me again. No, he didn't regret it. Yes, Wil had been right to take me. No, there was no going back.

I clung to my tree and wished time would freeze. Right now, Wil was alive. I wanted that to last as long as it could.

But then dusk arrived.

In the shadows, I climbed down, limbs aching from a day spent in a tree.

The men gathered around the hole, careful to avoid the smoke. Then came Father.

If anyone looked close enough, they would see me watching from the brush. I tried to stay low. My dull brown hair and my dirt-stained gown hopefully blended in with the forest floor.

Everyone watched Father.

He wore a satchel slung at his hip, and I could guess what was in it.

The bottle.

"Well," Father called down the hole. "Will you come out, lizard?"

As an answer, smoke curled forward. All the men had to leap out of the way, or risk inhaling poison. They knew what had happened to Guntor.

Guntor.

When the scuffle ended and the smoke settled, Father returned to the opening. The rest of the men stayed back. With a dry click, he unclasped the satchel.

From within, he pried a glass object, clutching it in his stiff fingers.

This bottle was larger than the one I remembered, though the same gold tint shimmered in the glass. Within, a mass of black liquid swirled.

And I knew what Father had done to get that much.

He gripped the bottle hard. Like before, the black liquid began to bubble. Soon, it would erupt into a torrent.

Instead, something erupted in me.

I knew I couldn't fight the dozens of men who stood around Father. I knew they would capture me, and I would never get away.

But I didn't care.

I had one moment to stop Wil from dying. This moment. If I could surprise Father and take the bottle from his hand, then I could throw it into the one place he couldn't go.

The tunnel.

It had to be fast, and it had to be now.

I burst from the trees and ran toward Father. He was facing away from me, his arm outstretched, clutching the bottle.

What would happen if the glass shattered? Would it trigger a flood?

The men saw me first, and must have reacted, because Father turned, and his eyes lit with recognition.

A thousand memories flooded back to me of those same eyes. The ones I had looked into as a child. The face I used to search for signs of love.

My resolve faltered for one beat, but I didn't stop moving. I fixed my sight on my goal.

I reached him sooner than I had anticipated, and my hand collided with his. As I passed, my fingers wrapped around cold glass. Before he could react, I wrenched the bottle from Father.

His too-familiar voice said my name.

"Gilde."

I would have expected shock in his tone. Maybe anger, or even hurt. But there was only my name. Plain, and almost soft.

It was the first time I had gone against him, and it broke me in a way I couldn't have guessed. I cracked. Not my chest, but my soul.

I didn't look back.

Two more steps. Then I would be close enough to place the bottle in the hole. I'd roll it, so it wouldn't break.

But I felt a jerking tug around my midsection. Father had snatched the trailing ribbons of my sash. It had been a beautiful gown before I destroyed it on my scramble over the mountain. Too elaborate for activities like running and fighting.

I gritted my teeth and pulled hard. It worked. The stitching ripped, and I barreled forward. My feet skittered over loose dirt, and I lost my balance, tumbling down.

Grit and sand flew into my eyes, and I hit the ground, cradling my body around the bottle. The little treasures sewn into my dress bit into my skin.

I wanted to get up and run, but the fall took the breath from my lungs. I couldn't see through the dirt and tears.

A tangle of voices roared above me. Men arguing. Father shouting orders over them, his voice furious.

"Someone get her. Find the embergold!"

Rough hands should have grabbed me. Hauled me to my feet. Taken the bottle. I braced myself, but nothing happened.

I coughed and took a breath. It tasted like smoke.

It wasn't too late. I was close.

Desperate, I tried to blink away the debris in my eyes, gripping the bottle as tight as I could. Which way was the tunnel? I needed to roll the bottle without being poisoned.

Tears streamed down my cheeks, and my eyes cleared, but I still couldn't see. The twilight had turned to darkness.

Black surrounded me.

I had fallen inside the opening of the hole. Into the billowing death.

21

AT FIRST, I TRIED TO HOLD MY breath. But my lungs were already full of the poison. I gasped, and involuntarily took another breath.

And that meant I would die. I lay there and let my lungs work against me, waiting for the pain.

But the air somehow met my need. It was smoky, yes, but no worse than being near a campfire.

I took another breath. Then another. I sat up, hidden beneath gusts of dark smoke. Why was I still alive?

Everything went silent outside the hole, then men spoke, their voices hushed and sharp. Was Father there, right above me?

"Get a rope," a man said. "Quick."

"How's that supposed to help?" another said. "I'm not going down there. And she's sure not climbing up."

"She can't have fallen far. Sharpen a hook so it catches."

They intended to fish my body out.

My lungs itched, and my side hurt where I had landed. But my heart thrummed steadily. I was still here.

Impossibly alive.

Shadows fell over the opening. The men were close. I could scramble into the fresh air, but then they would have me. I thought of Father's command. How he had demanded the men retrieve something, not that they save me.

What had he called it? Embergold?

If I went out there, he would be waiting.

Maybe there was another way. I took two deep breaths, testing the air. It burned, but it didn't feel like it would kill me.

I clutched the bottle. Why were the men whispering now instead of shouting?

Then I realized.

They didn't have a defense against the dragon anymore. They were scared.

Down was my only option, toward the mines, where no one could reach the bottle.

I crawled into the dark, away from Father, and my soul cracked a little more.

After a ways, I couldn't see at all. And there was another dreadful fact.

Guntor was down here.

If I kept going, I would encounter him. His body. My stomach threatened to heave.

I paused for a long time, frozen in the blackness. Scraping sounds came from the darkness behind me. The men had lowered their hook.

I kept going.

I crawled as far to one side of the tunnel as I could, feeling my way along the ground. I didn't encounter anything except dirt and support branches, but I was afraid of finding something cold and stiff and human.

Then an orange glow appeared through the tunnel ahead. I widened my eyes as far as I could, a relief after blindness.

The tunnel narrowed to a smaller hole, and I brought my face close to it. Heat wafted over me, and I longed for fresh air.

Through the hole, a wide cavern opened up with high

pillars to support the ceiling. This was the mine, where they had finally broken through.

Below, a crack in the ground flickered red. Fire, deep in the earth, illuminating the whole cavern.

Sand and pebbles crumbled away as I dug at the tunnel hole, widening it. My hands were scraped and sore. Surely Wil knew I was here now?

I wanted to cry out for him, but my voice would carry up the tunnel. The men would know I was still alive.

Why was I still alive?

I slid through the hole and down a rocky ledge, to the floor of the mine. Waves of heat engulfed me from the crack. My hand found its way to my chest, and I tapped my rhythm.

The glow lit the cavern to the ceiling, illuminating enough space for twenty dragons to fly. The mines were bigger than the castle by far. Smoke hung low in the room, hiding portions of the cave floor.

I was exhausted and bruised, and it had been a whole day since my water ran out.

I eyed the bottle in my hand.

Even if the water inside was drinkable, I couldn't ignore where it had come from. I held it away from my body, like a rotten kitchen scrap that I didn't want to touch. My feet carried me forward, and I scanned the cavern for the door that led into the castle.

There would be water there, and fresh air. My head hurt.

That's when I tripped on a stone. I couldn't see where I was walking through the smoke, and I stumbled forward, catching myself in a lunge.

The bottle slipped from my clammy fingers. I bit the insides of my cheeks and braced for the sound of shattering glass. For swirling water and boiling steam.

What had I done?

But the bottle didn't break. It thudded against the stone and rolled forward.

Straight into the fiery crack.

Flames leapt to meet the bottle, as if the fire were a mouth, ready to swallow the golden glass. Sparks shimmered and popped, and I threw an arm up to shield my face from the heat.

The fire turned yellow, then blue, and then a sickly shade of greenish black. After that, it sank back into the crevice, returning to an orange glow.

I leaned forward and peered into the liquid fire. The bottle had disappeared.

For a while, I stood there, waiting for magical steam to erupt, or enchanted water to flow, or something terrible to happen. But it didn't. I sank to one knee.

The bottle was gone for good.

A knot loosened in my stomach. Wil would live. They had no weapon against him. I had done it.

Then, a sound caught my attention from high in the cavern.

I looked up. Firelight glinted off something silver. An enormous metal door swung open at the top of a stone staircase. Until it opened, I would never have known where it was. The door I had been searching for.

Through it came the shape of a man.

I ducked into the shadows, behind an outcrop of rock at the edge of the crack. Was it one of Father's men? Had he seen me? I peered out from my hiding place.

The figure stifled a cough, then made his way down the staircase. He could breathe down here too. Had the smoke lessened somehow?

His steps were square and smooth, lacking the usual shuffle of the men from my childhood. I eyed the tunnel I had come from, but the man would see me if I tried to retreat there.

I had thought I was nearing the end of the battle. Wil was supposed to be here. To protect me.

When the man reached the bottom of the stairs, he turned in my direction. He was still too far away for me to see any detail. I sank deeper into the smoke, refusing to cough. My hands searched the floor for a stone to use as a weapon. If only I had taken my dragon scale with me on that evening walk from the castle. My last walk with Wil. I found a handful of gravel and gripped it hard, settling into a crouch.

He came nearer to the fiery crack. My whole body tensed. As he moved into the light, his features grew visible. He wore some kind of loose garment over his lower half, but his chest was bare. On his head, thick curls grew in ringlets toward his broad shoulders, glowing orange in the fire.

This man was young.

Younger than anyone camped outside the castle.

I couldn't see his face. He kept his head lowered, searching up and down the flickering crevice.

It was almost like he knew the bottle had fallen in there, but he hadn't been here when it happened. He couldn't have seen.

I didn't dare move.

He came closer, eyeing the fire, until he nearly reached the rock I hid behind. This close, I could see his face whether he lifted his head or not.

Firelight played over high cheekbones and long lashes. His face was well formed, and probably not much older than mine.

A jolt of recognition ran through me. Something about this man was familiar.

But I hadn't ever seen him before. He wasn't a gold addict, and he hadn't been in the encampment.

My mind searched for a memory. I leaned a hair's breadth forward, trying to see better without being seen.

Even that small movement gave me away.

His eyes darted to the shadows where I crouched. I was ready to strike with my fist full of gravel.

Then I met his gaze.

Yellow eyes stared back at me, with a rim of blue. Like the sun shining in a clear sky. Like the boy in the locket I wore around my neck.

The man didn't move, but his lips parted and emotion passed over his face. Something like shock. We both stared, unblinking.

"Gilde." He let out a breath and stepped toward me.

He knew my name.

I didn't know his, but I knew I was smaller than him.

I stood. "Don't come any closer."

He put a steady hand in front of him. "Gilde, you should have stayed—"

I launched one of my sharp pebbles as hard as I could.

It hit its mark, and the man flinched. Blood trickled from where the stone struck his bare shoulder.

I readied my fist to throw another piece of the rubble.

He took a step back, then surveyed me. "Are you hurt?"

I gave him a warning look. "I'm not injured."

And I would fight if needed.

His eyes stayed on me. "What are you doing here? Something fell in the fire . . ."

This wasn't right. Wil should have found us by now.

"It was the bottle," I said. "The only weapon against the dragon who lives here, and now it's gone. You should leave before the dragon finds you."

His face went still. "And you don't need to run away from the monster?"

"If I were you, I'd worry about myself."

"Well, you may not be me, but you are you. And you don't seem worried about yourself at all."

I looked into his eyes again. He was too human to be another ghost. Too whole to belong to the alchemist. Too similar to the boy in my locket.

Without realizing, I had lowered my fist of gravel. This man could hurt me. Capture me. Force me to face my father.

Why wasn't I afraid?

"Who are you?" I breathed.

"If you don't see it now . . ." He stepped closer again. ". . . how will you ever believe me?"

I didn't move.

Yellow eyes. Almost gold. Rims of blue.

There was something about the way he spoke. Not the timbre of his voice, but the pronunciation, as if he had spoken to me before.

Or read to me.

I felt my lip tremble as I spoke the impossible.

"Wil."

22

"YES." THE MAN'S FEATURES SOFTENED.
Wil's features.

I gave my head a shake and looked away, then back up at him. I knew this man, and yet I didn't know him at all. I didn't know anything.

He moved his hand as if to touch my shoulder, but stopped before he reached me. "Are you wearing your necklace?"

I slid the pendant from under my collar.

"Open it."

I did. Clumsily.

"It's me."

I nodded. "I know."

I looked at the little boy in the painting, then at the man in front of me. I searched him for any sign of the dragon. His feet were bare, and he wore velvet cloth tied around his waist. I recognized the fabric, a curtain from inside the castle. He had fashioned clothes for himself in a hurry.

"How?" My voice was raspy from the smoke.

The muscles in his jaw twitched. "It's the story I've most wanted to tell you. And the one I was too afraid to tell."

He did not continue, and silence lingered between us, interrupted by scraping noises from the tunnel behind me. They were dredging deeper for the bottle with their hook.

"Dragons aren't supposed to be afraid," I said. "Tell me. Please," I added.

He was watching the tunnel. "But I'm not a dragon right now. And we're surrounded by men. Follow me." He turned to the silver door. "You shouldn't have come down here."

He made a swift line for the staircase. I lingered a moment. Was I going to follow him?

My feet moved. They trusted him, and I caught up. "The bottle could have filled this whole mine with water. It was magic. That's why I came back. So I could tell the drag–" I faltered. "So you could know." I went on, "They'll come after it when they realize the smoke isn't poison anymore. Also, they may have heard us talking."

"You would have to be louder than that for them to hear you up there. Humans have small voices." He paused. "And the smoke still is poison."

I fought off a cough. "You're breathing," I pointed out.

"I'm immune to it." He glanced back at me. "You shouldn't be down here for one breath longer. Hurry." He took off again.

We climbed the stairs, and my lungs protested, but I kept up. The silver door swung easily when he opened it, no longer locked, the way it had been during my days in the castle. I took deep gulps of fresh air. He closed the door behind us, trapping the smoke inside the cavern. Didn't it burn him when he touched it?

My eyes went wide in the grand entry hall, the place that had been my shared home with the dragon.

It had once been swept and polished, with the first stars winking through high windows, and a soft breeze blowing through the dragon-sized entrance.

But it was dark now. I couldn't see anything, and dirt gritted under my boots. How much of this place was collapsed, like the entrance had been?

"I blocked out all the windows," Wil said. "It will be hard to see in here with human eyes."

When I couldn't see him, it was easier to hear the Wil I knew, though his voice was smoother now.

I thought of my first night in the castle, when I held onto his tail to avoid tripping in the shadows. Since then, I had learned to navigate the vast room with only slivers of moonlight to guide me. Now I had nothing.

I wanted my dragon. He was right beside me, but I didn't dare touch him.

My knees wobbled, and my mouth felt like dust.

"Can you drink water now?" I asked.

He took a moment to answer. "I think so, and we should try. I can guide you."

"You won't be able to see."

"The dragon never fully leaves. It's only suppressed. Take my hand."

So he was still a dragon inside.

I felt him near me in the dark. Slowly, I extended my fingers toward him, and tensed when they brushed against skin. He wrapped my hand in his, the hold firm.

My heart quickened.

We maneuvered through the darkness until he stopped, and I could hear the water bubbling in my little fountain. I knelt and scooped liquid to my dry lips, sipping at first, then swallowing mouthfuls. It cooled my hoarse throat.

I heard Wil do the same. He drank longer than me.

"It doesn't burn?" I asked.

"It's the only thing that hasn't in a long time." He took two more handfuls, then I heard him stand. "Have you had enough? We need to go upstairs."

I could have stayed beside the fountain for the rest of the night, drinking and sleeping on the cool stones. Instead, I dried my hands on my skirt as I got to my feet. "I have questions. How did you change? Who are you?"

"You weren't supposed to be here." That was not an answer. "You agreed to the plan."

My decision to return to the castle felt like a lifetime ago. I had accomplished what I came to do. Wil was alive. But he wasn't . . . Wil.

"I spoke with Hans and Petra," I said. "They told me how wizards get their power, and I couldn't hide from it anymore. I realized my fathe—the wizard—could gather more magic water. He had some already, but it was so small. I didn't tell you." My voice broke on the last word. "I didn't think it would be enough to hurt you."

There was a quick intake of breath.

"You climbed over the mountain and stole his gold?" Wil asked.

"A magic bottle. It fell in the fire."

He expelled the breath. "You once tried to fight a dragon with a knife. Now a wizard."

I was tired of fighting.

Wil took my hand again. "We have to keep going."

And then we were crossing the castle floor. When we came to a staircase, Wil helped me climb, his arm supporting mine.

"Where are we going? The castle is destroyed." I thought of the library with its walls of books and soft candlelight. Part of that tower had collapsed.

"The safest place I can think of for you right now. High ground. Not everything in the castle is demolished, though I tried to make it look like that from the outside."

After the stairs, and a few turns in complete darkness, we came to another set of steps.

"There's a third floor?" I stumbled up the stairs blindly.

"The castle doesn't reveal all its secrets at once. Even to wanderers like you."

The stairs seemed to spiral, and I supposed we were climbing into the very tip of a tower somewhere above the kitchens, on the backside of the castle. Then, a crack of the night sky illuminated a room in front of us. My eyes lingered on a small, bare window. Even that hint of light felt good.

The door to the room had been broken, leaving a space almost big enough for a dragon to squeeze through. We entered, and I peeked out the slitted window. Men stood below, their dark shapes gathered around the tunnel to the mines.

"You were watching from up here." I glanced back at the broken door. "When you were a dragon and made it look like the castle was full of rubble. Every window, except this one."

He would have had to wedge stones into the other windows with his snout and claws, breaking all the glass.

He nodded.

Something in me eased. "If they had flooded the mines, you would have survived."

"Maybe. Or maybe I would have been in the mines when they flooded them, having another shouting match with the wizard. I've never seen water magic before or read about it. I knew he had something planned, otherwise he wouldn't have come here. But I prepared for weapons, not water."

So Wil *had* been in danger. The bottle was gone now, and for that I was thankful.

I leaned against the wall. "I think the wizard had to . . . hurt a lot of people to get the power in that bottle."

Wil's mouth went tight in the moonlight. "I know."

"And then I threw it in the fire."

He turned away from me. "I need you to stay here. I'm going to get rid of the wizard."

"Wait—"

"I'll take a carpet square from downstairs and waft smoke up the tunnel from the mines as a sign of dragon life. Without the magic artifact, the smoke should be enough to scare them off. If you look, most have already left. Only the most loyal remain, scraping that tunnel."

The most loyal person wasn't standing out there anymore. I didn't know where he was, but I found I didn't want to speak of it.

Guntor's end made me realize something I had never allowed myself to admit. I hated him. And it wasn't right to hate. I didn't like that part of myself.

"I can help you," I said. "We can take two carpets."

"No. It's better to have someone watching from up here. You'll be able to see which way the men go. And I don't want you back in that smoke if it isn't necessary."

My lungs still itched, and I was exhausted.

"There could be a man down there in the mine." I couldn't bring myself to call Guntor a corpse. What if he hadn't died? I never found his body. "Some of them didn't come up."

"I'll be stronger than anyone in the smoke. I'm not afraid for me, but I am afraid for you." He faced me. "Will you stay and watch? Please."

"I'll stay."

At the broken door, he looked back. "You'll be alright alone?"

I could have asked him the same question. "We made it this far."

The man who should have been a dragon left, and I peered out the window.

His plan did work. Before long, dark smoke poured from the tunnel entrance. Not as much as before, but enough, and the men fled.

Four of them went into the forest and disappeared eastward. But one did remain behind. The man with black hair.

Father.

He strode toward the castle, examining the walls and windows. The only opening would be the slit I was looking out of. Wil had made sure of that.

Father should have been running. Did he sense that the dragon didn't want to fight him?

He looked up toward the tower. In the moonlight, I could see the distant outline of his pale face. Dark eyes, a strong nose, and a thin mouth.

My stomach hurt.

I had become an expert at reading the emotion on that face. Anger was the easiest to detect, and the most common. I could always tell when he was ready to tease Guntor. I used to glimpse fear at the mention of the dragon.

But the look on his face now was less familiar to me. I had seen it before, when he was bleeding from his arrow wound in the marsh.

Pain.

I pressed my face against the rough stone of the window, trying to look closer. The hard line of Father's mouth had deepened, turned down at the corners. His eyes were buried beneath knitted brows.

And I knew this wasn't physical pain.

Did he mourn the loss of the bottle? His failed attempt at stealing fire?

Then I saw the ribbons trailing from his fingers, fluttering in the breeze. The ribbons he had pulled from my gown.

I remembered the way he said my name when I snatched the bottle from him.

Soft.

The reward is worth the loss.

That's what he had told the dragon, and I knew he would sacrifice me again if he could do it all over.

But that didn't mean it wasn't a loss.

What toll would it take to give away your daughter for your own freedom? A fire that burns the one who holds it.

If he ever saw Isa again, he would tell her I was dead.

That thought made me want to double over. There was a hope in knowing Isa and I might find each other. If she heard of my death, the hope would be gone for her.

I couldn't take that from her.

I ran my fingers over the remaining ribbons on my bedraggled dress. I was safe in my tower with a dragon to guard me. Not a real dragon now, but Father didn't know that.

Before I could think, I tore three more ribbons free. They were dirty, and when I scratched them with my fingernail, it left a mark. Isa had taught me to sign my name, and hers, and I had copied Father's signature from his big ledger book when no one was looking.

I made those letters now by scraping soot from the ribbon.

His name, exactly the way he would write it.

My arm wouldn't fit into the window slit, so I poked the ribbons through and blew on them. The silk floated into moonlight, then fell toward my father.

Would he even see them?

But he was looking up, right at my tower, and the movement caught his eye. When the ribbons landed, he bent and gathered them. He added them to the others he held from before and turned the collection over and over in his hand. Then he paused and looked closer. His gaze darted from the silk to the tower.

He had found the signature that only the two of us could make.

I stayed pressed to the window. There was no way he could see me.

He gave the window a hard look, then turned and followed in the direction the others had gone.

I let out a breath and let myself sag.

Of course he had to leave. He was unarmed.

Father might have thought the dragon dropped the ribbons to antagonize him. How could I have survived the smoke that killed men? But the marking on the ribbon gave Father the truth. And would give Isa hope.

That was what I needed for her.

And maybe for him, if I dared to admit it to myself.

I slid to the floor. I wanted to think of Wil. To mull over his mysteries. But, after two nights spent in the open forest, sleep took me against my will. Dark, and thick, and dreamless.

23

I WOKE UP UNDER THE SCRUTINY of yellow eyes. Light poured through the window, and the man named Wil sat in its beam. He had found a pair of ill-fitting breeches and a tunic to replace his velvet cover from the night before.

My body felt stiff, and my dry tongue stuck to the roof of my mouth. I must have looked wild, with unkempt hair and unwashed clothes.

Wil reached out to hand me something—the old wine bottle I had used for drinking from the well.

"Thank you." I took the gift.

"How long did you go without water on the mountain?"

"Not long."

Not long compared to him. But I felt my thirst growing since we both last drank from the fountain.

I drank half the water without breathing, then offered it back to him. He smiled, and I noticed how straight and fine his teeth were.

I lowered my eyes. If it had been a dragon smile, I might have returned it. But I didn't know this version.

"I'm sorry I fell asleep." I looked up again. "Your plan worked. There was plenty of smoke and the men ran away."

Wil drank the rest of the water. "I tracked them down the mountain a ways. They're all together now, even the ones who ran away first. There's safety in numbers, and they're making camp in one of the caves with an underground spring. Somewhere defensible against a dragon."

"You think they'll keep going down the mountain?" What else could they do now?

"I do." His jaw went tight. "The wizard will go back to the cities of Xantic or Ulpia, so he can gather another weapon."

We both knew what that would require.

Wil sat on the stone floor across from me, and a large bag rested beside him. He must have carried it to the room while I slept.

"The wizard will be back as soon as he can," he said. "His tracking magic expired when he reached his destination. Now that he's left the castle, it will be shrouded from him again. But, the moment he can cast more tracking magic to find you, he'll have a map here. Even if he believes you're dead, he'll track your body. There are things in this castle no wizard should possess."

Wil said the spell required personal items from me, and Father had plenty of those. My old satchel and my cloak, and now the ribbons. But there was more to it than that. Magic always had a cost.

"What does the tracking spell require?" I asked. "If he's delaying using it, that means he needs something he doesn't have yet."

Wil only looked at me, sadness behind his eyes.

"I need to know what he's done," I stated.

He grimaced. "That spell takes death, not just blood. A fresh kill of two youths."

The water in my stomach threatened to come back up.

"We have to leave so he can't find this place." Now I knew what the bag was for.

"Yes."

But neither of us moved. We stayed in the stillness of morning for a moment, and I tried to make sense of the world.

When Wil looked down, his lashes brushed his cheeks. "You . . . didn't go with the humans."

I hadn't. When I came to the castle, I wanted nothing but escape. Everything had changed since then, and I wasn't ready to examine it all yet. For now, Wil was safe, and that was enough.

"As far as I can tell," I remarked, "I'm with a human."

"Gilde." Wil looked up. "I know what you did for me."

It had been for him. For his beautiful scales, and his ferocity against the ghost. For the gentle way he carried me on his back, and for his love of words.

But I didn't know how to say that.

My voice was just above a whisper. "I couldn't let the wizard have your fire."

For a blink of a moment, Wil's expression was unreadable as he regarded me. Then he rose to his feet and swung the large bag over his shoulder. "You slept through the morning. We should leave now. I don't know exactly how much time I'll have."

"How much time you'll have for what?" I pulled myself to standing.

"To be human," he answered. "It's been a long while since the last time, and I want to see water again. Lots of water. We'll head toward the sea."

He was right. We had to leave. Even if a wizard hadn't been trying to track us, we couldn't stay in the ruined castle. We had no sunlight. I imagined trying to bathe alone in the blackness. To live by firelight, and only have the mines as an exit. Human Wil wouldn't be strong enough to remove the stones he had placed as a dragon.

The room we stood in seemed to shrink, the walls too close.

I nodded. "I should get a new dress first. And soap. And my supply of oats, and—"

Wil interrupted me. "I gathered your things." He patted the bag. "Your blue dress and a cooking pot, an extra flint and a book of stories for the journey. It's a long walk."

A thought struck me.

"There are dragon hunters out there," I said. "If you turn back into the dragon, you won't have your shrouded castle to hide you."

He went to the door. "That's a problem I'll deal with when I'm the dragon again."

But even when he had been the dragon, he never strayed far from the castle.

"I could go alone." I tried to sound brave, though being alone was the last thing I wanted. I held my breath for his reply.

He gave a wan smile. "I want to see the ocean while I still can."

I let out the breath, and he held a hand to me, my guide through the darkness again.

I placed my hand in his. Had the calluses on his fingers developed while he was a dragon, or were they left over from the last time he was human? A previous life I knew nothing about.

Wil's hand warmed mine, and I was aware of every place our skin met.

We stepped into the absolute dark, and he became my tether to reality. I closed my eyes, then opened them. It didn't make a difference. I tried not to think of that nest of spiders he had mentioned, dried up in the second room to the left of this hall. My ears pricked at every footfall and every breath.

The silence pressed on me.

"Wil, can you talk to me while we walk?"

"What should I say?"

"Are you really a dragon?"

"The stairs begin here." His grip tightened, and we began an awkward descent.

I hoped he would still answer my question. I waited.

"What do you mean 'really'?" he asked when he finally spoke again. "I am real, and I am a dragon. Sometimes."

"Were you born that way?"

"No."

I let that truth sink in. He was a human from birth. A fact he had hidden from me during our time together in the castle. With my free hand, I touched the gold chain that hung at my collar.

"Your mother lived here. This is her necklace."

"She did. And it was."

"Wil, how did you—"

But suddenly he let go of me. I was stranded in the darkness.

A sharp groan came from his direction, and I blindly reached for him. He was doubled over, his shoulders where his waist should have been.

"Wil. What is it?"

He said nothing, and fear gripped me.

My hand raced over him, searching for a wound. A spider. Anything. The muscles in his face were tense and contorted under my fingers. He wasn't breathing, and his pulse raced.

I took the pack from his shoulders and threw it to the ground. Then, before I could think of anything else, the moment passed.

I felt Wil straighten and heard him take deep, shaky breaths.

"Are you hurt?" My hand was on his shoulder. Salty tears ran into my mouth, though I hadn't been aware I was crying. "Say something," I begged.

"I'm better. For now."

I heard him pick up his pack.

My heart skipped a beat. "For now?"

Wil only took my hand again and started to guide me

forward. It felt the same, like nothing had happened. But I didn't feel the same.

I stood still, forcing him to halt. "What just happened?"

"The fire."

I pictured the greedy flames in the mine, and a sick feeling came over me as I realized. "It burns the one who carries it."

"It wants me to change back, but I have more time. It won't win yet."

How could fire want anything? It wasn't alive.

I moved closer to Wil, and we began to walk again.

"It will hurt you when you change back." I didn't need to ask the question. I had felt his pulse racing during the attack.

"Very much."

I pictured Dragon-Wil, glittering and black. If something could hurt him, it was a terrible thing.

Wil's breath was still unsteady, and his hand had grown hot to my touch. There would be time for questions later, when I could look at him and read his eyes.

We went on like that through the dark. Wil guiding me. Me worried for him.

Then he stopped. "I'm going to open the gate to the mines. I need you to stay back from the smoke."

"I'll be alright."

"You survived it once. But I'm not taking that for granted. We'll test the smoke slowly. Take a breath at the edge of it and tell me what you experience. If you taste blood, that's your sign to move away."

I heard the door open and felt the gust of hot air. Then the orange glow of the fire below rescued me from darkness. I coughed as the metallic smoke hit my face.

Wil still held my hand, and he drew me away from the door. "What do you taste?"

My throat burned and my eyes watered, but I was fine. "It

feels the same as before. My lungs want fresh air, but I'll get through."

He looked down at me in the orange light, his eyes narrowed, then gave a nod. We headed forward, into the mine. Heat washed over me again, and sweat rolled down my arms and face. Our bodies would lose all the water we drank.

When I had entered the cavern before, I just wanted to find my dragon. Now, I didn't know what my goal was, except to get out of the smoke again.

The fire in the crack bubbled and swirled in a way I had never seen flames behave. A wave rippled through it and seemed to follow our progress across the vast stone floor.

I watched it.

Wil held my hand tighter. "Don't stare."

I turned his direction. "Are you afraid the glow will hurt my eyes?"

"The longer you look into fire, the deeper it can look into you."

"It can see?"

"And speak."

I had to fight to keep my eyes from the crack. "You hear it?"

"Always."

My unease deepened. What was the connection between dragon magic and this mine?

When we reached the tunnel, I slowed to a stop. "I think men died in there when the smoke first billowed."

"They did." Wil wiped the sweat from his brow.

He knew? A chill passed over me despite the heat.

"I tried to push them up the tunnel with my tail, so they could breathe," he said. "But it was too late. They were already poisoned by the time I touched them. I gave them a burial, deep in the caves. Did you . . . do you know their names?"

"I only knew one of them."

His voice came out dry. "Will you tell me the name?"

This dragon had laid my cousin's body to rest with more concern than Father showed.

"His name was Guntor." And that was all I wanted to say. How could I spend my whole life with a man and not mourn him now? I felt sorry for him. I didn't like that he had suffered. But I couldn't force myself to miss him.

Was I any different than my father?

Wil repeated the name. "Guntor." He stared up the tunnel. "They both deserved better."

He moved to climb through the hole, but I stopped him with a hand on his arm. He tensed.

"I know you didn't want it to happen," I said. "You're not like that."

"But I knew it would happen. So did the wizard. I carved a warning into the castle door." Wil pulled away and climbed into the tunnel. "Hurry. The less time you're in this smoke, the better."

I followed him into the dark.

The climb went much faster than the descent. Before long, we crawled out of the smoke into blinding-white sunshine. We sat on the dirt apart from each other, a ways from the entrance. I coughed and inhaled deep lungfuls of fresh air. When my eyes adjusted, I searched Wil, looking for signs of sickness.

His skin was smooth, with just a hint of stubble on his chin. A sheen of ash and sweat sat on his brow, and his chest rose and fell in long, even breaths. He looked healthy.

And he looked nothing like my dragon.

Then, a strained sound came from Wil, and he stopped breathing. He doubled over and wrapped his arms around himself.

It was happening again.

24

I LEAPT TO MY FEET. Wil twitched and rocked violently back and forth, his whole body straining.

I placed a trembling hand on his back, and he flinched.

Then it was over. He gasped and his breathing went back to normal, his muscles relaxed.

I sank down beside him. He brushed his hair back from his face.

We were quiet for a while.

"When it happens again," I said, "is there anything I can do to help?"

"It shouldn't happen again for a while. The fire pushes hard at first. When it realizes it can't win, it gives up until you're weak again. Then the change happens."

I looked at him. "Why did you change into a human if it hurts so much to change back?"

Wil stretched out his fingers and examined them. "I didn't make the change happen. You did."

I thought of the way the fire in the mines leapt up to devour Father's golden bottle.

"The dragon fire isn't just in you, is it?" I asked. "It's down in that cavern too."

"Yes."

"And when I dropped that bottle into the fire, it did something to you."

He shifted his whole body to face me. "Do you really want to know everything, Gilde? It isn't a good story. Or a happy one."

He wasn't angry. He wasn't even sad, as the dragon had often been. He was flat. His warning was purposefully neutral, leaving me to decide.

"But it's a true story," I said. "And those kinds are important."

He stared at nothing for a while.

Then he began. "A long time ago, that type of flame was sought by wizards, but whatever fire they found was lost, and it became a myth. Until this silver mine was quietly excavated, revealing a vein of dark fire. The master of this castle became a dragon. The first dragon before me."

But Wil wasn't a wizard.

"How does it work??"

His face went hard. If he had still been a dragon, smoke might have risen from his breath. "I don't want to tell you that. Not unless I tell you my own part in it first."

I imagined trying to tell my own story in full. How would I explain to someone about Father? About Isa? It would hurt too much.

"Tell it however feels right. I'm listening."

His face didn't soften, but he continued. "My mother was the daughter of a favored scholar. He had no money of his own, but the councils loved him and kept him at court. When he died, my mother stayed among powerful men, and I was born without knowing who my father was."

His words pricked at my old wounds. The mystery of my own mother.

He continued. "I was ten years old when a foreign scholar came to court. At least, that's what he said he was, and we didn't know there was more to him than that. Edric, tall and sharp, and full of eloquence. He didn't care that my mother had a child out of wedlock. She was beautiful, and he promised her a house of her own. We went with him. Here." Wil gestured to the ruined castle behind us. "He was a lord over the mountain, and this house was supposedly inherited from his family. But I think he built it himself a long time ago."

"This is more than a house," I said. "It feels like it was built with magic. How old was Edric?"

I was asking if Edric was a wizard. Someone who evaded death.

"Before you know the worst of Edric, I'll tell you the best." Wil's tone changed slightly. "My mother grew ill, and he searched the furthest cities for medicines or books that might help her. He hired servants to nurse her, and he made sure she was comfortable. He took care of her in ways I couldn't have. That was the best of him."

Wil had been a child. Of course he wouldn't have been able to provide for his mother.

"When my mother was gone, Edric went deeper into his books. And his magics. The fire had been uncovered for some time, and there were occasional sightings of the dragon. It was Edric, bound to the flames, but none of us knew that until later, when the transformation became permanent."

"How did he bind himself to it?"

So the dragon I had seen over the marsh really was Edric. The dangerous one.

"I don't know what kind of evil that required, but I'm sure it cost him. Before we lost my mother, Edric only used the blood from people with a spark to cast his spells. He didn't kill. But afterward, he started collecting golden items to burn from traders and practitioners. Dark people with dark artifacts."

"Other wizards," I said.

"Some, but not all," he said. "When a wizard kills someone with a spark, the blood has to be fresh for spells. But there is a way to preserve the death in gold. After that, the power can only be used in limited ways. The wizard has to decide what it will be when they preserve it, and then it works for only that specific magic. Like the bottle that makes water, or the alchemist's multiplying gold."

I wasn't sure I understood. "Then why would Edric burn the artifacts?"

"He called the treasures embergold, because the dragon fire made them special to him. When he burned embergold, he was able to absorb the power into himself because of his connection to the fire. The flames released the spark into him, fresh. He could use it for whatever he wanted."

Sickness washed over me. Wil had a connection to the fire also.

"The more he used the fire, the stronger it grew, until he couldn't change back into a man on his own. He needed embergold to do that too." Wil's voice was taut, "Edric tried to raise the dead. My mother. But it didn't work. He kept on, looking for more embergold, until he bypassed the items altogether and started burning something more precious. It was more than wizard killing. The fire let him absorb the sparks fully, no wasted power."

I had seen the skeletons.

"Toward the end, he grew weary. Being a dragon is . . . painful, and you're always thirsty. I should have left while I still could. He wasn't himself anymore, and that was the worst of him."

Wil stared into the sunlit forest, his gaze far away. "He found a way to transfer the fire to someone else, to free himself. He transferred it to the one person who never ran away from him. And then I never saw him again."

My throat knotted. Wil didn't just know about wizards in theory. He knew what they were capable of from experience.

I spoke, my voice choked. "So you absorbed all the power that was saved up in my father's bottle."

Wil turned his head away from me so I couldn't see his eyes. "I'll be human for at least seven days before I change back. Maybe more. There was a lot of power in that embergold. One strong girl, and sixteen lesser sparks."

Their lives and futures had been distilled into black liquid. And now they were gone.

"Wil," I said. "When you change back, will it be dangerous?"

He turned back to me. "Yes."

"But you survived it once already."

He said nothing.

"So you can survive it again."

He took too long to answer. "I don't know."

Those three words pierced me.

I had been alone, with only my stolen coins and my escape plans. But then there had been stories. And words. And most of all, Wil. I didn't care if he was a man or a dragon, or if he had kept a secret.

I didn't want to lose him too.

I felt the weight of the silver sewn into my ragged skirt. I would trade all of it. A whole castle full of treasure. All of Father's gold.

"There has to be something we can burn to help the change," I insisted. "Something in the castle. A book of spells? The golden stair rail?"

Wil shook his head. "There's no embergold left. And I would rather die than become a wizard."

"But what if we found a merchant—"

"No." He paused. "Being human again, I'm free for the first time in a long time. But, to get here, I used death. I don't blame you for burning the bottle, but I won't do something like that again."

I fixed my eyes on the pine needles at my feet. I hated the deaths too. So why was I angry at Wil?

"If the killing is already done, why not use it for good?"

"Good can never come from killing," he said. "And I might survive on my own."

Might.

That was all I had.

Birds chirped in the pines, and a soft breeze rustled the grass. It was too peaceful here. Too different from how I felt inside.

An urgency rose in me. I needed to move.

I stood and offered a hand to Wil. "If you want to see water, we're going to see water. Come on."

Once Wil was on his feet, I took off from the castle, down our usual trail. Wil stayed put, and when I looked back, he was smiling. How could he smile right now?

"You won't find water that way." He motioned to the right. "It's a three-day journey over that mountain. We're going to see the ocean."

"The ocean." I had read about the whales. "Are you sure you should walk that far?"

Wil's smile disappeared. "Your father has less influence on that side of the mountain. It's safer."

A lump rose in my throat. Safer for who? Wil would be better off staying on the mountain. Did he want me near people, in case something happened to him? Hans and Petra had already left for the valley. There was no one here.

"Are there cities near the ocean?" I asked.

"Small ones."

That used to mean freedom to me. Now, I wasn't sure.

But, if there were people at the ocean, there were traders. And I had treasure of my own. Buying an artifact wasn't the same as killing, no matter what Wil said. If embergold existed in our path, I would find it.

25

WE WALKED SIDE BY SIDE
through sunbeams.

The way someone walked said something about them.
Father always left me to trail behind him. Dragon-Wil had
usually flown overhead on our walks, or stalked behind me
where he could watch for animals.

But human Wil and I matched our steps.

Out of habit, my eyes darted up to check for him. I knew
he was beside me. But something in the back of my mind still
searched for wings and scales.

He was silent now, his face concentrated.

The path grew steep, then we lost it altogether and climbed
up slopes of loose pine needles. The wind picked up, and
clouds blocked the sun. At first, tree branches protected us
from the rain. After a while, the first droplets hit our heads,
smelling of sap.

It was warm, and I hated the way my dirty gown clung to
me. When would we find water for drinking and bathing?

I stole a glance at Wil, expecting to see more concentrated
distance.

But he had tipped his face back now, eyes half-closed. Big
rain droplets rolled down his cheeks, into the corners of his

mouth. He turned his hands palms-up, as if to feel every splash of water.

Where there used to be scorch marks, there was only fresh, human skin. He caught me looking, and he shook water out of his messy hair. It landed in wet strands against his forehead.

I looked away, embarrassed to be caught. Why did I feel the need to stare? He was a human now. An ordinary thing.

And yet he wasn't like any human I had known. He possessed a masculine beauty that I wasn't used to.

"You can travel to all kinds of places in books," he breathed. "But you can't feel the rain."

I wouldn't have minded not feeling the rain, but I kept that to myself.

"Hurry up then, before it ends." I ran past Wil.

"Hurry where?" his surprised voice floated after me.

I didn't answer.

The trees were sparse on the ridge ahead, and the rain fell without a barrier. Wil ran after me, and we reached the top of the hill.

I panted and held out my own palms. "Here. All the rain you could want."

It felt so good to run, now that my heart could take it.

He laughed, a soft sound. It was so different from dragon laughter that it startled me, but I found I liked it. And I liked that I had made it happen.

We caught eyes and held the glance for too long. This time, he was the first to break away.

"We've probably had enough for now," he said. "Two more hills, then we'll reach the cave for the night."

Wil had once told me that most of the drinking water on the mountain ran underground. Caves meant life up here.

My boots grew damp in the rain, though my feet stayed warm, and we slogged over two more hills. In a shallow ravine, we came to a grouping of boulders. I followed Wil through a maze of stone, then to a narrow opening between rocks.

He came to a stop. "I'm sorry it's not a nicer place to sleep. We'll make the best camp we can."

He knew I liked things clean.

"It's not the worst hole I've climbed through today," I said. "But how do you know it's unoccupied?"

"Dragon sense."

Wil went first, then I lowered myself into the crack. It opened into a wider space, and I smelled damp and heard splashing water. For a moment, I hesitated in the dark. There had been too much darkness lately. But then Wil spoke up.

"We're in luck," he said. "There's dry wood in here left by the workers from the old days."

Before long, Wil had a fire burning on the sandy floor of the cavern. Orange light flickered off the underground pool, casting ripples onto the stone above.

This fire was completely different from the glow in the mines. It danced like it should. Wood smoke filtered out the cave mouth, leaving clean air for our lungs.

I rifled through Wil's pack and found what I was looking for. My drinking bottle.

The vessel was empty now, all the water consumed on our walk. Wil had wrapped the whole thing in strips of cloth from the velvet curtains, so it wouldn't break if we dropped it. We needed to refill it as often as possible.

"Is the water safe?" I asked.

Wil glanced quickly up at me. Something flickered over his face, and he answered. "When it flows underground, the earth filters out impurities. Cave water is clean on my mountain."

I realized my mistake. Water hadn't been safe for him for a long time.

"I'm sorry. That was a stupid question," I said.

"You always ask questions." He poked at the fire with a stick. "Since when do you apologize for it?"

Since he had changed, but I didn't want to say that aloud. None of the humans in my life had liked questions.

I went to the pool and filled the bottle from a spring that flowed down the rocks, then brought the water to Wil for the first drink. He had been the thirstiest the longest.

"Thank you." He drank the whole thing without pausing for breath, then filled it up again and brought it back for me.

"We're out of the shrouding now, I think," he remarked. "If the wizard tracks you, the magic will take him to whatever location you were in when he cast the spell. He won't find the castle."

I wasn't a problem anymore. The fire would stay hidden.

"Good," I said. "And not good. You're unshrouded now too."

He said nothing but stared into the fire with his faraway look.

Beside the warm fire, my wet gown began to smell like earth and damp and something worse. I didn't have the dragon's stench to cover it.

I took off my boots and laid them out to dry. Then I fished the soap from the bag and went to the edge of the water.

I waded into this little pool with my clothes on, so I could scrub some of the mud out of my skirt. I could dry beside the fire.

Cold liquid lapped against my legs, causing little bumps to cover my skin. I bent and worked suds into the fabric beneath the water, submerging myself to my shoulders. The many trinkets hidden in the skirt weighed it down.

Shivering slightly, I stood. My dress hugged my body, and I hoped it wasn't sheer now that I was completely soaked through. I turned and found Wil's eyes on me.

He rose to his feet. "What are you doing?"

"Rinsing out the mud. I can dry beside the fire and—"

But Wil wasn't looking at me anymore. He turned his head away, intentionally focusing elsewhere. Without another word, he hurried out of the cave and disappeared into the rain.

I stood there dripping, and it felt like before. All those eerie days in the castle, when the dragon had left me. I wrapped my arms around myself, remembering the fever.

The hollow sounds of the cave echoed, and I felt hollow inside.

I trudged from the water and crossed the sand barefoot. Outside the cave entrance, Wil stood amidst the boulders, rain soaking his shirt and hair.

I climbed out, and he looked up, away from me.

"Where are you going?" My voice carried more emotion than I intended.

"Outside. I—"

"You can't leave me."

"What?"

"Tell me if I do something that makes you uncomfortable, and I'll stop it. Yell at me even. But don't leave without telling me. Not again." My throat tightened. "Warn me first."

Wil brought his eyes back to me. "You didn't do anything wrong."

Then why did it feel like I had?

"It's not that I don't want to be near you," he added, stiffly. "I want it too much. And it isn't proper for us to be alone."

I didn't know what to say to that.

"But I'm not going anywhere," he said.

I'd heard that from Isa every time she returned from running away. But then she left for good.

"People leave," I said.

Whether they thought they would or not.

We faced each other, both drenched.

"Not me," Wil said. "Not on my mountain."

I heard the words. I knew he meant them, and that sank into me.

The rain stopped, and the sounds of the forest took its place. Wil went back to the cave, and I followed.

I cooked a meal of hot porridge over the fire, and he ate more than his share. His first human food with me.

We both moved to clear the cooking pot at the same time, and our hands met on the handle. My heart fluttered at the unexpected touch, and not in an unpleasant way. He kept his hand on mine for the briefest moment, then stood.

"I'm going outside, and I won't come back until you call for me. I'll be near."

He didn't need to explain. He would wait in the dark and the wind so that I could take care of my personal needs.

I could finally bathe. I scrubbed my dress as quickly as I could, then laid it on the sand beside the fire to dry, running my fingers over the frayed bits where the ribbons had been torn.

The ribbons that Father might be holding now.

I washed my hair and put on my blue dress. It was wonderfully dry and fit well around my waist, but it was too short. Like all the dresses from the castle.

Did they belong to the lady of the house? Wil's mother?

The rain had stopped outside, and the night was still. I climbed up the rocks in my warm boots and poked my head out of the cave. Maybe I could collect pine needles to make tea.

Someone was there.

"Wil?"

A shadow moved among the boulders.

"Hello?" I tried again.

The moon passed from behind a cloud, lighting the rocky landscape, and I took in a sharp breath.

The shadow wasn't Wil.

It stalked through the boulders on four paws. Matted fur

covered its body, and reflective eyes glinted at me. Focused, inhuman eyes.

It was a true beast—an animal of the forest.

And it was right in front of me.

The scent of something rotting hit me. This beast was a killer, and it wore the stench of old blood.

I wanted a dragon scale, or a knife. Anything. But my hands were empty, and I was exposed. I wouldn't turn my back to run inside the cave.

Time slowed between breaths. My heart wasn't skipping, it raced.

The animal let out a low noise and raised its lip, showing fangs.

Time resumed. It crouched, ready to pounce, and I screamed. It was a sound of fear and anger, and a promise to fight.

The thing leapt forward, and I pivoted to the left. My shoulder hit rock with a sharp pain. I expected a crushing mass of fur and teeth to collide into me.

But the night was illuminated as a flame caught the animal in its path.

The creature fell, yipping, and its fur burned. Then it got up and ran away, smoke trailing behind it.

I watched it go, disgusted and relieved and a little sorry that it had to burn.

I scanned the rocks. My dragon was the only one who could make a fire like that.

But it was too soon for the change.

The human Wil ran toward me, sliding down a slope of loose gravel. He came to a stop when he reached me.

"Are you hurt?"

I stared at him in the faint light. Human hands. Human hair and skin.

He touched the place where my shoulder hit the rock. The sleeve was torn.

"I smelled blood," he said.

But my shoulder didn't hurt anymore. He pulled his hand back, clean.

"I'm fine," I said.

Wil kept his eyes leveled on me. "You almost weren't. That was a wolf."

I used to think Wil's stories of the beasts were a lie to keep me from running away. But Wil had never lied to me outright. He didn't tell me the whole truth about things either.

"The fire . . ." I said.

He didn't meet my eyes.

"You can still breathe flames. And smell blood. And see in the dark."

His response was quick. "I don't breathe fire right now. It came from my hands."

I tried to picture what that would look like. How far had he thrown the fire to hit the wolf?

"In the mines, you didn't waft smoke up the tunnel with a carpet, did you?" I asked. "You made smoke."

He gave a nod to confirm I was right.

"Why didn't you tell me?"

"I'm a human now."

That wasn't an answer. "I knew you as a dragon. You don't have anything to hide from me."

"And you still know me as a dragon. I wanted you to see me as . . . a man. Even if it can't last." He looked down at me, so close now.

"I see you as Wil," I said. "It doesn't matter if you're a man or a dragon."

"It matters to me."

It was my turn to pause.

"A human then," I said.

I couldn't bring myself to say man, because they were unsafe things.

"A human," he repeated.

Was there disappointment in his voice?

That night, we took blankets from the pack in the cave and made our beds on opposite sides of the fire. Even as a dragon, he didn't want to sleep close to me. Now I saw it was a concern for propriety.

"What if the animal comes back?" I asked.

"I won't let it."

And I believed him.

"Goodnight, Wil."

"Gilde . . ." He sounded hesitant. "I'm sorry I didn't tell you the truth about everything from the beginning. You should be angry at me."

I wasn't sure what I felt, but it wasn't anger. I understood not wanting to talk about certain things from the past. Still, there was so much he hadn't told me. Things I needed to know.

"It's fine," I said.

"It's not. You deserve honesty."

It was what I wanted.

But just because I wanted something didn't mean it was guaranteed. Some things had to be earned. And some things would remain elusive, no matter how hard you worked to earn them.

Like love.

We lay in silence, a dying fire between us. We weren't a girl and a dragon anymore, alone together on the mountain. This was something that should have been less dangerous.

Should have been.

26

WE BOTH DRANK AS MUCH
water as we could in the morning, then filled the bottle to carry
for the day. Wil said there wouldn't be another stream until
tomorrow, but luck was with us. Nestled among the firewood,
I found a crusty waterskin and filled that too.

I slung the extra water over my shoulder. "Just don't think
about who else has used it."

But Wil didn't look concerned about the cleanliness. Why
was I surprised?

That night, we made our camp under the stars. When it
came time to light the fire, Wil asked for my flint. I handed it
to him and glanced at his face. But he was focused on the fire.
He would never use his internal fire unless he had to. And yet
he had done it twice now to protect me. Maybe more than that.
There had been a fire in the castle hearth when I was sick with
infection.

We gathered branches and built the flames high. This
rhythm of making camp was becoming familiar. And it was
still strange.

I had slept outside plenty of times when Guntor and Isa
fought, and also on my journey with Father to the mountain.

But with Wil to keep guard, this camp was different from

the others. It felt like we were still inside a castle. Like he was the castle.

He stretched out on his blanket, closer to the heat than I dared. In the flickering light, his curls shone bright, and I tried not to watch him too much from my bedroll.

He held something in his hands. The book.

I stilled, waiting for him to read to me.

He turned the pages slowly as his eyes followed lines of words. Maybe he didn't care to read aloud, now that his claws were gone and he could hold the books for himself.

But then Wil put a finger on one page and cleared his throat. "This is the history of the southern wars, before the tribes formed cities."

He went on to read of battles. The people from the south were smaller than those of us in the north. But they came from a great nation and fought with shields.

They were called Rhufen, and we were the Elumennic peoples.

He read of vicious Rhufen generals who made war to gain political power back home. And northern warriors who were stolen away and forced to fight in Rhufen arenas.

Over many years, territories were won by our people, and treaties made with the south. Cities were built, and the Elumennic magistrates began their rule.

"If I were writing the story," I said, "I would make the southern general become friends with a northern maiden who saved his life. The general would grow to love the people he once fought. Then, together, they would rebel against the Rhufen emperor—his own king."

Wil smiled. "That would be a better story. But no one is making up this one. It really happened. Over two-hundred fifty years ago."

I let that sink in. The cities had always been a fact, solid and waiting for me. It was hard to imagine a time before they existed.

"No more fables, then," I declared.

We would only have the truth out here on the mountain.

Wil closed the book. "This book doesn't have gold filigree, but it's one of the most valuable in the library. There are fifty-seven true stories and accounts in these pages, compiled by scholars."

"Compiled by a wizard, you mean." Someone who sought knowledge and power.

Wil's expression shadowed. "All wizards are scholars. Or they start that way. But not all scholars become wizards. They can be good."

His grandfather had been a scholar. A man he had only heard stories about.

I thought a moment. "I've never known my father to love learning."

"Ah," Wil said. "People love to learn for different reasons. Some want to help others, as Edric tried to do once. Some learn out of fear, so they can know enough to stay safe. Others just want power. But it doesn't matter what the motivation is. If they turn to wizardry, it always involves harming others, and that changes a person. It makes them forget who they were."

"You said Edric didn't kill people at first. He only cut them."

"Yes. Even when he bled people against their wishes, Edric still believed he was better than the killing wizards. He hated their kind. Then he started buying embergold. And he killed."

Could that be why Edric had hated my father? He was the killing kind.

Wil grew distant. "I don't know when the tipping point was for Edric. When he lost himself."

I knew Wil was thinking of his own fire.

"You didn't choose to burn the bottle," I said.

He gave no reply.

"Thank you for reading to me." I shifted on my blanket. "I think I need more true stories in my life."

"Should I read another?"

I propped my chin up on my hands. "I'd like it if you told me a different story instead. One about you."

He gave a little laugh. "What kind of story?"

"Anything."

It took a while, but eventually he began.

"When I was a boy, I lived near the waters of Rijn. It's the largest river in this region, and it likely feeds the marshes you lived in."

Rijn. There was a name for the water I grew up with.

There were so many things Isa couldn't teach me. Or didn't think to teach me.

Wil continued. "A friend of my mother took me fishing when I was only seven years old, and I caught my fair share. Later, I wanted a boat like the fishermen, so I made my own out of twigs and rope. It didn't hold. I was a good swimmer, but the rapids took me over rocks, and I thought I would die. I breathed in a lung full of water, and I made a bargain with the river. If I survived, I would do only good in my life. Never anything bad. As soon as I made the promise, a current washed me toward the shore and I climbed out."

I peeked at him when he didn't go on. Again, he stared into the flames.

I thought of what I saw in the ghost's blackness. How I hadn't done good in my life.

But Wil was different than that. He hated violence and wouldn't have watched while Isa got hurt.

"The river should be happy," I said. "You've done better than most."

Wil shook his head. "It was too heavy of a promise. But I like remembering the child who didn't know any better."

His eyes drifted back to the fire.

I had seen that look on Wil's face too often, and it had begun to make me uneasy. It was like he was listening to something I couldn't hear.

"Wil . . . what does the fire say to you?"

He blinked, and the look fell away. "It talks about things we have both seen. Me and the fire."

"What things?"

"Things I'd like to forget."

"So it has the same trick as the ghost." I paused, then took a breath. "I lied to you about what I saw in his mouth. I saw my cousin who used to . . . suffer. And none of us stood up for her."

Wil said nothing, but there was an understanding in his expression that was better than words.

After a while, he spoke again. "Today, the fire is reminding me about the man in the tunnel. Guntor. It's angry."

"It has no right to be angry at you about that."

"The fire isn't angry that he died."

I waited.

"It wanted to burn his body. There was no spark in him after death. No reason for it. Still, it wanted to taste his death."

It wanted to consume human flesh. A shudder ran through me, and I hoped Wil didn't notice.

"Did he have a spark when he was alive?" I asked.

"I don't know."

And I wondered again if Guntor really was an oracle. If he had a spark, would my father have let him live?

"You buried him," I told Wil. "You did the right thing."

"I have to hear the fire. That doesn't mean I have to listen to it anymore."

Did he used to listen to it? But I looked at Wil's eyes and decided not to ask. Where had the golden sun in the blue sky gone? The eyes of the painted boy. His face was shadowed now.

I wanted to speak. Something to overpower the voice of the fire for him. But when I opened my mouth, I sang instead.

It started slow. A soft hum deep in my throat.

Wil's posture softened.

I went on, louder now. I didn't have lyrics tonight. No stories or poems to weave into my songs. I hummed the melodies I had known since I was a child and let them speak.

Wil closed his eyes, and he might have slept.

Until the attack came.

He went rigid, then curled into a ball. Veins throbbed in his hands and temples, and his skin was white. I flew to him, stumbling over my bedroll in the rush. At his side, I ran my fingers over his curls, whispering anything I could think of.

"I'm here."

This attack lasted longer than the others. Too long. Soon, my whole body ached from the tension of waiting.

He gasped, and it ended. I gasped too.

His head was cradled in my lap, and he looked up at me. Neither of us moved to separate.

"The change is coming soon," he said.

I swallowed tears. "You said seven days. It's only been three."

"I judged wrong. I may only have one more day."

"Then we can't go to the ocean tomorrow. The water will hurt you."

"Not if I don't touch it. I need this. To make more memories of it while I can."

I studied him and felt his warmth resting against my leg. How could something so perfect turn into something with claws and fangs?

"By sunset tomorrow, we'll reach the ocean," he said. "Gilde, I think you'll love it."

"Then I will."

He gave me an intent look. "Petra and Hans have left the mountain. Don't try to go back to them. If you follow the coast, you'll find people. You can find your cousin."

He meant alone. I could follow the coast without him.

I leaned forward and rested a hand on the earth, my head above his. My voice broke as I repeated my demand from the cave. "You can't leave me like that."

I meant he couldn't leave this life. He couldn't die.

But I also knew the truth.

It would be best for him to leave now, back to the castle. The attacks made him vulnerable, and he was away from safety.

He knew what I meant. "I'll fight the fire. I won't let it take me if I can help it."

Neither would I.

That night, we laid our bedrolls the same distance as usual. But we faced each other, and our eyes met as we tried to sleep.

"Can you smell it?" Wil stood on the grassy hill and leaned into the wind. We had followed an above-ground river for most of the day, and evening was approaching soon.

With his cheeks ruddy from walking, you would never know he'd had two more attacks since the night before.

"Smell what?" I inhaled through my nose. "Water and . . ." It was something else I couldn't name, though it seemed familiar.

"Salt," Wil said. "You can't drink ocean water."

We'd had more than enough to drink from the river. But I had imagined the ocean as a vast, clear pool. Not even the dirtiest parts of the marsh had salt in them.

White birds hovered above us, bobbing in the wind on stiff wings. They didn't peep or sing like forest birds. They let out sharp little screeches.

Wil noticed where I was looking. "They're seagulls. It's been a long time since I've seen anything like this. All the birds clear the air when bigger animals are in flight."

He had been the biggest.

We crested the next hill, and I halted. The world below us spread out into a flat landscape, reaching all the way to the horizon. Grassy hills gave way to a band of white sand. Beyond that, water filled the world.

But it didn't act like any water I had seen before.

Waves rolled and crashed, sending up sprays of white. Where the evening sun hit the surface, it sparkled blue. Bluer than the sky. A new definition of the word blue.

The ocean.

I glanced at Wil. He watched me instead of the water.

"What do you think?"

I took in a breath of misty air. "I have an easier time imagining whales now."

How many strange creatures existed in the world?

I scanned the coastline. From our vantage, I didn't spot one house or curl of campfire smoke. No signs of people.

"You said there would be cities here," I reminded Wil.

"There are always fishing villages, but it may take a day or two for you to find them." He looked at me intently. "Gilde, if you approach anyone, look for well-kept houses with well dressed women. They'll be the safest for you."

For me. Without him.

"We should start looking now," I said.

In my imagination, there was supposed to be a wealthy merchant I could barter with. A sailor with a chest full of artifacts. This couldn't be all there was.

"No," Wil said. "I need to rest before tonight."

His face glistened with sweat despite the pleasant breeze.

"Then you should rest in a house. In a bed with a proper meal." A knot formed in my chest.

"I want to touch the ocean first."

I followed him down the grass, toward the sand. When we reached the water's edge, he kicked off his boots and rolled up the hems of his breeches. He left the pack on dry ground.

The water came to him in a gentle wave, washing over his toes.

"Be careful of whales," I said.

His smile was wide. "Whales are the last thing I'm worried about. They don't actually attack humans, despite what the stories say."

"How would you know?"

"My mother brought me to the seaside when I was a child for a summer. It was a sweet time."

I removed my boots and copied him. The clear water tickled my feet as I sank into the sand. I eyed Wil. Would he think this was too private also?

But he looked content. The current made me a little unsteady, and I moved nearer to him.

We stood with our arms a breath from touching, looking out into the ocean. This was what he had wanted.

"I never thought I would see it again," he said.

"I never knew I would see it for the first time."

His smile faded. "I shouldn't have brought you. You deserve real houses and real beds with those proper meals. You deserve to see your Isadora again."

He remembered everything I ever told him.

Did Isa even have a bed and meals? She had married Guntor for shelter and food.

"It's good for me to keep moving like this," I said. "In case I'm tracked. And . . . I wanted to come with you."

Wil shifted his weight, and now our arms were touching as we stood together. His shoulder was so much higher than mine.

He took a breath. "When the wizard brought you to the mountain, it had been three years since I spoke to a human. By then, all the servants had fled."

"That must have been painful."

"It was no excuse to take you."

"You were protecting me," I said. "I know that now."

"No. That's what I'm trying to say. If I were protecting you, I would have given you to Hans and Petra right away rather than taking you to the castle. I wouldn't have isolated you here with me at the ocean. But I've been selfish." He turned to me. "From the first time I saw you on the cliff, I didn't want to let you go."

"Why?" I felt myself tremble. I had been nothing but trouble for Wil.

"When you brandished your little knife, I knew that you trusted the wizard. I hated it, because I hated myself for trusting a wizard once. And I . . . I loved it about you. Because you could care for someone as wretched as him. Everything in me said not to do it, but I wanted to know you."

My voice was barely audible over the waves. "Then I'm glad you were selfish."

"The fire wanted to hurt you." He looked pained. "Not just you, everyone else too. It's why I had to be alone for so long. But with you, I knew I wouldn't do what the fire said."

I asked my question again. "Why?"

"I'd never seen anything so beautiful."

At this, I looked down, unable to meet his eyes. Petra had called me pretty once. This was different.

But Wil reached out and tucked one strand of dark hair behind my ear, tilting my head up so he could see my eyes again. My face warmed where his fingers brushed against it.

"You deserve to be courted." There was sadness in his words. "With chaperones and flowers. And promises. In another life, maybe I could have done that. Instead, I brought you alone into the wilderness."

These were words between a man and a woman, not a dragon and his friend. But, as I looked into Wil's golden eyes, I found I wasn't afraid.

"I spent my whole life in the wilderness," I said. "This is the least alone I've ever been."

"There is so much more life for you, Gilde." His voice held a tenderness I hadn't heard before, as if a curtain had been pulled back between us.

We were close now, and his eyes moved to my mouth. Did he want to kiss me? Did I want him to do it?

Not if it were the kind of hard kiss Guntor gave Isa. But I knew Wil's would be nothing like that.

My heartbeat rose in my chest, and I didn't move for a long time.

But the moment passed, and Wil let his hand fall from my face.

I stood there, relieved and disappointed.

"I should get the pack before the tide changes," Wil said. "The waves could catch it."

The sun was setting.

We were knee deep in water now, and both of our clothes would be wet for a while, but it was a warm night. It had been a quarter day since his last attack. Was that a good sign?

Back on the sand, I let Wil retrieve the pack while I scanned the hills in the fading light. Which direction would be more likely to have a village? It all looked empty.

A noise came from behind me, where Wil stood. It was only a soft thud, but a jolt of dread ran through me.

I turned. Wil lay on the sand, his body rigid.

I wanted to scream for help, but there was no one to hear. There was only me. I ran to him and fell to the ground.

"No," I pled. "Not yet."

He took a deep breath, and his eyes opened.

"I need to tell you—" He convulsed and couldn't speak.

I smoothed his golden hair from his face.

The convulsion passed.

"I never burned a person," he panted.

"I know."

"But I burned all the embergold in the castle. It allowed me to be human again for a short time, in the beginning when I was alone, before I learned to bear the fire."

"Shh. It's alright. I understand."

"You don't." His voice was strained. "When I burned it, I felt the deaths. I consumed the people. And . . . it felt good."

I didn't know what to say, but I took Wil's hand in mine.

He gripped it hard. "I needed you to know. It's why I deserve this."

"You don't." My voice broke. "You've done good."

"Not for the dead."

"But for me." I kept my voice steady for him. "Don't I count?"

"You should leave. I don't want you to see what happens." Wil tensed again, and his eyes fluttered.

My vision blurred with tears, and I shook my head.

I wasn't going anywhere. No one could make me.

After that, there were no more breaks where he could speak. Waves of tremors came, and his body burned with a fever.

I held his hand to my heart and rocked back and forth.

I needed more time.

I needed embergold.

But Wil didn't want that, and so it had come to this. Even if I had something to burn, I had no dragon fire of my own, and Wil was incapacitated.

Tears fell from my eyes onto our entwined hands, and the scent of metallic smoke overpowered the ocean air.

His skin grew hotter, until it hurt to touch him. Still, I held on.

That's when I knew.

I never wanted to let go of his hand. I never wanted to be apart from him.

"Don't leave." I put my lips close to his ear. "Wil . . . I love you."

Smoke poured from his mouth, and black sores spread over

his skin. I thought of putting him in water, to soothe the heat, but it would hurt him now.

My skin turned red where we touched.

The black sores on his hands grew rough and thick. His round nails extended into sharp, dark claws.

The change was happening.

I wanted to close my eyes and look away, but I couldn't stop watching. Soon, Wil's body was unrecognizable as human or dragon. He became a mass of smoking, black scales that didn't seem to breathe at all. I had to move back to avoid being crushed, but I kept one hand on his scorching side.

I hadn't run out of tears, and when they fell on him now, they left little trails of white char. I dried my eyes for his sake.

"Wil, if you can hear me, you're not alone. I'm here with you, and I know you're strong. Not because of the dragon, but because of you. The man who doesn't listen to the fire."

His mouth, nose, and eyes had disappeared among the jumble of black. I stood very still, watching for any signs of movement.

That part of it seemed to last the longest.

Then the mass of scales began to look more and more like a dragon. The tail formed first and grew long enough that an ocean wave lapped over the tip, sizzling with heat.

I ran to the tail and took it in both hands. With all my strength, I lifted, leveraging my weight to curl it closer to Wil's body. Burns marked the scales.

Eventually, a snout formed at the head of the body, and black sludge escaped the nostrils. Air blew, and his sides rose and fell in rhythm. I almost collapsed from relief.

But the change wasn't over yet. Wings sprouted from his back, crumpled and thin.

It was dark now. The sun was gone.

Wil had reached his full size and stopped growing, but he was still misshapen.

I gathered driftwood from the grass and took my flint from the pack. The wood didn't ignite easily in the misty air, and when it finally burned, it steamed.

I spoke aloud as I worked, to myself as much as to Wil.

"Don't worry, I put the pack at the top of the beach where the waves won't get it."

"We have a fire now. Not a big one, but it's better than nothing."

Sharp, pointed ears began to emerge on Wil's head. Where his eyes should have been, there were deep pools of black fluid. But he was breathing.

He was still alive.

I kept the fire going through the night. When I grew thirsty, I delayed drinking for a long time. But it wouldn't help Wil if I became weak, so I gave in and finished the waterskin.

We were near the river mouth, and I thought of refilling my water, but then I would look at the dark hills and inch nearer to my fire. Twice, I thought I saw movement in the night, but no animals approached.

Dawn came, and I hadn't slept. The ocean water had receded, widening the stretch of dry land between Wil and the shore. Good.

His scales had organized themselves into a pattern now, more cohesive than the ugly mess they had been. Spines developed on the ridge of his back, and eyelids grew over the watery sockets in his face.

I felt the edge of one scale. It was sharper than ever. He was beginning to look like the dragon I had known.

"There's plenty of oats for several more days." I boiled porridge and spoke to Wil's sleeping form. "After that, I can catch fish with my hands. I used to do it in the marsh."

The easiest fish would be upriver, in the muddy banks. But I remembered the moving shadows in the hills. Most animals hunted at night, so why did I still feel the presence of something out there?

As the day went on, the ocean waves began to move closer again. At first, I hoped I was imagining it, but then the water overtook a marker stone I had placed in the sand.

The water crept closer to Wil's limp body, and I paced back and forth.

"You need to wake up. I need you to move." I rested a firm hand on his glittering forehead, between his eyes.

His breathing went on, steady and slow.

I found a stick and dug a trench in the sand around him. If the waves encroached, it would absorb some of the water. But not enough.

I had to keep trying, even if it was useless.

I gathered stones from the beach—the heaviest ones I could find. I stacked them into a wall behind the trench, one after the other. First two layers deep, then three, until it was a long mound of rock packed tight with sand.

The sun rose high while I worked, then began to sink, and the water came closer. It gushed into the trench, and crashed against my little wall, sending spray onto Wil's back. Each droplet sizzled white.

If not for my wall, it would be more than drops burning him.

I stood between Wil and the water, a hopeless barrier. How high would the ocean rise? The marsh never flooded this quickly.

By late afternoon, water seeped completely through the rocks and sloshed around my ankles. Each wave left a new burn on Wil's hide, flaring his scales to reveal bloodied skin.

I clung to what he had told me once. It would take a whole lake to drown him. Still, the white patches that grew on his body pained me.

Sometimes his breath caught when the water lapped against him. He could feel it.

I gritted my teeth.

"Hans thinks I have a spark," I told Wil. "If I did, I'd be able to help you. I would run fast enough to build a bigger wall. Or I would be strong enough to push you out of the way."

I leaned my back against his smooth scales and dug my heels into the sand, pushing. I might as well have pushed against the mountain.

Water crashed against us, and Wil's breath paused. I let out a frustrated scream and put all my weight against him.

His lungs filled.

"You'll make yourself tired." It was the deep voice of a dragon. "And then we'll both be exhausted."

27

I KICKED SAND INTO THE AIR as I scurried from Wil's side to his head. His golden eyes opened, now as large as my face.

"Can you move?" I asked. "The water is rising."

For one awful breath, his eyes closed again. But then they opened.

"I can try."

Slowly, he eased his body forward and curled his tail away from the water, onto the windswept grass. Such a small movement for him. It had been impossible for me.

I walked around him, inspecting the damage. His hind legs and tail were raw underneath. Red blood seeped from sores on the skin. It smelled metallic and bitter.

I dug my nails into my own skin.

Wil's head rested on the ground. Before I returned to his line of sight, I swallowed back emotion, wiping my face with my sleeve. He didn't need to know how bad it looked. I knelt beside him, laying a hand against his cheek.

"The water may keep coming. It's a flood."

"No. The tide will go out soon. It rises and falls in patterns."

He had known it would rise?

"You should have told me." My voice caught. "I could have moved you when you were—"

"I didn't think it would matter."

That hit me like a fiery wave. "You said you might live."

And he had lived. He was here, breathing and speaking.

"I wasn't the first one Edric tried to transfer the fire to." He moved his mouth carefully with each word, as if it pained him to speak through sharp teeth and a snout. "The others . . . they all died. I was the last resort, and the only one who knew to burn his treasures for power. I thought this time would be like when the others passed. It wasn't a pleasant thing to see. I'm sorry you had to watch me."

"Is it done?"

"Yes." His voice was flat.

"How did you survive?"

Wil's breath shuddered. "The fire's had me for too long. I don't think it would let me go so easily now."

As he spoke, I could see the man in the dragon. A sharp, smoldering version of the person he had been. The dragon was beautiful because he was terrible. The human had been beautiful simply because he was.

"You're badly burned." I couldn't wash his wounds with water like I would with anyone else. "Will you get an infection?"

"No. That isn't the way of dragons."

But I knew it hurt.

"You need to rest," I told him. "And I'll catch fish for you to eat."

"I won't be hungry. Last time, it took two days for me to recover. But then I had Edric's embergold still in me. Now I'm empty."

My hand began to overheat where it lay against him. I remembered Wil's own human fingers as they had brushed my cheek. This creature was something else, but not someone else.

"Was it much worse this time?" I asked.

"Yes." He closed his eyes. "And no. This time, I could hear your voice."

Had he heard everything I said?

I took a deep breath, and found it was my easiest in days. Wil was alive. He was out of the water. I could still hear it lapping and churning, something that should have brought life and instead brought only pain.

But we made it through the change.

Both of us.

Because if he died, I would have been broken beyond repair. I had lost my family. I couldn't lose this too. Not just protection, but kindness also. Not just a place to belong, but freedom too.

I kept my hand on Wil's cheek, despite the painful heat. "It's going to be alright."

But I watched as a single tear welled on his lower lid, sliding down his cheek with a steaming burn mark. I hadn't known he could cry, and it took everything to hold back my own weeping.

"Is it your burns?" I asked.

"The pain is bearable." His dragon voice held a tinge of sadness. "But I once was a man at the ocean, looking into the gray eyes of a girl named Gilde. Now I'm a dragon, filled with a fire that wants to burn her. How can anything be alright again?"

"You're alive." I rested my forehead against his scales. "So that means the story isn't over yet. Don't pretend you know the ending if you haven't read it."

He let out a long, smoky breath. "Thank you for staying with me."

I hesitated. Now that Wil was awake, a new worry arose. Should I have stayed?

"Wil, my father's men could find you if they tracked me."

"It would take them days to cross the mountains. How long have we been here?"

"A night and a morning."

"Then we're safe. I'll be able to move again soon."

My worry eased, but not entirely. Wil didn't look right. His whole body sagged, and no smoke curled from his nose.

"You should rest," I said.

We sat, engulfed in summer heat and dragon smell. After a while, he fell asleep. His breath was a pleasant sound, better than ocean waves and the wind in the grass.

Finally, I allowed myself to sleep, sprawled on the ground beside my dragon.

My eyes felt heavy when I opened them. What startled me awake? Everything sounded the same. Water. Seagulls. Dragon sleep.

I sat up. The ocean had receded past my stone wall. The trench was washed away. Wil's ears twitched as he slept, which was encouraging after his stillness in the change.

But something wasn't right.

Slowly, I turned to the hills, where I had seen the shadows the night before. Animals wouldn't come near a dragon, would they?

But it wasn't animals that came over the hill.

They were men.

Dozens of them, nothing like Father's servants. They were too organized for that.

They moved quietly, though I must have managed to hear the shuffle of boots in the grass.

I scrambled to stand, my back to Wil, searching for signs of gold-sickness among them.

They had already seen me. And Wil. Who would approach a dragon like this?

The men walked tall—shields and helmets protected their bodies, and long swords gleamed in the sunset.

I recognized the trappings of war, though I hadn't seen anything like them before.

Soldiers.

One of the men in the front wore a red feather on his helmet. He gave me a wary look and brought his finger to his mouth. The signal for silence.

They didn't want to wake the dragon, and I was a human, so they would assume I was on their side. I was not.

Wil should have heard them, but he was sick now. How much had the men seen?

I spoke low so only Wil could hear. "There are people."

His eyes shot open, and he lifted his head from the ground. There was a strain in the movement.

The men halted a stone's throw away, and their shields snapped up into place. Three men carried a long, metal tube between them. They anchored it in the grass, pointed at Wil. Was it an artifact?

I backed up against Wil. No one spoke, so I raised my voice. "Hello. We don't want any trouble."

The man in the front heard me but chose to address Wil with a shout. "Dragon, do you speak?"

His pronunciation was strange. Was that what a foreigner sounded like?

Wil answered, but he was quieter. "I speak as well as most. Better than some."

The man drew his sword from its hilt. "Then let the girl go with us and we won't harm you."

Smoke curled from Wil's nostrils above me. "I'm afraid I won't do that. She's not in danger from me, and I can't be certain if you're a threat. I won't tolerate a threat. You should leave while you still can."

A murmur ran through the men, but the one with the

feather raised a hand and they quieted. "We know you're weak. We've been watching. A messenger called us ashore, and he spoke of a monster with a captive."

A messenger? There was no one out here to see us. Who would have known where I was? This wasn't right.

This felt like magic.

"I'm not a captive." I made my voice loud. "The dragon saved my life, and he won't hurt me. You should listen to him and go."

The men stilled for a moment. Then the red-feathered man shouted, and chaos erupted.

A deafening crack came from the metal tube, and a bright light flashed. Something flew past my ear and crashed into Wil. He fell, and I dodged the sharp tip of his wing.

My ears rang as I spun to see Wil.

He slid on the beach, stopping before the tide line. A metal, fiery ball was lodged in his neck, surrounded by cracked scales and black fluid.

"Wil!" I screamed and tried to go to him, but the man with the feather blocked my way.

He caught me by the shoulders and pulled me in the opposite direction. His grip was strong.

"No." I tried to push the man away without success. "He's hurt. I have to go to him."

He turned me to face him and looked me square in the eyes. "Are you injured? We had to act quickly."

I squirmed to see my dragon.

Men swarmed him, removing the projectile orb and binding his wings with chains.

I looked back to the man, pleading with my eyes. "Please. Let me go."

He shouted something to the others in a language I couldn't understand. The words were fluid and nasal. Someone yelled back to him.

He addressed me again. "I don't enjoy restraining you, but it's for your safety. My men will secure the dragon's mouth shut so it can't breathe fire. Then you can go."

Secure his mouth? These people were the monsters. What kind of magic could hurt Wil like that?

I met the soldier's eyes and gave a slow nod, relaxing my stance. He loosened his grip, watching the others work.

I waited a heartbeat longer, then broke free of his hold and sprinted toward Wil.

The man ran after me, and I pushed harder, sand flying.

When I reached Wil, his mouth had already been chained, his head limp against the ground, unconscious. Hot anger flashed through me. My hands trembled as I reached out to feel his nostrils for breath. A small current of smoke ran over my fingers.

He was alive.

The weapon had only punctured the skin enough to bleed, not to cut deep. But he was missing scales, and the black flesh underneath was now tinted purple.

And then I knew who these men were.

Dragon fighters. From the south, on their summer tour of the western isles.

A long time ago, when I first heard of them, Isa's rumor filled me with hope. Now I was afraid, and furious.

I felt their presence behind me, and the red feather soldier drew close.

I brought my face to Wil's ear. "I'm here."

Then I turned to the man and stood as straight as I could, calming my breath.

He was older than Wil, but not by too many years. His smoke-colored hair was cropped short beneath his helmet, and he looked down at me with interest over a long, straight nose.

"My name is Gilde." I kept my voice firm. "And this dragon is mine."

His eyes went to Wil, then back to me. "I am Marcus, the prefect of this cohort."

I had never heard those titles, but I knew they meant he was a leader.

He cleared his throat. "The dragon is a wanted enemy of the Elumennic dominion, whom I serve under treaty. And I'm very sorry to question your logic, but I don't think a maiden can own a dragon."

"We belong to each other."

Marcus glanced at Wil again.

"There's been more than one dragon on the mountain," I said. "You have the wrong one."

"Every dragon is the enemy of mankind. And more specifically, the enemy of the Xantic magistrate."

My heart sank and my mind raced. Wil had mentioned Xantic as one of the cities my father would retreat to. A place to find victims with a spark.

"He isn't a dragon," I explained. "He's a man. When he's not a dragon." I knew that didn't make any sense. "He's under an enchantment."

Now that Wil was chained, the men had gathered around us. As I spoke, they muttered in their southern tongue and watched us.

Marcus addressed them. "I will speak to her alone."

The men left us, dispersing along the beach. I edged closer to Wil.

Marcus took his helmet off and tucked it under one arm. "I'm sorry this has been alarming."

Was he serious? The corners of his mouth were turned up, as if we had met beside a fire rather than beside a bleeding dragon.

I set my jaw. "If you wish to apologize, you'll continue on your way."

The man's smile fell. "I can't do that. But, I promise we mean you no harm, Gilde."

He pronounced my name in a way I had never heard before. "I'm not worried for myself." I looked back at Wil.

Marcus kept his tone conversational, a strong contrast to mine.

"Where I come from, we don't have enchantments," he said. "We also don't have girls who travel with monsters."

I disliked that word for Wil, but I needed to calm myself.

"What are you planning to do with him?" I asked.

"The best way to kill him is to put him in the ocean—"

"No!" The shrill word tore from me, and an ache filled my chest.

He held up a hand. "But that is not my plan."

I held my breath.

"I think it would serve us better to transport the beast to Xantic. The magistrate will be pleased."

"Alive?" My whole body felt weak.

"Yes. It will be difficult, but not impossible."

I met Marcus's gaze and tried to keep the vitriol from my eyes. "Why alive?"

"To stand trial. Also, for the magistrate. He has plenty of scales and horns in his collection—relics from the ancients—but he's never seen a live dragon."

People collected dragon horns? The thought of cutting the spines on Wil's back was disgusting.

Wil had been healing. He had survived. I could hardly grasp what was happening now, and tremors ran through me.

"Marcus." I used his name for emphasis. "He really is a man."

Marcus accepted my words without the weight they should have carried. "I won't decide his fate."

"But you could."

He could leave us alone and forget he ever saw us. It would be easier for him.

He examined me, eyes catching on my fine gown. "We need to decide what to do with you. Is your family nearby?"

He knew as well as I did that no one was nearby. And I had no family.

I placed my hand on Wil's cheek. "Where he goes, I go."

Marcus glanced out at the waves. "If that's what you want, it may be possible for you to come with us."

He couldn't have kept me from following either way.

His eyes went back to me. "I think you must have a story to tell."

28

I SAT WITH WIL AND CLUTCHED

our pack while the men made camp for the night. Wil remained unconscious, and the soldiers glanced over at us more often than I liked.

Especially Marcus.

Among them, one figure was smaller than the others. He stayed near Marcus and moved in an easy way, bouncing his steps. A child. I found myself watching him.

Wil was out of the tide line, but barely. If it came up again in the night, it would spray him. Even if they were small burns, he didn't need any more pain.

The sun went down. I built my fire, and the cohort built theirs. I ate oats. The men roasted fish.

I worried that Wil would never wake again, and that thought threatened to overtake me.

With so many people around, I didn't need a fire to scare the animals away. My dragon would have kept me warm. But I lit one to show Marcus I could care for myself.

He had already offered a private tent to me, and he tried to relocate my pack to their camp, away from the dragon.

I refused.

As I spread out my bedroll beside the fire, I noticed three

figures in the dark, moving toward me from their camp. I stood, a hefty stone in my hand.

Marcus had promised they meant no harm, but I was still a girl alone with strange men. I stood close to my fire, in the light where everyone could see.

It was Marcus. Again. And his companion, the child. There was also a soldier with them that I didn't know.

The boy wasn't as young as I had thought from a distance, though he still had the smooth skin of youth. A child, but not for long. He wore smaller versions of the same clothes as the others, minus the chest armor, and he looked up at me with bright eyes. His hair stuck up in the back.

"I saw you only had porridge for dinner." Marcus handed me a stick with a roasted fish on it.

My first instinct was to turn away his gift. I was on my own, and not under their control. But I also didn't want them to think of me as an enemy. And, in truth, the fish smelled good.

"Thank you." I took the stick with my free hand. "I didn't have time to catch my own tonight."

That was their fault.

I held the stick and waited for them to leave, but they didn't go. Instead, Marcus settled beside the embers of my fire, and the other two followed suit. I remained standing.

Marcus spoke first. "By tomorrow evening my full cohort should arrive. We've sent word. They're anchored up the coast."

"This isn't all your men?"

"We're one-hundred twenty in total. A specialized unit."

Specialized in harming dragons. That wasn't a skill I could admire. Except, if I had been taken by Edric instead of Wil, I might have been happy to meet this team of fighters. And that was the type of situation they had thought I was in.

"How long will it take to reach Xantic?" I asked.

Xantic, the same city that lay beyond the marshes, where

Father's men roamed. The place he would go to find more victims. The last place Wil or I should go.

It would be inland, over the mountain. Then maybe to the north, from what I could remember.

"Three days sailing north by ship," Marcus answered. "We'll have to figure out how to load the dragon without drowning him. After we reach port, I can't say how long it will take us on land." He glanced at Wil's unconscious form. "But, even without a dragon to haul, it's usually a two-day march to the city from there."

"Sailing?" I felt my face drain of blood. "But Xantic is over the mountain."

"It's northeast. You're right, we could go east over the hills, but it will be faster to sail up the coast and then travel on flat ground. All these lands belong to the magistrate. It makes no difference how we get to him, except to our own convenience."

Marcus was wrong on two accounts. Not all these lands belonged to the magistrate. The mountain was Wil's. And it made a world of difference how we traveled.

"He can't touch the water," I stated. "I won't allow it."

The boy smirked and shared a look with the other soldier, who laughed.

It wasn't funny, and I fixed the soldier with a cool stare. "Or do you make it a habit of torturing your prisoners?"

The boy spoke, his voice scratchy. "My apologies. We're not used to hearing anyone give orders to Marcus. That's all."

He had a mouth that seemed like it would smile more often than not.

"The dragon won't be harmed," Marcus promised. "We'll find a way. It's what we do."

I could tell his answer was final, no matter how much I disliked it. Wil would be trapped on a ship, surrounded by the one thing that could kill him.

And there were other things about this that weren't right. Things I needed to ask about.

Marcus read my face. "What is it, Gilde?"

"You mentioned a messenger. Someone who called you to shore. Can you tell me anything about the person?"

None of them moved to answer. They didn't move at all, and their eyes met. The smile fell from the boy's face.

I tried again. "Do you know the messenger's name?"

"He came and went," the boy said. "Strange like."

Marcus cleared his throat. "We believe he was a fisherman. He came in a boat."

"And what was strange about him?" I asked.

"It was mostly the eyes—" the boy began.

"He had an unusual demeanor." Marcus interrupted. "But there is a secret codeword the magistrate sends with his messengers, and this man used it. How he came to know the dragon's location, and how he reached us so soon, is still uncertain. There have always been things in the Elumennic regions that I can't explain. Talking dragons being one of them."

So the message had come from Xantic, spirited here by unnatural means. I couldn't explain it either, but I didn't know everything a wizard could do with a fresh kill.

Isa had made it clear Father wasn't liked in the cities. If he went there, it wouldn't be with the blessing of the ruling class. So how was the magistrate's secret word involved in this?

Marcus spoke again. "I'd still feel better if you let me give you a spare tent tonight."

I moved close to Wil's side. "As you can see, I'll be warm enough. But I appreciate the offer."

It felt like I needed some kind of formal gesture to end the conversation, so I gave an awkward curtsy. I immediately felt foolish.

Marcus stared a moment too long, and my cheeks warmed. I didn't know how to talk to humans.

The boy nudged Marcus with his elbow. Marcus blinked, then gestured, and all three men stood.

I caught the boy's eye. "What's your name?"

"Adrian." He grinned.

"You conscript children into your army?" I asked Marcus.

"I'm thirteen," Adrian announced.

"If anyone did the conscripting, it was him," Marcus said wryly.

Still, Marcus allowed it.

"Goodnight," I said. "And thank you."

"Goodnight," Marcus replied. "Maybe tomorrow you can join us at our fire. It would be good for the men to get used to you before we sail together."

"Maybe," I said.

After a final look from Marcus, the men left.

I dropped the rock and took a bite of the salty fish while I monitored each of Wil's breaths.

The moon rose high, and I couldn't sleep. I fidgeted with the stick Marcus had given me. It had been whittled straight, both ends sharpened to a point. A useful thing to have when cooking over a fire.

Wil's crusted blood glinted in the moonlight. His chains were padlocked together, and I had no idea where the keys might be.

I threw the stick down. I didn't want a gift from the people who did that.

I would give it back.

"I'll only be gone a moment." I reached up and touched Wil's head, between his ears.

Then I marched to the other camp.

When I reached the silent row of canvas tents, an accented voice came from the shadows. "What are you doing?"

I held up the stick and whispered. "Returning Marcus's cooking tool."

The soldier eyed me, then gestured to a tent at the end of the row, away from the others. "He's in there."

I didn't actually want to see Marcus, but I crept in that direction, stopping a few paces away. I bent to place the stick on the ground but froze when I heard low voices.

Adrian whispered first, his young voice unmistakable. "Well, if she hadn't refused the tent, it would have been the first time I ever saw you sleep under the stars."

So it hadn't been a spare tent that he offered after all.

Marcus laughed. "It wouldn't have been the roughest night I've spent on tour."

"In that case, it might not hurt for you to rough it a bit again. Ground yourself."

"What's that supposed to mean?" Someone shifted inside the tent, and I stiffened.

Adrian answered. "All I'm saying is, you were already a romantic before. Now you've gone and rescued a girl from a dragon." He lowered his voice to mimic Marcus. "Let her go and you won't be harmed."

There was silence for a moment, and I took a step away from the tent.

But Adrian spoke again. "I think the men will accept her if you take the lead. As long as you're not too distracted by her."

"Get some rest, Adrian."

No one spoke after that, and I snuck away, back to Wil.

It wasn't time for me to sleep. It was time to work in the dead of night, while no one was looking. I unpinned the largest silver brooch from the treasure inside my skirt, taking hold of the long needle. On the far side of Wil, away from the soldier's camp, I dug the sharp point into the lock on his chains.

I'd never seen locks like these, but I'd had to pick my way back into the house after Isa latched me out a few times.

I pressed carefully along the edges of the keyhole, trying to imitate what the prongs of a key might do. Nothing budged. I tried another lock that hung down from Wil's wing. This one looked different, but I didn't have any more success. I went from lock to lock, pressing harder with each one. Eventually, I broke the tip of the brooch pin.

The sky lightened, which would make my work easier, but it would also make me visible to any soldiers on watch. I needed to stop. My body wanted to lie down and sleep, which felt wrong. But I had to let the soldiers see me resting.

I lay facing Wil, and almost drifted off.

Then, in the gray light before dawn, my dragon opened his eyes, blinking and unfocused.

I sat up, and his vision narrowed on me.

I spoke quietly. "You're in chains. Don't struggle or they'll be alerted. There are two guards always on duty, and they have their weapon ready."

Little puffs of smoke rose from Wil's nostrils, and his jaw muscles tightened beneath the chains.

He spoke low, through clenched teeth, surprisingly articulate for someone who could only move their lips. "You need to escape."

His voice was hoarse.

"You don't get to worry about me right now. We need to get you out of here. Can you breathe fire? Or your poison smoke?"

The little curls of smoke were a different kind from the gusts that came from him in the mines.

"Not until I heal. It will be days before I control the fire again."

Those sentences were harder to understand, and I leaned in close. Out of the corner of my eye, I noticed one of the soldiers watching us.

"I tried all night to pick the locks, but I don't know how," I whispered. "I'll keep trying tonight. Wil, they want to transport you to Xantic."

"Xantic." His expression darkened.

We both knew what could be waiting for us there.

"And it's worse than that," I told him. "The magistrate of Xantic sent a messenger to bring the soldiers to you. But how could he have known where you were? And how could someone have reached them so quickly? It isn't natural."

His jaw strained at its chains. "Why are they transporting me?"

I hesitated. "To stand trial with the magistrate for your crimes as a dragon."

He closed his eyes for a long moment before they opened again.

Two more soldiers were looking our way now, alerted by the first.

I went on, speaking more quickly. "But we're going to get you free before then. And either way, you're innocent."

"Am I?"

I didn't like that response. "Yes," I said firmly.

I sensed movement behind me and turned.

Marcus.

He stood back from Wil, away from the dragon's head. Marcus was thinking of fire also.

A rumble came from Wil's throat, a sound I had never heard before.

"Dragon," Marcus addressed him. "You are the prisoner of the magistrate of Xantic, by delivery of the eighteenth cohort of the empiric legions. As long as it is up to me, you will be treated as a prisoner of war. That means humane nutrition and shelter until you leave my custody in Xantic. If you cooperate with us, things will go better for you."

Wil's tendril of smoke darkened as he exhaled.

"Is Gilde a prisoner also?" he slurred through his chains.

"Gilde has asked to accompany us to Xantic."

Wil's eyes slid to me.

And even I noticed that Marcus didn't clarify whether I was a prisoner or not. If they wanted to keep me, I didn't need chains. They knew I wouldn't leave Wil.

"Promise me." Wil swallowed, a dry sound. "Gilde won't be harmed."

Marcus looked between us, then gave a deep nod of his head, almost a bow. "That is a promise I am more than happy to make." He pointed toward the men's camp. "Do you see that lineup of metal tubes? They're called cannons. It's what knocked you out during our battle, and these weapons will be trained on you at all times. I'd like to promise that you won't be hurt either, but that depends on your actions. I can't risk the lives of my men. Do you understand?"

Wil's eyes searched the camp, taking in each soldier. Was he making a plan? I hoped so.

His teeth grated together. "Understood."

"Marcus," I said. "There's no need for threats. He's injured and weak from changing into a dragon. You have nothing to worry about."

"You saw him change into a dragon?" Marcus's expression was impassible. "From human form?"

Wil's breath quickened.

"Yes," I said. "And he'll be weak for a full cycle of the moon. He won't be able to breathe fire. It's how the magic works. Like I said, no need for threats."

Better for Marcus to underestimate Wil. Could he tell I was lying? Isa always could. She said my ears turned pink. I smoothed my hair.

But Marcus gave no indication. "They aren't threats. Only precautions."

And I wasn't plotting an escape. Only planning a departure.

I did not join the men at their fires that afternoon. Then, the ship came.

In my childhood, I crafted plenty of little rafts to float on the marshes, but I had never imagined a vessel like this. Long planks of smooth wood formed the body, and the front curved upward into an elegant spiral. Ocean wind pulled giant pieces of canvas tight, harnessed high above the ship.

It was so large, it couldn't come to shore. Men had to row smaller boats to the beach. They came in dozens, flooding the camp with more glinting armor and rolling accents.

We stayed on our dry patch of sand and watched the commotion.

Everyone reported to Marcus, who roamed the beach, grouping men and directing where to pitch tents. He never sat down, and I never saw him take a drink from the waterskin he carried.

None of the men came near us, though they did plenty of staring. Had Marcus ordered them to stay away? Or was a dragon enough to keep them at a distance?

I went about my routine. Gathering water. Making porridge. Keeping an eye on Wil. He went in and out of consciousness throughout the day. The tide never reached him, though, and that was one less worry.

The ship was more than big enough to hold him, but the boats that came to shore weren't. A sliver of hope ignited in me. Maybe they wouldn't find a way to load him. Maybe they would give up.

As long as that didn't mean execution without a trial.

At sunset, Marcus brought fish for me. Wil was awake.

Marcus raised his voice whenever he spoke to Wil, as if

trying to match his stature. "My men can bring you fish and loosen your chain to eat, but we'll have firepower at the ready. One wrong move and you'll—"

Wil interrupted, muttering through a closed jaw. "I'm not hungry. But thank you for the dinner invitation."

"You do eat fish, don't you?" Marcus asked.

He was making sure Wil wasn't saving an appetite for humans. I remembered when I had done the same.

"Rabbits, mostly," I said, answering for my dragon. "And a sheep, but only one time that I've seen. He paid the shepherd well above market price."

Anything to humanize Wil.

"Then we'll buy rabbits when we get to port." Marcus seemed to want to linger.

We were an awkward trio, and I had the urge to climb up onto Wil's back, out of sight. But I didn't know if that would hurt him right now.

"Well," Marcus said finally. "Goodnight then, Gilde. If you need anything, one of my men will direct you to me. I'm here to help."

"I'll keep that in mind."

He turned and left.

Wil raised his lip to show his teeth. "If you need anything, it's to get away from him. He's too helpful."

"If Marcus really wanted to help," I said, "he'd give me the keys to those chains. The magistrate may want you, but he's not the only one."

"I remember him. He would like to keep wizards out of his city, and he has an army. Your father may have still gone there discreetly, but he isn't a friend of the magistrate."

"Neither are you," I responded.

"We're on his lands now, off the mountain. A trial is better than being at the mercy of the wizard."

"It would be better to be free." I sounded harsher than I meant.

"I can't change my situation," Wil said. "The same isn't true for you. Gilde." He lifted his head to look at me, and I grieved at the effort it took. "You need to go before it's too late."

"I won't."

With that, neither of us spoke for a long time.

Eventually, I stooped and dug through our pack, rummaging through cloth until I found what I was looking for.

Our book.

Wil followed my movements. "It isn't easy to speak."

"Then I'll read to you."

It wouldn't be as good as his narration. But I had learned enough to make it through a sentence at a time, and we both needed this, whether he knew it or not. It would be something else to think of.

Something normal.

I settled beside the fire, close enough for the light to shine on the words. Most of the entries in the book went on for pages, far too long for me to tackle. Finally, I came to one that only covered half a page. The story header intrigued me.

The Beginning of All Things

My words came out stilted and slow, with plenty of mistakes, but I read. Wil listened, eyes closed but ears perked.

It was a strange story about the whole world. At the start, everything was empty, and water covered all the land. It made me think of the marshes. Then, with one breath, everything good came to the world. Plants and animals. The moon. The story ended when humans arrived.

"Well done," Wil said.

I closed the book, my head aching from the effort of sounding out all those letters. "I thought you said this was a history book. That story was a fable if I ever heard one."

Slowly, Wil's eyelids raised. "But did you like it?"

I thought for a moment. "Yes. I guess everything has a beginning and an end. It's interesting to think about the whole world like that."

"They say it's true."

"Who?" I asked.

"Priests. Worshippers."

I didn't know what a priest was.

"They think that someone breathed and made everything?" I had seen magic, but still it was hard to imagine. Magic could only destroy, not create.

"Not just someone." He said it as if he were sharing something he shouldn't speak of. Or something he didn't know how to speak of. "They say he's like a river of living water."

I watched his jaw muscles flex and wished I could loosen his chains.

"But if there is a creator," he said, "I don't think he made dragons. We're cursed."

I looked up into his sunshine eyes. "Wil, you're not really a dragon. Not even now. If there was a creator, I don't think this is what he would want for what he created."

His brow furrowed. "At least my size makes things difficult for Marcus."

"I'm going to pick the locks tonight," I informed him.

"You need to sleep. I can see it. And I need rest too, for what tomorrow holds."

Tomorrow they would try to get him on the ship.

Wil was at least twice as tall as any of the men, and much longer than that. I had seen him stretch and squish to fit through castle corridors, but this wasn't anything like that.

I did try the locks for quite a while that night, without any success. Eventually, I lay close to Wil, staring up at the moon and imagining a time before light. A time before people.

Like my life before I met Wil.

Whatever Marcus had planned, I would make sure he kept his promise to me. Wil wouldn't be burned.

29

I STOOD ON THE SHORE,
looking furiously between Marcus and the rowboats. "He'll
sink them."

The sea was quiet this morning compared to other days.
Still, I watched the waves roll in with dread, each one a
potential burn.

Marcus stood between me and the ocean, looking down
into my eyes. "Trust me. I can do this."

The cannons were always ready. For all his armor, Wil
might as well have been a captive man with a knife to his
throat. When would his own fire return? Once we were on the
ship, it would be too late, unless his wings were free for flight.
It was a prison for him.

"Please," I said to Marcus. "Wait another day to see if the
ocean calms. The winds are slowing and—"

"It won't get more calm than this. It has to be today."

He stood his ground, feet planted, back straight.

I said nothing and stared into the water, the breeze blowing
my loose hair.

Wil walked toward the boats under threat of firepower, his wings bound and his mouth chained. They had released his legs when I went into the hills to relieve myself. I shouldn't have gone. I should have stayed to see what kinds of keys they used, and where they stored them.

But they had waited on purpose. They wouldn't let me see.

Marcus was more aware of my thoughts than I liked.

Wil's movements were too stiff as he walked, still pained and weak.

The first two boats were already in the water. At the soldiers' commands, Wil put a leg in each boat, and tears slid from my eyes. But the boats held.

Men brought the vessels deeper into the sea, and Wil's body stretched, his hind legs still on land. The waves were so close to him. It took everything in me not to run and pull the boats inland.

Next, they positioned the last two in the water.

"Forward, Dragon," Marcus shouted.

Slow and awkward, Wil stepped fully into the boats. He wobbled and crouched, but held himself upright, his tail rigid to avoid the waves. His whole body was supported on the water now, floating.

I forced myself to breathe.

All the boats were tied together so they couldn't slide apart. A larger rowboat led the procession, full of men and two cannons. They would pull Wil to the ship.

Men ran into the water, waist deep, checking the knots. When Marcus was satisfied, he looked to me and gave a nod. My signal to board.

I wouldn't be allowed to ride with Wil. It would throw off the balance. I raced forward and climbed into the final boat.

With Marcus.

Men pushed us into the ocean, and the boat rocked, seawater misting my face. I lost my balance and sank onto a hard wooden bench. My bag tumbled into the bottom of the boat. Marcus caught it, and placed a hand under my elbow, balancing me.

"Careful," he said. "That pack is too large for someone so small."

But I knew I was tall for a woman.

I kept my eyes locked on Wil, wishing away the mist.

"Is it your first time at sea?" Marcus asked.

"Yes."

"They say it changes a man. Once you've lived on the ocean, it gets in your blood, and you keep coming back. Or it keeps calling you back. But maybe that's just men. You'll be the first maiden we've taken aboard."

Wil's legs strained and his tail was curled onto his back so he wouldn't have to hold it up. Still, it sagged dangerously close to the water. He was too weak for this.

"I don't suppose you've sailed with a dragon before, either," I said.

"I don't suppose anyone has."

An errant wave rolled toward us, causing all the boats to bob up and down. Wil's tail slipped, and a few spikes dipped into the sea. Steam erupted with a loud hiss.

I jumped to my feet and climbed to the front of our boat, stumbling over a coiled rope. Wil was only a few boat lengths ahead. So close, but what could I do?

I looked back at Marcus, pleading.

"Forward!" He was the first to grab an oar, pushing hard against the water below.

The other five men followed, and we lurched ahead.

We were lighter and faster than Wil's network of boats, so we caught up. I leaned over the front, reaching as far as I could.

My fingertips brushed against the scales of his tail, and I pressed my body against the wooden rim of the boat, using the leverage.

Then Marcus was beside me, lifting the charred spines that had fallen into the water. We both wrapped our arms around the tail, pulling. Wil must have helped us, or Marcus was stronger than I thought. Eventually, the tail rested between us, safe in the boat.

I looked at Marcus. "Thank you again."

"I promised he wouldn't be harmed. I gave my word."

But I knew men could lie. I would never take it for granted when promises were kept.

The whole ship tipped as Wil climbed on, and a few men cried out. I watched with a hand over my mouth.

Even chained, he took up more than his share of the ship's upper level. The deck, Marcus called it. As soon as I boarded, I went to Wil, our faces close together. The soldiers were near enough to hear us, even with lowered voices.

I spoke just above a whisper. "When they unchained you for the transport, did you see who had the . . ." I didn't want to say 'key' aloud.

"No. They stayed in my blind spots, which are many right now."

The chains around his neck and wings constricted the movement of his head. He wouldn't have been able to see behind himself at all.

"You should try to eat tonight," I said.

"I've gone months without before. The flame sustains me."

The men would sleep below that night in swinging hammocks. I would stay with Wil. It was the same as our nights on land, except I couldn't have a fire, and the ship rocked.

I wished we could be alone again.

In our castle. Flying through stars.

And I wished I could see human Wil again, though I would never say that aloud to my dragon.

Marcus brought dinner. Fish and some kind of beans in a tin cup. There were cups of water also, one for me and one for Marcus, despite the waterskin slung around his waist. With all his men to do his bidding, feeding me seemed below him, but no one else ever approached.

Wil had drifted into sleep already. He had said it might take longer to recover than the last time he changed.

But he would recover eventually, and then he wouldn't be such an easy captive. He could be flaming and terrifying.

The thing he hated most about being a dragon was the fire. And we needed it.

"Are you seasick?" Marcus asked.

I shook my head, though I didn't know what seasickness was. I felt fine, physically.

Marcus gestured to the sleeping dragon. "Do you think he gets seasick? That could be unpleasant."

"None of this is pleasant. Your life would be easier if you let him go."

Marcus shot me a look. "If I weren't an officer with a duty, I like to think I'd take your request seriously."

"If you weren't an officer, you wouldn't have the power or position to help."

I awoke in the night, too hot from Wil's proximity. Stars shone overhead in a black sky, and the water spread out beyond the ship, black also. A man stood watch on the deck. When I looked at him, he turned his head away. He had been watching me.

I stood and turned. I couldn't see the land. A terrible, trapped feeling came over me, and I moved away from Wil to get cool air.

I had known we would be imprisoned by the water, but this sailing was worse for Wil. If I jumped in the ocean, I would swim, but he didn't have that luxury. I couldn't let him see my panic.

We would be on the ship for three days. In that time, I would be strong for Wil.

I settled back onto the hard, wooden deck, determined to sleep.

꧁꧂

At dawn, Wil opened his eyes and pricked his ears forward. I sat facing him with my back against the rail of the ship.

"You hear something?" I asked.

His dragon voice was a low rumble. "I can't hear far, but I hear everything close to me. They're right below us. Mostly they speak in their language, though sometimes they return to an Elumennic tongue."

"Did you know any southerners when you were . . . a child?" I'd almost said *when you were still human.*

"I saw their kind in the city, and I've heard the accent before. But I didn't know any of these men."

I thought a moment. "Is there anyone in Xantic who will remember you? Who might help?"

"The way we left—my mother and I—it wasn't a respectable thing to do." He closed his eyes and flicked his ears. "Some of the soldiers aren't bad men. When I hear them talk, they're worried for you."

"If you haven't eaten me by now, they should know you won't."

His eyes opened. "I heard one of them say the book in your pack is full of spells, and he thinks I'm controlling your mind with magic."

The wind blew my hair into my face, and I had to pull it back to see Wil again. "Can magic even do that? The alchemist strings his men along with gold, but he can't make them into puppets."

Father had never needed to control me with magic.

"Magic can manipulate someone who wants something, like with the alchemist's gold. But they have to be weak, and it makes them sick. You're not sick or weak."

"Then the soldiers have nothing to worry about."

Wil looked toward the men. "Still. Perhaps you should keep your distance from me for a time. For appearances."

I tried to keep my voice even. "Is that really what you want? To be away from me?"

His answer came as the barest whisper, something vulnerable in the breath. "Never."

I leaned against his tail and rested a hand on his scales.

The sun warmed my back as I looked to the east. For the first time in days, I saw land. I had left Wil's side to get a better view in the bow of the ship, one of the rare times we were parted.

Marcus found me right away. He was always watching, and his eyes lingered in a way that made me uneasy.

"We'll arrive this evening," he said. "I'm always a little sad when a sea voyage comes to an end, though the food in port is better. What did you think of sailing?"

It had been a lot of work for everyone but me. The men secured ropes and climbed rigging in the heat, keeping a constant eye on the sails. And an eye on the dragon.

Ships were dirtier places than you would think, full of dust and salt and sweat. We all needed a bath, though it was difficult to smell anything but Wil. I could feel the oil in my hair.

"You told me once that the sea gets in your blood and calls you back," I replied. "But it didn't quite work on me like that. I think I'll always love the shoreline, but not the open water." I glanced at the cannons pointed at Wil—and the soldiers who manned them today. "It's well enough. I think your men will be more comfortable once I leave."

"Why do you say that?"

"They avoid me, except for Adrian. Which I don't mind."

Adrian found every excuse to bring me a water ration. It usually came with a smile and a wise remark.

But I had started noticing the wide berth most of the other men gave, even when I wasn't beside Wil. It was more than fear of the dragon.

"I've asked them to respect your space," Marcus said.

"And they think I'm enchanted."

Marcus stiffened. "So you know."

I went on. "Your men aren't fond of magic. Neither am I. I wonder if we could say the same for your magistrate, who sends strange messengers."

"Gilde." Marcus's tone changed. "If there is one thing the magistrate despises, it's magic."

His intensity took me aback, and I was tempted to be comforted. But still there were things that couldn't be explained in all of this.

"My book is full of stories," I informed him. "Not spells. Feel free to tell the others." I didn't want those rumors spreading to land. Wil didn't need any more accusations against him.

"I know," Marcus said. "I've looked over your shoulder once or twice as you read."

"You can read?" I had thought only scholars learned.

"Almost every citizen in the empire reads. It's only rare here in the Elumennic region. How did you learn?"

I looked back at Wil. "He taught me. And I'm still learning."

"Oh." Marcus followed my line of sight. He changed the subject. "All his burns are healing now, for the most part. When we unload him tomorrow, I'll be sure to plan for the tail. He won't get wet again."

I looked at the blue sky. "As long as the weather holds."

We'd had clear skies for days. I was always watching the horizon, looking for signs of rain clouds, but so far nothing. It was our only piece of good luck.

"We'll purchase a wagon for him at port so he won't have to walk," Marcus said.

I frowned. Marcus wasn't worried about Wil getting tired. He was worried about him getting away.

"Good." I kept my tone flat. "He's still weak. I'm worried."

But that was another lie, and I felt my ears go pink.

More than just Wil's burns had healed. He was alert now, and the smoke in his breath had thickened. We never said it aloud because the others would hear, but I could see his fire was returning. As soon as we left the water, he would be something to fear.

"Well," Marcus said. "I, at least, was very glad to have you on the voyage."

I turned my head to him. "I'm glad you brought me along."

His mouth turned upward. "I don't leave lost things behind."

I wasn't sure I liked the way he saw me.

Still, there was more kindness in the world than I had ever guessed when I was younger. Marcus didn't enjoy hurting Wil. He kept his promises, and he took care of his soldiers. He was a good man.

But Marcus also had a job to do. And that job came before kindness.

I looked at the soldier beside me. During our time on the

ship, I'd grown more comfortable in his presence, and I didn't like that.

All the times I thanked him for helping me had become more than just words. I felt grateful to him when I should have felt anger for the chains around Wil's mouth.

But perhaps this was my scar from the marsh. Being under a commander was too familiar to me after a lifetime of Father's rule. Old patterns were easy to fall into, and young Gilde was too used to being captive.

Young Gilde had let things happen to her.

No more.

I was the Gilde who made choices. And now I had a dragon on my side.

Buildings lined the shore of Port Hafen. They were much finer than our marsh cottage, with thatched roofs and brick walls. Though nothing was as fine as the wizard's castle in the mountain, which had been constructed by magic.

The mountains were visible to the south, and open sky to the east.

Wil's transport went smoother this time, partly because we were experienced. Partly because he was stronger now. Could Marcus see it? I wished Wil would at least pretend to tremble a little as he balanced in the rowboats.

The cannons were always present. But the soldiers didn't know how fast Wil could be when he was well.

Marcus helped me step from the boat to a brick walkway that ran along the shoreline. The water here was a lighter blue, with a rocky bed beneath the surface.

I moved to a dry part of the path, planting my feet. If Wil

made a move, I would try to jump on the boat with the cannons, directing it away from shore.

But Wil simply climbed onto the bricks and allowed chains to be fastened around his ankles. The locks closed into place with a cruel snap, and I never saw the keys. They were only needed for unlocking.

Marcus was near me when Adrian approached. He had gone ahead the night before with two of the other soldiers. He really was part of the military. Marcus had stayed behind, with the dragon always.

"The men are at their stations for crowd control." Adrian straightened his shoulders, mimicking the stance of the older men. "We should relocate to the fields as soon as possible, before the locals gather. The nineteenth cohort has secured a wagon and will meet us shortly."

He sounded older than his years, like Isa had been, and I worried for him.

The men I was with were called the eighteenth cohort. I didn't like the sound of another group.

Marcus gave his approval, and Adrian left us.

"How long has Adrian been with you?" I asked.

"Two years."

I watched Adrian go. "How did he come to the cohort?"

"That isn't my story to tell," Marcus said. "You shouldn't be concerned."

"He's a child surrounded by weapons."

"I promise you, he'd seen worse days than this before he came to us." He regarded me. "I should offer silver to pay for an inn for you tonight, but I don't think you'd stay there while your dragon is in a field."

"You're right."

Even if I needed a room, I didn't need his silver. Though I didn't know how far gems and silver buttons could stretch in the cities.

The wagon came, along with men I didn't recognize. Their armor was unstained from ocean water. The nineteenth cohort.

Chains rested on the wagon. Thicker ones than they'd had before.

I bit the inside of my mouth and watched as they chained Wil to a wooden cart that was barely large enough to hold him. More locks clinked shut.

There were twice as many men in the field as there had been on the ship, but Wil and I finally had space to ourselves. No one camped beside us, and I wanted to talk to Wil. To make plans. But he fell asleep fast, and I couldn't bring myself to wake him.

The horses disliked being near Wil more than the men did. There were six of them, purchased to pull the wagon.

They were lovely. White and dappled and strong.

They whinnied and their eyes rolled back when Adrian first hitched them to Wil's cart. Eventually, they resigned themselves to pulling the dragon. Now, in the camp, they stayed at the ends of their tethers, grazing as far from us as possible.

I awoke in the morning to whinnies as Adrian brought the reluctant horses back to Wil's cart. I rose from my blankets.

Wil's voice rumbled. "They should be free to run."

"So should you," I said.

Adrian greeted me. "Marcus says I'm good with animals." He tugged at a harness, managing to move a creature much larger than himself. "Can't say the same for you . . ."

I had tried to pet the horses, and even to feed them a bit of fruit the night before. But they shied away.

"They're not used to me yet," I said. "That's all."

Adrian rolled his eyes. "You smell like a dragon. It's easy enough for me to look past it, but they're horses. They can't tell you look alright. They're all nose."

It made me think of the way Father never kept livestock, and the birds didn't fly when Wil was in the air.

Even animals knew to stay away from dark magic.

I would have liked to feel the horses' glossy manes for myself, but there was no time to bathe away the dragon smell. I was exactly where I needed to be. Alone with Wil.

Soldiers led the way ahead, and the cart of cannons stayed behind us. The horses followed without direction, accepting their place in line. No one traveled beside us.

With Wil awake, this was my chance.

"Your fire is back," I told him. "I can smell it."

He frowned.

"It's time to use it." I kept my voice low. "Before we get to a bigger city with more soldiers. You could melt the cannons when they open your mouth to eat, and then melt your chains—"

He mumbled through his bindings. "I would destroy my own body if I tried to melt my chains. It doesn't burn me from within, but on the outside, the flames become something apart from me. My skin wouldn't hold up under that heat."

Like Marcus's firepower could hurt him.

"Your smoke then," I persisted. "I could run away, and you could poison—"

"No." Wil's tone was sharp. "Gilde, hear yourself. These men aren't wizards. Should I take fifty lives to save my own?"

I opened my mouth but said nothing. I didn't want anyone to die either, but there were ways to scare enemies off. Guntor only died because of Father's greed. He should have known to stay away.

"There has to be a way to make them leave." I looked directly into his face, my cheeks hot.

"I'm scared of what I might do with my fire. If you were in danger, Gilde, I'd do anything. But you're safe for now, and there's time for you to get away from these men. I'll stand trial and tell the truth. That's justice, and I made a promise to the river when I was a boy."

It wasn't justice. It wasn't anywhere close to fair, but Wil couldn't see that now. What was the fire whispering to him at night?

I brought my face close to his as I walked. "If there were no chains . . ." My voice softened. "If they all disappeared, would you fly us away from here?"

"If I were free, I would fly you anywhere you wanted to go. The other side of the ocean. The furthest star."

I laid my hand between his eyes, and he closed them.

"But that will never happen," he said.

It had to.

30

I HAD BEEN WRONG. THERE were places finer and grander than Edric's castle. Xantic sprawled alongside the river Rijn, a white city, shining and alive.

Instead of dirt pathways, smooth stones paved the streets. One building stood as tall as a castle, though it was square and wide, rather than tall and pointed. Intricate carvings lined the pillars that held it up, and there were statues that looked exactly like men.

I had always imagined the city. I had never known it would be so beautiful, or that men could make places like this. There were more houses and structures than I could count, all encased by the high walls we had entered through. Soon, I was lost in the maze of streets, and for a moment, I wanted to cry.

It was everything I had wanted. People. Culture. Society. But I couldn't want it anymore. Not with Wil at stake, and not with the overwhelming amount of soldiers pressed in around us.

Marcus walked beside me now, though no one had asked him to. The team of horses pulled Wil, their muscles straining. Both cohorts were present in the streets, all two-hundred forty men.

If my father was here, there would be an army between him and Wil. That was my only comfort.

I didn't want to see him again, yet I couldn't stop picturing his face in the crowd that was forming beyond the soldiers. It was a feeling between terror and longing.

Marcus nodded to the pillared building. "That's the temple. They built it hundreds of years ago for the old gods. It's just a piece of history now."

"Old gods?" I asked.

"They were like men. Some brought luck, some vengeance. Others were tricksters, but no one prays to any of them anymore."

Why would anyone want to pray to a trickster god? Or a god that was like a man? The idea was very different from Wil's story, where a creator was powerful enough to breathe the world into existence.

It was so loud here, I couldn't think. Soldiers kept the citizens of Xantic back from us, but the people still pressed in as close as they could, jostling and shouting to see the captive dragon. I could only understand a few words in the sea of voices, but what I heard, I didn't like.

Words like *monster*. And execution.

The city smelled of onions and dirt. Perfume and woodsmoke. All of it was too much, and I knew it would be worse for Wil with his powerful senses.

I hadn't found the keys on our journey. I'd snuck into empty tents and even spent time around campfires with the men, searching discarded satchels and garments when no one was looking. One night, I'd even hugged Marcus under the pretense of thanks, feeling his jacket for hidden pockets. I'd found nothing, and he'd hugged me back for longer than I'd anticipated.

Then, after two days of walking, we came to the city gate.

Even now, my eyes flickered over the men, always searching for jingling metal.

Marcus had promised Wil a meal in the city, which would require releasing some of the locks. This time, I would make sure to be present.

We rounded a corner, and people parted to make way for Wil's cart. Ahead, a wide building stood with large, arched gates. Gates big enough for Wil.

"Is that our destination?" I asked Marcus.

"It's a safe place for us to keep him in the city."

Were they keeping Wil safe from the people? Or the people safe from a dragon?

Marcus moved nearer to me, walking close and speaking low. "We'll present him to the magistrate there."

I glanced at the building and then at Marcus. "I've been thinking. How does the magistrate decide who's innocent in a trial?"

"He'll question the prisoner and hear testimony from the families affected by his crimes, as well as anyone who might speak on behalf of the prisoner."

This was what I had been thinking of. "I can speak on his behalf. There are things the magistrate doesn't know about dragons . . ."

I trailed off, seeing the discomfort on Marcus's face.

"Is there a problem?" I asked.

"I haven't spoken with the magistrate yet, but we've shared correspondence through messengers on horseback. And he's heard the rumors by now."

"Ah." I knew what he meant. "About my enchantment."

"There's always talk, and I suspect more than letters traveled with the messenger. You may not be considered a reliable witness."

But I had to try. "He'll see I'm in my right mind."

Marcus bent his head to me. "I want to make sure the

magistrate is sympathetic before I present you. Let me show him the creature, and you can watch from afar. Let me gauge—"

"And what about you?" I interrupted. "If you believe I'm not cursed, you can speak on my behalf."

"It may not be that simple."

"What do you believe about me, Marcus?" I finally asked it outright.

His answer was too quick, as if he'd rehearsed it. "You wouldn't align yourself with a monster if you knew him to be one. You're a kind soul to have compassion on a creature, and you're as brave as any of my men. I can't imagine everything you've been through."

My face warmed with frustration.

"You believe in me," I challenged. "But you don't believe what I've told you is reality."

"It's not my job to decide."

He didn't want to know what was true. He would defer to higher authority, the magistrate, because it was safe. Marcus was me when I lived in the marsh, following Father blindly.

I looked straight ahead. "Truth matters," I said to him. "Whether it matters to you or not."

Neither of us spoke again until we reached the iron gate of the structure ahead.

"Stay in the shadows with Adrian, behind the other men," he said. "With any luck, you won't be seen. I'll find you after."

I looked up into his face, dark lashes rimming earnest eyes.

"Marcus, if you do value compassion, please do what you can for Wil."

Marcus blinked at my use of the dragon's name. "I will try my best."

I didn't know what his best would be, but I clung to it.

"Before we go in, I need to speak with Wil alone." We were surrounded by soldiers. "As alone as we can be."

Marcus scanned the men around us. "Quickly."

He stepped away, and I came closer to my dragon.

Wil didn't look tired anymore, or weak. He was full of fire, tendrils of smoke curling from his nostrils. His eyes softened when I neared his face, and he lowered his head close to mine. I spoke into his ear. "I'll be hidden behind the soldiers while they present you. I need to follow Marcus's rules if I'm going to be a witness in the trial."

Wil spoke in a low rumble. "Gilde, now is the time for you to leave while you still can."

I blinked back tears. He was the one in chains, and still he meant to protect me.

"If the worst happens," he said, "Marcus has given me a promise while you slept, and I believe he will keep his word."

They had a conversation without me?

"What is it?" My heart rose.

Wil spoke close and heat enveloped me from his breath. "He'll guard my body for two days until the fire goes out. Everything I have read said it can't outlast death for any longer than that. No one will get my fire, and I know you'll keep the mountain's secret."

I stared at Wil, unable to speak. This couldn't be the best we could dream of. This wasn't anywhere close to being good news.

The arched gate opened in front of us, metal grinding on hinges that were as tall as me.

Marcus came up beside me. "It's time."

He had to pull me back from Wil. The cart rolled forward, and Marcus ushered me along, his grip on my arm firm.

Wil's chains didn't allow him to stand, but even if he had risen to his full height on the wagon, his spine ridge wouldn't have come close to scraping the arch.

The size of the gate made me wonder.

"Did they build this place to hold dragons?" I asked.

"No," Marcus answered. "They built it to be impressive. But it is conveniently large."

We passed into the cool shadows of the building, and it took a moment for my eyes to adjust. Then our path opened into sunlight again. We had walked through the outer structure into a wide enclosure in the center, surrounded by walls. Torches burned along the perimeter, even in daylight. Were the flames meant to impress also? I could see no other purpose. Above the walls, rows of stairs stretched upward toward nothing.

Not stairs, I realized. Empty seats. They were built for people to view this field below.

There were two gates. The one we had entered through, and one on the other side. Both had men stationed on either side of each gate and above on a walkway. Guards. They all followed Wil with their eyes. Had there been guards outside as well? It would have been difficult to notice with the crowds pressing in.

At the center of the enclosure, in the distance, several more men waited. They didn't wear uniforms like Marcus's soldiers, but they looked just as proud, longswords drawn.

Those swords would do nothing to defend them against Wil if he wanted to hurt them. Which he didn't.

Among them, one man stood out. His graying beard grew all the way to his midriff, and his sword remained sheathed.

How had I ended up in the world of so many men, without any women around me?

There was no sign of my father.

As we stepped into the light, Marcus quickened his step, leaving me behind. Adrian appeared at my side, and soldiers surrounded us until I was lost in a crowd, shielded from those who waited.

The cohort always followed orders, whether they thought I was cursed or not.

Adrian offered me an apologetic smile as everyone pressed in close. "Not a lot of personal space, eh?"

I tried to look past the soldiers to keep an eye on Wil, but it was difficult to see anything except helmets and legs and backs. We crossed the dirt toward the center of the field, and all voices silenced. The only sounds were boots on earth and the creaking of the wagon. One of the horses whinnied, and it echoed off the surrounding walls.

When the men around me halted, I had to stop also, too far from Wil.

A voice came from somewhere ahead. It was deep and crackly, and I suspected it was the man with the long beard. He sounded Elumennic, like the people in the encampment rather than the accent of the cohort.

"The creature's smaller than I remember."

Marcus spoke, though I couldn't see him. "He felt big enough on our ship."

The man laughed. "And he's ugly enough too. Well done, Marcus. You've silenced those who said the empire sent you up here for show. You're a real dragon hunter now, and I'm glad to have you back in Xantic."

"I'm glad to be here if it pleases you, sir."

It had to be the magistrate. Marcus wouldn't show that level of deference to anyone else.

"And you still haven't sustained any casualties?" the magistrate asked.

"None. The prisoner was cooperative once he was arrested."

"Arrested?" There was a pause. "More like captured. I would have liked to see it."

"My men followed their training well."

"I'm sure they did." There was a sound, as if the magistrate had clapped Marcus on the shoulders.

The older man went on. "We'll keep the beast as I discussed

in my letter. It should be easy enough to lower him in if he's really so cooperative."

Lower him where? I fought the urge to press forward so I could see what was happening.

"We could put him there now, if you wish. But when will the trial begin?"

"Yes, lower him in," the magistrate said. "The sooner the better."

"Since the trial will be held near water, it might be best to keep him there until a decision has been reached. The less we transport him—"

"No need to worry about things like that." There was an edge in the magistrate's voice now.

"The safety of Xantic is my first priority," Marcus said. "And your safety. The more we move him, the more—"

"We won't be moving him until I say so."

"The trial has been delayed?"

The magistrate spoke carefully. "Citizens have rights to a trial. What does this thing look like to you?"

"He's a dragon." Marcus had lost his assured tone.

"Exactly."

"What will you do with him then?"

"I'll let you know when I decide."

That's when I realized what the man was saying. There would be no trial.

I suddenly felt weak. How could I speak for Wil? How could the magistrate learn the truth?

And what role could my father be playing in this?

Above the soldiers' heads, smoke rose into the air. Not the black, toxic smoke that would poison people. It was the kind that let me know Wil was unhappy.

I couldn't stand back any longer. Turning sideways, I squeezed between the two soldiers who stood in front of me.

They looked down, surprised, but they didn't move to stop me. The one in front of them stepped in my path.

I gave him a long look, daring him to make a scene. Marcus had ordered them to keep me hidden. Apprehending me would draw attention. I made it past another soldier, but Adrian was with me, following my trail through the crowd of men.

He caught me by the wrist, and I turned.

"Not yet." He mouthed the words, hardly making a sound.

"I have to," I insisted.

I tugged at Adrian's grip.

He whispered this time. "Do you want to ruin your chances?"

I paused. I had to do something, but that something needed to be effective. Reality sank in.

Currently, I was muddy and worn from travel. A strange, bedraggled girl defending a dragon.

If I interrupted now with a wild story from a wild maiden, the magistrate would think the worst.

Adrian was trying to help.

"At least let me see him," I mouthed back at him.

He grimaced, but we made our way nearer to the front, leaving two rows of men between us and the wagon. I could see Wil's back, and if I crouched a bit and peered between the soldiers' ankles, I had a view of the magistrate's fine leather shoes.

Beyond the magistrate, a metal grate was laid into the ground. With a shuffling of soldiers and a loud scraping, it slid to one side, revealing a dark pit underneath. I couldn't pull my eyes from that pit. Had the magistrate prepared something like this in case they ever caught Edric?

They freed the team of horses, then pushed the wagon closer toward the hole.

Wil was still chained to it, along with the chains that bound his wings and legs. They would have to partially release him in order to lower him down.

I would finally see it. The unlocking.

I crouched even lower and recognized Marcus's tawny legs and hands, though my view of his face was obstructed. He moved behind Wil, closer to me, where the largest lock was fastened. I watched Marcus's hands. Was there a secret pocket? A slot in his helmet for the key?

Slowly, his body stiff, he opened the top of his drinking skin and upturned it. Instead of water, a long iron key fell from the flasket onto Marcus's palm.

I ground my teeth. That drinking skin had never left his side once. It was the place I'd never had a chance to look.

With a smooth click, the lock turned. Wil's restraints wouldn't let him move his legs, though he wasn't tied to the wagon anymore. He turned his neck as far as it would go, scanning the soldiers with his golden eyes until they landed on me. Even crouched, I was visible from his height, where he could see down into the ranks.

There was pain in the look he gave, but also a softness that spoke of gentler times between us. I swallowed past the lump in my throat and tried to send courage in my own expression. Would the magistrate follow the dragon's gaze?

A host of men gathered at the back of the wagon, positioning to lift it. I stifled a cry as they strained to tip the wagon, letting Wil's chained body free-fall into the pit.

There was an awful moment before he hit the bottom.

Then a thud.

Chains rattled, and dust rose up around us from his impact. Everything went silent.

I realized I was supporting myself with a fistful of someone's tunic. It was Adrian's. He had moved close to me, a hand resting on my shoulder. Did he mean to comfort me, or was it a restraint so I wouldn't run to Wil? I let go of his clothing, balancing myself.

Marcus's legs moved back into my view. I stood and raised myself onto my toes, catching his gaze between those in front of me. As soon as he saw me, he looked away.

The magistrate's creaky voice broke the silence, and he sounded pleased. "Rocks don't burn. He could breathe fire all day down there and the city will be safe."

"If you'll allow it," Marcus said respectfully, "I can climb down and remove the restraint over his mouth."

"And get burned yourself?"

"I don't believe he'll try to hurt me. He hasn't so far."

If Wil had wanted to, he could have poisoned everyone by now, chains or no chains.

"Leave it," the magistrate commanded.

"I've promised him a meal of rabbits, which is more than fair under penal treaty. If he's going to eat, I'll need to—"

"I said leave it." The magistrate's tone hardened, and I tensed.

"Yes, sir." There was nothing in Marcus's tone to indicate he had been reprimanded.

"Now, let's discuss arrangements. As always, only half your men can be accommodated in the barracks, so you'll have to make camp or find lodging for the rest. You'll be allotted a generous purse at the treasury for your service. I suggest you see to it before nightfall. And . . ." The magistrate drew out the word. "I hear your cohort picked up an additional companion."

The soldiers in front of me stood a little taller, and I wondered if the magistrate was surveying the men. It was frustrating not to see anything.

"You know we prefer to stay together," Marcus said. "We'll make camp in the usual place until autumn."

"And you'll keep the girl there?" The magistrate clicked

his tongue, chiding. "You must enjoy being the focus of much gossip."

"Of course not. There's lodging for Gilde at a proper boarding house."

"Gilde."

My stomach turned at the sound of my name.

"And where is she now?"

Adrian leaned forward in the slightest motion, then stilled. The soldiers in front of us went rigid.

"She has friends in the city," Marcus said. "She's with them."

I glanced at Adrian. I didn't consider any of these people friends, but Marcus had lied for me to his superior, and that was something.

"We'll discuss the situation further in the morning," the magistrate announced.

There must have been a dismissive gesture, because the soldiers began to move. Adrian shuffled me deeper into the rows of men, and we turned back toward the gate.

At first, they all moved while I stood motionless. I would be left in the open if I didn't join them, but still I couldn't get my legs to work. Gently, Adrian pressed me forward, and I walked to keep from stumbling.

My body moved, but my mind stayed behind, stuck at the pit and the thud Wil's body made against the ground at the bottom.

If Marcus had offered to climb down and loosen Wil's chains, there must be a ladder. Something too small for a dragon to climb, but useful for a human.

Every step I took away from the pit felt wrong, like my body was betraying me, but I would find a way back there during the night.

That would be my proper lodging.

31

OUTSIDE, THE MEN FOLLOWED
the street back the way we came. I let myself be swept along
with them.

There was a lightness in the way they stepped and the
glances they shared with each other now. The dragon had
been delivered, and their job was complete. They were headed
toward tents, and campfires, and roasted chickens purchased
in the city.

People still gathered to watch us, but not as many as when
Wil had been there. Some of the soldiers exchanged greetings
with them. It was evening, and the large buildings cast shadows
over the streets, making it seem later.

Adrian stayed beside me, and his presence forced me to
keep pace with everyone else. A small anchor to the rest.

We passed a narrow alley with a vegetable garden. Adrian
stopped and pulled me aside, his arm linked in mine.

I looked down into his round face. It was somber.

"You're not going to the camp?" I asked.

"We'll wait here for Marcus."

He led me all the way to the back of the little garden where
a shade tree grew. When we stopped, he let go of my arm.

I was with Adrian, but my mind was somewhere else.

I watched the last of the soldiers pass us, then noticed the people on the far side of the street. There was a gray old woman and a young man with yellow hair. A girl my age carried a basket full of radishes.

None of their clothes were as luxurious as the gown I wore, though they were much cleaner.

I had an irrational feeling that I should recognize the people. That there couldn't possibly be so many strange faces in the world.

They chattered to each other and watched the soldiers go down the street. No one looked at me, an unwashed girl sitting in a garden.

All the soldiers passed us by and disappeared from view. A shaggy dog followed after, its little tail raised high as it padded along.

I leaned forward to watch it go.

Adrian followed my line of sight. "If you want people to think you belong here, you'll have to stop staring at dogs like you've never seen one."

"I've seen a dog before. Once."

He shook his head.

I didn't belong here. These people had friends and families that weren't dragons and wizards.

But I did need the magistrate to think the best of me, so I took Adrian's advice and looked away from the dog.

"I can take you to the field tomorrow if you'd like," Adrian offered. "To see the horses, after you have a chance to clean the dragon smell off. I think I've only seen you smile with a real smile once. And it was when you were watching a horse."

I knew the time he was talking about. We were camped, and the horse had rolled on its back in the dust, the way Wil used to sometimes. It looked so free, I had almost forgotten about things like chains and cannons for a moment. I almost forgot about wizards even.

"You told me their names," I said. "But it's still hard to tell them all apart, except for Potato because he's fatter than the others."

"You just need to get to know them."

The street began to empty as the shadows grew. One figure walked down the middle, toward us. Marcus.

He no longer wore his chestplate, and his red-feather helmet was nowhere to be seen. Clean garments had replaced his traveling clothes, and his longsword was gone, though I suspected there would still be a dagger sheathed beneath the hem of his shirt.

I looked him up and down, searching for the most important thing. But his water flasket was missing also.

As he approached, his face brightened. Adrian stood up straight.

Marcus stopped in front of us, and he gestured around, indicating the garden. "Do you like it?"

"Um . . . yes." It was a well-tended little square with shade and a summer berry patch. Isa and I used to have a garden, and it wasn't so different from this one.

But it was hard to think about gardens and horses now. My thoughts were still in that fortress, with the dark pit in the ground.

"I sent word ahead," Marcus told me. "You'll be staying here."

I looked up at the stone house beside us. It was two stories tall, and a breeze rustled white curtains in an open window. In Xantic, they used shutters like our cottage had. There were no glass panes like I saw in the castle.

My eyes were drawn back to the street. Once again, I mentally traced all the steps and turns that had brought me here from Wil's prison. The distance wasn't as far as it could have been.

"Good," I said.

Marcus seemed encouraged. "The proprietor here is a southerner and a friend of the cohort. She'll be discreet about gossip and fair with the price. You'll like her, I think."

"And what is the price?" I asked.

"Nothing for you to worry about."

I could tell Marcus expected his answer to be a comfort. And I should have been grateful. But Isa had married Guntor so someone would take care of her. What did it mean if Marcus paid for me?

I reached up into my sleeve and freed a stolen brooch I had pinned there a lifetime ago. Even after Wil said I could have anything in the castle, I had left the treasures hidden in my gowns. They were already sewn in, and it was a convenient way to carry the wealth on our trek across the mountain.

This particular brooch was an ornate, silver pentagon, set with a sizable green gemstone. It wasn't comfortable to wear.

I held it out to Marcus. "Will this cover the cost?"

His eyes widened when he saw it, then narrowed. "Is that real? It's not glass?"

"Wil said it's called an emerald."

I held it flat on my palm, and Marcus went still for a moment, staring at the gem. Adrian took it, holding the brooch close to his face.

He whistled. "Looks real enough to me."

"Give it back to her," Marcus ordered.

Adrian did, but I extended the brooch to Marcus again. "Take it as payment."

"I can't. With that piece you'd be able to buy a lot more than a few nights in a boarding room. It's wise to keep it hidden."

"You've given me plenty of fish," I said. "And transport on your ship. I owe you, and I'd like to settle."

Marcus reached down to close my fingers over the gem, pressing it away from him. He cradled my fist for too long. "You owe me nothing."

I took his hand and forced the treasure into it. "I want you to have it."

He met my eyes, and I held his gaze.

"Alright." He pinned the brooch to the inside of his collar where no one would see it. "I'm proud to wear it. But when you need it back, it's yours."

"I won't need it back. Our debt is settled."

He didn't know about all the silver buttons in my tattered gown. The silk looked worthless now, but apparently it was worth more than I knew.

I had a question to ask. "Marcus, what can silver buy in the city?"

He pulled out his collar and looked down at the gem again. "That's not just silver. There's craftsmanship to it. This would buy you a whole team of horses, or a year's lease in a townhome."

Was it mined and crafted with magic, like everything in the castle?

"What about freedom?" I asked. "Would there be a price high enough to release Wil?"

Marcus frowned. "Maybe if the magistrate were a different man."

My heart fell a little. "He's wealthy, then?"

"The magistrate of Xantic built his fortune when he was young, leading mercenaries to fight in empire conquests. Barbarians from the north can change the tide of a battle."

Adrian raised his brows and lifted a hand over his head, indicating the height difference between southern Rhufen and my people. The cohort was smaller and swarthier than anyone in the city.

"Then what motivates him, if not money?" I wanted to know.

"Once a man gathers wealth, he has to keep it. Xantic is protected from thieves and armies, but dragons can overcome those defenses. And dragons love gold."

No, wizards loved gold.

"I promise you," I said, "Wil is not interested in the magistrate's treasure."

"It's more than that. He's become a collector of ancient dragon relics. Most of them are fakes, if you ask me. But he talks of the beasts more than he should."

So the only price the magistrate wanted was Wil, and that was the one thing I couldn't part with.

"It's how we ended up in this city," Marcus said. "Our cohort was trained in firepower, and the magistrate used all his favor with the empire to bargain for us."

"You didn't choose to come here?"

"There is little choice in the life of a soldier."

Adrian interjected. "No one bothered to mention before I came that this place freezes over every winter. Almost lost my toes the first season." He wiggled his feet in his sandals and grinned.

Marcus led the way to the front of the house. A little bell rang above the door when it opened, and a woman came to greet us, a broom in her hand. She was small, and her silky black hair was tied into a knot. I wouldn't have called her face beautiful, but I still liked looking at it.

"Marcus." She spoke in the smooth accent of the empire. "This must be Gilde."

He introduced her to me as Cybele, the owner of the boarding house.

"I'm normally more busy than this," she said. "We are one of the first establishments to fill up every winter."

"I'm sure," I responded. "It's lovely."

"Right now, you'll get the big room to yourself." She eyed Marcus, then looked back to me. "You will be by yourself?"

I rushed to answer. "Of course."

"There's a textile merchant traveling through. He's on the second floor with his daughter. I'll put you across the hall."

"Thank you." I gave an awkward little bow of my head.

A merchant and his daughter. I had once been a girl traveling with her father.

Cybele showed us up the stairs to the room. She kept a clean home, with floor tiles scrubbed white.

"There'll be hot rolls for breakfast," she said, then left.

I stood there with Marcus and Adrian, feeling crowded in the hall. Through the open door, I could see the room had a mattress on a wooden frame and a chamber pot on a little table. All the furniture gleamed with polish, and the linens were crisp.

I scraped at the dirt under my nails.

Marcus nodded at me. "We'll come for you at sunrise. Tomorrow, you can stay with Adrian while I meet with the magistrate."

One side of Adrian's smile tilted up. "I hear Potato needs his mane combed."

My eyes flickered over Marcus, looking again for his water flasket.

"If I need you before then, you'll be at the campsite near the river?" I asked. "Outside the city gate?"

Marcus shared a look with Adrian. "Albrecht—the magistrate—informed me that he and his attendants are personally staying at the barracks in the arena. With the dragon. I thought someone else should be there too. So I will now be staying there with a selection of my own men."

This was it. The promise Marcus had made to do what he could for Wil.

And it meant he would be close to where I was. They would be only streets away.

"Thank you."

"Adrian." Marcus kept his eyes on me. "Will you go see if Cybele has any of those rolls ready for us to take?"

"A lady like her probably bakes them fresh in the morning—"

"Go check," Marcus reiterated.

Adrian looked between us. "Ah. Yes."

He headed down the stairs, and then Marcus and I were alone.

His expression grew serious. "Gilde, I know this isn't easy for you, and I want you to know I'll be here for you through it."

I was startled by the intensity in his voice. It matched the warm stares he had given me on our journey. I realized we had never spoken alone together until now.

"You've been kind to me."

It was true, in a way. And he had also taken everything from me.

He seemed to stand straighter, if that were possible. "Finding you was the most interesting thing that has happened to me on tour. Not only did I discover a dragon, but also a maiden who isn't afraid of dragons."

Did he hear himself? I hadn't wanted to be found. And I wasn't as brave as he might think.

There was a pause, and I thought he would leave.

He didn't. "I want to say something to you."

I waited.

"Gilde, you can't blame them for thinking you're enchanted. You're tall and untamed. You could stop a man in his tracks with those gray eyes. They don't know whether to fear you or to want you, but I see past that, to a lost girl underneath."

I opened my mouth, but he stopped me.

"I don't want you to say anything. Not yet. Soon all of this will be over, and you'll have to start your life again. I hope to be part of that life, and to help you find your way. I'm stationed here for at least five more years, and I don't have any attachments in my country."

I needed to say something. "Marcus, I don't think—"

He interrupted a second time. He was used to being listened to. "You're not in a place to discuss this yet. I've said my piece, and I'll wait until the dragon's fate is carried out. Will you do that for me? Wait until then?"

I couldn't speak. What future was he imagining for Wil?

Marcus took my silence as agreement. "It will be over soon."

That's when I knew he wanted Wil to die. Not just out of duty to the magistrate.

"Soon," I agreed.

When Marcus left, I sat on the bed to wait for darkness.

Night came, but it was still too early. Cybele had left a candle on the small table, and I could have lit it with the flint in my bag. Instead, I opened the gauzy curtains and let in the moonlight. My eyes needed to be ready for shadows.

I could have settled under the covers or sought a bath and clean clothes.

But I sat there with my boots still on my feet. My mind circled over everything that had happened and everything that was coming.

There was a task ahead of me.

A left. A right. Another left. Would I recognize the streets in the dark? How many people would be out in the city at night?

There came the sound of footsteps in the hall.

The merchant's room was closer to the stairs than mine, so he had no reason to pass outside my door. A knock came, deafening in the silence. I was startled and stood, but it was probably just Cybele.

"Yes?" I raised my voice.

The door began to open. I hadn't locked the latch.

An image of the ghost came to me. An opening door. A gaping jaw.

"Cybele?" I tried again.

The door swung inward, revealing candlelight, and my breath caught.

I had expected a stranger. Or an almost stranger. But the face that stared back at me now was one of the few in the world I knew.

One of the only faces I had known in childhood.

"Isa."

She wore a plain dress, and her hair was tied back in a thick braid. But Isa didn't need nice things to be lovely. Her eyes shone pale blue and clear, illuminated by candle she held.

Those eyes took me in for a moment, and then burst into tears.

I don't know who moved first, but before I could think, we were holding each other, our arms wrapped tight.

Arms that had held me when I was a child.

You don't ever forget that feeling.

It took a long time for both of us to stop crying, and we wiped tears from each other's cheeks.

Eventually, Isa stepped back and looked into my face. "It's you."

"How did you find me?" my voice was choked. "I had no way of knowing where you were."

Isa gave me a look that was so familiar, it made my heart ache. It was the kind of look she used to give when I asked a stupid question.

"The whole city is talking about the dragon," she said. "And they say a girl came with the fighters. I would have to be a raving idiot not to guess who the girl was. Or at least hope. I've been dodging around to every house I could think of since high noon, asking for you. That southerner downstairs was the most tight-lipped, which clued me in more than anything. She caved when I let a few tears slip, though." She smiled.

There were so many things I had wanted to tell Isa. So many times I wondered if I would see her again. But now that we were here, I just wanted to look at her for a while.

She seemed less thin than I remembered. She never used to

eat after a bad fight with Guntor. And the bruises on her face were gone, replaced by even, rosy skin.

She inspected me too, and her eyes lingered on my forearm where my sleeve ended. I pulled my hand away, but she had seen the red scars where the ghost bit me.

"It was hard to hope," she whispered. "But I couldn't stop." For an instant, I saw pain behind Isa's eyes. Then her smile returned, and she took in a deep breath, blowing it out dramatically. "But here you are, alive and kicking."

"I thought about you every day," I told her. "I didn't know if you were safe, or if Guntor found you . . ."

And then I closed my mouth. Isa didn't know about Guntor, and I would have to be the one to tell her.

"The city isn't the same as before, when I was ten and on my own," she said. "I know the types to avoid, and I found myself a respectable job too." She raised her chin. "I'm a laundress for my rent now."

My heart lifted by a fraction. It was what I had hoped for her. And, at the same time, I mourned that her life with me hadn't been respectable.

"I'm sorry you had to come here alone," I said. "I should have gone with you."

Though I couldn't regret meeting Wil.

Her face went still. "You're alive. But I think there's more to it." Her eyes darted to my scars again. "Guntor never came after me. Then your father's spies disappeared from the city and I . . . I didn't know what was happening." She looked up with a haunted expression. "Did . . . the dragon take you?"

So she suspected the full truth from the beginning. She knew what I had been heading toward.

"Yes." I barely said the word.

Isa seemed to shrink in stature. "How are you alive?" she asked. "And what of the others?"

"Guntor . . ."

Our eyes met, and I shook my head. "He didn't make it."

Her face hardened. "How did it happen?"

"They wanted to steal from the dragon. Guntor climbed inside a tunnel at the dragon's home, and there was poisoned smoke in the air."

Isa went still and quiet.

"I'm sorry," I said.

"Don't be," she said curtly. "I don't know how I feel, but it isn't sad. Not yet."

"However you feel, you have a right to it."

I had learned that in the castle, where I shouldn't have been happy as a prisoner. But I was.

She walked past me into the room, looking around at the rich furniture and the ornamental chamber pot. "So you found a soldier to buy you lodging."

"No." I spoke quickly. "I paid for it myself."

She stopped and faced me. "You have alchemist gold?"

She was worried.

I reached into my other sleeve and located a precious button. I had done a good job of stitching it. It took a strong tug to dislodge. This one was silver and molded into the tiny shape of roses. I handed the button to her.

"I stayed with the dragon well into summer. He . . . gave me things."

She took hold of my wrist gently and pulled up the sleeve. "He gave you scars."

"Not him. A creature in his house. The dragon defended me from it."

Her brow furrowed, and she pulled me over to the mattress, sinking down beside me like she might have done when I was little.

"Gilde, tell me everything."

And so I did. The beginning was the hard part. I had never said aloud the way Father gave me over.

Isa listened without comment while I got through the worst of it. Father was the one who had done something wrong. So why did I feel ashamed?

When I finished that part, she had a question.

"Do you think it was his plan for a long time, to wait until you came of age and make a trade for his freedom? Or did something change?"

But I couldn't give her an answer. "I don't think I ever knew what was in his mind."

"I should tell you, Guntor had a lot of dreams toward the end. He started talking in his sleep about the dragon."

"What did Guntor say?"

"I heard two phrases again and again. I didn't want to believe they were oracle dreams."

I braced myself.

Isa's lip trembled. "Out of the two phrases, the worst one was the most vague."

"You have to tell me."

"He said 'it wants her'."

But that wasn't as bad as I had imagined. It was true. Wil had wanted me from the moment we met on that cliff. We were both discarded creatures. He had kept me, and now I wanted him too.

"Guntor really was an oracle." It was the first time I believed it fully.

And I didn't even know what an oracle was. Some kind of wizardry? Or a spark?

"Of course he was," Isa said. "Didn't I do everything he predicted?"

"But wouldn't he have seen his own death?"

"It's the one thing they can never see." And then she did look sad.

I suspected Isa could hate Guntor and love him at the same time, even now. I knew what that was like.

I went on and told her the rest of the story. About the castle and the ghost. About learning to read. The locket and the boy. Father's return, and everything that happened after.

Almost everything.

I described Wil's goodness, but I felt shy to talk about our moment at the ocean, when I had seen him as more than my dragon friend.

I also didn't tell her about the unguarded fire in the mines. It was too dangerous of a secret to ever be spoken aloud. I told her Wil burned the bottle, but I wouldn't mention the other artifacts he had burned.

"And you saw him change with your own eyes?" Isa stared at me.

"Yes."

She slouched into the soft bed and blew out another breath, disturbing the silken hairs that framed her face. "I remember I warned you once to stay away from men. You went and found the worst one you could have."

My cheeks went hot. I had forgotten how quickly I could get angry at Isa. "He's the best one."

"The worst ones always are."

I didn't want to fight with her. Not now. "You said Guntor kept repeating two phrases. The first one made sense. What was the second?"

Isa wouldn't look at me as she answered. "If it has her, it will drown."

Now all of me went hot, and I repeated the words over in my mind.

I didn't want to hear them, but I needed to.

Anxiety filled me, and I stood. How did oracle dreams work? Could they be changed?

They had to.

"I have somewhere I need to be," I said.

The night had grown deep while we talked.

Isa rose also. "Where? Nothing good happens on the streets in these hours of night. Especially with an alchemist in the city."

"You think my father is in Xantic now?"

"His men have returned, and they don't look well. A sure sign of fresh gold. He isn't welcome in open society, but that won't stop him from sneaking around."

A lump formed in my throat, but I tried not to show it. "If he wants to find me, he can do it easier here, the same way you did. I'm going."

Isa went rigid and her eyes glistened. "It's the same as before."

There was anger in her tone.

"Nothing is the same," I countered. "Wil's in danger."

"You're the same." Her voice cracked. "You're leaving me in order to make someone love you."

I felt her words burn through my whole body.

"Isa, I went to that mountain with Father because I thought he needed me, and I loved him. And yes, I wanted to be loved by him more than anything." The lump in my throat rose higher, and I turned my face away. The scene I had witnessed in the ghost's mouth returned to me. "But you needed me too, and I didn't see that. From the beginning . . . he hit you, and all of us pretended it was normal. But it wasn't, and I should have—"

"No." Isa shook her head, her face white. "You were a child, and I pretended too. I taught you to pretend. I should have left, and I should have taken you before it was too late. I once said you were the thing that kept me with Guntor all those years. The truth is, you were the thing that kept me sane." Her voice hushed. "I never wanted you to give yourself away like I did. And that's exactly what this looks like."

But Wil wasn't Guntor.

"My father used me." I trembled as I spoke. "But I wasn't wrong for loving him. Just because someone exploited that part of me doesn't mean I should destroy it."

"You should."

I could understand why she would say that, but I pictured Wil's face, dusty with freckles. "I can't."

"Do you?" she asked.

"What?"

"Love this dragon?"

Love was the thing I had wanted most. I had even said the words. But did I really know what it was?

I knew one thing. I couldn't let him drown.

I took too long to answer, and Isa got tired of waiting.

"I should offer to go with you this time," she said. "But I don't think you'll accept."

The offer made my heart ache. I had just gotten Isa back, and I didn't want to be alone. But she didn't want to come. Not really. And I couldn't ask her to go against an army with me.

"One person slips through the dark easier than two," I said.

Isa nodded. "If you're successful, you won't be coming back here, will you?"

"We'll have to fly away tonight. But I'll come back when it's safe. I promise."

I didn't know what our lives would look like after that. Could Isa join us?

"And if you're not successful tonight?" she asked.

"I'm not worried for myself."

"And that's the problem."

Our goodbye was different this time. I knew my way back to her now, and she knew I would come. We didn't understand each other, but that didn't matter.

We had shared too much life together to let it matter.

Isa brightened when she described the location of her new home. "In the north quarter. Not the slums. Never there again."

I had never stood up for her to Guntor. Even if she absolved me, that didn't make the past right. But now that I had found my voice, she didn't need me anymore. Neither of us were children.

We hugged, and both held on longer than we ever used to. I would have liked more long hugs like that when I was little. Maybe Isa would have liked them too. We had both known too much coldness.

It would be different in the future. We could make it that way.

"I'll be at home," Isa said. "You can be there too, anytime you want."

It struck me that she had never offered my silver button back to me. It was nestled somewhere in her pockets.

That was the Isa I remembered.

She took her candle to light the way as we descended the stairs into the dark garden, and I saw her eyes dampen again before we parted ways.

With one last squeeze of her hand, I left the warmth of her candle and became a shadow in the street.

32

NO LIGHT SHONE FROM THE
window shutters in the houses. The people inside were asleep,
maybe dreaming about the dragon that had arrived in their city
the day before. For them, the dreams would be nightmares.

More likely, though, the people weren't thinking of the
dragon at all, or the girl who ran through the streets below.
They were in their homes with their families, resting for a day
of work tomorrow. Tonight, the dragon made little difference
to their lives.

Everything looked different than it had during the day, and
I began to doubt my own directions. Had I turned left on the
correct street? But then I saw the temple with its statues, and
I knew where I was.

In the dark, the stone men were too real, their forms exactly
like the soldiers I had come to know. It made me feel a tingling
sensation, as if I were being watched.

The statues stood beside the temple pillars in the exact
same position I remembered from earlier. Casual and pensive.
I padded past, landing on the balls of my feet so my boots
wouldn't clack against the street pavers.

The carvings had been made in service to a trickster god.

That seemed about right. An illusion of humanity without a beating heart.

Wil was the opposite. A human heart that looked indestructible. But he wasn't.

I rounded the corner and spied my destination. It was the only structure where fire burned, flickering in mounted torches outside the front gate. There, a real soldier stood, arms crossed, his back against the wall. Pale hair brushed his shoulders, and his sword was longer than Marcus's. This man belonged to Xantic, not the cohort.

He wasn't looking in my direction, and I melted into the darkness, pressing my body into a crevice between windows. A ledge blocked me from view, but if I leaned forward, I could see the guard.

There was only one, and the gate was already cracked open. Only one guard was needed, because who would dare to steal a dragon from an army in the middle of a city?

But even one guard would be a challenge for me.

I looked up and down the edges of the building, inspecting for loose stones. In the wilds, pebbles were always available. But in the city, everything was cut straight and solid.

Finally, I found what I was looking for a few paces to the right. I crouched and dug my fingernails underneath a dark line in a broken paver, prying a sizable piece away.

My aim had always been good enough to kill a rabbit, but I didn't want to fight anyone tonight.

I stepped back into the alley and threw the paver as hard as I could. It hit its mark over a low wall in an adjacent street. The landing echoed in the stillness, louder than I had anticipated.

Perfect.

The guard straightened, alert. His head tilted toward the sound, and I held my breath, waiting for him to investigate. It would be a short window of time to slip through the gate.

He stood tense. I was poised to run the moment he left.

But he never went.

Eventually, his shoulders relaxed, and he sat against the wall of the fortress again.

I gritted my teeth, and I wanted to let loose a swear word I had heard from the soldiers.

Of course the man had disregarded a random noise down the street. This was a city full of people. Not a marsh or a forest, where a sound like that would mean something more.

I returned to my window crevice to think. Eventually, my legs grew stiff in the cramped space.

I leaned forward to see the guard. He must have been uncomfortable too, because his head now rested against the wall.

His breath slowed, his chest rising and falling.

This was the time for normal people to sleep, even if I couldn't feel tired. Urgency raced through my veins.

I waited. I counted his breaths, timing each one. They grew longer and deeper, and I almost smiled in the dark.

When his eyes had fully closed, I unlaced my boots and tiptoed barefoot from the shadows. I didn't breathe. I even tried not to think too loudly.

Gravel dug into my feet, which had grown soft from wearing such quality shoes.

The worst moment happened when I reached the opening to the gate. The man was close enough to touch the hem of my skirt, and he coughed. I leapt through the door, spinning back to see if I was caught. But the guard was still asleep, his sword glinting in torch light.

I shuddered and moved deeper into the fortress.

I had only made it past one guard, and it wasn't even because of anything I did.

How many more would I encounter? But I couldn't think like that. I would take each step as it came.

If there was a good god, the living water kind, he had to be on my side of things tonight.

Now to find the barracks.

I headed to the back of the fortress, following the hall around the edge rather than cutting through the arena where I would be seen. In my limited experience, bedrooms were always in the back of the house.

The hall was dark, with only an occasional window to let in moonlight between iron bars. After a while, in one patch of light, I spied rows of discarded boots, all lined along the wall in neat rows.

Soldiers' boots—the kind Marcus's men wore.

They never tracked mud into their tents. The barracks would be the same.

I was here.

The magistrate might sleep in his own quarters, but I knew Marcus would be with his people. Always.

The hall ended at a large wooden door. Were there guards on the other side? There had always been soldiers set to watch Wil through the night, but things were different now.

I pressed the door lightly, and it moved.

Inside, open windows let cool night air into an enormous room, casting shadows on beds. There must have been fifty bunks, stacked three levels high in some cases.

Sounds of sleeping men filled the room. Deep snores and heavy breaths.

They wouldn't be disturbed by one figure moving in the dark. Not with this many people together.

Then I saw Marcus.

Asleep in his bed near the door.

I paused. His face was peaceful, the usual lines in his brow smoothed. The blanket only came up to his waist, leaving his chest bare. He was well shaped, and nice to look at, and I didn't like that thought.

He wasn't handsome to me when he was awake. There was always something unsettled behind his eyes, as if he were looking for the next thing to set right. It was a striving.

I thought of all the meals he had brought me. The promises he kept. Now I was stealing from him.

He was good, but the wrong sort of good. And I had to do this.

As I watched him breathe, I wished things could be different between us. Not the way he hoped. But different.

The water flasket hung over his wooden bed post, and one of Marcus's hands was wrapped around the strap.

As gently as I could, I edged the cork from the mouth and slid my finger into the opening. It was as dry as smoke inside, and I felt the tip of something cool and metal.

Marcus remained steady in his slumber.

Out came the key, into the palm of my hand.

The thing I had searched for all this time. The key that meant freedom.

I stood and turned, gripping it tight.

And there stood Adrian. His eyes were not smiling.

I wanted to run. I wanted to shrink under the bed and hide. Had he guessed what I was doing?

Adrian's sharp glance jumped to Marcus's bed, then back to me.

"The key?" He whispered, almost silent.

Why was he being so quiet? If he was on watch, he should wake everyone. There was an intruder.

"I have to." I mouthed back.

We stared at each other, and then something strange happened.

Adrian's lips moved. "I know."

A different kind of shock coursed through me as he stepped aside, clearing a path to the exit.

He followed me out and eased the door closed behind us. Then he stopped, letting me go on without him.

After two steps, I turned. He was watching me with big, round eyes. Was this a trick?

"Why are you helping me?" I still whispered, even with the closed door to muffle the sound.

Adrian shrugged and looked down. "Don't know."

"You do." I should have been running.

He lifted his eyes. "Did you know that most of them have no family? It's how they get assigned out here." His already quiet voice dropped. "But I used to have a mother . . ."

"Used to." I understood terms like that. "I'm sorry."

He shrugged again. "She . . . went mad. I was eight." He crossed his arms over himself. "She's gone now, but I know what madness looks like, and you're not it. You're not a wizard, either, or else you'd know I have a spark. Neither you nor the dragon took an interest."

I inhaled a breath. "What's your spark?"

"How would I know? I'm not of age. And even if I was, there are some things a soul keeps to himself. Before Marcus found me, there were others. Bad men who would have charged a price for me."

"And Marcus stopped that from happening." I knew.

Adrian nodded. "I owe him, and I should have stopped you in there. But if you're not mad and you're not evil, you're probably telling the truth. And that means something bad is happening to someone you care about. It's not in me to keep you from trying to help."

I gripped the key and felt a swell rise in my chest. Isa had warned me about people in the world. But then there were these ones. Hans and Adrian and even Marcus.

The ones who helped.

"Thank you, Adrian." My voice was husky.

"Don't thank me yet," he warned. "There are about twelve men stationed around the dragon pit."

"I'll find a way."

His smile returned, and he shook his head. "You know, I think you actually might. But if Marcus asks, I was relieving myself out the window when you stole that key."

I felt myself smile back. "He won't get a chance to ask me anything. I'll be flying."

Before Adrian could change his mind, I took off down the hall.

I turned the corner and raced through the corridor on my bare feet. Eventually, I paused in the hall and inspected the stolen key. It weighed heavy in my hand. The dark iron had been imprinted with the ugly likeness of a dragon. Wild eyes and flared nostrils. It looked nothing like Wil.

Twelve guards.

Men of Xantic.

And I had nothing but a key and a gown full of valuable buttons. I reached into the bodice of my dress, tugging on an especially precious button. This one was gold—a rare thing in the castle, where gold had been used for more than ornament. Would these little treasures be enough to bribe twelve men in a wealthy city?

I held the button up and it glinted in the dim light between window bars.

A man's voice came from down the hall. "And now she has gold of her own."

I froze.

The man stepped into the moonbeam where I could see his face. High cheekbones, dark hair trimmed neat. Plain brown clothing without embroidery or a collar, worn for utility.

A wizard. An alchemist. My father.

33

THE GOLDEN BUTTON FELL FROM

my fingers and clinked against the floor, bouncing toward
Father and then landing.

He bent to pick it up, and then he came close, holding the
button out to me.

My heart raced, and I couldn't move. I couldn't look away
from his face, which was dangerously still. It was my old habit,
always watching for undercurrents.

I had expected to see him at every turn in Xantic. Now that
it was really happening, I still wasn't prepared.

When I didn't take the button, Father reached into his
pocket and pulled something else out, adding it to his offering.

I looked down.

It was the ribbon from my dress. The one I had written his
signature on. It was faded now, and even dirtier than it had
been when I tore it loose in the castle tower.

My hands moved, though I didn't remember telling them to.
There was no magic in this obedience. It was learned. I took
the treasures from him and held them in my palm, not feeling
the weight.

"The bottle," he said. "You broke it?"

The sound of his voice returned so many memories, but

they felt like days from a different life. A different me. So why was I lowering my gaze? I looked up.

"Yes."

His jaw went tight with anger. It was like nothing had changed for him, even after everything that happened.

He held back. "I will forgive it."

But I hadn't asked for forgiveness. I looked past him into the black hall. I used to have so many questions for the man in front of me. Things I wanted to know. But now, I wanted to be somewhere else. Anywhere else.

"I need to go." I took a step to move around him, but he blocked my way.

"You wouldn't have given me that scrap of your dress if you didn't want me to find you." He reached out and grasped at the dirty ribbon I held.

"I wanted to save you from grieving." The words spilled from my lips, a raw edge to them.

He said nothing.

There was a little shake in my voice. "But I don't think you have ever grieved."

Something flashed across his face, marring his confidence like a crack in a paver.

"I hoped you were alive." His voice was low, rough.

That break in his surface threatened the defenses I had built up around my heart. The stones that kept me safe from anger.

Once, I had been a survivor, alone on a mountain with a beast. Then I was a student, learning a softness I had never known. Now I was a girl with her father again, and I was torn open.

"You were supposed to keep me alive." I couldn't stop my chin from trembling.

"And you are—"

But I hadn't said everything yet. "You knew what you were going to do for years before it happened."

He fixed me with a steady look, standing firm against my accusation.

My whole face heated. "Even once–just one time–did you try to think of another way?"

It was a foolish question. He couldn't have an answer that would make things better, but I still wanted one.

His mouth made a thin line before he spoke. "There was never going to be another way to kill the dragon. Guntor saw it, and he wasn't wrong."

That hurt worse than I had imagined.

"There were ten different ways to survive," I said. "We could have stayed in the marsh. You could have gathered an army."

I was still pretending that things were the way I had once believed them to be. That he wasn't a wizard with blood on his hands, and we weren't a tainted family. That I had been happy.

"Guntor was never wrong," he repeated. "But he never saw your death. So I always knew there was a chance for you if you were strong enough. I made sure you were strong, and I never went easy on you."

He never did.

"Did Guntor see me alive in his vision?" I demanded.

"You've always been full of questions." He was growing impatient, and that meant the answer was no.

But now I knew things he didn't.

"You weren't hunted anymore," I said. "Did you know that? The dragon with the grudge is gone, and this one didn't know you existed until you went to his mountain. Why do you think you were able to leave the marsh finally?"

"He told you that?"

"Would the dragon you knew have kept me alive?" I asked.

His mind worked behind his eyes.

He spoke. "It was the only way, no matter what you claim."

"How many did you have to kill to fill your bottle?" I demanded. "Now that you're free to hunt for sparks?"

He gritted his teeth. "So you knew what it cost me, and still you took it."

I was horrified to hear it from his lips.

I might have had the same fate if he had traded me to Edric instead of Wil. I didn't have a real spark, or else I would have used it to save Wil. Or maybe my spark was broken. But Father didn't know that.

He hadn't kept me hidden in the marsh because I was hunted. He had kept me as a buried treasure, until it was time to use me.

"Even after you were free, you wouldn't give up," I said. "Did you really hate the dragon so much? Why?"

These were questions I could never ask before. Part of my history that was blank. But I wasn't afraid to lose his love anymore.

And he knew it.

He answered. "People like me live more than one lifetime, but we never forget the first one. The first time someone you knew died, and you realized you would die too."

What memories lay in his past? My grandmother? My grandfather? People he had never spoken of.

"Who was it?" I asked.

But he ignored that question. "People like me stop death from happening to us. And the longer you live, the more you see there's limited power in this world. Bits and fragments that only a few have the wits to recognize. The dragon and I wanted the same bits for years. Lifetimes. He was a man once."

"I know." My stomach churned. The bits and fragments were people's lives.

Father's look sharpened. "And now you tell me someone else has dragon fire. After all this time."

"It's not what you think it is. It destroys you."

Wil had already tried to explain it to Father.

He laughed. "Tell me, what price would you pay to stop

your skin from sagging off your bones? To stop your vision from fading and your mouth from becoming a decayed and sucking hole? Without a cost, your body goes into the ground, and worms tear away your flesh until you're nothing but dirt. If any unseen part of you carries on, it's a haunted existence. Your soul is punished for just wanting to live."

This was the most I had ever heard Father talk, and the words dripped with the same black as the ghost's teeth. I didn't know what death would be like, but I knew aging wasn't what he described. Hans and Petra sagged and faded, but there was a sweetness in it. A bond between them and a beauty to the lines in their skin.

I had hardly moved since Father approached me, a rabbit in a snare. But my eyes darted past him now, toward the hallway where I wanted to run.

He noticed.

Father snatched the ribbon from my frozen hands. It felt like a slap, and I shrank back.

"I gave you everything." His voice was sharp. "Life and breath. But you've lived seventeen short years, and you think you're justified to hate me now."

"No." As I said it, I found it was true. "I don't hate you. But I can't live your way."

If there was a potion that would turn him into the father I used to think he was, I would have given it to him. At one point, I might have taken it myself so I could go back to believing. I would never stop wishing he could be that man.

"I kept you safe all those years," he said. "Do you know what happens in the world to girls like you who aren't protected?"

But he was the one I was afraid of. He had protected me from friendship and learning and love.

"I have to go."

Father's jaw tensed.

I was disobeying. I was hurting him. Things I used to consider the worst transgressions.

The way he saw me was upside-down and twisted, and I knew that now, but it still dug knives into my heart.

He could stop me from leaving. He had done it a hundred times before, strong fingers digging into my skin. He had done it for lesser reasons than this.

I took a step toward the shadowed hall, closing my eyes and bracing myself. I heard him move to intercept my path, but pain didn't come. Instead, he took my hand, almost gently.

Startled, my eyes flew open.

And that's when he slid the key out of my grasp.

My hands went after his, but he was too quick. He had always been faster than me.

"Give it back," I hissed.

He held the key high, above where I could reach. "Unfortunately, I need to make sure you don't leave here with this particular key. Why do you think I've been following you?"

Now was not the time to argue. It wasn't time to submit or to wait. He couldn't have that key. I wouldn't let it happen.

So I threw my body into his as hard as I could and used my fists to hit his arm. He staggered a half-step.

The key fell to the floor.

For the briefest flicker, I met his eyes. Dark, like mine. Did mine ever hold that bitter edge?

Then we were both after the key. Or, at least I was. Father went after me. He grabbed a fistful of my hair with one hand, and with the other, he found the nerve in my forearm and pressed down until it took my breath away.

I tried to pull free.

"Let go." I had never said those words to him before.

He dragged me down by my hair, until my face was against the ground. Stone grit dug into my cheek.

I could see the key, and I reached out a hand toward it, but Father's boot pinned my fingers to the floor.

Why did he want it? I couldn't think of any reason he would unchain a dragon, unless Wil was dead.

My heart had been weak. There was never anything wrong with my voice.

I took a deep breath and screamed as loud as I could.

I expected Father to try to quiet me. We were both sneaking around in a fortress full of soldiers. As far as they would know, he had stolen that key from Marcus. But he held me steady, as if I had made no sound.

When I stopped to take another breath, he bent to my ear.

"So be it."

I screamed again.

Running footsteps pounded on stone. Soldiers' boots. But the sound came from the wrong direction.

It wasn't the cohort who rounded the corner and swarmed us in the hall. Dozens of Xantic's men reached us, crowding in, and then I heard a crackly voice I recognized from yesterday.

The magistrate.

He stood in front of his men, and now that I could get a good look at him, I saw he was younger than I had thought from afar in the arena. His white beard aged him, but his frame was still firm and muscled. Even dressed in a sleep shirt, he carried an air of authority.

He addressed Father, "I told you not to come here."

Father didn't loosen his grip on my hair, or his foot on my hand.

"I know what you told me," he said.

"I should kill you now." The magistrate's words snapped. And his men tensed.

"Like you killed me last time?" Father asked.

How could he speak like that to a man who had him surrounded by soldiers?

Father's tone darkened. "I came back. I'll always come back."

To my surprise, the magistrate didn't make a move, and the soldiers seemed to relax. "Why did you come today?"

"There were circumstances I needed to address."

I was the circumstance.

The magistrate's eyes raked over me. "This is the dragon girl?"

The way he said it made me want to protest, but what could I deny?

"Yes," Father answered.

No further explanation. No defense.

The magistrate spotted the dragon key on the ground, inches from my fingers. He picked it up, and I almost sobbed as it moved further from me.

That was when Marcus pushed his way through the circle of men. There I was, pressed against the floor, reaching for a key I shouldn't have had.

"What is this?" Marcus demanded.

The magistrate held up the key. "I believe it's yours."

Marcus's eyes narrowed on the little piece of iron, but he didn't reach to take it.

The magistrate sighed. "I'm going to give you the benefit of the doubt and assume you didn't mean to part with it tonight."

"No, sir. I did not."

I twisted against Father's grip to look up at Marcus, and he met my eyes. There were questions in his, and I expected to see anger. Instead, something in him deflated.

"Apprehend her." The magistrate spoke to one of his guards.

Father's foot moved from my hand, and I was hoisted to my feet by a rough grip. The guard pulled at me, and I stumbled into a group of the men.

Marcus stepped forward, but then stopped himself.

"Be careful." He spoke to the men who held me.

"She's a thief," Father stated.

"She's still a maiden. I don't care what else she might be."

But Marcus did care. He wouldn't look at me again.

"It's late." the magistrate made a point of sounding tired.

"Take her to a cell so we can get some peace."

The guards on either side of me gripped my arms tighter, pulling me through the gathering of men. Their hands would leave bruises. Marcus moved to follow.

"Where are you going, Prefect?" the magistrate asked.

"I'll escort them."

"No." He handed the key to Marcus, and I felt a stone settle in my stomach. "You'll put this back where it belongs. And you'll be more vigilant from now on."

The men dragged me further. They weren't fast, but they jostled me up and down so it was difficult to keep my footing.

I squinted to look back, and saw Marcus take the key.

I wanted to call out to him, but I had lost that right when I became a thief. Adrian was nowhere in sight, but I wouldn't have spoken to him if he was.

I was alone. Captured.

And out of ideas.

If there was an unseen god, and he wasn't on my side, how could he be good?

Father was following me and the guards. The magistrate yelled after him.

"Alchemist, I expect you to leave here tonight. Do not return until it's time, and after that, I never want to see you again."

I felt everyone's eyes on us until we rounded the corner in the hall. Father drew closer.

"You shouldn't have screamed. You made it worse for yourself."

I tried to walk with as much dignity as I could, despite the human vices wrapped around both my arms. The guards said nothing, keeping their eyes forward.

"At least you don't have the key now," I said.

"Ah, but I never said I wanted it. I just didn't want you to have it."

Something like despair threatened to rise up in me.

"Why did the magistrate tell you to come back when it's time? What did he mean?"

Father smiled. "We've made a deal."

The guards jostled me, and a sharp pain ran through my arm. We started down a set of damp steps, away from the windows. The rough stone scraped my bare feet, and torches burned to light the way.

"What kind of deal?" I needed to know.

"Wealthy men like him don't like my gold. It devalues theirs. He'd like to keep me out of the city, and I'll leave without bloodshed. For a price."

My body chilled with cold sweat. I looked at Father, and he already knew what I wanted.

"The dragon's body," he said. "I was the one who helped the soldiers find him, vulnerable outside his castle." There was satisfaction in his voice. "It was a simple tracking spell to locate you, and then we cast a message to a nearby fisherman. The magistrate stayed out of the magic, but he gave me his code word. Tomorrow night, the beast drowns. Of course, the magistrate will want to keep a piece or two as a trophy."

I stopped walking for a moment, then went on.

"You'll never be able to drink water again," I said. "But you'll always be thirsty."

It was the only thing I could think of, and I knew it wasn't enough.

"That's all of life," he growled. "Always hungry, never full."

I thought of my time with Wil, tucked away in the library. Our shared moment on the shoreline when he was a man. My heart had been full.

I thought of Petra and Hans. Their shared cottage, their children and grandchildren. They were full.

"Life doesn't have to be that way." My words were choked. "I gave up believing in stories more than a lifetime ago. You should too."

One of the guards swung open a door with iron bars. Firelight flickered on discolored stone, and the air was chilled. They shoved me through and closed the door behind me, locking the handle.

"I hope to see you again someday." Father rested a hand on the bars.

Now that I had been with other people, I saw him more clearly. There was something tired behind the young eyes. Like his mind had gone on too long, whether his body aged or not.

"I hope you never get what you want," I replied. "For my sake, and for yours."

His face hardened, and he followed the guards back up the stairs. I watched through the bars, and he never turned back.

34

THERE WAS ONLY ONE PLACE
to sit—a stone shelf at the back of the cell. Mildew grew on the
surface, and it left slimy residue on my finger when I touched it.

I remained standing and paced. Back and forth, faster
and faster.

I wanted to walk out of the cell and into the arena. But that
wasn't possible, so I settled for walking in circles. My feet grew
icy against cold floor tiles.

The sun might have risen already, but there was no way
to tell from inside the cell. I never wanted to be underground
again. This was just another cavern.

Whether I could see it or not, time passed. The sun would
reach its peak and start to fall. Then it would be night. The
night when Father expected payment from the magistrate.

I walked faster.

Footsteps sounded on the stairs, and I rushed to the bars
to see. The magistrate descended, flanked by two men. One of
them I recognized. He had forced me to this prison by my left
arm. He smelled better than the one on the right.

The other guard I didn't recognize. Not that it mattered.

I took a step back from the door, out of reach, and waited
for the magistrate to come. Hidden for a brief moment, I

straightened my dress and tried to put on a pleasant expression. The kind that looked obedient, no matter how I felt in my heart.

The magistrate came into view, inches from the bars now. His expression was impassive.

I had to force myself to blink.

"You're the girl who came here with the cohort?" He examined my bare feet and strange attire.

"Yes." It felt like I was admitting to something.

The barest smile came to his mouth, then disappeared. "I've had enough of wizards and enchantments in my city."

"I'm not a wizard, but I'd be happy to leave if you unlock the door."

He shook his head and eyed me again. "I won't have you stealing from me anymore."

I kept my stance demure.

He sighed. "I'll have to keep you here for now, until I know if what they say about you is true. I wanted to see you again for myself."

I moved closer to the bars. "You're wondering if the dragon can control people with magic."

He lowered his voice. "Yes."

"I'm not enchanted—"

"What else can I think?" But his tone didn't invite an explanation.

I would give him one anyway. "This dragon is named Wil and he's not the one who committed the crimes. He's a young man under a curse. I can't prove it right now, but if—"

"Exactly," the magistrate interrupted. "You can't prove it. You want me to let a beast go and then face the families of the people who went missing into the mountains. This is a city who lost daughters and sons."

I clung to the bars between us. "I promise Wil didn't hurt anyone. He didn't take any children."

His expression flinched at the word children, unfocused for

the briefest moment. It was barely noticeable, but I saw it, and I wondered at the magistrate's own story.

His vision cleared again. "Your arguments are proof he's controlling you."

My heart fell. "Please—"

"If your curse doesn't lift tonight when he breathes his last, I'll have to lock you up again. I can't have humans in my city fighting on behalf of demons." He turned to the guards. "Bring her up to witness the execution. If his death won't set her free, I don't know what can."

He strode back toward the stairs.

"Wait!" I called. "You can't give the alchemist Wil's body."

There was a pause in the footsteps.

"The wizard can have his flesh," the magistrate said. "I'm keeping the horns."

"No! He'll become a dragon. You'll never have peace in Xantic again."

But he and the men were already gone. The torch light flickered against the dark walls.

A sob ran through me, and then I collapsed in on myself. When my tears subsided and I could breathe more evenly, I straightened, holding onto one fact.

When it was time, the guards would bring me up.

I would be near Wil.

If he knew what my father was planning, he might use his fire to break free. It could kill soldiers, but I didn't want to think of that. It would save everyone from a worse beast than they could imagine. It would save lives, so there had to be a way.

I had to tell him. The tears came again.

I sat in the mildew and cried until my mouth was cotton and my eyes were swollen. Wil would never forgive himself if he had to harm anyone.

Sooner than I hoped, the guards came. They treated me the same as before, as if I might break free at any minute. As if I weren't a slight girl who was exhausted and thirsty.

"Can I look for my boots?" I asked. "I left them at the gate." But the men kept their eyes forward and ignored me.

We trudged up the stairs and left the fortress. My eyes smarted in the daylight, and the streets scuffed my feet. A few people watched and whispered to each other as I passed. I looked at all their faces, wishing to see Isa.

The guards led me through the city gates.

Outside the walls, crowds had gathered in the fields beside the river Rijn. I didn't know if there were hundreds or thousands of people. Had all of Xantic come to watch?

Wind blew against my face, and I caught a hint of dragon stench. They had moved Wil out here. He would be chained beyond the crowd.

The roar of water and the sounds of people combined to make an overwhelming hum. Now, in the soft grass, I quickened my steps, and the guards moved with me, pressing through the gathering.

Children ran among the people. Why would children come to something like this? They were too young to see death. But then I realized that for them, it was the end of a beast. Something to celebrate. People smiled and greeted each other. Some ate meals that had been packed in cloth hampers.

My mind raced. How many might Wil have to harm if he used his fire? Could he target only the soldiers of Xantic? Even they were husbands and fathers, though.

Then I saw him in the distance, and my heart fell.

He was a long way downriver from where the people gathered. One wingtip and flank trailed in the water, and even from such a distance, I could see a hint of white char on his scales.

Did they think he couldn't feel pain? Or did they wish more suffering on him? Tears blurred my vision, but I blinked them away. I needed to see everything.

Chains glinted all over his body. It was hard to tell from so far away, but it seemed like more than before. There were thin lines of rope attached, and they extended into the waters of the river. I could barely make out the rows of men that lined the shore on the other side, ready to drag him in. Was Marcus among them? Was Adrian?

Beside Wil, I recognized the silhouette of a cannon. The soldier who manned it would die if the dragon decided to blow toxic smoke.

He could burn the ropes and keep everyone away. But he couldn't fly or walk with those chains around him. After enough death, they might unchain him. Or they might hold my life as a ransom. I couldn't let that happen. There were already too many impossible choices ahead of Wil.

Every step forward closed the distance between us. It shrank the time until I would speak and he would hear, and that would change everything.

But then the soldiers who held me stopped.

We were only a few paces in front of the crowd. Wil was still too far away.

The guards forced me to my knees beside a boulder slab with a chain wrapped around its base.

"No." I tried to struggle against their grip, which only bruised me more.

A third man came and latched manacles around my

ankles. The sun-heated metal burned my skin and dug into my ankle bones.

I looked up at the man. "Can you move me closer? I need to speak with him . . . one last time." Tears streamed from my eyes.

He turned to the others. "They weren't making it up. Her mind's gone."

And they left me.

I stood and moved to the end of my chain, stumbling and catching myself in grass and mud. On the ground, I clawed at the manacle, and it broke the nail on my index finger below the quick. I bled, but Wil wouldn't smell one drop among all these humans.

I regained my feet. "Wil!"

The river and the crowd kept up their rumble. My voice was too small. Wil's distant form didn't move or acknowledge my shout. Did he even know I was here?

I waved my hands, and he lifted his head. He had enhanced sight, but I was too far out of range for his hearing.

"*The wizard is coming for you!*" The bellow hurt my throat.

The people near me backed away and shot dark glances in my direction. Their murmurings grew.

Wil put his snout in the air, and it looked like he might be trying to call out to me, but I heard nothing.

He saw me and knew I was unharmed. He wouldn't fight for his own life.

I turned to a woman in the crowd who stood closest to me. "How long until it happens?"

She took in my wild state, then shrank away into the arms of a man beside her.

"Please." I raised my cracking voice so more people could hear. "An innocent man is about to die."

No one answered me. They looked away, as if the sight of me were shameful. I wiped my damp face on my sleeve.

A boy much younger than Adrian held onto the woman's

crisp, linen skirt. He was a lovely child, with dark hair and milky skin.

He pulled on the hem until she looked down.

"Is that the girl the dragon hurt?"

The woman's face went tight, and she picked up the boy. The family moved further into the crowd.

Good.

They shouldn't have been out here. None of them.

My eyes went back to Wil. Even if I could get a message to him somehow, there would be death. There was no way out of this without someone's death.

I pulled at the edge of my tether, metal biting into my legs.

If only Wil could be a man for the briefest minute. If they could see his sunshine curls and his honest face.

I wished for the barest sliver of embergold, and fire of my own. But even embergold meant someone had died.

I wished for a hundred different things. A way out. But wishes wouldn't help me now. I needed something real.

All the stories had turned out to be true. Treasures in mountain caves.

Ghosts.

And then the eerie words came back to me. The ones I hadn't thought of since that day in the castle.

I see things. And I hear things. If you ever need a wish, call for me.

I hadn't been desperate enough to think of them again. Not until now.

My body chilled. Wil said a wish from the ghost would harm me. But there was no way out of this without harm.

I closed my eyes and saw black jaws. I paced back and forth and counted my breaths. This idea didn't feel like hope. It felt like dread.

But I couldn't stop myself.

Everyone here already thought I was insane, so I raised my voice. "Ghost, I need you."

Did he have a name? How would he hear me?

I took a breath and tried louder. "Ghost! I'm ready to claim my wish. You owe me."

The crowd seemed to give me even more space.

My body was exhausted, and I had no more tears to cry. Part of me wanted to sit in the grass and stop thinking for a while.

Instead, I tried again. "Ghost, you made me a promise. If it weren't for me, you'd still be starving in that room. You said you'd hear me if I asked—"

My words caught in my throat.

"I'm happy to keep my promise . . ." a syrupy voice spoke, though I couldn't tell where it came from.

It was here.

I had done it.

Out of the corner of my eye, I saw the flicker of a translucent man standing beside me. I spun, but when I looked directly at it, it disappeared. Only when I glanced sideways could I see the outline.

No one in the crowd seemed to notice.

My whole body tensed. The air felt wrong, and the figure breathed in a way that made me want to get away from it.

"I'm here now." It sounded too eager. "I can free you from your chains. Would you like that?"

I imagined myself with severed legs. Free, but dying. Was I really going to do this?

I spoke low now. "What would you do if I asked you to unlock the dragon's chains . . . secretly . . . and make sure we were both unharmed?"

"That's three wishes. Possibly four. You have to choose just one."

"I'm not making a wish yet," I informed him. "I just want to know how you would do it. Do you really have the power?"

"I can do many things."

"But if I wished for you to unlock the dragon's chains?"

There was an oily smile in its voice. "I said I would give you a wish. Not any wish."

Was he trying to trick me? "What does that mean?"

"I'm not going near the dragon. I'll help you, but not at my own expense. I can separate you from those shackles . . ."

Even if I got loose from my chains, I would have to make it past soldiers to speak with Wil.

But there was another idea forming in my mind.

"Embergold," I ventured. "Can you bring me embergold?"

The ghost let out a dry laugh. "You think something like that is just lying around? I'd have to find a wizard. Not a wise decision for someone like me. Wizards have a history of trapping and using my kind."

If Wil fought, dozens might be hurt. If he didn't, there would be another dragon on the mountain, and even more people would come to harm. But there was a way where only one person would be injured.

And it was a wish that the ghost couldn't corrupt. Because it was already grim.

"Can you bring me fire . . ." My voice faltered. I took a breath. "From the mine under the dragon's castle?"

I was completely still, waiting for his reply.

"Oh." The ghost's voice was honey and poison. "Oh, that is an interesting wish. Will you burn a treasure with those flames? For the sake of the dragon?"

I swallowed the bitter taste rising in my throat. "Yes."

"Hmmm. It would take me some time. I travel faster than most, but I can't get there and back in a blink."

"Would it be fast enough?"

"Yes. I think so, though I can't guarantee anything. Is this your wish? I need you to say it."

"Yes." It was a hoarse whisper.

"Say the words," he coaxed. "I wish for you to bring me fire from the dragon's mine."

I repeated the phrase exactly, and then added on my own clause.

"And I wish for you to never reveal the fire to anyone else again." It had to be kept away from the wizards of the world. Away from my father.

"Ahh," the ghost said. "That is two wishes. But I don't have any love for wizards, and that's what the fire creates. You couldn't force me to give it to anyone who wants to consume it. But you want it to consume you. And that I will happily do. Both your wishes are acceptable."

He paused, as if waiting for thanks.

"Go," I said.

"Between you and me, I hoped you'd come to this conclusion."

Then his flickering outline disappeared, and I collapsed into the grass. What was I doing?

35

WIL RESTED HIS HEAD ON THE ground. I knew he wasn't sick anymore, only resigned.

My mind filled with questions again. Why hadn't I been more specific with the ghost? What did fast enough mean? When was the execution happening?

The sun neared the horizon, threatening to touch the green hills beyond the river.

I tried not to think, but my mind centered on the task ahead.

If I somehow had a spark, then I was like embergold. Wil had said once that the fire consumed what it burned. What part of myself would I give? What would be enough to transform him back into a human?

I didn't even know if it would work, but it was all I had.

I filled my vision with Wil and remembered him with eyebrows and eyelashes and stubble on his face.

There were hundreds of voices behind me, but one startled me by using my name.

"Gilde."

I shifted and saw an elderly woman behind me.

Petra. Her eyes and mouth looked even more wrinkled than I remembered, if that were possible. What was she doing here?

I stood, clumsy in the manacles. "I thought you would be on the coast with your granddaughter."

In truth, I had thought I would never see her again.

Petra set down her basket and surprised me with an embrace. She was so short, the top of her head barely grazed the underside of my chin. The hug ended almost as soon as it had begun, but she kept her knobby hands on my waist and peered up into my eyes.

"We hoped it was you they were talking about." She looked down at my chain and let me go. "Not that I like to see you this way, but it's a better fate than we thought you might find."

I searched the crowd. "Where is Hans?"

"Twisted his ankle on the way down the mountain. It took us forever to make it this far, and now he's healing up at an inn. We'll have to winter in Xantic before we head on."

I should have been glad to see her. Part of me was. But I didn't have much time left, and I couldn't do what I needed to in front of her.

I thought of sending her to Wil. Maybe an elder would be able to get past the soldiers and pass a message. But then Wil would have to burn them all.

No. There was only one way.

"Are you here for the execution?" I asked.

As an answer, Petra opened the flap at the top of her basket. "I'm here to see if you're hungry." She pulled out a bundle.

"Thank you, Petra." I tried a weak smile.

My stomach felt sick, and I couldn't imagine eating, but the intention behind that bundle of food strengthened me in a way I hadn't known it could.

"You look terrible. Here." She handed me a soft bread roll with nuts baked on the top.

Petra watched me as I took it. "They say you'll probably be released after tonight."

If I denied Wil. If I betrayed my dragon.

"Do you know what time it's supposed to happen?" I tipped my head in Wil's direction.

"Sunset."

Any time now.

She grimaced. "We went straight to the magistrate when we heard about everything. Gave our testimony to the councilman. But I don't think it did any good." She glanced at Wil. "I thought . . ." She cleared her throat. "Well, Hans didn't want you to be alone when it happens. We know how you feel about the creature."

My throat tightened. "That was kind of Hans. It's hard to explain, but the two of you were some of the first people I've met out in the world, and I couldn't have asked for better."

She stood a little taller. "Decent folks don't approve of locking up girls like this. That's all."

"That's more than decent." I had thought all my tears were used up, but they filled my eyes again. "Petra . . . I can't eat this bread."

She dug through her basket, ignoring me. "I think there's cheese in here too—"

I reached out and caught her wrist gently. "I need water. I haven't had any in days. Could you get some and come back in a while?"

"I have milk."

"No." There was desperation in my voice now. "It has to be water. I'll see you again . . . after it's over. It would be better to talk then."

She looked again at Wil and then gazed up at me. Her mouth thinned and she gave a short nod. "I'll find you after. You can count on that."

She left me beside the boulder, waddling in her stiff way toward the crowd. People gave her space as she passed. She was tainted now, because of me.

I watched her go, and I wondered if she understood what

she had done for me. A person out of this crowd had risked their reputation to bring me a meal. I was separate from the people, but no longer alone.

The sun touched the hills as I sat on the ground with the boulder between me and everyone else. "Ghost, where are you?"

I hoped for his sickly glimmer. It didn't come.

The crowd began to quiet. My heart quickened, and I moved to stand at the edge of my chain. The air was still, and soon all the voices completely died away, leaving only the sound of the river.

A faint shout came from Wil's direction. A soldier's voice, though I couldn't make out what he said.

The men on the far shore began to pull their ropes. It took half an army to heave Wil's chained body into the river.

"*No!*" My scream split the silence.

It wasn't supposed to happen yet. I needed more time.

Wil sank into the water until only his head was visible, and white steam rose in a cloud. I smelled it from where I stood. That scent I used to hate.

The men pulled harder.

Water rushed over him. The same water flowed beside me, all the way down to the place where Wil was dying. I couldn't build a wall of sand this time. I couldn't do anything.

Wil's head slipped beneath the surface until only his snout showed. I screamed again. I couldn't feel anything in my body. Not the ground under my feet. Not the manacles on my legs. All I could do was watch.

It was almost over. The ghost hadn't paid his debt to me. He probably never intended to. He was the kind of thing that enjoyed the suffering of others.

But then the air around me shifted, and a glimmer appeared. A flickering that only I could see. Except one thing was bright and present.

Fire.

It rippled over the end of a branch, eating away at the wood with a dark hunger. Metallic smoke drifted into the air.

People saw it, but I didn't care.

"Give it to me!" I stretched my arms as far as I could, but the ghost was outside my reach.

He laughed. "You're sure you want—"

"Yes!" The word tore from me. "Now," I begged.

Wil's snout still protruded from the water, a speck in my vision. The tip of his tail had made its way to the surface also. If he could breathe, would the water still kill him?

"You're willing to die for him," the ghost said. "Why shouldn't he die for you?"

"I can survive this."

I had decided to burn the skin on my forearm. If I lost a leg, I wouldn't be able to walk. An arm was farthest from my face and my lungs.

"But would he do the same for you if he had the choice?"

The ghost solidified, and his worst details came into focus. Long, dirty nails grew from his fingers. His jaw opened wide, and I saw the black substance that coated his pointed teeth. The poison that had almost killed me.

As I looked into the black, images appeared in my mind. I didn't see Isa this time.

I saw myself brandishing a knife to protect my father from a dragon. Then I saw him walk away as I was taken.

The next image was me falling into a smoky hole, a golden bottle in my hand. I had fought to save Wil. Then the image changed. We were in the cave with the spring, and Wil left me alone. I was shameful and he couldn't be near me.

I saw him become the dragon, and the soldiers chain him. His fire returned, and he wouldn't fight to set us free.

Next, I saw Isa pocketing the button I had shown her.

I gave and gave, and everyone else took.

"You see?" the ghost asked. "I've brought you the fire, but you don't have to use it."

When he spoke, his jaw closed, and the trance broke. My mind was my own again.

Those images had been real. The message was a lie.

Wil had given me more than I could measure.

He would die to keep from hurting the soldiers. His enemies. What more would he do for me? Wil's voice came to me at my own bidding, a memory.

I'm scared of what I might do with my fire. If you were in danger, Gilde, I'd do anything.

He couldn't help me now. His snout still fought for breath in the distance.

This was my choice. I was chained, but more free than I had ever been.

Love couldn't be demanded or coerced, only given. This was the right kind of sacrifice.

The ghost still held back. He was stalling. Did he hope that Wil would die and I would still be burned? Two victories in one.

"Now." I demanded. "Give me the fire now."

"But—"

"It's my wish and it has to be now."

The thing grinned, showing an unnatural amount of teeth. "As you wish."

And it threw the fire at me, a flaming projectile.

36

I CAUGHT THE BRANCH IN MY
hands, but the flames touched my skirt. Instantly, the cloth
ignited, and the fire grew.

Smoke engulfed me.

People shouted, but I barely heard them.

I beat the skirt to put it out, but then my sleeve caught fire,
and pain seared my arm.

It was what I had wanted. But not like this.

I had thought it would be a controlled burn, but this fire had
a mind. I could feel it. It wanted to consume.

I stole a glance downriver.

Before I could locate Wil, the fire got through to my leg, and
I let out a cry. I fell to the grass and rolled.

I tore at mud and flung it onto my dress.

Nothing worked. The fire continued to eat away at the silk,
and then at me. I gasped against the pain and threw myself into
the dirt. When would it have enough?

The burn spread up my arm to my shoulder, and I smelled
my hair catch fire.

Then a loud noise rang out beside me. I squinted through
streaming tears and saw Isadora heaving a stone against
the chain.

Had she been watching me?

The stone wouldn't work. The shackles were built by dragon fighters.

"We have to get you to the water!" Her words sounded distant.

The pain was becoming everything. Smoke began to cloud my vision.

Then Petra was beside me. She splashed a jar of water over my body, and it steamed.

"Stay away," I slurred.

This fire would destroy everything it touched.

I heard the ghost laugh. Screams accompanied the sound. Could the people see him now?

"Your dragon has slipped beneath the water," he said. "You should have wished to be unchained. Not that it will help now."

I felt the pressure of the manacles release from my ankles. It was a cruel gesture, given to mock me.

"Goodbye." The ghost laughed one last time.

I needed to get to the river.

I tried to crawl, but it was difficult to move now. I couldn't see, and my breath came in shallow heaves. The left side of my body was nothing but pain, and I couldn't feel my hand.

With my other arm, I pulled myself in what I hoped was the right direction. The flames reached the side of my face, and I fell.

Then something pulled repeatedly on my right arm. I was being tugged in short bursts over the ground.

It was Isa, and maybe Petra too.

I couldn't yell at them. I couldn't tell them not to breathe the smoke.

The pain was less now on my left leg, and that scared me. I was numb in too many places.

Now there was cold all around me. Water pushed at my body, and whoever held me lost their grip on my arm.

"Gilde!" It was Isa's cry.

Isa, who had never learned to swim. She didn't follow me into the river, and for that I was grateful.

The heat on the back of my head disappeared, but the pain surged. Water filled my nose, and I fought with my right arm. One eye managed to open, and I kicked my left leg toward the light.

For one moment, I had air. Then I was beneath the water again. It rushed me along, down the river to the place Wil had been.

Time slowed. Without the flames fighting against me, my thoughts cleared.

Was Wil under here with me, floating? He would have shrunk small enough to escape his chains, and then he could swim.

Swim. I needed to kick my legs.

I did for a while, and then I forgot again. It felt better to let my body rest. Everything hurt.

Was I dying? Was Wil alive?

If so, my father would never have the fire. Not even the ghost would give it to him.

The water pressed in on all sides, like the god Wil spoke of. A living river that never let me have my way. I'd wanted the key. I'd wanted to speak to Wil again. I'd wanted peace and freedom and love.

But that god had other plans.

Now I wanted to breathe.

And the river wouldn't let me do that, either.

It entered my mouth and then my throat. This was my end, and I didn't have the strength left to stop it.

I was dying. But for a time, I had been free. Maybe even loved.

Then something tugged at me, and the pain flared. I was

moving the wrong way in the water, against it rather than with it. This wasn't right. It was too hard, and it hurt too much.

I was lifted from the water and laid on something solid.

"Breathe, Gilde!"

It was a man's voice.

I tried but couldn't. The water wasn't around me anymore, but it was inside me.

Hands rolled me over and struck my back. I vomited. That part seemed to last a long time, and the ground beneath me felt like razor blades cutting my skin. Finally, I coughed. Then came the first breath.

Something brushed against the right side of my face. The side that hadn't burned. I forced my eyes open again, and my vision returned, but it was like looking through a narrow crack.

A face was close to mine. Tangled ringlets dripped water onto my cheek.

Wil.

Breathing and perfect.

When I looked at him, he let out something like a laugh, but it was too anguished. His golden eyes were red-lined.

"Gilde . . ."

I took a shuddering breath and tried to speak, but only gurgles came out, and I couldn't move my lips the right way. The fire had touched me even there.

I would have embraced him and shouted that he was alive. I would have taken his hand and run away into the forest. We would have made a woodfire and talked about everything that had happened and everything that would happen.

Instead, I lay there on the ground, unmoving.

Another voice spoke from out of my sight. It was heavy with emotion.

"You've only prolonged her pain. She can't live."

I thought it might be Marcus.

More men shouted in the distance. Were soldiers coming?

Wil glanced away from me for the briefest moment. "You don't know what she can do." His voice was hard, then it softened as his eyes moved back to me. "Neither do I."

His tone warmed me even through the pain. And then I realized what I must have looked like to him. To anyone.

Bloody and ruined.

He whispered now, only to me. "Why, Gilde?"

I tried to speak.

"Shh," he said. "No." His voice cracked. "It should have been me. You should have let it be me. You can't leave me . . ."

I wanted to stay for him, but a darkness was coming over me. My vision narrowed, then disappeared. I was aware, but I couldn't see anymore.

"No." He held me, careful not to touch where I had been burned.

I wished it could last.

"Gilde, my love . . ."

My love.

I had nothing left to give, but he had just given me everything.

I wanted more, of course. More days together.

But this would be enough for me.

And then I fell into a black sleep. There were no dreams. Only pain.

37

I KNEW IT HAD BEEN A LONG
time since the burns. I felt every moment of my sleep, and
waking came in stages.

First, I heard muffled voices, and knew I was lying on
something softer than ground. That part only lasted for a
while, and eventually I began to catch snippets of conversation
as my sleep faded in and out.

"She needs to eat, though."

"Give her time."

"You should rest too, you know."

I was aware of my body, and I didn't think it hurt, but I was
afraid to move. Finally, full consciousness came, and I lay there
with my eyes closed. Everything was silent, and daylight filtered
through my eyelids.

I tried my right hand. It was the safest. It curled and
uncurled without incident.

Next, I did the harder thing. I moved my left hand, and to
my surprise, my fingers bent.

I was still too scared to try my legs. Most of all, I was afraid
of my mouth.

I took a deep breath through my nose and opened my eyes.
I could see.

Gauzy blankets covered my body, and I lay on a bed with a wooden frame. The room was familiar. This was Cybele's home, where Isa had found me that night.

It must have been early morning, from the light in the window.

In the corner, in a wooden chair, sat Wil. Asleep. His head rested against the wall, and he breathed softly. An untidy pile of books rested at his feet.

I took the image in. No cuts. No bruises. No scales. Just Wil, alive and beautiful.

We were both alive.

For a moment, it was too much. Too good to believe.

I knew I should make a sound to wake him. But I thought of my burns, and I let the silence linger.

Once, when I was young, I burned my elbow on the hearth in our cottage. It blistered, and the purple scar stayed with me.

I had never hoped to be the most beautiful. I was a dark, clumsy thing. But I had discovered I was pretty enough.

Gilde, my love . . .

He loved me. And now that meant he loved a broken, ugly thing.

I wanted to let that moment of waking go on forever, before I would have to face how badly I was injured. I could have watched Wil sleep for a long time and been content.

But the door opened, and in came a petite girl with a long yellow braid. Isadora and Wil in the same room. They felt like they belonged in different worlds.

Her face paled when she saw me, then brightened.

Before I could say anything, she marched to Wil and gave his shoulder a push. He started and woke.

"Better try to look like you didn't sneak in for the whole night again before Cybele comes up." Then she nodded toward me with a broad smile. "And Gilde's awake."

Isa proceeded to plop down on the edge of my bed, and she

took hold of my left hand. Her ocean blue eyes were glassy, but no tears fell as she looked down at me.

In the daylight, I noticed little creases had begun to form at the corners of her eyes and between her brows. The first lovely signs of aging.

"So," she said, "you did it."

What had I done? Saved Wil? Burned myself? Survived.

Then Wil came to my other side. He reached beneath the blanket and took my hand. The one that would be ruined.

"Gilde."

There was so much heart in that word, I felt myself smile. It wasn't painful, so I got braver.

I closed my hand around his. "Wil."

And my mouth moved like it should.

Isa sank back against my pillows, jarring the bed more than I thought she should have with an injured person in it.

"Never would have believed it," she said. "Except you didn't die, so we kind of knew something was going on. But then it took forever. Did you know you've been passed out for twenty-three days? And you've only eaten what could be dripped into your mouth. Cybele will make that right soon enough. What do you fancy? There's bread in the kitchen with cinnamon." She sat upright and looked down at me. "You must be thirsty."

I was.

She sprang up from the bed. "I'll be back." She shot a look at Wil. "Not that you'll be alone. I could barely keep Wil out of this room for a minute when you were asleep. Now that you're awake it'll be impossible."

Isa brushed a piece of hair out of my face. "Don't fall asleep again." There was something afraid in her tone, but then it passed, and she left the room.

Wil sat on the edge of the bed more gingerly than Isa had.

"I know you must have so many questions," he said. "But

we don't need to rush into it until you're ready. We have time."
He smiled. "Which is new for us."

But that was the most pressing question. Isa had said twenty-three days. Wil had been a human for all that time.

"How long of a time?" My voice came out clear and high. I had expected it to be raw. "Wil, you'll be a dragon again. We need to get out of the city."

There was something so light in Wil's expression, it made him look younger than I remembered. Like someone I had never met.

"I don't think I'll ever be the dragon again." He said it slowly, as if savoring each word.

I used my right hand to push myself up to a sitting position.
"The fire?" I asked, breathless.
"It's gone from me."

And when he spoke the words, I knew they were true. There had been a darkness over Wil before. Now he seemed smaller, but not diminished. Like some covering had been peeled away, and this was Wil as he always should have been.

"But . . ." I stopped to think. "I burned myself so you would have strength to transform. But how can the fire put itself out?"

"What you did saved my body from dying. But something else saved me from the fire. Or maybe it was a mix of all of it." He looked at me carefully. "Are you ready to hear this now? You need to rest."

"I've done nothing *but* rest." If I wasn't afraid of the pain and the scars, I would have gotten up from bed and paced the floor. "Tell me everything. Please."

"There are pieces I can only guess at. I think you called on the ghost . . ."

"Yes," I whispered.

Pain filled Wil's eyes.

"It was a wish he couldn't corrupt." I swallowed and kept

my face still as I tried to explain. "And I would do it again. I don't care how twisted and burned I am. Wil . . . we're alive."

I did care. But I would never let him carry the burden of that grief.

Wil regarded me for a moment. "There's something you need to see." He let go of my hand and went to a wooden desk across the room. He picked up a small, flat item. As he came back to me, the thing glinted in the sun, reflecting light, and I realized what it was.

A mirror.

I squeezed my eyes closed and felt Wil sit beside me.

"Open your eyes, Gilde." His voice was gentle.

"I can't."

"Please," he said. "This is the most important thing for you to know, more than anything else. And you'll know it best by seeing."

He sounded so sure. I couldn't hide from this forever.

I took a shaking breath and opened my eyes.

In the mirror, a girl with round cheeks and rumpled brown hair looked back at me.

All her hair was there. It hadn't been burned away.

Her mouth didn't twist and pull with mottled scars. Her cheeks were smooth, and not purple. Even her neck curved pleasantly into an unblemished collar.

I pulled my left hand from beneath the blankets and examined it. The one that should have been burned beyond use.

It was whole.

I realized my legs didn't hurt, and I wriggled them under the blanket. I kicked away the covers and found myself dressed in a modest white nightgown with little ribbon bows stitched down the front.

Wil watched me. "Do you remember the burns?"

"When I woke up just now, they were all I remembered.

Like they had been my whole life before I fell asleep. What happened?"

I couldn't stop inspecting my hands.

"You first came to the castle when you were almost seventeen," Wil said. "The age when a spark manifests. I sensed it in you."

How many times had I resented that nonexistent spark? I needed strength to move a dragon. Speed to steal Father's bottle. I'd had none of it.

"I'm immune to fire," I realized. "It's why I didn't die in the mine."

"That was part of it, but I think it's much more than that. I think you can heal your body from anything. Smoke. Cuts. Illness. It's a powerful spark, more so than most."

That didn't make sense.

"But I got sick when the ghost scratched me. You had to bring silver salts to cool the infection."

"The spark was in you, but sometimes it can be slow to show itself. Do you remember when you first came to me, you used to tire easily? You would struggle to breathe, and your lips turned blue. I worried about it often."

"I was always that way," I said. "Even as a child. But then, over the summer, I"—my voice slowed—"grew out of it."

"Your spark showed. But that was after your fever from the ghost scratch. And you never bled much when you cut yourself on my scales. I smelled it, but then it would go away." His face shadowed. "I didn't like thinking about your spark. The fire inside me would speak of it often, and I refused to bring it up to you. The flames were hungry enough."

I searched his eyes, but there wasn't the shame that used to be there when he spoke of the fire's voice.

"Is it really gone?" I asked.

"The water cut into me, and it hurt more than anything I had ever known. Except, in another way, it was better than anything. As I sank deeper, the fire panicked. And I realized it was the fire that burned me when I touched the water, not the water itself. The flame was afraid, and that gave me hope."

"You could have drowned out the fire at any time?"

He shook his head. "It was so painful, and the fire fought so hard. I don't know if I could have made myself do it before that night. Even if I had, it would have destroyed my body. But to be free . . ." His voice trailed off.

And I understood.

"I would lose myself a hundred times again to find what was in that water," he said.

"You found yourself."

"More than that." Wil looked over his shoulder at the door, then lowered his voice. "I don't really know how to speak about it yet. I'm still figuring it out. But . . . there was a voice in the river. It spoke to me, and it sounded nothing like the voice of the fire."

"What did it say?" I'd had my own dying thoughts beneath the rapids.

"It remembered the promise I made as a child, to never do anything wrong again. It knew about my struggle against the fire, the way I battled in my mind every day. And it knew I was tired. It was the voice of a man, and it asked me if I was ready to lay down my burden. I had never been capable of extinguishing the fire on my own. '*If you trust me,*' it said, '*I will set you free*.'"

Wil believed what he was saying. I could see that. Whatever had happened in the water, it did something to him.

"And what did you say?" I asked.

"There was nothing else I could do but trust. I had come to the end of my strength. When I made that decision, the fire died inside me. I was dying with it, and . . . I know it sounds wrong, but there was so much peace, and the voice was with me. It was almost a joy to die, except that I thought of leaving you. Then he spoke to me again. *'Gilde has given you a gift. It was an evil thing, but I will use it for good'.* After that, I was a man again, and I swam out of the chains."

I tried to picture what he was saying. "But someone must have seen you come out of the water."

"It was getting dark at that point, and I swam to the opposite bank from where the soldiers were. But Marcus was on that side, running with the river. He was chasing after your body . . . he wanted to catch you to give you a burial. You floated to me. I don't know how I would have found you in the water if it hadn't happened like that. I pulled us both out among the bushes. The soldiers saw someone with Marcus, but only a figure in the twilight. I was dressed in nothing but a cloth fishing net I snagged when I transformed. A gift from the river."

His cheeks turned a ruddy shade.

His clothing was the last thing I would have thought of that night, as I lay there bleeding.

"I didn't see," I reassured him.

"I found better clothes in a soldier's pack. We brought you here, and the magistrate's men came for me. There were suspicions about my involvement in everything that night, and they held me in a cell beneath the fortress for two days. I was mad with worry for you."

I knew that cell. "You escaped?"

"They let me go. Marcus never testified that he saw me come out of the water. As far as most people in this city know, the dragon died in the river and was carried off by soldiers at a later time. Of course, when the cohort pulled the chains out, they were empty, but no one else was there to see that, and the magistrate has sworn them to secrecy. There was no proof that I had done anything to free the dragon, or that I used to be him."

My eyes went wide. "That's a big secret."

"A lot of people saw you get burned, Gilde. Everyone

thought you were mad, but no one could hear those screams and not take pity. Word spread of your recovery." He smiled. "Isadora made sure of that. They're calling it a miracle, and they're impressed by your spark. You'll be a hero now that you're awake, and I was the one who pulled you out of the river. In light of that, the magistrate set me free."

I found that hard to believe, and my face must have shown it.

"He has his suspicions," Wil admitted. "He may not let me leave the city. We'll see. But I'm not what he wanted. I have no horns or scales for him to collect anymore. I'm a man now. With rights. They have no evidence against me."

Because of Marcus. He hadn't testified, even after I betrayed him.

I had been right. If the people could see Wil was a human, things would be different. They were different now.

Another thought came to my mind. "Has there been any sight of my father?"

Wil shook his head. "I expected to see him before now, but he hasn't been here. We're being watched by gold addicts, though. I've seen them."

I felt Wil had the right to know what almost happened. "The magistrate made a bargain with my father. He was going to give him your body. I don't think Marcus could have stopped it."

Wil's eyebrows rose. "And what did the magistrate want in exchange?"

"He wanted my father to leave."

Wil shifted on the edge of the bed, uneasy. "There's a new bounty on the alchemist's head. The magistrate has been killing gold addicts who are proven to be working for him."

I shuddered. "How many have died?"

"At least six. Cities protect themselves against wizards, but it sounds like the magistrate was trying to do it through deal-making. A smarter way. Wizards are easy to injure, but they're not easy to kill forever. Now that the deal is impossible, the magistrate won't tolerate magic."

And that's when I realized. My father had always been hunted, whether by dragons or by men. You couldn't live as a wizard and not make enemies. My dream of a normal life had never been real.

"I wanted to tell you about the deal," I said. "I tried to sneak into the fortress, but they caught me."

I recounted the entire night to him.

"If I had known what they would do with my body . . ." Wil stiffened.

I looked at his very human face. "I know. It would have been bad."

"If I had known what would happen to you, I would have fought."

We were close now, sitting side by side. He reached for my hand, and our fingers intertwined.

"You already saved me enough times," I said.

"No more than you saved me. Even in the beginning, you made me start to believe I didn't belong to the fire." He looked down at me.

I wanted to tell him that I belonged to him. All my heart. If he still wanted me.

But Isa chose that moment to return with my cup of water.

I thanked her and drank no more than half, then held out the cup to Wil, offering him the rest.

His mouth turned up at one corner. "I'm not thirsty."

I smiled, and Isa looked between us. Her eyebrow lifted.

"Well," she declared. "Better get you caught up."

She proceeded to tell the whole story from her point of view, which started when she heard I had been captured. She had come to the execution and found me just before the ghost appeared. Isa described my burns too vividly, and my stomach soured.

"I didn't know Petra yet, but I could see we were both determined to do the same thing. We tried to hold onto you, but the current was too fast." Her words held so much regret, I knew they were an apology, even though she wouldn't say she was sorry.

There was nothing to forgive. If she and Petra hadn't acted, I would have been consumed.

Then Isa's story contained lots of details about her changing my bandages, and how everything healed suspiciously fast.

"And so I guess you do have a spark. A big one too." She shook her head. "All that time in the marshes, when someone like you should have been in a fine house like a lady, rubbing shoulders with the top of society." She gave a short laugh. "That's probably where you'll end up too, especially with all those little gems and bits of silver we found in your gowns."

Wil interjected quickly. "All your possessions have been deposited in a safety box." He kept his eyes on Isa while he spoke. "You can access it any time through city officials, and there's plenty there to provide for your needs."

Had some of my buttons gone missing before the deposit?

I understood stealing. I had done it myself, before I knew that Wil didn't care to keep his own silver. But that had been before he was human.

"It's your treasure," I told him. "All of it."

"It was a gift." His tone was final. "And less than you deserved."

From what Isa said, Marcus had tried to pay for my boarding, but Wil beat him to it. With the combination of the two, Cybele was paid in full for at least ninety more days of housing me.

Isa leaned forward. "And you know there are men from the cohort posted outside the house here? A night watch. Marcus himself comes to visit more often than I would have thought."

Wil's voice went flat. "They know Gilde has some association with the alchemist. They're watching for him. And Marcus has been concerned for her recovery."

That brought more questions. Slowly, I sat up. "I am associated with the alchemist. A man who doesn't die. How is my spark of healing so different than that?"

He gave me a quiet look. "Your spark will last through the prime of your life, then fade. You'll pass at your proper time. That is nothing like a wizard. When wizards heal, people disappear. There is rot and death. Too many people saw your healing to call it anything other than a spark."

"How much does everyone know about my connection to the alchemist?"

"Don't look at me," Isa said. "I don't speak a word in this city about my past or yours. Better not to mention the alchemist in my circles."

"They must have guessed something," Wil mused. "Maybe because you were caught together in the fortress. But I doubt anyone knows the full truth."

The three of us passed the morning that way, discussing everything I had missed. Cybele came eventually and scrutinized me more than once.

"I'm happy to have you here as long as you like," she beamed. "This will put my boarding house on the map."

She left us with spice bread. I ate a whole loaf by myself, with butter and walnuts. Wil ate too, and I tried not to keep watching him. This was human food, other than meat, and I enjoyed sharing it with him.

After a while, I grew tired again and my eyes felt heavy. I found myself leaning back into the pillows while Isa went over every person she had told about my recovery, and who they had told, and which city officials had visited me to see for themselves.

I didn't think Isa really understood about the fire and what my burns had done, and she didn't seem curious. But she had always been like that, with few questions for Guntor or Father. She was happy just to live.

I wanted more. I wanted to read all the books in Wil's pile, and all the books I could find after that. The world was finally open to me.

My eyes drooped closed once, but I sprang them back open.

"You should sleep," Wil said gently.

"I've slept enough." But my fatigued voice wasn't convincing.

"You came back from death, Gilde. That's bound to be exhausting, even if you look healed on the outside."

"And I'd better get back to the laundry," Isa announced. "Some of us still have work to do." She turned to Wil. "Remember, out before nightfall. Gilde's a good girl, and I'll keep her reputation that way."

Wil gave a cheerful nod. "Now that she's awake, I'll make sure to follow the rules. Leave the door open when you go."

She left it wide open. "You're both the good sort."

That was the highest praise Isa had ever given a man.

I felt myself blush. Wil and I had been alone on the mountain together, and I had never considered my reputation. This room in the heart of a city was public compared to that.

Wil grinned. "There are more people who will want to see you. Petra came often to visit. And to boss everyone around. She kept throwing out the vases of flowers I brought up because she said they smelled like weeds."

I laughed at that.

"Even the magistrate may come now to see the miracle of your spark," Wil cautioned. "Adrian was here most days when you slept. And Marcus . . ."

"Oh."

A silence lingered.

"You should know . . ." I began. "I've been able to meet more humans now. I'm not the sheltered girl from the marsh who didn't know anyone."

Wil watched the curtains blow in the breeze. "And how have you found humanity to be?"

"Some of them are very kind. Especially Petra. Some of them are surprising. Like Adrian . . . and Marcus."

Wil's face stilled.

"But out of all of them," I told him. "You're my favorite human."

His blue-rimmed eyes looked into mine. "I'd rather not talk of other people right now. There are more important things before I leave you to sleep."

He brushed a finger down my cheek, along my jawline. With that one gesture, I was back at the shore with him, the sun setting over glistening waters.

We each moved nearer to the other. He whispered close enough to my cheek for me to feel his soft breath.

"My love."

And Wil brought his lips to meet mine. It was careful at first, and then more. I reached up and ran my fingers through his curls like I had longed to do.

When we parted, we were changed. No longer a girl and her dragon, but something I didn't have words for. Something I knew could only grow and never die.

"I should go," Wil's voice was low. "But I won't go far away. Not ever again. If you need me, I'll be on the armchair in the sitting room downstairs."

I didn't tell him that did feel far away.

With one last kiss on my forehead, Wil left the room.

"Sleep," he said at the doorway.

I was tired, but I didn't close my eyes.

That kiss felt like lying on a grassy slope in the sunshine when apples were in season. My whole body was full of light.

But there were harder things to think of also. Like Wil's experience with the voice in the water.

Gilde has given you a gift. It was an evil thing, but I will use it for good.

If the voice was real, it didn't approve of my wish, and I couldn't blame it. The fire was a hungry, rageful thing. But still the voice honored my intention as a gift.

Everything that happened had been painful and terrifying, and I had made desperate choices. But somehow Wil and I ended up here. Both healed. Both whole.

I had once thought a good god had to be on my side of things. But none of my plans would have been this good. After Wil's story, if there really was a god like that, I was starting to think I ought to be on his side.

What kind of a god could use my ghost wish for good? And why had I never called on him for help?

There were bound to be more books on the subject, and I planned to read them all. As soon as I wasn't so tired.

My eyelids fell closed, and I slept in the true sense. Not the injured, healing kind of slumber, but the kind of rest my mind needed after fighting for so long.

38

SOMETHING IN THE ROOM wasn't right. I opened my eyes and found myself in darkness. The sun had set.

When Wil left me, the window shutter had been cracked open. Now, it was open all the way, and a night wind blew in, rustling the blankets nestled around me.

I swung my legs off the bed and let my bare feet touch the floor. How long had it been since I walked? My last steps had been in chains.

I stood. My legs felt as if no time had passed in a sick bed.

Movement caught my eye in the windowsill. It had been empty before. Now, a small object rested there with some kind of trailing string that fluttered in the wind.

I went over and saw it was not string. They were ribbons, pinned to the sill by a coin, large and round and golden.

I raced to my pack, which had been left here the night I went to steal Marcus's key. Inside, I found my flint. The first gift Wil gave me.

I lit Cybele's nightstand candle and brought it to the windowsill.

The ribbons were green.

Like the ones I once tore from my dress.

My heart raced, and I turned slowly in the room, searching every corner. I was alone. The garden and street below my window were deserted.

Words had been penned on the ribbons in black ink, far more legible than the scratchings I had thrown from the castle tower.

Only one person could have left this on my windowsill.

There were six long ribbons stacked in order under the coin, each numbered in bold strokes. I forced my breathing to slow and brought the candle close enough to read.

1. *Gilde. The fire is gone from the boy. I haven't figured out how you did it yet, but I watched it happen that night. My anger may fade in time.*
2. *You stole my future from me. In that way, keeping power from others, you are my daughter.*
3. *Someday, you'll need a father again. Or a wizard. I'll find you then.*
4. *Guntor was right. The dragon did drown.*
5. *Don't ever meet with a spirit again. Even I know better than that.*
6. *Don't tell them who your father is. It won't serve either of us.*

I read it over again. And then again. I tried to harvest all the meaning I could from each word on the ribbons.

I focused on the word *someday*. That sounded distant, and I needed time.

Father was older than I could guess, and more learned than I could imagine, but I knew he was wrong. I would never need a wizard.

As for a father, that was more difficult. Without him, I would have been alone as a child, like Isa had been. There were things she faced that I couldn't imagine. But I wasn't a child anymore.

I thought of Petra and Hans. Marcus and Adrian. Wil and Isa. I wasn't alone anymore, either.

The message shook me, and I couldn't bring myself to touch the gold. But it was a comfort in one way. Father wasn't after Wil anymore.

And he wasn't after me. For now.

We could breathe for a while.

I looked out the window and searched the garden below again. Someone had climbed up to leave the message. If not Father, then one of the gold addicts. There was no sign of anyone now.

Or Father had used some unknown magic to get it to me.

Either way, Wil would want to know.

I took my spare dress from my pack. It smelled like smoke and damp. Like our travels over the mountain to the sea. The garment fit well over my nightgown, and all the uncomfortable treasures had been removed from the lining. They were deposited in a safety box.

I tugged Father's ribbons out from under the coin on the sill, then took the candle and crossed the room to the door.

Once I made it to the stairs, I paused as footsteps sounded below.

Another light appeared around the corner, and with it came two men.

First Marcus, carrying a lantern, then Wil close behind.

"You're awake." Marcus's face lit, and he climbed the stairs, then stopped a few steps down from us.

"Why are you awake in the middle of the night?" Wil's voice was stern.

"It's morning," Marcus said before I could speak. "Just very early."

I couldn't explain with Marcus here. It would lead to more questions than I was prepared to answer.

"I . . . heard a noise." I balled the ribbons into my fist.

Wil gave Marcus a displeased look.

Marcus didn't seem to notice. His attention was on me. "I came as soon as I heard. No one sent word that you were awake yesterday, but gossip made it to me from the laundry where Isadora works."

"Oh," I replied, then remembered to say, "I heard you visited me while I was recovering. Thank you."

"I'm glad to see you awake," he said. "I'm sorry if I disturbed you too early."

"I was up." I glanced at Wil.

Marcus climbed one stair step closer to my level. "Isadora informed me she's known you since childhood, and that you weren't aware of your spark. Is that true?"

I answered slowly. "Yes . . ."

"Then I didn't want to make you wait one moment longer to hear the information I've gathered." His eyes darted to Wil, then back to me. "But it's personal to you, and I would prefer to talk with you alone."

I hesitated. Whatever Marcus shared, Wil could hear it too. But after everything Marcus had done for me, it felt wrong to deny him this request.

Wil must have had a similar thought. "It would be more appropriate for you to speak down in the front room. As I suggested when you arrived."

Wil was apparently helping to enforce Cybele's rules now.

"Of course." Marcus held the lamp a little higher, lighting the path as he moved down the stairs.

"Wil," I said. "I heard the noise outside my window . . ."

He briefly studied my face, then, with a nod, headed up that direction. I knew he would find the coin. I would explain as soon as I could.

Soon, Marcus and I stood in Cybele's front room, facing each other stiffly.

I spoke first. "I wouldn't have taken your key if it wasn't a matter of urgency. I'm sorry I had to do it."

It wasn't much of an apology. But it was the best one I had.

"You almost died." His lowered voice carried intensity.

"I didn't die. No one did."

Marcus fixed his eyes somewhere past me. "At least you proved everyone wrong. Even me."

Maybe that was his attempt at an apology also.

His rigid posture softened. "Last time we were in Cybele's home, I spoke of our future."

I swallowed and held my breath.

"I know things are different now," he said.

Wil was alive. It wasn't what Marcus planned, but he wouldn't fight it now. His silence to the magistrate proved that.

"Still," he continued. "I found you out there on the coast, a lost thing. I ought to return you where you belong."

"You don't owe me anything." I said. "And I'm not lost anymore."

"You are. Gilde, where's your family?"

I said nothing.

"When I saw your burns healing, I knew it was some kind of spark magic—"

I stopped him. "It's not magic. Wizardry causes harm, not miracles. A spark is something different. Something that's part of me, made by the creator."

And as I spoke the words, I finally owned what had always been mine.

Marcus listened to me but didn't respond directly. Instead, he said, "So I asked around. Your kind of a spark has the strength of the far north. There are landowners up there with well protected clans."

"There are other people in Xantic with a spark too," I said. "It's somewhat common."

"Not like yours. Certain abilities run in bloodlines, and there's only one region you could come from."

I went still.

"What do you mean?" I breathed.

"I sent a party of my men in that direction. They've just sent a messenger back. I think I've found your family."

My legs felt weak, and I sat in Wil's armchair.

Marcus went on. "There's a rumor of a woman whose clan had healing sparks in the past. She lost her child at birth, but there was suspicion around the midwife."

Lost.

If a woman lost a child, then that child lost a mother too.

But it had never been like that for me. I had never had a mother to lose. It was like I wasn't allowed to believe one existed.

When I spoke, I hardly recognized my voice. "The father?"

"There are rumors around that too. We know that she was pregnant out of wedlock, and there were deaths in her family . . ." He hesitated. "I won't say more. It's hearsay."

My father was my blood relative. Wil had always questioned it, but that doubt never felt right, despite everything.

I could only imagine the circumstances of my conception.

Father killed people who had a spark. If there was power in the north, it made sense he would have been there. He worked his way into their community. And people died.

And then I was born.

Did he love her? He couldn't have, if he took her child.

A mother who lost her baby.

But my thoughts stopped there. If I went any further, I would lose myself, and Marcus was still with me.

"Gilde?" he asked. "What is your connection to the alchemist?'

Father had come to Xantic hungry. Now that the fire was gone, he might go elsewhere.

I didn't think my spark was in danger from him. He had crossed every other line, but not that one. There was a small difference between what he had done and killing me outright. But there was a difference.

"I don't think any of us will be seeing the alchemist again soon," I said finally.

It wasn't really an answer.

Marcus sat on the edge of the armchair beside me, keeping a respectful distance.

"If you want, I can send word. My men can approach the woman and ask her about you."

"No." He seemed surprised at my abruptness, and I surprised myself with my answer. Why wouldn't I want to know for sure? Why wouldn't I want to be known?

It was too much too fast.

"I need time," I amended. "When I'm ready, would your men be able to tell me how to get there?"

"Yes. But it's a three-day journey on the open road."

That made me smile. "I think I could handle that."

"I suppose you could." Marcus's expression stayed neutral. "Adrian will still want to see you."

"He's the first person I'm going to visit now that I'm awake. Is he in the camps?"

"Where else would he be?"

"Marcus," I said. "I'm grateful I got to know you. Not just because of all the ways you helped, but because you're someone who wants to find a home for lost things."

Whether they were lost or not.

He commanded a small army, and he hunted dragons despite their innocence. But he was also a protector in his way. And he had surprised me in the end.

A person could be more than one thing.

A father and a killer. An oracle and an abuser. A human and a dragon.

But I wanted to know one more thing. "Why didn't you testify against Wil?"

Marcus rose and moved a couple of paces away, his back to me. He was silent for a moment before he turned and spoke. "I've never withheld testimony before. But then I thought I saw you die. It changed things."

It changed my whole life.

I stood also. "I hope to see you again . . . with Adrian."

"With Adrian," he agreed.

He left out the front door, taking his lantern with him. The sun had risen outside, and I didn't need his light anymore.

Wil came in from the hall.

"Were you listening?" I asked.

"I wanted to be nearby. Especially after I found this." He held a small cloth in his hand, unfolding it to reveal the coin from my window. He hadn't wanted to touch it, either.

"I'm glad you were," I confessed. "I wanted you to hear."

He held the coin up again, and his face was pale. "The wizard was this close to you, and there was nothing I could have done. I don't have fire anymore. Not even smoke."

"Good." I wrapped my hand over his, closing the cloth around the coin, then held out my own fistful of ribbons. "He left a message."

We sat close on the armchair and read them together.

"I think he'll leave me alone for now," I said.

"For now." Wil glanced at the front door and the window. "But he said he would find you again someday."

It was true, and it reminded me of the ghost. "That spirit found me easily when I called on him."

"If you hadn't called, he might have forgotten about you eventually. There's a whole world full of more convenient prey for him. Now that his debt is paid, though, the tether between you is broken. He'd have to search for you. But the alchemist can still find you with divination."

Wil took my hand, and I clung tight.

"I do share his same blood," I told him. "I'm sure of it now."

"There are spells for finding family." A pained look crossed his face. "I wish I didn't know things like that."

We had both lived with a wizard through childhood, but he hadn't been spared seeing the brutality of it. There were rooms for killing in his home.

"I've been thinking about the castle," I said. "Even if no one knows about the mines, Father might still be curious to investigate. Is there any other way to get past the shrouding?"

"I've been thinking about it too. A lot." He paused. "Gilde, can you remember the way there?"

"It's on the mountain."

"But which mountain? Where?"

The instant I thought about it, my head began to hurt. I could picture our time in the forest. Our night in the cave. My desperate climb from Petra's house. But had it been north or south? I couldn't remember the horizon or the shapes of the hills.

I couldn't remember where it was at all.

"That's the shrouding," Wil said. "And it's the same for me now that the fire is gone. I spent eight years there as a child, but I never left. Then, when I was the dragon for two years, the fire always brought me back. But I don't think I'll ever find it again."

It was truly hidden. I had been Father's guide, and I couldn't return. No one would ever find it.

I took a long, deep breath, then exhaled, releasing one more worry. "It's safe."

"I wish I could say the same for you." His hold tightened on my hand.

He had been a creature that could protect me from anything, even himself. The dragon always knew what to do.

It was my turn to reassure him.

"Wil," I said gently "I'm free and I'm alive. So are you. That's more than I hoped for. We can't control the future."

Wil's mouth curved. "There is one thing we can do. We can stay together."

That was exactly what I most wanted to do.

It was different leaving Cybele's house this time. Today, I wasn't slipping into the city in darkness. Morning light cast soft shadows on the white street pavers. Birds sang in the garden.

I wore fresh slippers and a new dress, provided by Cybele herself as a gift. The clothes were simple and clean, but lovely. Isa had plaited my hair into an intricate braid.

And this time when I left the house, I wasn't alone.

Wil walked beside me, dressed in a linen shirt. As we passed people, a few eyes seemed to linger on us, but it was nothing like the procession when we had first entered the city.

I smiled up at him. "It's much easier to get through the streets unnoticed when you don't have scales."

"It's probably easier too, when you're not caked in mud." He gave me a warm look and reached over to brush back one tendril of hair that hadn't made it into my braid.

We both paused our steps, and I wished we were alone again instead of in a street full of people.

Then someone approached, and the moment ended. It was a woman with large, round eyes and a well-used apron. I had never seen her before.

She came closer than I expected. "You're her, aren't you?"

I knew what she meant, but I didn't know how to respond.

"The survivor." The woman lifted her brows, as if we were sharing a secret between us. She reached into her basket to pull out a popover pastry and held it out to me. "For you. I sell them, and they're the best in Xantic if you believe my customers."

I hesitated. "I don't have any money with me."

"It's free." She offered the pastry. "I saw you that night. It was terrible." Tears welled in her eyes. "But here you are."

She wouldn't lower the pastry, so I took it from her. She smiled.

"Thank you," I said.

Her eyes roved over me. "Not a scar. Like they said."

Then she seemed to realize she was staring. She hoisted her basket a little higher. "If you ever need a baker, my name's Maria. Remember that."

"I will."

"My lady." Maria gave a little curtsy, then continued down the street.

I stood there with the pastry in my hand.

"She called me a lady," I said.

"You could be. With your spark, doors will be open to you."

I knew what he meant, and I didn't like it. Isa had made it clear. Prominent families wed their children to people with a spark, the stronger the better. I could marry into land or wealth or power.

I broke the pastry in two and handed half to Wil. "If my spark gets me berries and sugar-crust, fine. Beyond that, I have enough doors of my own."

At the look in his eyes, I slipped my hand into Wil's, and we made our way through the city. It was like that, quiet and comfortable, all the way to the south gate, where the cohort camped in the fields.

I had a promise to keep to Adrian.

We found him beside the river with the horses. Where I had hoped he would be.

He held a muddy stick in one hand and knelt behind one of the animals, cleaning dirt from the underside of a hoof.

I stayed back but called out a greeting and waved. Adrian saw us and threw down his stick. He ran to meet me, then stopped.

"Adrian—" I began.

"I didn't snitch on you," he started. "In case you thought I did."

"I never thought that," I assured him. "Not even for a moment. Though you would have been justified."

Our eyes met, and he gave a nod. "Good."

He leaned in close and sniffed. "Like I thought. You smell incredible compared to before. Which isn't saying much. Come on." He pulled me by my arm toward the horses.

They didn't flinch as we approached, and Adrian led me to the fattest one. He pushed my hand up and laid it against Potato's velvet white cheek. The horse pressed into my touch, asking to be scratched. I did what I was told.

I felt the feathery hairs between Potato's ears. "They're not afraid anymore."

"They don't have any reason to be." But Adrian wasn't watching me.

Wil had approached a horse also. One with a square face and defined legs. He ran a hand along its mane.

I watched him too. How many times had I laid a hand against Wil's dragon cheek, or climbed on his back to ride?

He stroked the animal with a soft touch.

Adrian turned his head toward Wil. "I won't snitch on anything else either. Even if it is weird as hades."

"I've heard of hades in a story once," I said. "It's a place of darkness. This is the opposite."

Adrian's face went serious, and his eyes swept over me. How much of my burns had he seen before I began to heal?

"I can tell," he said. "Darkness doesn't bring people back from death."

My father was alive. But that didn't mean he was living.

"Adrian . . ." I tried to find the right words to say. "I know you've seen your share of darkness."

He grew intent on untangling a knot in Potato's mane.

"And I know this cohort has been a place of light for you. But someone your age should have family. Not just comrades."

I wanted to say that a child didn't belong in the military, but he wouldn't like being reminded of his youth.

Adrian let go of the horse's mane. "They are my family. More than anyone has been."

How could I argue with that?

"I would have stayed with a dragon," I remarked.

"Then you know."

We turned our attention to the horses. Adrian reminded me of each of their names. Potato, Icicle, Snowy, Cloud, Milky, and Flour. All named after their similar color.

"Now that you can get close, you'd better remember the differences."

"I promise I will."

"And," he said proudly, "I can ride Cloud now. Want to see?"

"Yes." And I really did.

He hoisted himself onto Cloud. The horse pranced and tossed his head, but settled once Adrian was seated. They trotted off, circling the field.

Wil came to watch beside me. "I would never wish the fire on anyone, and I wouldn't take it back for anything. But part of me will always miss flying."

I remembered the rush of stars and the wind. "In his way, the dragon was amazing. And I don't know how that could come from something so evil."

"I've been going over it in my mind, Gilde," Wil said. "I don't think the fire made the dragon. I did. It was my only defense to stay alive when I burned the hottest. It was powered by evil, but it's about how the human will to survive channels the power. For me, and for Edric, and maybe for the ancient dragons too. Our will to live can be an amazing thing. And an ugly thing."

"You made your own armor." I brought my shoulder close to his.

"So did you, I think."

Adrian returned and slid off of Cloud. "Want to try?"

I laughed. "I just finally got to touch them. I don't want to push it too far. Maybe next time I come?"

"Don't wait too long. Marcus is selling them this fall when the grass dies. He says they'll eat too much, and the magistrate's lowering our wages. Which seems unfair after we actually caught a dragon." He shot a crooked smile at Wil. "No offense."

"Even I agree." Wil scratched Cloud behind his ears. "Completely unfair."

Adrian grinned.

In the end, Wil took a turn riding Cloud, and raced faster than I liked across the field. Was he feeling the wind on his face again?

Once, I caught Marcus watching us from the tents, and I lifted a hand in greeting. He acknowledged me with a wave of his own, but then turned away.

Wil and I left that afternoon without the chance to speak to him.

The sun warmed our backs on the return walk to the gate.

"Wil?" I asked. "Do you think we have enough money to buy Cloud and feed him over the winter? For Adrian."

"You have more than enough." He wrapped an arm around me while we walked. "They counted eighteen gems among your treasures."

"Our treasures," I corrected.

Wil entered into one of his silences. The ones I had grown accustomed to when he was a dragon.

"Are you thinking of the castle, and how I stole from you?"

"No." He was quick to reply. "None of it ever belonged to me, except the pendant you're wearing. And it makes me happy seeing you wear it."

I felt the blossom-shaped locket at my throat.

Wil took a breath. "I'm thinking of words like *ours*. And *us*. Of how two people make a life together."

We reached the gate and stopped. There were shade trees here, and soft grass. A good place for talking. I turned my face up to Wil, ready to hear what he would say next.

And afraid to hear it.

We had survived together, fought together, and crossed mountains. But there were words we had never spoken.

He brushed his thumb along my cheek, and my heart raced.

"I don't know when I fell in love with you, Gilde. It could have happened in the library, when you learned everything faster than I hoped. Sometimes I wonder if it was when I fought the ghost, or when you came back after I sent you to Petra."

I laughed, because he had seemed so angry that I returned. And I laughed to keep tears at bay. Some tears don't come from sorrow.

Wil remained intent. "It probably happened at some unimportant moment, when we shared a rabbit or when we cleaned the castle. But the truth is, from the very first, I knew I wanted to be near you. I've changed since then. Everything has. But that has stayed the same, and it always will."

"I'm not going anywhere," I whispered.

He shook his head. "But you have to."

My heart sank, and he took my hand.

"I told you once you deserve to be courted. It's still true. You deserve a beautiful wedding with harvest flowers braided into your hair. And you deserve to have your family be there."

And then I saw where he was going with his speech. "I'm not ready for them."

"But you will be. I justified taking you because the man you would have run to was dangerous. But now you have family out there. People I should ask for your hand, if only you knew them and trusted them. And I need to give you that chance."

I reached my hand up to run my fingers through Wil's golden hair. "I don't need anyone's permission to be with you, Wil. We fought for that together."

His eyes were glassy now, and his voice came out husky. "I don't have anything for you. No family. No heritage."

"Don't you see it?" I lay my hand on his cheek. "If I have a family, then so do you."

A single, human tear spilled from his eye as he pulled me close. Our lips met. This was a kiss made of salt and water. Memories and promises.

ACKNOWLEDGMENTS

It takes a team to bring a book into the world. Without them, you would never have met Gilde and Wil.

Firstly, I'd like to thank my mom. She taught me to read, and then she taught me to love reading. Both of my grandmothers have passed away, but they loved words too, and they each invested in my education in their own ways. Never underestimate the power of grandparents.

My sweetheart husband, Jared, has his fingerprints all over this book, and I would have never made it through without his honesty and patient encouragement. Thank you for putting up with me.

I owe so much to Lisa Laube, my editor. She has believed in my stories and brought them to readers, which means more than I can say.

Makenna Albert is the best beta reader in the world, and there would have been a couple of very fuzzy details in *Embergold* without her expert eye.

The amazing Enclave Publishing and Oasis Audio family are a powerhouse behind the scenes. So much thanks to Trissina, who has answered my endless marketing questions, and who is talented in many creative fields. Steve Laube oversaw the whole project with care, and he is behind the visionary publication of more beautiful books than I can count. Lindsay Franklin is a wonderful production manager.

The line and copy editors for *Embergold*, Avily Jerome and Coralie Terry, are such a blessing with their firm command of commas. Jamie Foley created the gorgeous interior layout. If my books ship to a house, library, or store, the joyful Charmagne Kaushal likely made it happen. Thank you for your work in the warehouse. I'm sure there are others who have helped, so if you've had an unseen hand in *Embergold*, I thank you also. You are a gift.

Kirk DuPonce crafted a perfect cover for Gilde and Wil, and I am so grateful.

Victoria McCombs, Moriah Chavis, and Clare B. Dunkle are incredible authors, and I am beyond humbled to have their endorsements on a book I wrote. Clare B. Dunkle filled my teen years with magic, and her stories helped inspire me to write fantasy.

Most of all, I want to thank Jesus, who is the Truth in every story.

About the Author

Rachelle grew up reading fantasy novels and getting her clothes muddy in the pine forests of Idaho. These days, she still loves hiking through forests and libraries, though she's a bit less fond of mud. Her debut novel, *Sky of Seven Colors,* released in 2023 through Enclave Publishing and won both the Carol Award and Christy Award. Rachelle doesn't write true stories, but she does write about truth. When she's not doing that, she sings in a band with her husband, who makes her happier than should be legal. If you like good food and honest conversations, you're her favorite kind of person.

If you enjoyed *Embergold*, feel free to say so! Reviews mean the world to authors.

For a free novelette eBook download, visit RachelleNelson Author.com

ALSO FROM RACHELLE NELSON

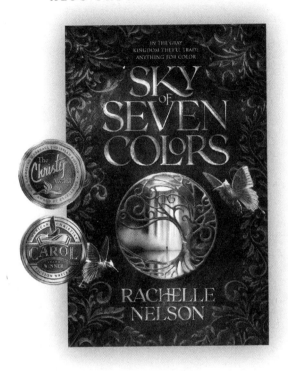

Sky of Seven Colors

IN THE GRAY KINGDOM,
THEY'LL TRADE ANYTHING FOR COLOR

www.enclavepublishing.com

IF YOU ENJOYED

EMBERGOLD

YOU MIGHT LIKE THESE OTHER NOVELS:

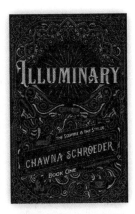

www.enclavepublishing.com

,